PRAISE FOR TIME STORM AND GORDON DICKSON

"SCIENCE FICTION THAT SEDUCES . . . A masterful science fiction story told by a masterful science fiction writer."

—*Milwaukee Journal*

"TIME STORM . . . It's one of those rare books that holds your attention constantly. The suspense at some points is almost unbearable, leaving the reader breathless and glad the crisis has passed."

—*New Orleans Times-Picayune*

"IT TAKES A MASTER to handle the concepts involved here with clarity and interest, and Dickson has done a superb job."

—*Publishers Weekly*

"DICKSON AT HIS BEST . . . One of the notable science fiction novels of the year."

—*Booklist*

D0552946

Bantam Science Fiction
Ask your bookseller for the books you have missed

FANTASTIC VOYAGE by Isaac Asimov
MONUMENT by Lloyd Biggle, Jr.
ROGUE IN SPACE by Fredric Brown
WHAT MAD UNIVERSE by Fredric Brown
BEASTS by John Crowley
DHALGREN by Samuel R. Delany
NOVA by Samuel R. Delany
TRITON by Samuel R. Delany
UBIK by Philip K. Dick
TIME STORM by Gordon Dickson
ALAS, BABYLON by Pat Frank
HELLSTROM'S HIVE by Frank Herbert
DEMON SEED by Dean Koontz
NEBULA AWARD STORIES ELEVEN edited by Ursula
    K. LeGuin
THE DAY OF THE DRONES by A. M. Lightner
DRAGONSONG by Anne McCaffrey
DRAGONSINGER by Anne McCaffrey
A CANTICLE FOR LEIBOWITZ by Walter M. Miller, Jr.
HIGH COUCH OF SILISTRA by Janet E. Morris
THE GOLDEN SWORD by Janet E. Morris
WIND FROM THE ABYSS by Janet E. Morris
LOGAN'S RUN by William F. Nolan & George Clayton
    Johnson
LOGAN'S WORLD by William F. Nolan
MAN PLUS by Frederik Pohl
CRITICAL MASS by Frederik Pohl & C. M. Kornbluth
THE FEMALE MAN by Johanna Russ
THE JONAH KIT by Ian Watson
NEBULA AWARD STORIES NINE edited by Kate
    Wilhelm

DEDICATION: TO THE LIBRARIANS

During the 1930s and 1940s anyone writing science fiction did so almost exclusively for magazines. Then in the early 1950s the magazine market began to die and paperback books took over. But the paperback books were on the stand one week and gone the next. By the time an author's newest book came out his older books had disappeared.

As a result, during these later years, when the magazines were mostly gone and the paperback books were coming and going, there were only a few of us who could afford to be full-time writers of science fiction; and the fact that this was possible at all was only because libraries continued to be the only real market for hardcover science fiction. The libraries alone bought science fiction books on a regular basis, shelved them, and made them continuously available to readers; and in this way libraries kept both science fiction and those of us who wrote it, alive.

To librarians everywhere, therefore, this book—the youngest of my literary children to see the light of day—is dedicated.

TIME STORM

The leopard—I called him Sunday, after the day I found him—almost never became annoyed with the girl, for all her hanging on to him. But he was only a wild animal, after all, and there were limits to his patience.

What had moved me to pick up first him, then her, was something I asked myself often without getting a good answer. They were nothing but encumbrances and no concern of mine. My only concern was getting to Omaha and Swannee. Beyond that point there was no need for me to think. But . . . I don't know. Somehow out of the terrible feeling of emptiness that I kept waking up to in the mornings, I had gotten a notion that in a world where nearly all the people and animals had vanished, they would be living creatures I could talk to. "Talk to," however, had turned out to be the working phrase; because certainly neither of them was able to talk back. Crazy cat and speechless girl and with them, myself, who before had always had the good sense never to need anybody, dragging them both along with me across a landscape as mixed up and insane as they were. But, of course, without me they would have been helpless.

This time, the trouble erupted just as I pushed the panel truck over a rise in late summer wheat country, which I figured had once been cornland, a little below the one-time northern border of Iowa. All the warning I heard was a sort of combination meow-snarl. Not a top-pitch, ready-to-fight sound, but a plain signal that Sunday had had enough of being treated like a stuffed animal and wanted the girl to leave him alone. I braked the panel sharply to a stop on the side of the empty, two-lane asphalt road and scrambled over the seat backs into the body of the truck.

1

"Cat!" I raved at him. "What the hell's got into you now?"

But of course, having said his piece and already gotten her to let him go, Sunday was now feeling just fine. He lay there, completely self-possessed, cleaning the fur on the back of his right forepaw with his tongue. Only, the girl was huddled up into a tight little ball that looked as if it never intended to come unwound again; and that made me lose my temper.

I cuffed Sunday; and he cringed, putting his head down as I crawled over him to get to the girl. A second later I felt his rough tongue rasping on my left ankle in a plea for forgiveness—for what he did not even understand. And that made me angry all over again, because illogically, now, I was the one who felt guilty. He was literally insane where I was concerned. I knew it, and yet I had taken advantage of that to knock him around, knowing I was quite safe in doing so when otherwise he could have had my throat out in two seconds as easy as yawning.

But I was only human myself, I told myself; and here I had the girl to unwind again. She was still in her ball, completely unyielding, all elbows and rigid muscle when I put my hands on her. I had told myself I had no real feeling for her, any more than I had for Sunday. But somehow, for some reason I had never understood, it always damn near broke my heart when she went like that. My younger sister had had moments of withdrawal something like that—before she grew out of them. I had guessed this girl to be no more than fifteen or sixteen at the most, and she had not said a word since the day I found her wandering by the road. But she had taken to Sunday from the moment I had led her back to the truck and she first laid eyes on him. Now, it was as if he was the only living thing in the world for her; and when he snarled at her like that, it seemed to hit her like being rejected by everyone who had ever loved her, all at once.

I had been through a number of crises like this one with her before—though the others had not been so obviously Sunday's fault—and I knew that there was nothing much to be done with her until she began to relax. So I sat down and wrapped my arms around her, cuddling her as close as her rigidness would allow, and began to try to talk her out of it. The sound of my voice seemed to help, although at that time she would never show any kind of direct response to it, except to follow orders.

So, there I sat, on the mattresses and blankets in the back of the panel truck, with my arms around her narrow body that was more sharp bones than anything else, talking to her and telling her over and over again that Sunday wasn't mad at her; he was just a crazy cat, and she should pay no attention when he snarled, except to leave him alone for a while. After a while I got tired of repeating the same words and tried singing to her—any song that I could remember. I was aware it was no great performance. I may have believed at that time that I was hell on wheels at a number of things, but I knew singing was not one of them. I had a voice to scare bullfrogs. However, that had never seemed to matter with the girl. It was keeping up the human noise and holding her that helped. Meanwhile, all the time this was going on, Sunday had crept up as close to us as he could and had his forepaws around my left ankle, his forehead butted against my knee.

So, after a while, illogically, I reached down and patted his head, which he took as forgiveness. I was a complete fool for both of them, in some ways. Shortly after that, the girl began to stir. The stiffness went out of her. Her arms and legs extended themselves; and without a word to me she pulled away, crawled off and put her arms around Sunday. He suffered it, even licking at her face with his tongue. I unkinked my own cramped muscles and went back up front to the driver's seat of the truck.

Then I saw it, to the left of the highway. It was a line of sky-high mist or dust-haze, less than a couple of hundred yards away, rolling down on us at an angle.

There was no time for checking on the two back there to see if they were braced for a racing start. I jammed the key over, got the motor started, and slammed the panel into motion down the narrow asphalt lane between the brown-yellow of the standing wheat, now gently wind-rippled by the breeze that always preceded a mistwall, until the plant-tops wavered into varying shades of gold.

2

No mistwall I had seen, with the time change line its presence always signalled, had ever moved faster than about thirty miles an hour. That meant that unless this one was an exception, theoretically, any car in good working order on a decent road should have no trouble outrunning it. The difficulty arose, however, when—as now—the mistwall was not simply coming up behind us, but moving at an angle flanking the road. I would have to drive over half the length of the wall or more—and some mistwalls were up to ten miles long—to get out of its path before it caught us, along with everything else in its way. I held the pedal of the accelerator to the floor and sweated.

According to the needle on the speedometer, we were doing nearly a hundred and ten—which was nonsense. Eighty-five miles an hour was more like the absolute top speed of the panel truck. As it was, we swayed and bounced along the empty road as if five more miles an hour would have sent us flying off it.

I could now see the far end of the mistwall. It was still a good two or three miles away; and the wall itself was only a few hundred yards off and closing swiftly. I may have prayed a little bit at this point, in spite of being completely irreligious. I seem to remember that I did. In the weeks since the whole business of the time changes started, I had not been this close to being caught since that first day in the cabin northwest of Duluth, when I had, in fact, been caught without knowing what hit me. I had thought then it was another heart attack, come to carry me off for good this time; and the bitterness of being chopped down before I was thirty and after I had spent nearly two years putting myself into the best possible physical shape, had been like a dry, ugly taste in my throat just before the change line reached me and knocked me out.

I remember still thinking that it was a heart attack, even after I came to. I had gone on thinking that way, even after I found the squirrel that was still in shock from it; the way Sunday had been later, when I found him. For several days afterwards, with the squirrel tagging along behind me like some miniature dog until I either exhausted it or lost it, I did not begin to realize the size of what had happened. It was only later that I began to understand, when I came to where Duluth should have been and found virgin forest where a couple of hundred thousand people had lived, and later yet, as I moved south, and stumbled across the log cabin with the bearded man in cord-wrapped leather leggings.

The bearded man had nearly finished me. It took me almost three minutes too long after I met him to realize that he did not understand that the rifle in my hand was a weapon. It was only when I stepped back and picked up the hunting bow, that he pulled his fancy quick-draw trick with the axe he had been using to chop wood when I stepped into his clearing. I never saw anything like it and I hope I never see it again, unless I'm on the side of the man with the axe. It was a sort of scimitar-bladed tool with a wide, curving forward edge; and he had hung it on his shoulder, blade-forward, in what I took to be a reassuring gesture, when I first tried to speak to him. Then he came toward me, speaking some kind of Scandinavian-sounding gibberish in a friendly voice, the axe hung on his shoulder as if he had forgotten it was there.

It was when I began to get worried about the steady way he was coming on and warned him back with the rifle, that I recognized suddenly that, apparently, as far as he was concerned, I was carrying nothing more than a club. For a second I was merely paralyzed by the enormity of that insight. Then, before I could bring myself to shoot him after all in self-defense, I had the idea of trying to pick up the bow with my free hand. As an idea, it was a good one—but the minute he saw the bow in my hand he acted; and to this day, I'm not sure exactly how he did it.

He reached back at belt-level and jerked forward on the handle-end of the axe. It came off his shoulder—

spinning, back, around, under his arm, up in the air and over, and came down, incredibly, with the end of its handle into his fist and the blade edge forward.

Then he threw it.

I saw it come whirling toward me, ducked instinctively and ran. I heard it thunk into a tree somewhere behind me; but by then I was into the cover of the woods, and he did not follow.

Five days later I was where the twin cities of Minneapolis and St. Paul had been—and they looked as if they had been abandoned for a hundred years after a bombing raid that had nearly leveled them. But I found the panel truck there, and it started when I turned its key. There was gas in the filling station pumps, though I had to rig up a little kerosene generator I liberated from a sporting goods store, in order to pump some of it into the tank of the truck, and I headed south along U.S. 35W. Then came Sunday. Then came the girl. . . .

I was almost to the far end of the mistwall now, although to the left of the road the haze was less than a hundred yards from the roadway; and little stinging sprays of everything from dust to fine gravel were beginning to pepper the left side of the panel, including my own head and shoulder where the window on that side was not rolled up. But I had no time to roll it up now. I kept pushing the gas pedal through the floor, and suddenly we whipped past the end of the wall of mist, and I could see open country clear to the summer horizon.

Sweating, I eased back on the gas, let the truck roll to a stop, and half-turned it across the road so I could look behind us.

Back where we had been, seconds before, the mist had already crossed the road and was moving on into the fields that had been on the road's far side. They were ceasing to be there as it passed—as the road itself had already ceased to be, and the farm land on the near side of the road. Where the grain had rippled in the wind, there was now wild, grassy hillside—open country sparsely interspersed with a few clumps of trees, rising to a bluff, a crown of land, less than a quarter of a mile off, looking so close I could reach out and touch it. There was not a breath of wind stirring.

I put the panel back in gear again and drove off. After a while the road swung in a gentle curve toward a small town that looked as normal as apple pie, as if no mistwall had ever passed through it. It could be, of course. My heart began to pound a little with hope of running into someone sane I could talk with, about everything that had happened since that apparent heart attack of mine in the cabin.

But when I drove into Main Street of the town, between the buildings, there was no one in sight; and the whole place seemed deserted. Hope evaporated into caution. Then I saw what seemed to be a barricade across the street up ahead; and a single figure crouched behind it with what looked like a rocket launcher on his shoulder. He was peering over the barricade away from me; although he must have heard the sound of the motor coming up the street behind him.

I pulled the truck into an alley between two stores and stopped it.

"Stay here and stay quiet," I told the girl and Sunday.

I took the carbine from beside my driver's seat and got out. Holding it ready, just in case, I went up behind the man crouched at the barricade. Up this close I could see easily over the barricade—and sure enough, there was another mistwall, less than a mile away, but unmoving. For the first time since I had come into the silent town, I became conscious of a steady sound.

3

It came from somewhere up ahead, beyond the point where the straight white concrete highway vanished into the unmoving haze of the mistwall—a small buzzing sound. Like the sound of a fly in an enclosed box on a hot July day such as this one was.

"Get down," said the man with the rocket launcher.

I pulled my head below the top line of the makeshift barricade—furniture, rolls of carpeting, cans of paint—that barred the empty street between the gritty sidewalks and the unbroken store windows in the red brick sides of the Main Street building. Driving in from the northwest, I had thought at first that this small town was still living. Then, when I got closer, I guessed it was one of those places, untouched but abandoned, such as I had run into further north. And so it was, in fact; except for the man, his home-made barricade, and the rocket launcher.

The buzzing grew louder. I looked behind me, back down Main Street. I could just make out the brown, left front fender of the panel truck showing at the mouth of the alley into which I had backed it. There was no sound or movement from inside it. The two of them in there would be obeying my orders, lying still on the blankets in the van section, the leopard probably purring a little in its rough, throaty way and cleaning the fur of a forepaw with its tongue, while the girl held to the animal for comfort and companionship, in spite of the heat.

When I looked back through a chink in the barricade, there was something already visible in the road. It had evidently just appeared out of the haze, for it was coming very fast. Its sound was the buzzing sound I had heard earlier, now growing rapidly louder as the object raced toward us,

8

seeming to swell in size, like a balloon being inflated against the white backdrop of the haze, as it came.

It came so fast that there was only time to get a glimpse of it. It was yellow and black in color, like a wasp, a small gadget with an amazing resemblance to a late-model compact car, but half the size of such a car, charging at us down the ruler-straight section of highway like some outsize wind-up toy.

I jerked up my rifle; but at the same time the rocket launcher went off beside me with a flat clap of sound. The rocket was slow enough so that we could see it like a black speck, curving through the air to meet the gadget coming at us. They met and there was an explosion. The gadget hopped up off the road shedding parts which flew toward us, whacking into the far side of the barricade like shrapnel. For a full minute after it quit moving, there was no sound to be heard. Then the whistling of birds and the trilling of crickets took up again.

I looked over at the rocket launcher.

"Good," I said to the man. "Where did you get that launcher, anyway?"

"Somebody must have stolen it from a National Guard outfit," he said. "Or brought it back from overseas. I found it with a bunch of knives and guns and other things, in a storeroom behind the town police office."

He was as tall as I was, a tight-shouldered, narrow-bodied man with a deep tan on his forearms, and on his quiet, bony face. Maybe a little older than I; possibly in his late thirties. I studied him, trying to estimate how hard it would be to kill him if I had to. I could see him watching, doubtless with the same thought in mind.

It was the way things were, now. There was no shortage of food or drink, or anything material you could want. But neither was there any law, anymore—at least, none I'd been able to find in the last three weeks.

4

To break the staring match, I deliberately looked away to the gadget, lying still now beyond the barricades, and nodded at it.

"I'd like to have a look at it close up," I said. "Is it safe?"

"Sure." He got to his feet, laying down the rocket launcher. I saw, however, he had a heavy revolver—possibly a thirty-eight or forty-four—in a holster on the hip away from me; and a deer rifle carbine like mine was lying against the barricade. He picked it up in his left hand.

"Come on," he said. "They only show up one at a time; on a staggered schedule, seven to ten hours apart."

I looked down the road. There were no other wrecked shapes in black and yellow in sight along it.

"You're sure?" I said. "How many have you seen?"

He laughed, making a dry sound in his throat like an old man.

"They're never quite stopped," he said. "Like this one. It's harmless, now, but not really done for. Later it'll crawl back, or get pullled back behind the mist over there—you'll see. Come on."

He climbed over the barricade and I followed him. When we got to the gadget, it looked more than ever like an overlarge toy car—except that where the windows should be, there was a flat yellow surface; and instead of four ordinary-sized wheels with tires, the lower halves of something like sixteen or eighteen small metal disks showed through the panel sealing the underbody. The rocket had torn a large hole in the gadget's side.

"Listen," said the man, stooping over the hole. I came

close and listened myself. There was a faint buzzing still going on down there someplace inside it.

"Who sends these things?" I said. "Or what sends them?"

He shrugged.

"By the way," I said, "I'm Marc Despard." I held out my hand.

He hesitated.

"Raymond Samuelson," he said.

I saw his hand jerk forward a little, then back again. Outside of that, he ignored my offered hand; and I let it drop. I guessed that he might not want to shake hands with a man he might later have to try to kill; and I judged that anyone who worried about a nicety like that was not likely to shoot me in the back, at least, unless he had to. At the same time, there was no point in asking for trouble by letting any misunderstandings arise.

"I'm just on my way through to Omaha," I said. "My wife's there, if she's still all right. But I'm not going to drive right across that time change line out there if I've got a choice." I nodded at the haze from which the gadget had come. "Have you got any other roads leading south or east from the town?"

"Yes," he said. He was frowning. "Did you say your wife was there?"

"Yes," I answered. For the life of me, I had meant to say "ex-wife," but my tongue had slipped; and it was not worth straightening the matter out now for someone like Samuelson.

"Look," he said, "you don't have to go right away. Stop and have dinner."

Stop and have dinner. Something about my mentioning a wife had triggered off a hospitality reflex in him. The familiar, homely words he spoke seemed as strange and out of place, here between the empty town and the haze that barred the landscape to our right, as the wrecked gadget at our feet.

"All right," I said.

We went back, over the barricade and down to the panel truck. I called to the leopard and the girl to come out, and introduced them to Samuelson. His eyes widened at the sight of the leopard; but they opened even more at the sight of the girl behind the big cat.

"I call the leopard 'Sunday,' " I said. "The girl's never told me her name."

I put out my hand and Sunday stepped forward, flattening his ears and rubbing his head up under my palm with a sound that was like a whimper of pleasure.

"I came across him just after a time change had swept the area where he was," I said. "He was still in shock when I first touched him; and now I've got his soul in pawn, or something like that. You've seen how animals act, if you get them right after a change, before they come all the way back to being themselves?"

Samuelson shook his head. He was looking at me now with some distrust and suspicion.

"That's too bad," I said. "Maybe you'll take my word for it, then. He's perfectly safe as long as I'm around."

I petted Sunday. Samuelson looked at the girl.

"Hello," he said, smiling at her. But she simply stared back without answering. She would do anything I set her to doing, but I had never been able to make her seem conscious of herself. The straight, dark hair hanging down around her shoulders always had a wild look; and even the shirt and jeans she was wearing looked as if they did not belong on her.

They were the best of available choices, though. I had put her into a dress once, shortly after I had found her; and the effect had been pitiful. She had looked like a caricature of a young girl in that dress.

"She doesn't talk," I said. "I came across her a couple of days after I found the leopard, about two hundred miles south. The leopard was about where the Minneapolis-St. Paul area used to be. It could have come from a zoo. The girl was just wandering along the road. No telling where she came from."

"Poor kid," said Samuelson. He evidently meant it; and I began to think it even more unlikely that he would shoot me in the back.

We went to his house, one block off Main Street, for dinner.

"What about the—whatever-you-call-them?" I asked. "What if one comes while you aren't there to stop it?"

"The buzzers," he said. "No, like I told you, they don't run on schedule, but after one's come by, it's at least six and a half hours before the next one. It's my guess there's some kind of automatic factory behind the mist there, that takes that long to make a new one."

Samuelson's house turned out to be one of those tall, ornate, late-nineteenth century homes you still see in small towns. Two stories and an attic with a wide screen porch in front and lilac bushes growing all along one side of it. The rooms inside were small, dark and high-ceilinged, with too much furniture for their floorspace. He had rigged a gas motor and a water tank to the well in his basement that had formerly been run by an electric pump; and he had found an old, black, wood-burning stove to block up in one corner of this spacious kitchen. The furniture was clean of dust and in order.

He gave us the closest thing to a normal meal that I'd eaten—or the girl had, undoubtedly—since the time storm first hit Earth. I knew it had affected all the Earth, by this time; not just the little part west of the Great Lakes in North America, where I was. I carried a good all-bands portable radio along and, once in a while, picked up a fragment of a broadcast from somewhere. The continuity—or discontinuity—lines dividing the time areas usually blocked off radio. But sometimes things came through. Hawaii, evidently, was unique in hardly having been touched, and I'd occasionally heard bits of shortwave from as far away as Greece. Not that I listened much. There was nothing I could do for the people broadcasting, any more than there was anything they could do for me.

I told Samuelson about this while he was fixing dinner; and he said he had run into the same thing with both the shortwave and long-wave radios he had set up. We agreed that the storm was not over.

"We've only had the one time change here in Saulsburg, though," he said. "Every so often, I'll see a line of change moving across country off on the horizon, or standing still for a while out there; but so far, none's come this way."

"Where did all the people go, that were in this place?" I asked.

His face changed, all at once.

"I don't know," he said. Then he bent over the biscuit dough he was making, so that his face was hidden away from me. "I had to drive over to Peppard—that's the next town. I drove and drove and couldn't find it. I began to think I was sick or crazy, so I turned the car around and drove home. When I got back here, it was like you see it now."

It was clear he did not want to talk about it. But I could guess some of what he had lost from the house. It had been lived in by more than one adult, and several children. There were a woman's overshoes in the front closet, toys in a box in one corner of the living room, and three bicycles in good condition in the garage.

"What did you do for a living?" he asked me after a moment.

"I was retired," I said.

He frowned over that, too. So I told him about myself. The time storm had done nothing in my case to leave me with things I did not want to talk about, except for the matter of Swannee, down in Omaha; and somehow I was perfectly comforted and sure that she and that city had come through the time storm changes unharmed, though I had heard no radio broadcasts from there.

"I started investing in the stock market when I was nineteen," I said, "before I was even out of college. I struck it lucky." Luck, of course, had nothing to do with it; but I had found I could not tell people that. Because the word "stocks" was involved, it had to be luck, not hard research and harder-headed decision-making, that had made money for me. "Then I used what I had to take over a company that made trailers and snowmobiles; and that did all right. I'd be there yet, but I had a heart attack."

Samuelson's eyebrows went up.

"A heart attack?" he said. "You're pretty young for something like that."

"I was damned young," I said. "I was twenty-four."

I discovered suddenly that I had been wrong about not having things I did not want to talk about. I did not want to tell him about my heart attack. He looked too much like a man who'd never had a sick day in his life.

"Anyway," I said, "my doctor told me to take it easy and lose weight. That was two years ago. So I sold out, set up a trust to support me, and bought a place up in the woods of northern Minnesota, beyond Ely—if you know that state. I got back in shape, and I've been fine ever since; until the time storm hit three weeks ago."

"Yes," he said.

The food was ready, so I helped him carry it into the dining room and we all ate there; even Sunday, curled up in a corner. I had thought Samuelson might object to my bringing the leopard into his house, but he had not.

Afterwards, we sat on his screened porch at the front of the house, with the thick leaves of the sugar maple in the yard screening us from the western sun. It was after six by my watch, but now in midsummer, there were at least another three hours of light left. Samuelson had some homemade white wine which was not bad. It was not very good either, but the town was apparently a dry town; and of course, he had not left it since he had first come back here and found his people gone.

"How about the girl?" he asked me, when he first poured the wine into water glasses.

"Why not?" I said. "We may be all dead—her included —tomorrow, if the wrong sort of time change catches us."

So he gave her a glass. But she only took a small sip, then put it down on the floor of the porch by her chair. After a bit, while Samuelson and I talked, she got out of the chair itself and sat down on the floor where she could put an arm around Sunday, who was lying there, dozing. Outside of raising a lazy eyebrow when he felt the weight of her arm, the leopard paid no attention. It was amazing what he would stand from her, sometimes.

"What is it?" Samuelson asked me, after we'd been talking for a while about how things used to be. "I mean—where did it come from?"

He was talking about the time storm.

"I don't know," I said. "I'll bet nobody does. But I've got a theory."

"What's that?" He was looking at me closely in the shadow of the porch. A little evening breeze stirred the lilac bushes into scraping their upper branches against the side of the house.

"I think it's just what we're calling it," I said. "A storm. Some sort of storm in space that the whole world ran into, the same way you could be out driving in your car and run into a thunderstorm. Only in this case, instead of wind and rain, thunder and lightning, we get these time changes, like ripples moving across the surface of the world, with everything getting moved either forward or back in time. Wherever a change passes over them."

"How about here?" he asked. "The town's just where it was before. Only the people . . ."

He trailed off.

"How do you know?" I said. "Maybe the area right around here was moved forward just a year, say, or even a month. That wouldn't be enough to make any change in the buildings and streets you could notice, but it might have been beyond the point where everybody living here, for some reason, decided to get out."

"Why?"

"Those buzzers, as you call them," I said. "Seeing one of them come at the town would be pretty good reason to me to get out, if I was someone living here."

He shook his head.

"Not everybody," he said. "Not without leaving some kind of message."

I gave up. If he did not want reasonable explanations, there was no point in my forcing them on him.

"Tell me," he said, after we had sat there without talking for a while, "do you think God had something to do with it?"

So that was his hang-up. That was why he stayed here, day after day, defending a town with no people in it. That was why he had carefully adapted the well in the base-ment to the new conditions and set up a wood stove so that he could give a regular meal at a moment's notice to a complete family, if they should return unexpectedly, showing up at the front door, tired and hungry. I wanted to tell him neither God nor human had ever changed things much for me; but now that I knew what his question meant to him, I could not do it. All at once I felt the pain in him—and I found myself suddenly angry that someone I did not even know should be able to export his troubles to me, like that. It was true I had lost nothing, not like him. Still . . . .

"Who can tell?" I said, standing up. "We'd better be going."

He stood up also, quickly. Before he was on his feet, Sunday was on his, and that brought the girl scrambling upright.

"You could stay here overnight," he said.

I shook my head.

"You don't want to drive in the dark," he went on.

"No," I said. "But I'd like to get some miles under our belt before quitting for the day. I'm anxious to get to my wife."

I led the leopard and the girl out to the panel, which I had driven over and now stood in his driveway. I opened the door on the driver's side, and the other two got in, crawling back into the body. I waited until they were settled, then got in myself and was about to back out, when Samuelson, who had gone in the house instead of following us to the truck, came out again, almost shyly, with a pair of large paper grocery sacks. He pushed them in through the open window at my left.

"Here," he said. "There's some food you could use. I put in a bottle of the wine, too."

"Thanks." I put the two sacks on the empty front seat beside me. He looked past me, back into the body of the van, where the girl and the leopard were already curled up, ready for sleep.

"I've got everything, you know," he said. "Everything you could want. There's nothing she could use—clothes, or anything?"

"Sunday's the only thing she wants," I said. "As long as she's got him, there's nothing else she cares about."

"Well, goodby then," he said.

"So long."

I backed out into the street and drove off. In the side-view mirror I could see him walk into the street himself so that he could look after us and wave. I turned a corner two blocks down and the houses shut him from view.

He had given me a filling station map earlier, with a route marked in pencil, that led me to the south edge of the city and out at last on a two-lane asphalt road rising and dipping over the land, with open, farmers' fields on either side. The fields had all been planted that spring; and as I drove along I was surrounded by acres of corn and wheat and peas no one would ever harvest or use. The sky-high wall of haze that was the time change line, holding its position just outside of Samuelson's town, now to the left and behind us, grew smaller as I drove the van away from there.

In a car we were pretty safe, according to what I had learned so far. These time lines were like lengths of rod, rolling across the landscape; but as I say, I had yet to encounter any that seemed to travel at more than thirty miles an hour. It was not hard to get away from them as long as you could stick to a road.

I had been keeping my eyes open for something in the way of an all-terrain vehicle, but with adequate speed. Something like a Land Rover that could make good time on the roads but could also cut across open country, if necessary. But so far I had not found anything.

I became aware that the engine of the van was roaring furiously under the hood. I was belting us along the empty asphalt road at nearly seventy miles an hour. There was no need for anything like that. It was both safer and easier on the gas consumption to travel at about forty or forty-five; and now and then gas was not easily available, just when the tank ran low. It was true I had four spare five-gallon cans-full, lashed to the luggage carrier on the van's roof. But that was for real emergencies.

Besides, none of the three of us had anything that urgent to run to—or away from. I throttled down to forty miles an hour, wondering how I had let my speed creep up in the first place.

Then, of course, I realized why. I had been letting Samuelson's feelings get to me. Why should I cry for him? He was as crazy from the loss of his family as the girl was—or Sunday. But he had really wanted us to stay the night, in that large house of his from which his family had disappeared; and it would have been a kindness to him if we had stayed. Only, I could not take the chance. Sometime in the night he might change suddenly from the man who was desperate for company to a man who thought that I, or all of us, had something to do with whatever it was that had taken his people away from him.

I could not trust his momentary sanity. Samuelson had talked for a while like a sane man; but he was still someone sitting in a deserted town, shooting rockets full of high explosives at out-size toys that attacked at regular intervals. No one in that position could be completely sane. Besides, insanity was part of things, now. Sunday was the definitive example. I could have cut the leopard's throat, and he would have licked my hand as I was doing it. The girl was in no better mental condition. Samuelson, like them, was caught in this cosmic joke that had overtaken the world we knew—so he was insane too, by definition. There was no other possibility.

Which of course, I thought, following the idea to its logical conclusion, as I drove into the increasing twilight, meant that I had to be insane, too. The idea was almost laughable. I felt perfectly sane. But just as I had not trusted Samuelson, if I were him, or anyone else looking at me from the outside as I drove across the country with a leopard and a speechless girl for companions, I would not trust myself. I would have been afraid that there could be a madness in me too, that would overtake me sometime, suddenly and without warning. Of course, that was all nonsense. I put the ridiculous thought out of my head.

5

When the red flush of the sunset above the horizon to our right began to grow narrow and dark, and stars were clearly visible in the clear sky to the east, I pulled the van off the road into a comfortable spot under some cottonwood trees growing down in a little dip between two hills and set up camp. It was so warm that I had the tent flaps tied all the way back. I lay there looking out at the stars, seeming to move deeper and deeper in the night sky, becoming more and more important and making the earth under me feel more like a chip of matter lost in the universe.

But I could not sleep. That had happened to me a lot, lately. I wanted to get up and go sit outside the tent by myself, with my back to the trunk of one of the cottonwoods. But if I did, Sunday would get up and come out with me; and then the girl would get up and follow Sunday. It was a chain reaction. A tag-end of a line from my previous two years of steady reading, during my hermit-like existence above Ely, came back to me. *Privatum commodum publico cedit*—"private advantage yields to public." I decided to lie there and tough it out.

What I had to tough out was the replaying in my head of all the things that had happened. I had almost forgotten, until now, my last summer in high school when I started teaching myself to read Latin because I had just learned how powerfully it underlays all our English language. Underlays and outdoes. *"How long, O Cataline, will you abuse our patience?"* Good, but not in the same ball game with the thunder of old Cicero's original: *"Quo usque, Catilina, abutere patienta nostra?"*

After the sweep of the first time change that I thought was my second heart attack come to take me for good

20

this time—after I had found I was not dead, or even
hurt—there had been the squirrel, frozen in shock. The
little gray body had been relaxed in my hands when I
picked it up; the small forepaws had clung to my fingers.
It had followed me after that for at least the first three
days, when I finally decided to walk south from my cabin
and reach a city called Ely, that turned out to be no
longer there. I had not understood then that what I had
done to the squirrel was what later I was to do to Sunday
—be with it when it came out of shock, making it totally
dependent on me . . . . Then, a week or so later, there
had been the log cabin and the man in leggings, the
transplanted Viking or whoever, who I thought was just
anyone cutting firewood with his shirt off, until he saw
me, hooked the axe over his shoulder as if holstering it,
and started walking toward me . . . .

I was into it again. I was really starting to replay the
whole sequence, whether I wanted to or not; and I could
not endure that, lying trapped in this tent with two other
bodies. I had to get out. I got to my feet as quietly as I
could. Sunday lifted his head, but I hissed at him between
my teeth so angrily that he lay down again. The girl only
stirred in her sleep and made a little noise in her throat,
one hand flung out to touch the fur of Sunday's back.

So I made it outside without them after all, into the
open air where I could breathe; and I sat down with my
back against the rugged, soft bark of one of the big cottonwoods. Overhead the sky was perfectly clear and the
stars were everywhere. The air was still and warm, very
transparent and clean. I leaned the back of my head
against the tree trunk and let my mental machinery go.
It was simply something I was stuck with—had always
been stuck with, all my lifetime.

Well, perhaps not all. Before the age of seven or eight,
things had been different. But by the time I was that
old, I had begun to recognize that I was on my own—and
needed no one else.

My father had been a cipher as far back as I could
remember. If someone were to tell me that he had never
actually realized he had two children, I would be inclined
to believe it. Certainly I had seen him forget us even
when we were before his eyes, in the same room with
him. He had been the director of the Walter H. Mann-
heim private library in St. Paul; and he was a harmless

man—a bookworm. But he was no use either to me or my
younger sister as a parent.

My mother was something else. To begin with, she
was beautiful. Yes I know, every child thinks that about
its mother. But I had independent testimony from a number of other people; particularly a long line of men, other
than my father, who not only thought so, also, but told
my mother so, when I was there to overhear them.

However, most of that came later. Before my sister
was born my mother was my whole family, by herself.
We used to play games together, she and I. Also, she
sang and talked to me and told me stories endlessly.
But then, after my sister was born, things began to
change. Not at once, of course. It was not until Beth
was old enough to run around that the alteration in my
mother became clearly visible. I now think that she had
counted on Beth's birth to do something for her marriage; and it had not done so.

At any rate, from that time on, she began to forget
us. Not that I blamed her for it. She had forgotten our
father long since—in fact, there was nothing there to forget. But now she began to forget us as well. Not all of
the time, to start with; but we came to know when she
was about to start forgetting because she would show up
one day with some new, tall man we had never seen, who
smelled of cigars and alcohol.

When this first started happening, it was the beginning
of a bad time for me. I was too young then to accept it,
and I wanted to fight whatever was taking her away from
me; but there was nothing there with which I could come
to grips. It was only as if a glass window had suddenly
been rolled up between her and me; and no matter how I
shouted or pounded on its transparent surface, she did not
hear. Still, I kept on trying to fight it for several years,
during which she began to stay away for longer and longer
periods—all with my father's silent consent, or at least
with no objections from him.

It was at the close of those years that my fight finally
came to an end. I did not give up, because I could not;
but the time came when my mother disappeared completely. She went away on one last trip and never came
back. So at last I was able to stop struggling; and as a result I came to the first great discovery of my life, which
was that nobody ever really loved anyone. There was a

built-in instinct when you were young that made you think you needed a mother; and another built-in instinct in that mother to pay attention to you. But as you got older you discovered your parents were only other humanly selfish people, in competition with you for life's pleasures; and your parents came to realize that this child of theirs that was you was not so unique and wonderful after all, but only a small savage with whom they were burdened. When I understood this at last, I began to see how knowing it gave me a great advantage over everyone else; because I realized then that life was not love, as my mother had told me it was when I was very young, but competition —fighting; and, knowing this, I was now set free to give all my attention to what really mattered. So, from that moment on I became a fighter without match, a fighter nothing could stop.

It was not quite that sudden and complete a change, of course. I still had, and probably always would have, absent-minded moments when I would still react to other people out of my early training, as if it mattered to me whether they lived or died. Indeed, after my mother disappeared for good, there was a period of several years in which Beth clung to me—quite naturally, of course, because I was all she had—and I responded unthinkingly with the false affection reflex. But in time she too grew up and went looking somewhere else for attention; and I became completely free.

It was a freedom so great I saw most people could not even conceive of it. When I was still less than half-grown, adults would remark on how strong-minded I was. They talked of how I would make my mark in the world. I used to want to laugh, hearing them say that, because anything else was unthinkable. I not only had every intention of leaving my mark on the world; I intended to put my brand on it and turn it into my own personal property; and I had no doubt I could do it. Free as I was of the love delusion that blinkered all the rest of them, there was nothing to stop me; and I had already found out that I would go on trying for what I wanted as long as it was there for me to get.

I had found that out when I had fought my mother's withdrawal from us. I had not been able to stop struggling against that until it had finally sunk in on me that she was gone for good. Up until that time I had not been able to accept the fact she might leave us. My mind simply refused to give up on her. It would keep going over and over the available data or evidence, with near-idiot, unending patience, searching for some crack in the problem, like a rat chewing at a steel plate across the bottom of a granary door. A steel plate could wear down a rat's teeth; but he would only rest a while to let them grow again, and then go back once more to chewing, until one day he would wear his way through to where the grain was. So it was with me. Pure reflex kept the rat chewing like that; and, as far as I was concerned, it was a pure reflex that kept my mind coming back and back to a problem until it found a solution.

There was only one way to turn it off, one I had never found out how to control. That was if somehow the knowledge managed to filter through to me that the answer I sought would have no usefulness after I found it. When that happened—as when I finally realized my mother was gone for good—there would be an almost audible *click* in my mind, and the whole process would blank out. It was as if the reflex suddenly went dead. But that did not happen often; and it was certainly not happening now.

The problem my mind would not give up on at the moment was the question of what had happened to the world. My head kept replaying all its available evidence, from the moment of my collapse in the cabin near Duluth to the present, trying for one solid, explainable picture that would pull everything together.

Sitting now under the tree, in the shade of a new-risen quarter moon and staring up at the star-bright sky of summer, I went clear back to reliving my college days, to the paper I had written on the methods of charting stocks, followed by the theoretical investments, then the actual investments, then the penthouse suite in the Bellecourt Towers, hotel service twenty-four hours a day, and the reputation for being some sort of young financial wizard. Then my cashing out and buying into Snowman, Inc., my three years as president of that company, while snowmobile and motor home sales climbed up off the wall chart—and my marriage to Swannee.

I had never blamed Swannee a bit for what had happened. It must have been as irritating to her as it would have been to me to have someone hanging on to her the way I ended up doing. The way I had decided to get married in the first place was that I had gotten tired of living in the penthouse apartment. I wanted a real house, and found one. An architecturally modern, rambling building with five bedrooms, on about twenty acres of land with its own small lake. And of course, once I had decided to have a house, I realized what I really needed was a wife to go along with it. And I looked around a bit and married Swannee. She was not as beautiful as my mother, but she was close to it. Tall, with a superb body and a sort of golden-custard colored hair, very fine, that she wore long and which floated around her shoulders like a cloud.

By education she had been headed for being a lawyer; but her instincts for work were not all that strong. In spite of the fact that she had done well academically in law school, she had never taken her bar exams and was, in fact, working as a sort of ornamental legal assistant to a firm of corporation attorneys down in St. Paul. I think she was glad to give up the pretense of going to the office every day and simply take over as my wife. She was, in fact, ideal from my standpoint. I had no illusions about her. I had buried those with the memories of my mother years before. So I had not asked her to be any more than she was; ornamental, good in bed, and able to do the relatively easy job of managing this home of mine. I think, in fact, we had an ideal marriage—until I spoiled it.

As I said, occasionally I would become absent-minded and respond as if other people really mattered to me. Apparently I made the mistake of doing this with Swannee; because little by little she drifted off from me, began disappearing on short trips almost as my mother had done, and then one day she told me she wanted a divorce and left.

I was disappointed, but of course, not much more than that; and I decided that trying to have an ordinary, live-in wife had been a mistake in the first place. I now had all my time to devote to work, and for the next year I did just that. Right up to the moment of my first heart attack.

At twenty-four. God damn it, no one should have to have a heart attack after only twenty-four years in this world! But again there was my rat-reflex mind chewing

away at that problem, too, until it broke through to a
way out. I cashed in and set up a living trust to support
me in style forever, if necessary; and I went up to the
cabin to live and make myself healthy again.

Two years of that—and then the blackout, the squirrel,
the trek south, the man with the axe . . . and Sunday.

I had almost shot Sunday in the first second I saw him,
before I realized that he was in the same sort of trance
the squirrel had been in. We ran into each other about
twenty miles or so south of the Twin Cities, in an area
where they had started to put together a really good
modern zoo—one in which the animals wandered about
almost without restriction; and the people visiting were
moved through wire tunnels and cages to see the creatures
in something like their natural, wild, free states.

But there was no zoo left when I got there; only
half-timbered country. A time change line had moved
through, taking out about three miles of highway. The
ground was rough, but dry and open. I coaxed the panel
truck across it in low gear, picking as level a route as I
could and doing all right, until I got one rear wheel down
into a hole and had to jack it up to get traction again.

I needed something firm to rest the jack base on. I
walked into a little patch of woods nearby looking for a
piece of fallen tree limb the right size, and literally
stumbled over a leopard.

He was crouched low on the ground, head twisted a
little sideways and looking up as if cringing from something large that was about to attack him. Like the
squirrel, he was unmoving in that position when I walked
into him—the time storm that had taken out the road
and caught him as well, must have passed only minutes
previously. When I stubbed my toe on his soft flank, he
came out of his trance and looked at me. I jumped back
and jerked up the rifle I had had the sense to carry with
me.

But he stepped forward and rubbed along the side of my
upper leg, purring, so much like an overgrown household
pussycat that I could not have brought myself to shoot
him, even if I had had the sense to do so. He was a
large young male, weighing a hundred and forty pounds
when I later managed to coax him onto a bathroom scale
in an abandoned hardware store. He rubbed by me, turned
and came back to slide up along my other side, licking at

my hands where they held the rifle. And from then on, like it or not, I had Sunday.

I had puzzled about him, and the squirrel, a number of times since. The closest I had come to satisfying my search for what had made them react as they had, was that being caught by a time change jarred anything living right back to its infancy. After I first came to in the cabin—well, I had generally avoided thinking about that. For one thing I had a job to clean myself up. But I do remember that first, terrible feeling of helplessness and abandonment—like a very young child lost in a woods from which he knows he can never find his way out. If someone had turned up then to hold my hand, I might have reacted just like the squirrel or the leopard.

Then there had been our meeting—Sunday's and mine —with the girl. That had been a different kettle of fish. For one thing, evidently she had passed the point of initial recovery from being caught in a time change; but equally evidently, the experience—or something just before the experience—had hit her a great deal more severely than my experience with the time change had done.

But about this time, the stars started to swim slowly in a circular dance, and I fell asleep.

I woke with the sun in my eyes, feeling hot and itchy all over. It was a bright cloudless day, at least a couple of hours old, since dawn; evidently the tree had shaded me from the sun's waking me earlier.

Sunday lay curled within the open entrance to the tent; but he was all alone. The girl was gone.

6

My first reaction, out of that old, false, early training of mine, was to worry. Then common sense returned. It would only be a relief, as far as I was concerned, to have her gone; with her fits of withdrawal and her pestering Sunday until he, in turn, became a bother.

Damn it, I thought, *let her go.*

But then it occurred to me that something might have happened to her. It was open country all around us here, except for a screen of young popple, beyond which there was a small creek. I went down through the popple and looked across the creek, up over a swelling expanse of meadow lifting to a near horizon maybe three hundred yards off. There was nothing to be seen. I went down to look at the creek itself, the edges of which were muddy and marshy, and found her footprints in soft earth, going toward the water. A little further, one of her shoes was stuck in the mud and abandoned.

The creek was shallow—no more than knee deep for someone her size. I waded across, picked up the shoe, located her tracks in the mud on the far side and saw them joined by two other sets of footprints. Bare feet, larger than hers. I began to feel cold and hot inside at the same time.

I went back to the tent, strapped on the belt with the holstered revolver and took the carbine. The carbine held thirteen shells and it was semi-automatic. My first thought was of following the tracks up the hill; and then I realized that this would be more likely to alert whoever the other two people had been than if I drove. If they saw me coming in the panel, they might figure I'd given up the girl and left her. If they saw me coming on foot, particu-

larly with Sunday, they wouldn't have much choice but
to think I was chasing her down.

I packed the gear. It would be hard to replace, maybe;
and there was no guarantee we'd be coming back this
way again. Then I got into the panel, letting Sunday up
on the seat beside me for once, but making him lie down
out of sight from outside. I pulled out on the highway
and headed up the road parallel to the way I had last
seen the footprints going.

We did not have far to go. Just up and over the rise
that belonged to the meadow across the creek, I saw a
trailer camp with some sort of large building up in front
of all the trailers. No one had cut the grass in the camp
for a long time, but there were figures moving about the
trailers. I drove up to the building in front. There were a
couple of dusty gas pumps there, and a cheerfully grinning, skinny, little old man in coveralls too big for him
came out of the building as I stopped.

"Hi," he said, coming up within about four feet of
Sunday's side of the car and squinting across through the
open window at me. "Want some gas?"

"No thanks," I said. "I'm looking for a girl. A girl
about fourteen, fifteen years old with dark hair and
doesn't talk. Have you seen—"

"Nope!" he chirped. "Want some gas?"

Gas was something you had to scrounge for these
days. I was suddenly very interested in him.

"Yes," I said. "I think I'll have some gas. And . . ."

I let my voice trail off into silence. He came closer,
cocking his left ear at me.

"What'd y'say?" He stuck his head in the window and
came face to face with Sunday, only inches between
them. He stopped, perfectly still.

"That's right," I said. "Don't move or make a sound,
now. And don't try to run. The leopard can catch you
before you can take three steps." He didn't know that
Sunday would never have understood in a million years
any command I might have given to chase someone.

I jerked my thumb at the back of the panel. Sunday
understood that. He turned and leaped into the back, out
of the right hand seat in one flowing movement. The old
man's eyes followed him. I slid over into the right hand
seat.

"Now," I said, "turn around. Give me room to open the door."

He did. I opened the door on that side of the panel a crack. The baggy coverall on his back was only inches away. Vertically in the center of the back, about belt level, was a tear or cut about eight inches long. I reached in through it and closed my hand on pretty much what I expected. A handgun—a five-chamber .22 revolver—stuck in a belt around his waist under the coveralls.

"All right," I said, picking up the carbine and getting out of the panel behind him. "Walk straight ahead of me. Act ordinary and don't try to run. The leopard will be with me; and if I don't get you, he will. Now, where's the girl? Keep your voice down when you answer."

"Bub-bu-bu——," the old man stammered. Sounds, nothing understandable. Plainly, as his repeated offer of gas had shown, whoever lived in this camp had chosen one of their less bright citizens to stand out front and make the place look harmless.

"Come on, Sunday," I said.

The leopard came. We followed the old man across the drive, past the pumps. The large building looked not only closed, but abandoned. Darkness was behind its windows, and spider webs hung over the cracked white paint of its door frame. I poked the old man with the carbine muzzle, directing him around the right end of the building and back into the camp. I was expecting to be jumped or fired at, at any second. But nothing happened. When I got around the end of the building, I saw why. They were all at the party.

God knows, they might have been normal people once. But what I saw now were somewhere between starving savages and starving animals. They were mostly late adolescents, rib-skinny every one of them, male and female alike barefoot below the ragged cuff-edges of the jeans they wore and naked above the waistband. Everyone of them, as well, was striped and marked with black paint on face and body. They were gathered, maybe thirty or forty of them, in an open space before the rows of trailers began. It might have been a stretch of show lawn, or a volleyball court, once. At the end of it, tied to a sort of X of planks set upright and surrounded by burnable trash, paper and bits of wood, was the girl.

Whether she had come there willingly, I do not know.

It is not beyond the bounds of possibility that she had finally despaired of ever having Sunday love her; and when she met those two other pairs of feet by the creek, she had gone off of her own free will with them. But she was terrified now. Her eyes were enormous, and her mouth was stretched wide in a scream that she could not bring forth.

I poked the old man with the gun muzzle and walked in among them. I saw no weapons; but it stood to reason they must have something more than the revolver that had been hidden on the old man. The back of my neck prickled; but on the spur of the moment the best thing I could think of was to put a bold front on it, and maybe we could just all walk out of here—the girl, Sunday and I—with no trouble.

They said not a word, they did not move as I walked through them. And then, when I was less than a dozen feet from the girl, she finally got that scream out of her.

"Look out!"

For a part of a second I was so stunned to hear her utter something understandable that I only stared. Then it registered on me that she was looking over my shoulder at something behind me. I spun around, dropping on one knee instinctively and bringing up the carbine to my shoulder.

There were two of them, lying on the roof of the house with either rifles or shotguns—I had no time to decide which. They were just like the others, except for their firearms. The girl's shriek must have startled them as much as it had me, because they were simply lying there, staring down at me with their weapons forgotten.

But it was not them I had to worry about, anyway, because—I have no idea from where—the crowd I had just passed had since produced bows and arrows; perhaps a bow for every five or six of them, so that half a dozen of them were already fitting arrows to their strings as I turned. I started firing.

I shot the two on the roof first, without thinking—which was pure foolishness, the reflex of a man brought up to think of firearms as deadly, but of arrows as playthings—because the two on the roof did not even have their guns aimed, and by the time I'd fired at them a couple of arrows had already whistled by me. They were target arrows, lacking barbed hunting heads, but nonetheless deadly for that. The rest of the ones being aimed would certainly not all have missed me—if it had not been for Sunday.

There was nothing of the Lassie-dog-to-the-rescue about Sunday. The situation was entirely beyond his understanding; and if the two on the roof or the bow-wielders had shot me quickly and quietly enough, probably he would merely have sniffed sadly at me as I lay on the ground and wondered why I had stopped moving. But the girl had screamed—and I must suddenly have reeked of the body chemicals released by fear and fury—so Sunday operated by instinct.

If I was frightened, he was frightened, too. And in wild animals, as in man himself once he is broken down to it, fear and fury are the same thing. Sunday attacked the only fear-making cause in view—the group of archers and their friends before us; and they found themselves suddenly facing a wild, snarling, pinwheel-of-knives that was a hundred and forty pound member of the cat family gone berserk.

They ran from him. Of course they ran. All but three or four that were too badly clawed or bitten to get away. I had plenty of time and freedom to get the girl untied from the planks and start to lead her out of the clearing. By that time Sunday was off in one corner of the open space, daintily toying, with one hooked claw, at a bleeding, moaning figure that was trying to crawl away from him. It was a little sickening; but so was what they had planned for the girl. I called the leopard. He came—if reluctantly—and followed us back to the truck. We got out of there.

Half a mile down the highway I had to pull over to the shoulder and stop the car, again. Sunday was still prickly from the adrenaline of the battle. He wanted to lie in the back of the panel all alone and lick his fur. The girl, rebuffed by him, was suddenly sick. I helped her out of the car and held her head until it was over. Then I got her back into the front seat of the car, curled up there with a blanket over her.

"They were going to EAT me," she whispered, when I covered her up.

It was the second time she had spoken, and all in one day. I looked at her, but her eyes were squeezed shut. I could not tell if she had been talking to me, or only to herself. I got the panel moving again and let her sleep. That evening when we camped, I tried talking to her myself. But she had gone back to being dumb. She would neither speak nor look at me. Foolishly, I even found myself feeling disappointed—even a little hurt at that. But of course that was just the wrong-headed early training at work in me again. I had been feeling good over the fact that she was coming out of her mental prison—as if that really mattered, one way or another.

The next day we headed south by west again. It was a bright, hot day, and I was feeling good. We had gotten off the asphalt on to a stretch of superhighway, and there was no one to be seen—not even anything on the road as inconsequential as an abandoned car. We were making good time; and Samuelson had helped me to fix myself on the map. We were close enough to the location of Omaha that, barring unforeseen delays along the road, we would reach it by sunset. When noon came, I picked a ramp and pulled off the freeway—just to be on the safe side in case someone unfriendly should be cruising it about the time we were having lunch—and found a patch of shade under some large, scraggly-limbed trees I could not identify.

We had hardly glimpsed the mistwall of a time change all morning—and the few we had seen had been far off, so far off that in the bright daylight it was impossible to tell whether they were standing still or moving. But obviously one had passed by where we were sometime since the storms started. About four hundred yards from the exit ramp of the highway the cross road ended abruptly in a clump of tall mop-headed palms, the kind you find lining the street boulevards in Los Angeles.

The palms and the big scraggly-limbed trees signalled that we were into a different time-changed territory than we had been earlier. Now that I stopped to notice it, for some time there had been a different kind of dampness to the air than that which comes from midwestern, midsummer humidity. The softness of the atmosphere was more like that of a seacoast; and the few white clouds that moved overhead seemed to hang low and opulent in the sky, the way they do in Florida, instead of being high and distant like piled up castles, as they are in temperate zone mid-continental skies during the warm months.

It was a hint, I thought, to be on our guard against

strange company. As far as I had been able to determine, it was only everything below the animal level that got changed by the time storms when they passed. I had begun to add up some evidence in what I saw to reach the conclusion that much of what I came across was several hundred, if not several thousand, years forward from my own original time. There was some evidence of extensive storm damage and geological change, followed by considered reforestation in a majority of the landscapes I moved through. There must have been massive loss of life in most areas at the same time or another, which accounted for the scarcity of most warm-blooded creatures, except for birds. Certainly topography and vegetation changed when a time line passed; and I had noticed fish in lakes that had not been lakes before the time change. But just where on the scale of life the dividing line was drawn, I had no idea. It would pay to be watchful. If, for example, snakes were below the dividing line, then we might suddenly encounter poisonous varieties in latitudes or areas where such varieties had never existed before.

I spent part of the lunch hour trying to get the girl to talk; but she was back at being voiceless again. I kept chattering to her, though, partly out of stubbornness and partly out of the idea that if she had loosened up once, she could again; and the more I tried to wear down the barrier between us, possibly, the sooner she would.

When we were done with lunch, we buried the tin cans and the paper. The girl and I ate a lot of canned stuff, which made meals easy; and I had fallen into the habit of feeding Sunday on canned dog food or any other meat that could be found. He also hunted occasionally as we went along. But he would never go very far from me to do it, and this restricted what he could catch. We buried our trash just in case some one or something might find the remains and take a notion to trail us. We got back in the panel truck and headed once more down the superhighway.

But it was exactly as if stopping to eat lunch had changed our luck. Within five miles the superhighway disappeared—cut off by some past time storm line. It ended in a neat lip of concrete hanging thirty feet in the air with nothing in the shape of a road below or beyond it but sandy hills, covered with cactus and scraggly trees.

I had to backtrack two miles to find an exit ramp that led down on to a road that appeared to keep going off at an angle as far as I could see. It was asphalt, like most of the roads we had been travelling earlier, but it was not in as good shape as the ones that had led us through Samuelson's small town and past the trailer camp. It was narrower, high-crowned, and weedy along the edges. I hesitated because, although the road angled exactly in the direction I wanted to go, there was something about it that filled me with uneasiness. I simply did not like the look of it. Here and there sand had blown across it, a smudge of gold on black—but not to any depth that would slow down the panel truck. Still, I slowed on my own and cruised at no more than thirty miles an hour, keeping my eyes open.

The road seemed to run on without end, which did nothing to allay that uneasiness of mine. There was something about it that was unfamiliar—not of any recognizable time—in spite of the fact that it looked like a backwoods road anywhere. The sandy hillscapes following us on either side were alien, too, as if they had been transported from a desert somewhere and set down here. Also, it was getting hotter and the humidity was worse.

I stopped the panel, finally, to do a more precise job of estimating our position on the map than I could do while driving. According to the compass I had mounted on the instrument panel on our vehicle, the asphalt road had been running almost exactly due west; and the outskirts of Omaha should be less than twenty miles southwest of us.

As long as we had been on the superhighway, I had not worried; because a road like that, obviously belonging to our original twentieth century time, had to be headed toward the nearest large city—which had to be Omaha. Just as on the asphalt road at first I had not worried either, because it headed so nearly in the direction I wanted to go.

But it was stretching out now to the point where I began to worry that it would carry me to the north and past the city, without letting me catch sight of it. Certainly, by this time we had gone far enough to intersect some other roads heading south and into the metropolitan area. But we had crossed no other road. For that matter, we had come across nothing else that indicated a city nearby, no railroad tracks, no isolated houses, no fences, no sub-urban developments in the bulldozer stage of construction. . . . I was uneasy.

Laying out the road map on the hood of the car, I traced our route to the superhighway, traced the super-highway to what I believed to be the exit by which we had come down off it, and along the road that exit tied into—headed west. The road was there; but according to the map, less than a dozen miles farther on, it ran through a small town called Leeder; and we had come twenty miles without seeing as much as a road sign.

I went through the whole thing twice more, checked the compass and traced out our route, and checked the odometer on the panel to see how far we'd come since leaving the superhighway—and the results came out the same. We had to be bypassing Omaha to the north.

I got back in the truck and started travelling again, driving slowly. I told myself I'd give myself another five miles without a crossroad before turning back. I drove them, and then another five. But I saw no crossroad. Nothing. Only the narrow, neglected-looking strip of asphalt which looked as if it might continue unchanged around to the Pacific Ocean.

I stopped the panel again, got out and walked off the road to check the surface of the ground to the south. I walked back and forth and stamped a few times. The surface was sandy, but hard—easily solid enough to bear the weight of the panel truck; and the vegetation was scattered enough so that there would be no trouble driving through it. Up until now I had been very careful not to get off the roads, for fear of a breakdown of the truck which would strand us a distance from any hope of easily finding another vehicle. On foot we would be at the mercy of the first moving time storm wall that came to-ward us.

But we were so close now—we were just a few miles away from getting back to normal life. I could see Swan-nee in my mind's eye so clearly that she was almost like a mirage superimposed on the semidesert landscape around us. She had to be there, waiting for me. Something inside me was still positive, beyond all argument, that Omaha had survived; and that along with it Swannee had sur-vived in the sanity of a portion of the world as it had been before the time storm. In fact my mind had toyed a number of times with the idea that since Omaha, like Hawaii, had survived, it might mean there might be many other enclaves of safety; and the fact that there were such enclaves would mean there was a way of beating the time storm, by applying to all other places the special conditions or whatever unusual elements had kept these enclaves protected.

In those enclaves she and I could still lead the reasonable and normal life we could have had before the time storm hit; and somehow I felt sure that the experience of the time storm would have straightened her out on what had gone wrong between us before. Time would have brought her to the realization that it was simply an old reflex on my part that had made me act like someone literally in love with her. Also, she would know how tough life could be outside the enclaves like the one she now lived in—or even there, for that matter. She would have a new appreciation of what I could do for her, in the way of taking care of her. In fact, the more I thought, the more confident I was that by this time she would be ready to indulge these little emotional lapses of mine. All I had to do was find her and things would go well.

—But that was something to think about when there was time to think about it. The big question now was—should I take the panel cross-country, south, away from the road, to find a highway or street that would bring me to the city?

There was really no argument about it. I got Sunday and the girl back into the panel—they had followed me outside and wandered after me as I stamped on the ground to make sure it would not bog down the panel—then we got back in the truck, turned off the asphalt and headed due south by the compass.

It was not bad driving at all. I had to slow down to about five to ten miles an hour; and I kept the panel in second gear, occasionally having to shift down to low on the hills, but generally finding it easy going. It was all up and down, a roller coaster-type of going for about nine-tenths of a mile; and then suddenly we came up over a rise and looked down on a lakeshore.

It was just a strip of whitish-brown, sandy beach. But the shallow, rather stagnant-looking water beyond the beach stretched out as far as I could see and out of sight right and left as well. Evidently the time storm had moved this whole area into the northwest of the metropolitan area, pretty well blocking off access from that direction. The problem for me now was—which way would be the shortest way round the lake? Right or left?

It was a toss-up. I squinted in both directions but for some reason, just while I had been standing there, a haze of some sort seemed to have moved in, so that I could not see far out on the water in any direction. Finally I chose to go to the right, because I thought I saw a little darkness through the haze upon the sun-glare off the water and sand in that direction. I turned the nose of the truck and we got going.

The beach was almost as good as a paved road to drive on. It was flat and firm. Apparently, the water adjoining it began to shelve more sharply as we went along, for it lost its stagnant, shallow appearance and began to develop quite a respectable surf. There was an onshore wind blowing; but it helped the heat and the humidity only a little. We kept driving.

As I watched the miles add up on the truck's odometer, I began gradually to regret not trying in the other direction. Clearly, I had picked the long way around this body of water, because looking ahead I could still see no end to it. When the small, clicking figures of the odometer rolled up past the twelve mile mark, I braked the truck to a halt, turned around and headed back.

As I said, the beach was good driving. I pushed our speed up to about forty, and it was not long before we were back at the point where we had first come across the lake. I kept pounding along; and shortly I made out something up ahead. The dazzle of sunlight from the water seemed to have gotten in my eyes so that I could not make out exactly what it was—something like a handkerchief-sized island with a tree, or a large raft with a diving tower out in the water, just a little way from the beach. But there were the black silhouettes of two-legged figures on the sand there. I could stop to get some directions, and we could still be pulling into Swannee's driveway in time for dinner.

The dazzle-effect on my eyes got worse as the panel got close to the figures; and the glitter of sunlight through the windshield was not helping. I blinked, and blinked again. I should have thought to pick up some dark glasses and keep them in the glove compartment of the panel for situations like this—but I just had not expected to run into water-glare like this. I must have been no more than thirty or forty feet from the figures by the time I finally braked the panel to a stop and jumped out of it on to the sand, blinking to get the windshield-glitter out of the way between us—and I still could not see them clearly. There were at least half a dozen of them on the beach, and I saw more out on the raft or whatever it was.

I started toward them.

"Hey!" I said. "I'm lost. Can you put me on the road to Omaha? I want to get to Byerly Park, there."

The figures did not answer. I was within a few steps of them now. I stopped, closed my eyes and shook my head violently. Then I opened my eyes again.

For the first time I saw them clearly. They had two legs apiece all right; but that was the only thing people-like about them. As far as I could see, they wore no clothes; and I could have sworn they were covered with greenish-gold scales. Heavy, lizard-like features with un-blinking dark eyes stared directly into my face.

I stared back at them. Then I turned and looked out at the raft and beyond. All around were the beach and the water—nothing more. And finally, finally, the truth came crashing in on me.

There was too much water. There was no way Omaha could still exist out there beyond the waves. I had been wrong all the time. I had been fooling myself, hugging to my mind an impossible hope, as if it was the fixed center of the universe.

Omaha was gone. Gone completely. Swannee was gone. Like so many other things, she had been taken away forever. I had lost her for good, just as I had lost my mother . . .

The sun, which had been high overhead, seemed to swing halfway around the sky before my eyes and turn blood red. The water seemed to go black as ink and swirl up all around me and the watching lizard-humans. My mind felt as if it was cracking wide open; and every-thing spun about me like liquid going down a drain, suck-ing water and beach and all, including me, away down into some place that was ugly and frightening.

It was the end of the world. I had been intending to survive anything for Swannee's sake; but all the time she had already been gone. She and Omaha had probably been lost in the first moment after the time storm hit. From then on, there had only been the illusion of her in my sick mind. I had been as insane as Samuelson, after all. The crazy cat, the idiot girl and I—we had been three loonies together. I had flattered myself that the mistwalls were all outside me; but now I could feel them breaching the walls of my skull, moving inside me, wiping clean and destroying everything over which they passed. I had a faint and distant impression of hearing myself howling like a chained dog; and of strong hands holding me. But this, too, swiftly faded away, into a complete and utter nothingness. . . .

7

The world was rocking gently underneath me. No . . . it was not the world, it was the raft rocking.

Waking, I began to remember that there had been moments of clarity before this. But they had been seldom. Most of the time I had been in a world in which I had found Swannee—but a changed Swannee—after all; and we had settled down in an Omaha untouched by the time storm. But, slowly, that world had begun to wear thin; and more and more often there had been moments when I was not in Omaha but here, seeing the raft and the rest of it from my present position. Now, there was no doubt which world I lived in.

So I was back for good. I could feel that; along with a grim, aching hunger in my belly. For the first time I began to wonder where the raft was going, and to worry about Sunday and the girl.

I looked around, identifying things from the hazy periods earlier. It was a beautiful, clear day at sea, or at whatever equivalent of a sea it was upon which we were afloat. A few inches from my nose were saplings, tree branches or what-have-you, that had been woven into a sort of cage about me. Beyond the cage, there was a little distance—perhaps ten feet—of open log surface to an edge of the raft, studded with the ever-sprouting twigs that tried to grow from the raft logs, though these had been neatly and recently bitten off for this day. Beyond the logs was the restlessly heaving surface of the gray-blue water, stretching away to the curve of the horizon.

I rolled over and looked out in the opposite direction, through another cage-side of loosely woven withes, at the rest of the raft.

It was about a hundred or so feet in length. At one

end was a stand of—I had to call them "trees" for want of any better name—their thick-leaved, almost furry-looking tops taking advantage of whatever breeze was blowing to push the raft along before it. Around their base grew the carefully cultivated stand of shoots from which my cage, and just about everything else the lizard-people seemed to make with their hands, had been constructed.

Behind the trees and the shoots were a couple of other cages holding the girl and Sunday, plus a pile of shells and stones that apparently had some value for the lizards. They looked all right. They were both perhaps a little thinner; but they seemed lively enough; and, in fact, the girl was looking brighter and more in charge of herself than I could ever remember seeing her. From her cage on back, except for piles of assorted rubble and junk—everything from sand itself to what looked like a heap of furs—were the various members of the crew. I found myself calling them a crew for lack of a better term. For all I knew, most of them may have been passengers. Or perhaps they were all members of one family; there was no way of telling.

But in any case, there were thirty or forty of them, most simply lying on their bellies or sides, absolutely still in the sunlight, but with dark eyes open and heads up, not as if they were sleeping. The few on their feet were moving about aimlessly. There were only four who seemed to have any occupation. One was an individual who was working his way down the far side of the raft on all fours, delicately biting off the newly sprouted twigs from the logs of the raft as he went, and three others at the rear of the raft. These three were holding the heavy shaft of a great steering oar, which evidently gave the raft what little directional purpose it could have while floating before the wind.

In the very center of the raft, back about twenty feet from my cage, was a roughly square hole in the logs, exposing a sort of small interior swimming pool of the same water that was all around us. For several minutes, I stared at the hole, puzzled. The sight of it triggered off a nagging feeling in the back of my mind, as of something that ought to be remembered, but which, annoyingly, refused to surface from the unconscious. Something half-recalled from one or more moments of earlier temporary return to rationality. As I watched, one of the recumbent lizard-people got up, walked over to the pool and stepped into it. He splashed down out of sight and stayed invisible for what must have been at least four or five minutes before his head bobbed to the surface momentarily, and then he disappeared again.

There were several more splashes. A few of the others had joined him in the pool. I watched the water there for a while, but the lizard-people stayed mainly below the surface. After about fifteen minutes or so, one of them climbed back out and lay down on the bare logs once more, scales wet and glistening in the sun.

From my earlier brief moments of sanity, I remembered seeing a lot of this swimming pool activity, but without speculating about it. Now that my mind was back in my head for good, the old reflex in me to gnaw away at answers I did not have went to work. The most obvious reason for their continual plunges was to keep the outside of their bodies reasonably damp. They had the look of a water-living race; either one which had evolved in the sea, or whatever we were on, or humans who had returned to an aquatic environment. If it was the latter, then it could be that this part of the earth had been moved very far into the past or future indeed, either far enough back to find the great Nebraska sea—that shallow ocean that had occupied the interior of the North American continent in the Permian period, or far enough into the future to find a time when that sea had been geologically recreated.

A shift that far forward would have given time for humans to deevolve and make a genetic shift to the form of these who had captured us. I studied them.

I had not really looked closely at them before, but now that I did so, I could see clearly that there were, indeed, two sexes aboard, and that the females had a mammalian breast development—although this was barely perceptible.

The genitals of both sexes were all but hidden in a heavy horizontal fold of skin descending from the lower belly into the crotch; but what I could see of these external organs was also mammalian, even human-like, in appearance. So it looked strongly as if a far futureward development of this area under the time storm influence was a good guess.

Outside of the slight bodily differences, the sex of the

individual creatures around us seemed to make little difference in the ordinary conduct of their daily lives. I saw no signs of sexual response between individuals—no sign even of sexual awareness. Perhaps they had a season for such things, and this was not it.

They were clearly used to spending a good share of their time in water; and that perhaps explained their periodic dunkings in the raft pool. It could be that they were like dolphins who needed to be wetted down if they were out of water for any length of time.

It seemed strange to me, though, that they should go to the trouble of cutting a hole in the center of their raft, rather than just dunking themselves over one of the edges, if that was their reason for getting in the water. I was mulling this strangeness over, when something I had been looking at suddenly registered on me as an entirely different object from what I had taken it to be.

Everybody has had the experience of looking right at an object and taking it for something entirely different from what it really is—until abruptly, the mind clicks over and recognizes its true nature. I had been staring absently at a sort of vertical plane projecting from the water alongside the raft and perhaps half a dozen feet off the edge, and more or less half-wondering what usefulness it had, when the object suddenly took on its true character, and my heart gave an unusually heavy thump.

I had been allowing the plane's apparent lack of motion relative to the raft to deceive me into thinking it was a surface of wood, a part of the raft itself. Abruptly, I recognized what it really was—I had seen enough of the same things charter-fishing on my vacations to South America, back when I still owned Snowman, Inc. What I was watching was a shark's fin, keeping pace with the raft. There was no mistaking that particular shape for the fin of a sailfish, a tarpon, or any other sea denizen. It was the dorsal of a shark—but what a shark!

If the fin was in proportion to the body beneath it, that body must be half as long as this raft.

Now that I saw it clearly for what it was, I could not imagine what had led me to mistake it for a plane of wood. But now my mind had clicked over and would not click back. If monsters like that were about in these waters, no wonder the lizard-people wanted to do their swimming inboard.

On the other hand, it was odd . . . once one or more of them were in the water, the shark should be able to get at them as easily underneath the raft as alongside it. Unless there was some reason it would not go under the raft after them. Or did the lizard-people figure that by the time the shark started under the raft, they would have time to get back out of the pool and back up on top of the logs of which it was built? Now, that was a good theory. On the other hand, I had seen no evidence of unusual haste in those getting out of the pool.

Was it possible that in the water the lizard-people could outswim the shark? That did not seem likely, although obviously, our captors were at home in the water, and obviously, they were built for swimming. They were thick-bodied and thick-limbed, their elbows and knees bent slightly so that they stood in a perpetual crouch; and both their hands and feet were webbed to near the ends of their fingers and toes. They looked to be very powerful, physically, compared to a human, and those teeth of theirs were almost shark-standard in themselves; although none of them were much more than five feet tall. But in relation to a shark that size, the strength of any one of them would not be worth considering.

I was puzzling about these things, when a change came in the schedule. One of the lizard people approached the cage holding the girl and opened up some sort of trapdoor in one end of it. The girl crept out, as if she had been through this before and knew the procedure, and, without hesitation, got up, walked to the pool, and jumped in. She stayed there, holding onto an edge.

The same lizard who had let her out was joined by another, and the two of them went over to the cage of Sunday, who snarled as they approached. They paid no attention to him but lifted up his cage easily between them—evidently I had been right about their strength—carried it to the edge of the pool and opened its end.

Sunday, however, showed none of the girl's willingness to leave his cage for the water. But evidently the lizards had encountered this problem before. After a moment's wait, one of them got down into the pool, reached up with a scaly arm, and pulled cage and Sunday under the surface with him.

For a moment there was no sign of leopard, cage, or lizard. Then the head of Sunday broke water in the exact

center of the pool, snorting, and swimming strongly. He
swam directly to the edge of the pool by the girl, crawled
out, and sat down in the sun to lick himself dry, looking
as furious as only a wet cat can look. The lizard rose
behind him, towing an empty cage and climbed out on the
other side.

The two made no immediate attempt to recage him,
and I was still watching him when a sudden squeaking
sound behind me made me turn my head to look. A door
in the far end of my own cage was being lifted. I turned
around and crawled out. A lizard-man was standing facing
me, and I caught a sickish, if faint, reek of fish-smell
from him before I turned and went toward the pool. But
at the edge I stopped, looking once more to my right
where the shark fin was still on patrol.

My escort picked me up and dropped me in the water. I
came up sputtering, and grabbed hold of the edge to haul
myself out. Then I saw the girl, still hanging on to a
log, in the water near me, watching. Evidently, she considered it safe enough where we were.

I turned and tried to look down through the water;
but the shadow of the trees at the front of the raft was
on it and made it too dark to see. I took a breath, stuck
my head under the water and looked about. Then I saw
why the shark was nothing to worry about when you were
in the pool. The underside of the raft was a tangle of
tree-growth; either roots or saplings of the same sort I
could see growing upwards from the top of the logs.

It was growth that had run wild, a veritable nightmare
jungle of straight and twisted, vine-like limbs, some of
them almost half as thick as the logs of the raft itself.
The roots grew everywhere but in toward the pool area
itself, until about fifteen feet down or so, they curved in
and came together in a mat, like the bottom of an underwater nest. I assumed the lizards kept the pool area clear
underwater by biting off the new suckers emerging from
the logs, as they did in the clean areas topside. Plainly,
even something the size of the shark companioning this
raft could not get at us through that tangle below.

So, the pool was safe territory after all. Not only that,
it occurred to me now, but the heavy mass of vegetation
underneath must act as a sort of keel for the raft. I
pulled my head back up out of water and looked around
in the air.

The girl was still in the pool. Sunday was still out of it and licking his fur, undisturbed. The two lizards who had turned us out of our cages had wandered off and become indistinguishable from their companions. I wondered what would happen if I got out of the pool myself. I did so—the girl imitating my action a second later—and found that nothing happened. The lizards ignored us.

I was startled suddenly to feel a hand slip into mine. I turned and it was the girl. She had never done anything like that before.

"What is it?" I asked.

She paid no attention to the words. She was already leading me toward the back of the raft. I followed along, puzzled, until a nagging sense of familiarity about our actions sprang an answer out of my hazy memory of those earlier brief returns to consciousness. She was leading me —the two of us completely ignored by the lizards—to the back edge of the raft; and the back edge was what was available to us by way of sanitary conveniences on this voyage. Apparently, while I had been out of my head, she had acquired the responsibility of leading me back there to relieve myself, after each periodic dip in the pool.

When this memory emerged, I put on the brakes. She and I had been living under pretty close conditions from the moment we had met. But now that my wits were back in my skull, I preferred at least the illusion of privacy in matters of elimination. After tugging at me vainly for a while, she gave up and went on by herself. I turned back to the pool.

Sunday was nearly dry now, and once more on good terms with the world. When I got back to the pool edge, he got up from where he was lying and wound around my legs, purring. I patted his head and sat down on the logs to think. After an unsuccessful—because I wouldn't let him—attempt to crawl into my lap, he gave up, lay down beside me and compromised by dropping his head on my knee. The head of a full-grown leopard is not a light matter; but better the head than all of him. I stroked his fur to keep him where he was; and he closed his eyes, rumbling in sheer bliss at my giving him this much attention.

After a little while the girl came back, and I went off to the back of the raft by myself, warning her sternly to stay where she was, when she once more tried to accompany me. She looked worried, but stayed. When I came back, she was lying down with her arm flung across Sunday's back and was back to her customary pattern of acting as if I did not even exist.

I sat down on the other side of Sunday, to keep him quiet, and tried to think. I had not gotten very far, however, when a couple of the lizards showed up. The girl rose meekly and crawled back into her cage. I took the hint and went back into mine. Sunday, of course, showed no signs of being so obliging: but the lizards handled him efficiently enough. They dropped a sort of clumsy twig net over him, twisted him up in it, and put net and all in his cage. Left alone there, Sunday struggled and squirmed until he was free; and a little later a lizard, passing, reached casually in through the bars of the cage, whisked the loose net out and carried it off.

So, there I was, back in the cage—and it was only then that I realized that I was hungry and thirsty. Above all, thirsty. I tried yelling to attract the attention of the lizards, but they ignored me. I even tried calling to the girl for advice and help; but she was back to being as unresponsive as the lizards. In the end, tired out, I went to sleep.

I woke about sunset to the sound of my cage being opened again. Before I knew it, I was being dumped in the pool once more. This time, I got a taste of the water into which I had been thrown. It was not ocean-salty—it had a faint taste that could be a touch of brackishness, but it was clearly sweet enough for human consumption. If this was the Nebraska sea, it was open to the ocean at its lower end. But as I remembered reading, it had been very shallow; and like the Baltic in my time, this far north, in-flowing rivers and underground springs could have diluted it to nearly fresh-water condition. I climbed out of the pool and went to the side edge of the raft to drink, just to avoid any contamination there might be in the pool. I could not remember water tasting quite so good.

I lay on the logs of the raft with my belly full until the liquid began to disperse to the rest of my dehydrated body, then got up and went looking for something to eat. A quick tour of the raft turned up coconuts, which I had no way of opening, some green leafy stuff which might or might not be an edible vegetable, and a stack of bananas—most of which were still green.

I helped myself to the ripest I could find, half expecting the lizards to stop me. But they paid no attention. When I had taken care of my appetite, I thought of the girl and took some back to her.

She gave me one quick glance and looked away. But she took the bananas and ate them. After she had finished, she got up and went a little way away from me and lay down on her side, apparently sticking her arm right through the solid surface of the raft.

I went over to her and saw that she had found a place where two adjoining logs gapped apart; and her arm was now reaching down through the gap into the water and the tangle of growth below.

Something about her position as she lay there struck an odd note of familiarity. I straightened up and looked around the raft. Sure enough, the lizards who were lying down were nearly all in just the position she had taken. Apparently, they too had found holes in the raft.

I wondered what sort of a game she and they were playing. I even asked her—but of course I got no answer. Then, just a few seconds later she sat up, withdrawing her arm and held out her closed fist to me. When she opened it up, there was a small fish in the palm of her hand—hardly bigger than the average goldfish in a home fishbowl.

She held it out to me with her head averted; but clearly she was offering it to me. When I did not take it, she looked back at me with something like a flash of anger on her face and threw the fish away. It landed on the raft surface only inches from Sunday. The leopard stretched out his neck to reach it and eagerly licked it up.

The girl had gone back to her fishing. But whatever she caught next, she put in her own mouth. Later on, she made a number of trips to feed Sunday with what she caught. Full of curiosity, I went looking for another gap in the logs, lay down and put my eye to it.

In the shadow under the raft I could at first see nothing. But as my vision adjusted, I looked into the tangle of growth there and saw a veritable aquarium of small marine life. So this was how the lizards provisioned themselves. It was like carrying a game farm along with you on your travels. The small fish and squid-like creatures I

saw through the gap in the logs did not look all that
appetizing to me, at first glance. But after my third day
on bananas, I found myself eating them along with the
girl and the lizards—eating them, and what's more, enjoying them. Protein hunger can be a remarkably powerful conditioning force.

Meanwhile—on the days that immediately followed—I
was trying to puzzle out a great many things, including
why we had been brought along on the raft. The most
obvious answer that came to me was the one I liked
least—that, like the bananas and the coconuts, we three
represented a potential exotic addition to the ordinary
lizard diet, a sort of special treat to be eaten later.

I also toyed with the thought that we had been picked
up as slaves, or as curiosities to be used or traded off at
some later time. But this was hard to believe. The lizards
were clearly an extremely primitive people, if they were a
true people at all, and not some sort of ant-like society
operating on instinct rather than intelligence. They had
shown no sign of having a spoken language; and so far I
had not seen any of them using even stone tools to make
or do anything. The extent of their technology seemed to
be the weaving of the nets and cages, the gathering of
things like coconuts (and the three of us) and the building
of this raft; if, indeed, this raft had been deliberately
built, rather than being just grown to order, or chewed
loose from some larger mass of vegetation of which it
originally had been a part.

No, I was forgetting the steering oar. The next time I
was let out of my cage, I went back to the stern of the
raft to look at it. What I found was on a par with the
rest of the raft. The oar was not so much an oar as a
thinner tree trunk of the same variety as those which
made up the logs of the raft. It had no true blade. It
was bare trunk down to the point where it entered the
water, and from there on, it was mop-like with a brush
of untrimmed growth. It was pivoted in a notch between
two logs of the raft, tied in place there with a great
bundle of the same flexible vine or plant with which the
lizards had made the net they used to restrain Sunday.
This tie broke several times a day, but each time, it was
patiently rewrapped and reknotted by the nearby lizards.

Whatever their cultural level—in fact, whether they had
a culture or not—they had clearly collected the three of

us for their own purposes, not for ours. It struck me that the sooner we got away from them, the better.

But here on a raft in the middle of an unknown body of water, getting away was something easier to imagine than do. For one thing, we would have to wait until we touched land again; and there was no telling when that would be. Or was there? I puzzled over the question.

It was hard to believe that the lizards could be trying to follow any specific route with their clumsy sail of trees and their mop-ended steering oar. At best, I told myself, they could only impose a slight angle on the path of their drift before the wind. But, when I thought about this some more, it occurred to me that the wind had been blowing continually from the stern of the raft with about the same strength since I had gotten my senses back. We were, of course, still in the temperate latitudes of what had been the North American continent, well above the zone of any trade winds. But, what if here on this body of water, current climatic conditions made for seasonal winds blowing in a certain direction? Say, for example, winds that blew east in the summer and west in the winter, from generally the same quarters of the compass? Judging by the sun, we were now headed generally east. With a continuous directional breeze like that to rely on, even the crude rig of this raft could follow a roughly regular route depending only on the season of the year.

That evening I marked on one of the logs the angle of the sunset on the horizon to the longitudinal axis of the raft, by cutting marks in one of the logs under my cage with my pocketknife. It set almost due astern of us, but a little to the north. The next morning I again marked the angle of the sunrise—again, a little to the north of our long axis. A check of the angle of the steering oar confirmed this. The three lizards holding it had it angled to guide the raft slightly to the north from a true east-west line. It was not until then that I thought of checking the stars.

So I did, as soon as they came out that evening; but they were absolutely unfamiliar. I could not recognize a single constellation. Not that I was very knowledgable about astronomy; but like most people, I was normally able to pick out the Little and Big Dippers and find the pole star from the Big Dipper. Such a difference in the patterns of the heavens I saw could only be strong evidence that a time change had moved this part of the world a long way from the present I had known—either far into the future or far into the past.

If so . . . a new thought kindled in an odd back corner of my mind.

If it was indeed the Permian period, or a future one like it, through which this raft was now sailing, then one thing was highly likely. We were almost surely moving along roughly parallel to the northern shore of the inland sea since the beach where we had first run into the lizards had to be that same northern shore; and it now seemed probable we had been holding a steady northeasterly course ever since. I had seen a geology textbook map of the Great Nebraska Sea once, years ago. It had shown the land area of the southern and middle states depressed, and that part of the continent drowned, so that the Gulf of Mexico, in effect, filled most of the lower middle region of North America. That meant, almost certainly, we should be running into land again before long. We were not, as I had originally feared, off on some endless voyage to nowhere, as we were perfectly capable of being, while an endless supply of food swam underneath us and water all around us that was drinkable.

The prospect of coming to land again before too long meant we ought to at least get a chance to escape. I cheered up at the thought and, with immediate anxieties out of the way, remembered the rest of what was still heavy in my mind.

The insane belief I had had in the survival of Swannee was, of course, still with me, like the mistwall of a time change line in the back of my thought.

But the rest of my brain recognized it for the illusion it was. Evidently, while I had been out of my head, what was left had been coming to terms with this matter. I was now ready to admit that there had been something more than a lingering knee-jerk reflex of the affection response operating in me. The plain truth of the matter was that I had flipped over Swannee. Not only had I flipped, but I had done it after I married her, not before; and the thing that had driven her off was the fact that I had tried to change the rules of the game after the game was started. I had let myself go with the idea that I loved Swannee; and made up in my mind a completely imaginary image of her as someone who was lovable.

Of course she wasn't. She was an ordinary self-seeking human being like all the rest of us, and when she acted like one and took off to escape my trying to make her into something she was not, I literally set out to work myself to death, and almost succeeded with the heart attack.

I suppose, in a way, I had never really let go of Swannee—even then. So that when the time storm hit, the one thing I could not accept was that it could have touched her in any way.

But I now had met, and survived, the fact of her death. The madness, of course, was still back there in the recesses of my mind, and still virulent; but it was dying, and time would kill it off entirely. Just as time had healed my first sense of loss when she had gotten married. Now that it was dying, locked in my wooden cage most of the time and going nowhere, I had plenty of leisure to begin looking more sanely at the world around me. Out of that look came a couple of recognitions I had been refusing to make earlier. One was that we would have to work hard to survive on this raft. Sunday and the girl were not only thin, as I had noticed, but getting thinner. Sunday himself required the equivalent of four pounds of meat a day to keep him alive. I needed about two thousand calories, or nearly half that amount; and the girl, because she was not yet at her full growth, probably the same. We two, of course, could make use of carbohydrates—like the bananas—as well, as long as those lasted. But getting Sunday the equivalent of four pounds of protein daily through the cracks between the logs of the raft, was impossible; even with both the girl and I doing our best—which we did as soon as I realized what the situation was. The lizard-people showed no interest at all in providing food for us. We would need to reach land soon if we wanted to live.

The second recognition was that only a few people, relatively, had escaped the time change. A few people and a few animals. Apparently the changes had been like great rakes that swept away most of the population, but here and there let an individual like me, the girl, or Sunday, slip through their tines. Either that, or some of us simply were natural survivors—statistical immunes.

Whether the greater number of the population of my time had been carried off to some other continuum, or destroyed by the suddenly changed conditions, there was no telling. But one fact was becoming more apparent day by day—there was no reasonable hope of their ever coming back. *The moving finger writes . . .*

I, and the girl, and Sunday, along with a relative handful of others, possibly including these lizard-people, were stuck with making what we could out of the world as it now was. What we had at the present, of course, was chaos, with the time lines still moving and different times coming into existence behind each of them. But maybe if I was right about some of us being statistical immunes, we would learn eventually to live with the lines, passing from zone to zone and becoming a new civilization which took constant time changes for granted.

Unless, that is, there was some way of bringing the time changes to a halt. . . .

Now, that was a new thought. It exploded in me silently, one night as I lay there on my back, looking up through the bars of my cage at the unfamiliar star-patterns, while the raft rocked gently under me. I lay there, turning it over and over in my head, examining it. That relentless part of my mind had fastened on the idea the second it emerged, like the jaws of a boa constrictor on part of a prey the snake intended to swallow, and now I knew I could never let it go, until I had succeeded with it, or proved its impossibility.

8

Ten mornings later we saw land, and by noon it was obvious we would reach it the same day. I was ready to blow kisses at it from the first second it had appeared like a dark smudge on the horizon. Try as the girl and I might, we could not keep the three of us properly fed with the small underraft waterlife; and I had lived with a sharp-toothed fear that we would have grown too weak to try escaping by the time our chance for it came. Our goal was a curving bay with a wide beach shelving gently down to it, some hills hazy in the background, and one or two large rocks or small rocky islands just beyond the mouth of the bay.

Shortly after noon the lizards lined up along the side of the raft facing the shark fin and began to roll up the vegetable-like leaves I had seen and throw these small green balls at the shark. Where the balls of vegetable matter touched the water, a milky stain spread immediately and was still spreading, like the blossoming of some underwater flower, as the motion of the raft left the spot behind us. As the lizards continued to pelt the water around the fin with the balls of green stuff, a milky rime gradually gathered around the base of the fin itself.

Suddenly the fin moved, changed angle in the water and moved off rapidly until it was lost from sight. Looking back along the wake of the raft, I saw the shapes of small fish come to the surface belly-up through the whitened water where the green stuff had fallen.

So we half-drifted, half-steered at last into the bay without our overside companion. In the bay the water was as calm as a lake on a still day, and startlingly clear. I could look down at a sandy, plant-and-shell strewn bottom, finally, that must have been fifty feet below, although it looked much shallower.

I was able to estimate its true depth because the full extent of the growth on the underside of the raft was now visible; and it stretched down almost as far, if not as far, as the trees that were our "sail" stretched up from the deck of the raft. A good two hundred yards or more from the beach we grounded, the lowest extensions of the growth under our raft touching against the bottom of the bay and stopping us from going further inshore.

The lizards immediately began diving for what seemed to be some sort of large shellfish. The shells were a good foot in length, and when I picked up one of the first that was brought on board, I was startled by the heaviness of it. The whole thing must have weighed twenty pounds.

In the sun and the air, the shells soon opened of their own accord; and the lizards scooped the interior creatures out and swallowed them more or less whole.

So did the girl, Sunday and myself. They were delicious; and we would have stuffed ourselves if I had not stopped, and made the girl stop, feeding herself as well as Sunday, for fear of intestinal upset in all of us after such a period of semi-starvation.

But beyond a few mild stomach cramps an hour or so later, I had no bad effects, and the girl and Sunday did not even seem to have that. So, I left them to eat or not as they wished; and during the next few days, we ate our persistent hunger out of existence through steady snacking on the shellfish.

We were free to do this around the clock, because Sunday, the girl and I had been let out of our cages some time before we came to anchor, so to speak; and since then, none of the lizards had bothered to put us back in. As my hunger diminished, I began to think less of that and more about escaping. I could stand on the edge of the raft and look at the sand of the beach. Only a couple of hundred yards away, as I said; but it might as well have been a couple of hundred miles away. There was no way to get ashore except to swim there. And even if the girl could, and Sunday would make it through the water with me, any one of the amphibious-looking lizard-people could probably let us get nine-tenths of the way to the beach and still reach us in time to bring us back before we could wade ashore. They shot through the clear underwater like green rockets. But there had to be a way. It was bad enough to have to figure out a way of escaping by myself. The headache would come in bringing the girl and Sunday safely with me. But I could not leave them behind. Neither one was able to survive alone. It had to be the three of us, together.

I was standing looking down into the water at them, even envying them in a way, when something like a swiftly moving dark shadow suddenly intruded on the scene; and all at once lizards were literally leaping out of the water back on to the surface of the raft. All but one. Down in the transparent depths, that one was being swallowed. Either our original shark, or one just like it, had joined us; and once more we had a deadly companion alongside.

The lizards stood on the deck and stared down at the shark. I did not blame them. In the beautifully clear water the huge sea predator loomed like a nuclear submarine. It was patrolling the water about the raft now, in short runs and turns back and forth, as if impatient for another victim.

I looked at the still-large pile of green vegetation on the raft. But none of the lizards made a move toward it, and after a second I realized why. Clearly the stuff, in water, was a potent poison. They could safely throw it overside when they were moving before a breeze, away from the place where the poison would linger. But here in this bay, once the water was poisoned, they would not be able to return soon to their diving for shellfish.

I waited. The shark stayed. The lizards waited. I fumed. The shark's presence was one more obstacle in the way of escape for the girl, Sunday and myself. At the same time I was amazed at the apparent helplessness of the lizards. I had assumed without thinking that they would have some kind of plan to deal with a situation of this sort. But apparently not—unless their technique was to simply wait out the shark, sit on the raft until it got tired and went away.

However, if it was the same shark—or even of the same breed and temperament as the shark that had dogged the raft earlier—it was not likely to leave in any reasonable length of time. The fin that had followed us earlier had been with us for days on end.

The eerie part of the whole business was that there was

no visible sign of an attempt at consultation among the lizards. From the beginning they had shown no indication of having a spoken language; and I had not been able to make out any other method of signs or signalling they might be using between themselves. But I had always assumed that in some way, if they had to, they could communicate with each other. Now it seemed they could not even do that. A handful of them stood and watched the shark for a while; but eventually, all of them went back to acting as if they were still out at sea, resting on the logs, hunting between them in the growth under the raft in search of small marine life to eat, and so on. The only sign that there was anything at all unusual about the situation was the fact that still none of them came to put us back in our cages.

Night came with no change. A day after that followed with the shark still waiting and the lizards still all on the raft. Around noon of the third day, however, something new began to happen.

Just before the sun was full overhead, one of the lizards lying near the edge of the raft, beyond which the shark was presently patrolling, got to his feet. He stood facing down at the shark in the water, and then he began to bounce as he stood, not moving his feet, but bending his knees slightly so that he bobbed up and down like someone on a diving board getting ready to dive.

Once started, he continued the bobbing steadily and with a sort of reflexive monotony of pace. The other lizards seemed to be paying no attention to him; but after perhaps half an hour, when I looked back over at where he was, after having my attention elsewhere for a while, I saw that another of the lizards, about ten feet from him, was now also on his feet and bobbing. The two of them matched their rhythms precisely, rising and falling together as if the same invisible spring was actuating them both.

An hour later, there were four of them on their feet and bobbing. Gradually, more and more of the others joined them in silent, continuous movement—until by mid-afternoon all the lizards on the ship were performing the same soundless, feet-in-place dance.

The shark, meanwhile, either having seen them on the edge of the raft, or—what is more likely—having been attracted by the vibrations of their movements through the logs and the water, was now patrolling in very short runs back and forth, almost within touching distance, it seemed, of the raft edge.

Suddenly, as the shark passed, one of the lizard figures leaped into the water upon its back . . . and all at once the air was full of lizards taking to the water.

I ran to the side of the raft and looked out—and down. The shark was already at the bottom of the bay, moving rapidly away from the raft. But the lizards were all over him, like green-scaled dogs clinging to a bull. Their heavy jaws were tearing chunks out of the shark's incredibly tough hide; and a filmy cloud of blood was spreading through the underwater. Not merely shark's blood, either. I saw the huge selachian catch a lizard in its jaws and literally divide him in half.

Then the whole struggle moved away out of my sight, headed toward the open sea, as the shark evidently followed its reflex to go for deeper water.

For some moments I simply stood, staring—then the implications of the situation exploded on me. I ran to the girl and grabbed her by the arm.

"Come on," I said. "Come on, now's our chance! We can get ashore now, while they're all gone."

She did not answer. She only stared at me. I looked over at Sunday.

"Come, Sunday!"

He came. The girl came also. She did not hang back; but on the other hand, she only let me pull her toward the shoreside of the raft, which was its forward end.

"We've got to swim for the beach!" I shouted at her. "If you can't swim, hang on to me. You understand?"

I roared the last two words at her as if she was deaf; but she only stared back at me. She was not hindering, but neither was she helping. The cold thought came through me that, once more, I was being put in a concerned situation. Why didn't I go off and leave her—her and the leopard both, if it came to that? The important thing was that I live, not that I save other people's lives.

But, you know, I could not. Somehow, to go ashore by myself and leave both of them here was unthinkable. But she would have to do something more than just stand there, not making an active effort to get ashore. I tried to tell her this; but it was at once like talking to someone who was deaf and someone who had given up thinking.

I was reaching the desperation point. I was about to throw her bodily into the water when the first of the lizards started coming back aboard the raft, and our chance to escape was past.

I gave up and turned back to watch them climb out of the water onto the logs. Those who had been hurt were the first to return. They crawled back up into the sunlight, one by one, and dropped down, to lie as still as if each of them had been knocked on the head.

Lizards kept coming back over the next half hour or so. The last dozen or so to come aboard had been very badly bitten by the shark. Three of these later died, and the surviving lizards simply pushed the bodies overside. The tide took them out in the late afternoon, and in the morning they were gone. There would be plenty of scavengers waiting for them.

The lizards did not go immediately back to their shell-fishing when day broke the following morning. They had evidently won their battle with the large shark—though my guess was that it had cost them at least a dozen of their number. But they seemed exhausted by the effort; and as the sun rose, the clear water of the bay showed itself to be full of small sharks, not more than two or three feet long but dashing around madly as if still excited by the gore and torn meat of the day before. Sunday, the girl and I were still uncaged; and I began to hope that, possibly, this would become the permanent state of affairs. If so, I appreciated it; although of course, I could always have cut myself out of my woven cage with my pocket-knife and then freed the girl and Sunday.

I could not decide what was keeping the smaller sharks around us. There was nothing for them to feed on that I could see. Then that night the first storm I had ever known to ruffle that sea blew up, a heavy, tropical rainstorm type of atmospheric explosion; and I found out why they were still with us.

The wind began in the afternoon, and the sky piled up with white clouds which crowded together and darkened until we had an early twilight. Then the breeze died and the water beneath us became viscid and heavy. The raft rocked, rubbing on the floor of the bay with its undergrowth, swayed by a swell that came in on us from far out on the airless water, even though we felt no wind where we were.

Then lightning and thunder began to flicker and growl —high up in the clouds above us, but also far out, over the open water. A new, cold breeze sprang up, blowing shoreward, strengthening as the daylight faded; and the sound and activity of the storm grew, approaching us and coming lower, closer toward the surface of the sea. As the last of the sun's illumination went, leaving us in a pitch darkness, the storm broke over us with its full power; and we clung in darkness to the now heavily pitching and rolling raft.

I had found a place to wedge myself among the trees of our "sail," with one arm around the girl and the other holding on to Sunday. The girl trembled and shivered as the cold rainwater poured down on us; but the leopard took it stoically, pressing close to me but never moving. Around us, also wedged in among the trees, were some of the lizards. Where the rest of them were, I had no idea. It was impossible to see someone in the total darkness unless they were right beside you. In the total darkness, vision came only in brief glimpses, every few seconds or so, when there would be a crack of thunder and a vivid lightning flash that lit up the whole surface of the raft, streaming with the rain and plunging like a tethered horse as the black waves all around us tried to drive us up on the beach, and the raft's undergrowth, grounded on the sand below, resisted.

The lightning flashes were like explosions in the mind. After the sudden brilliance of each was gone, the scene it revealed would linger for a second on the retina and in the mind before fading out. I got wild glimpses of the struggling raft—and wilder glimpses of the waters of the bay, not merely their surface but their depths, as sometimes the raft heeled over to hold us in a position staring almost directly down into the heaving sea.

The water was alive with marine life of all kinds, visible in the lightning flashes, dashing about in a frenzy. I had wondered what had brought all the small sharks into the bay after the fight with the big shark was over. Now I suddenly saw why. Like a great waterlogged mass bumping and rolling along the very floor of the bay, impelled by the storm and by the fly-like swarm of smaller fish tearing at its carcass, the huge shark, now dead, was with us again.

It could not have died at the time the lizards abandoned

their fight with it, or its skeleton would have been stripped clean long before this. It must have survived, weakly fighting off the smaller members of its own species who were ready to devour it while it still lived, until just a few hours past, when loss of blood and strength had finally let it down into death.

Now, like a dead man returned to the scene of the crime, it was back with us, courtesy of the storm and the onshore wind. A freak of that wind and storm was bringing it back, not merely into the bay, but right up against the roots of our raft itself. Clinging to the tree-trunks on either side of me, looking down into the water with each flash of lightning, I was less than fifty feet or so in a straight line from where what was left of the carcass was being torn apart—now, by larger sharks and other fish up to fifteen or twenty feet long, still small compared to the sea corpse, but big enough from my point of view. I fretted over their presence. Even if another chance to escape should come, with all the lizards off the raft, we could not hope to make the swim ashore in safety, through those swarming shark jaws.

Then, suddenly, there was a lightning flash and the underwater scavengers were all gone. The half-eaten body of the large shark lay rolling to the sea-disturbance and the tearing it had just been getting by its devourers, but now it was alone on the floor of the bay. I blinked and waited for the next flash. I could not believe what I saw.

With the next flash came enlightenment; and with it, an end to shark carcass, raft, lizards, and everything. The next glare showed the shark overshadowed by a shape twice its size—a dark body, like an underwater cloud. And it also showed, out of the water and white against the black of the waves, a gray-white tentacle as thick as a cable used to tie up a superliner. The tentacle was out of the water. It stood erect in the air, like a telephone pole, twenty feet above the deck at the far end of the raft. A moment later the raft shuddered, as if to the blow of an unthinkably huge axe, and the end where we were began to rise in the air.

Another flash of lightning showed the great tentacle now gripping the whole far end of the raft and pulling it over, down into the waves.

There was no more time for waiting, nor any time to

talk the two of them into coming with me. I yelled in Sunday's ear to come, pulled the girl after me, and jumped for the water. Its choking wetness closed over my head; but I came up still holding on to the girl, and taking a sight on the beach with the next flash, began to swim ashore.

I do not remember how I made it. It seemed I swam forever holding up the girl. But eventually the wet blackness that enclosed us threw us forward into a blackness that had no substance, and a split second later we slammed against hard, level sand. Even with most of the breath knocked out of me, I had the sense to crawl as much farther up the beach as I could, dragging the girl. Then I collapsed. I let myself drop on the beach, one hand still holding an arm of the girl. The damp, grainy surface beneath me went soft as a mattress and I fell into sudden, deep sleep.

I woke to daylight and warming air. The girl was only a few feet away. So was Sunday.

In the bay there was no sign of any raft, or anything, for that matter. We were as alone as if we had been lost in the desert for weeks. I lay there, slowly letting our new situation become real to me.

We were free again, but without food, weapons, or transportation. In addition, I felt as if I had been drawn through a whole series of knotholes, one after another. By contrast, the girl and Sunday looked as rested and cheerful as if the storm and all the rest of it had never happened. Well, their reactions were nothing to be surprised at, I told myself, grumpily. I was twice the age of the girl or nearly so and probably five time the age of Sunday. It didn't matter. By God, the three of us had made it!

The minute I tried to sit up, they noticed me. In a second they were all over me. Sunday gave one large leap to land beside me and started to rub himself up against my chest, knocking me flat. The girl reached me a split-second later and picked me up.

"Stop that," she scolded Sunday, out loud, in actual and unexpected words. I was sitting up again now, but her arms were still around me, her head against my chest; and I got the strange impression that she was hugging me. This sort of response by the two of them made me feel absurdly warm inside; but when I tried to pat the girl on the head, she broke away at once, scrambling to her feet, turning her back and walking off a few steps. Sunday, purring loudly, was doing his best to knock me down again; but I was braced for him.

I leaned heavily on his back with one arm and pulled myself creakily to my feet. Seen from the shore, the place we had ended up had much less of the California look than the beach where we had first run into the lizards. Back from the stretch of open sand were some kind of pine-needle trees with a northerly look and a tree like a willow, with fairly thick-standing grass in the open spaces.

I patted Sunday on the head and spoke to the girl's back.

"We'd better look around," I said, hoarsely.

I led the way and the other two followed. Behind the immediate fringe of trees there was a small bluff. We went up to the top of that and looked out at what seemed to be a stretch of midcontinental prairie spottily overgrown with clumps of trees. There were not quite enough trees to call it a forest and an almost total lack of undergrowth. In the open patches it was mainly high grass, green and brown, with just an occasional, scattered, lone sapling or bush.

Nowhere in sight was there any sign of civilization.

I stood on the top of the bluff and did some pondering. I did not like the semi-arid look of the country before me. We were on foot now, and we could survive without food for a few days, if necessary; but what I was looking at did not have the appearance of being either lake or river country, and drinking water was a constant need. Add to that the fact that we were now completely unarmed except for my pocketknife; and it might not be just wild animals we would have to worry about encountering out there.

In the end, I decided against leaving the only drinking water in view, which was the lake. We went east along the beach, the route in which the lizard raft had been headed anyway, for three days, living off shellfish and whatever small creatures we could find in the sand or shallow water just offshore. Our diet of small things from the underside of the raft had done my sensibilities a world of good in that area of diet. I could now eat anything that didn't look as if it would poison me—and eat it raw at that. The girl was equally open-minded, I noticed; and as for Sunday, he had never had a problem about the looks of his food to begin with.

The third day we hit the jackpot—well, a jackpot of sorts. It must have been somebody's lakeshore home, on a lake that had now become part of the inland sea. There were no people in sight around it, and no other lakeshore houses or cabins nearby. But this place must have cost someone a good deal of money. It had a large house, with attached garage and a separate pole barn—that is, a type of barn-size building, made of metal roof and siding that were literally hung on wooden posts the thickness of telephone poles, set in the earth. It also had a dock and a boat. A road that was dirt, but well-graded and well-kept, led from the house and the lake away into the country beyond the beach. The country here was treed thickly enough to be honestly called forested.

The home looked as if it had been abandoned less than a week before. Some of the food in the refrigerator still looked edible; and the food in the large, chest-type freezer in the double garage would probably have been edible if the electric power had stayed on. We must have crossed a former mistwall line, some way back; because this was the kind of trick the time storm played. A few miles off, we had been several geologic ages in the past, here we were only in yesterday. Tomorrow we might be in any future time, I supposed. As it was, I trusted none of it. But there was a wealth of canned goods on shelves—also bottled goods. It gave me a peculiar feeling to mix myself a scotch and soda—even an iceless scotch and soda—and sit sipping it in the overstuffed chair of a carpeted living room.

The only drawback to the place was that it had neither of the two things we needed most—weapons and transport —a car or truck in which we could travel.

I searched the place from dock to driveway. There was not even a canoe in the boathouse. There was, in the pole barn, a 1931 all-black Model A Ford roadster somebody had been restoring; but it was not in drivable condition, nor were there parts lying around that could be put in to make it drivable. It held only the block of a motor, with the head off and the cylinders, crankshaft and oil pan missing. There were a couple of bicycles in

the garage, a battered girl's singlespeed, and a man-sized
three-speed Raleigh, which had been kept in only slightly
better condition.

In one end of the pole barn, however, was a gasoline-
driven electric generator, in beautiful condition under its
protective coat of grease, and a good deal of wood and
metal-working tools—power and otherwise—also in fine
condition. I got the generator cleaned up and going; although after about fifteen minutes I shut it off again. The
three of us were used to doing without the luxury of
electric lights and appliances; and there was, I judged
after measuring it with a stick, only ten or fifteen gallons
of gas left in a drum by the generator. I did not yet
know exactly what I would use the gas for, but it was
too useful a material to be wasted. Later, I found some
empty pop bottles with screwtops and filled them with the
gas, then tied rags around their necks, so that they could
be turned into Molotov cocktails in a hurry. That gave us
one kind of weapon.

Meanwhile, the girl and Sunday were settling in. There
were two bedrooms with closets holding women's clothes,
and the girl, for the first time, began to show some interest
in what she wore. She still stuck to shirt and jeans, generally, but I caught her a couple of times trying on things
when I came into the house unexpectedly from outside.

Sunday liked the carpets. He slept and ate. We all ate
—and gained back some of the weight we had lost on
the raft.

I was determined that we would not stir from where
we were without some means of protecting ourselves. I
had two ideas about weapons I might be able to make. I
had rejected the thought of a bow and arrows. I was a
mediocre-to-poor archer; and no bowyer at all. Making a
really effective bow was beyond me. Other alternatives
were, first a homemade, muzzle-loading gun using a length
of metal water pipe wrapped with wire, if I could find
any, and using match heads for the explosive element. In
short—a zip gun. Second, a crossbow using a leaf from
one of the springs of the Model A. There was enough gas
to let me run the generator and get the wood and metal-
working power tools operating in the pole barn.

In the end, I chose the crossbow, not because it was
simpler, but because I couldn't find any wire; and I had a

vision of the water pipe blowing up in my face. I found a dry chunk of firewood that looked to me to be maple or oak, sawed it roughly to shape and then worked it on the lath to an approximation of a stock and frame for the crossbow. I cut a slot across the frame, sank the leaf spring (the smallest of the leaf springs) into it crosswise and did as good a job of gluing it there as I could. Modern glues were miracle-workers, given half a chance. I glued a separate, notched bar of hard wood along the top of the frame for the cord of the crossbow, and set up a lever-crank to allow me to tighten the bow cord, notch by notch.

I had more trouble making the short, heavy arrows—quarrels—for the thing than I did putting together the crossbow itself. It was not easy to make a straight shaft from a raw chunk of wood, I discovered.

But the day came when I had both crossbow and quarrels. Both had been tested. There was no lack of power in the crossbow. The problem was with my quarrels. Their shafts broke too easily when they hit something hard. But, they would do on any flesh and blood target. The morning came when we mounted the two bikes, the girl and I—happily she had evidently ridden a bicycle before, and the skill came back to her quickly—and wearing backpacks, we started off down the empty road, away from the lake, with Sunday footing it alongside us.

The weather was pleasant, with the temperature in the high sixties, Fahrenheit, and the sky was lightly spotted with occasional clouds. As we got away from the water the humidity began to fall off sharply, until the day was almost like one in early autumn up near the Canadian border. We made good time, considering—considering Sunday, that was. Dogs are generally content to trot steadily alongside the bikers they belong to; but Sunday had a cat's dislike of regimentation. Sunday preferred that the girl and I travel at the equivalent of a slow walk, so that he could make short side excursions, or even take a quick nap and still catch up with us. When we did stop finally, to give him a break, he lay down heavily on top of the girl's bike and would not be moved until I hauled him clear by sheer muscle-strength and a good grip on the scruff of his neck.

In the end we compromised with him, riding along at

hardly more than a walking speed. As a result, it was not surprising that I got more and more involved in my own thoughts.

The road we were on had yet to lead past any sign of civilization. But, of course, we were not covering ground at any great speed. Eventually our route must bring us to someplace where we could get the weapons and wheels I wanted. Then, once more mobile and protected, as it were, I meant to do a little investigating along the thought I had come to, lying on the lizard raft, nights. If the world was going to be as full of potential threats, as we had just seen it, it was high time we set actively about the business of learning the best ways to survive in it. . . .

We hit no signs of civilization that day, but late afternoon, we crossed a creek hardly larger than a trickle, running through a culvert under the road. In this open territory it looked as though it probably contained clean water; but I boiled it to make sure, and we set up camp for the night by it.

Midway through the next morning on the road, we rode past a chunk of a suburb. I mean exactly that—a chunk. It was some two hundred yards off our asphalt highway, a roughly triangular piece of real estate with lawns, garages, streets and tract houses looking as if it had been sliced off at random and dropped down here in the middle of nowhere.

There were no people about it any more than there had been people about the lakeshore home. But these buildings were not in the untouched condition of the house by the lake. The area looked, in fact, as if a tornado had passed through it, a tornado, or else something with the size of a dinosaur and a destructive urge to match. There was not one building that was whole and weathertight, and some were all but flattened.

Nonetheless, they represented a treasure trove for us. I went through all the houses and turned up a sixteen gauge shotgun and a carbine-type .22 rifle. There were no shells for the shotgun and only one box of shorts for the .22. But the odds on picking up ammunition for these two common caliber firearms were good enough to count on. The suburb-chunk also contained eight cars. Five of these had been made useless by whatever had smashed the buildings. Of the remaining three, all were more than a few years old, and one would not start at

all. That left me with a choice between a two-door
Pontiac hardtop in relatively good shape and a Volvo
four-door sedan that was pretty well beaten up.

I chose the Volvo, however. Not only for its extra
carrying capacity, but because the gas mileage should be
better. There was no filling station among the homes in
the suburb, but I drained the gas tanks of all the other
cars that proved to have anything in them; and when we
started out in the Volvo, we had a full tank plus another
fifteen gallons in cans tied on to a makeshift rack on top
of the trunk. Also, I had found two three-speed bikes in
good shape. They were tied to the top of the car.

The suburb had a fine, four-lane concrete road leading
out of it, but that ended about two hundred yards from
the last of the smashed houses. I drove the Volvo, bumping and bucking across a lumpy open field, to get it
back on our familiar asphalt and turned left into the
direction in which we had been originally headed. We
kept going; and about an hour later, I spotted a mistwall
to our right. It was angled toward the road we were on,
looking as if it crossed the asphalt somewhere up ahead
of us.

9

My heart jumped when I saw it; but after watching it closely for a little while, I calmed down. Clearly, the wall was standing still. We continued on up along the road, with its vertical, white face getting closer and closer, until finally we were far enough along to see where it ended. It did indeed cut across the road at last, about a quarter mile ahead of where we were; but it only continued beyond that point of intersection for about a hundred yards. By going off the asphalt to the left just a short distance, we could get around the end of the cloud-high curtain. Not only could we bypass it safely; but after going a little further, we would be able to get where we could see what was behind it, without ever having to set foot in what might be dangerous territory. I kept us moving.

We stopped finally and left the road, a good fifty or a hundred feet short of the point where it was intersected by the mistwall. Up this close to the wall, we could see it seeming to reach clear out of sight above us; and we could feel the peculiar breeze and the dust that always eddied from it, like the peppering of a fine spray on our face and hands. We struck off into the trees and brush to the left of the road, with the car in low gear and moving along level with the face of the wall.

It did not take long to reach the end of it. I kept on a little further, however, not wanting to turn the corner until I could see behind it. But though we kept going further and further, we still did not seem to quite clear the end. Finally, I saw why. We were not going to be able to see behind that mistwall after all. Here at what I had thought was its point of termination, it had either bent to the right and continued, or run into another mist-wall going off at an angle in that direction.

At first, all I felt was disappointment that I was not going to get a look behind it. Then it occurred to me that perhaps the reason neither mistwall nor mistwall section had been moving had been because each had butted up against the other; and the two time change lines coming together had somehow created an unusual state or condition that had halted them both.

The moment that I thought it, I was hungry to see what was behind the intersection of those two mistwalls. Ever since, lying on the lizard raft, I had come up with the idea that perhaps those of us who were still here on the earth might be individually immune to the time changes, I had been playing with the idea of not avoiding the next mistwall we met, but deliberately walking into it, to see if I could get through and survive. Now I had a double reason to try going through the one before me. It was not merely to find out if I could get through with nothing worse than the unconsciousness I had experienced the first time, but to discover if there was something special or strange about the situation where one time change line ran into another. I stopped the Volvo.

I got out and looked at the wall. I also looked forward along the other angle of the second, or continued, mistwall to see where the road emerged once more from it, only about a couple of hundred yards away. It occurred to me that all I had to do was get back on the road and keep going, and the three of us would continue to stay safe, united, and happy. Or, I could turn and go through the mistwall; and I might, just might, learn something—that is, if I made it through all right.

I stood there. And the longer I stood, the stronger grew the desire in me to try going through the wall. It was exactly the way it had always been, from my earliest childhood, when my mind fastened on to a question and would not let it go without finding the answer. The phenomenon was like every time since I'd first let that relentless mental machinery in my head get its teeth into a problem. I remembered perfectly the terrible feeling I had felt during the initial seconds of that first time change, when I had thought I was having another heart attack. I remembered the miserable, helpless, empty sensation all

through me after I had come to. I remembered every bit
and part that had been bad about it; and still . . . still . . .
as I stood there the wanting to go through that wall and
find out what I did not know was like a sharp, sweet
taste on my lips and a hunger that used me up inside like fire.

I turned back at last to look at the girl and Sunday. If I
went through the wall and never returned, what would
happen to them? I told myself that I owed them nothing,
and something inside me called me a liar. At the same
time, the thought of any responsibility I might have toward either of them had about as much deterrent effect
on the hunger that was eating me up as a cup of water
tossed on a burning building. I had no real choice. I had
to go through that wall if I—and they—died for it. I
turned back to the leopard and the girl, both of whom
were still sitting in the car.

"Stay here!" I said. "You understand me? Stay right
here. Don't take as much as one step after me. *Stay where
you are!*"

They both stared at me silently. One of the girl's hands
twitched—that was all. I turned and walked away from
them, toward the mistwall, until I had to squint my eyes
against the flying dust of it. Just before I reached the
actual mist of the wall, I turned and looked back. The
girl still sat with Sunday beside her, both watching me.
Neither had moved a muscle.

I turned back again, closed my eyes to the sting of the
dust, and walked blindly forward.

But the hard part was not the dust. The hard part was
that it was like walking into an emotional tornado. It
was bad. It was very bad. But, somehow, it was not as
bad as I remembered it from the first time, outside my
cabin. Maybe this was because my first time through had
left me with a sort of immunity; as if I had been inocu-
lated against the effects I felt. Maybe it was easier because
I now had some idea what to expect and was braced for
it. Basically, I felt as if my soul had been ripped out of
my being. I felt naked, sick and frightened. But, you
know, it was not the kind of fear I feared—if that statement makes any sense to you. I stayed on my feet and
came out the other side, walking.

I was suddenly assaulted by the clamor of dogs barking
not far in front of me. I opened my eyes and saw them—
more than a dozen of them, all tied to short leashes, but

all barking, snarling and leaping against their tethers to get at me. They were tied to leashes anchored to thick stakes driven into the earth, in front of a slice of a house about fifty yards away, a house sitting on a chunk of a lawn in the interior angle of the two mistwalls. Behind the house was forest, and the house itself was a two-story frame building that looked as if it would be at home surrounded by a midwestern farmyard. As I looked, the door opened, and a woman came out with a rifle already at her shoulder, pointed at me.

"Drop your gun." Her voice was a low, carrying soprano, soft but positive.

"Wait a minute," I told her. "How about talking about this?"

I had no intention of dropping my gun. She was standing behind the dogs, in the open, with no rest or other support for her rifle, but with the weapon up and aimed. If I had to shoot her to live myself, I would. At that distance, unless she was a natural markswoman, holding her gun steady enough to hit me would not be easy. Even from where I stood, I could see the end of the barrel waver slightly in the sunlight.

I was more concerned about her dogs; and I was not about to drop the one weapon that could defend me against them. In fact—the situation framed itself in my mind and produced its own inescapable conclusion—if she turned the dogs loose on me, I was going to shoot her first. They were dogs of all sizes, but the least of them must have gone at least forty pounds, which is heavy enough to be a potential man-killer. I could shoot three-quarters of them, and there would still be enough left to pull me down and finish me off. Nor did I think she would be able to pull them off in time to save my life, once she had set them on me.

"Listen!" I called to her. "I'm just here by accident—"

"I said put down your gun!" she cried. Her rifle went off, and a bullet whistled wide of me into the mistwall beside me.

"Quit that!" I said, raising the .22. "Or I'll have to start shooting back."

She hesitated—or if it wasn't hesitation, at least she did not pull her trigger again. Perhaps the first shot had been more accidental than otherwise. I kept talking.

"Look," I told her over the noise of the dogs. "I don't

want to bother you. I just happened to stumble on your
place here, and I'll be glad to be on my way again. Why
would I want to be any trouble to you anyway? You're
armed, you've got your dogs; and I'm all alone. Now,
why don't we just both point our rifles to the ground and
talk for a moment—"

Her gaze, which had been focused on me, shifted suddenly. Her rifle barrel changed its aim slightly.

"Alone?" she shouted back. "Do you call that alone?"

I turned to look; and sure enough, her question was a
good one. If there was one thing I could count on—if
there was one damn thing under the sun that I could absolutely be sure of with Sunday and the girl—it was that
they would do exactly what I had told them not to.
Somehow they had worked up the courage to come
through the mistwall on their own, and now they were
standing right behind me.

Of course, this changed the situation entirely. The woman had three times as much target, now. She might not hit
me, but her chances of hitting one of our group was
tripled. I felt a touch of something not far from panic.
Add to what was happening the fact that with Sunday in
view and scent, the dogs were now really going crazy;
while Sunday's own back was beginning to arch like the
stave of a drawn bow. He did not like dogs.

But for all that, he would not leave me to face them
alone. He pressed close against my leg and snarled softly
in his throat, watching the dogs. It was magnificently
touching and, at the same time, monumentally exasperat-
ing to know that the crazy cat would stay beside me, even
if I tried to drive him back with a club.

I looked again at the woman—just in time. She had
grown arm-tired of holding the rifle to her shoulder and
was moving now to untie the nearest dogs. There was
no time for me to debate the ethics of the situation. I
put a shot from my own rifle into the dirt between her
and the animal she was approaching. She froze.

"Don't try letting any of them go!" I called to her. "I
don't want to hurt you; but I'm not going to let us be
chewed up by your animals. Step back now and put your
own gun down."

She backed up, but without letting go of her rifle. I
put another shot from the .22 into the frame of the door-

way behind her. She checked, hesitated, and let the gun slip from her hands to the earth at her feet.

"All right!" I said. "Now, I'm not going to hurt you, but I've got to make sure you're not going to hurt us. Stay where you are and don't move."

She stood still. I turned to the girl.

"Hold, Sunday!" I said. "Stay right where you are, both of you. This time, I mean it!"

I went forward, holding the .22. The dogs had their tethers stretched taut, trying to reach me, so that it was possible for me to see where I needed to walk to stay out of reach of each one of them as I went through their pack. I came up to the woman, bent and picked up her gun. It was a 30.06, a good, clean, hunting rifle. With that in my hands, I felt more secure.

I knew what I had to do, then—and that was shoot the dogs while they were all still safely tied up. But when I raised her rifle I found I could not do it. It was not just that the woman would be vulnerable without them once I had taken her rifle and gone on. It was also the matter that I was still too civilized. I could not get over thinking of them as pets, instead of as the four-legged killers she had turned them into. I twisted about to face the woman.

"Look," I said. "I'm going to have to kill your dogs to make sure they won't hurt us, unless you can think of some way to fix things so I can trust them not to attack us."

She sighed and shivered at the same time. It was as if all the strength in her had suddenly run out.

"I can do it," she said, in a dead voice. She looked away from me, to the dogs. "Quiet! Down—all of you. *Down!* Be quiet!"

They obeyed, to my astonishment. Their barking and snarling fell gradually into silence. They stared at the woman, licking their muzzles, and lay down one by one until they were all on the ground and silent, watching.

"That's pretty good," I said to the woman.

"I used to run an obedience school," she answered in the same dead voice. "You don't have to worry. You can go now."

"Sorry," I said. "But I don't know what else you have in the way of guns or dogs inside that house of yours. Let's go inside. You first."

She stiffened.

"No!"

"Calm down, damn it!" I said. "I just want to look round."

She was still stiff.

"Just a minute," she said. She turned her head and called back through the open doorway into the dark interior behind her. "Wendy, come out here."

"My daughter," she said, harshly.

We waited, and after a second, a blonde-haired little girl of early grade school age came out and pressed herself up against the woman, who put her arm around the child.

"It's all right," the woman said, "We're just going to show this man our house."

She turned then, and with one arm still around her daughter, led the way inside. I followed, carrying both rifles. There was not a great deal to see inside. A time change line had cut the house very nearly in half. A portion of the living room, all of the kitchen and bathroom, plus one bedroom and a half, remained. The bright sun coming in the uncurtained windows of the rooms that were still whole made the spartan existence that the two of them had been living here all very clear and plain. I went over the rooms carefully, but there were no other guns and only some kitchen knives that might have possibilities as weapons.

The woman said nothing all the time I was looking around. She stood by the living-room window and glanced out from time to time. I thought she was checking on the dogs, because they stayed quiet. But I was wrong.

"Is that your wife out there?" she asked at last.

"Wife?" I said.

For a second, the question made no sense at all. I looked out the window where she was looking and saw only Sunday and the girl. Then, of course, I understood.

"No!" I said. "She's just a kid. I picked her up after she'd just been through a time change; and it mixed her up pretty badly. She's not right yet, for that matter. I—"

I broke off. I had been about to go on and tell her about my previous conviction that Swannee had escaped the time changes, and a lot more that was purely personal. But it was none of her business. For that matter, the girl was none of her business, either. The fact of the matter was, I had long since drifted into ignoring any sexual quality in the girl; if I had ever paid any attention to that, in the first place. My mind had been full of my own personal problems. But I could hardly try to explain that to this woman without confusing the matter more than I would clear it up. I was a little surprised at the strength of the sudden urge in me to talk about it; then I realized that she was the first rational, adult human I had met since the beginning of the time storms. But it was still none of her business.

I looked once more around the living room of the house, ready to leave now. The woman spoke quickly, as if she could read my mind.

"Why don't you ask her to come in?"

"Ask her in?" I said. "If she comes in, the leopard has to come in, too."

She grew a little pale at that and held the young child closer to her side. But then she tossed her head back.

"Is he dangerous?" she asked. "The leopard?"

"Not if the two of you stay well back from him," I said. "But if he comes in here, he's got to pass by those dogs of yours, and I can't imagine that happening."

"I can," she said, flatly. "They'll obey orders."

She walked with her daughter to the door, which was standing open, and through it. I followed her.

"Come on in!" she called to the girl and Sunday. Of course the girl neither moved nor answered, any more than Sunday did.

"It's all right," I told the girl. "You and Sunday come in." I turned to the woman. "And you'd better control those dogs."

The girl had already started toward the house; but Sunday held back. Seeing he would not come, she turned back to him. I had to go out to both of them.

"Come on," I said. I took a fistful of the loose skin at the scruff of Sunday's neck and led him with me toward the house. He came; a little reluctantly, but he came. The dogs tied nearest to his path shrank back from him as we approached, but those farther off whined and crawled forward to the limit of their tethers, white-toothed and panting.

"Down!" said the woman from the doorstep, and, hearing her, if I'd been a dog I would not have delayed doing what she said. The soft soprano now had a knife-edge to it. It lifted and cut. It carried clearly without her seeming to have to raise the volume. "All of you—down! *Quiet!*" The dogs followed the girl and Sunday with eyes and wet breath; but they neither got to their feet nor raised a clamor.

We all went back inside the house and the woman shut the door behind us. One lone bark sounded from the yard as the door closed. The woman opened it again and looked out. There was silence. She closed the door once more and this time the silence continued.

"Hello," she said to the girl. "I'm Marie Walcott, and this is my daughter, Wendy."

The girl—my girl—said nothing. Her face had a look that made it appear merely as if she did not understand, but which I knew well enough to recognize as an expression of stubbornness.

"She doesn't talk," I told the woman. "I mean, she can talk, but she doesn't like to—part of the shock she went through, I suppose. But she hears and understands you, all right."

The girl stepped to my side, at that, then went around me and knelt down on the other side of Sunday, putting an arm around the leopard's neck.

"Poor thing," said the woman, watching her. The expression on the girl's face did not change. The woman looked back at me. "What are you going to do now?"

"We'll move on," I said. "I told you that. And I'm taking this rifle of yours. I'll leave you my .22 rifle—I'll drop it about five hundred yards out, so we'll be well gone by the time you get to it. It's a lighter gun and it'll suit you better in any use you've got for a rifle. The dogs are your real protection, and I'm leaving you those, alive. But try to track us down with them, and I'll shoot every one of them that Sunday doesn't tear up."

"I wouldn't come after you that way," said the woman. "Where are you going anyway?"

"Into the futuremost segment of time-changed country I can find," I said. "Somewhere there must be somebody who'll understand what's happened to the world."

"What makes you so sure there's anyone like that?"

"All right," I said, "if there isn't we're still going to be looking—for the best piece of time to stay with, or some way of living with the time changes, themselves. I've been running away from the mistwalls; but now I'm going through any one I meet, so I can find out what's on the other side."

She looked out her window toward the two mistwalls overshadowing her dogs and her home.

"What is on the other side out there?" she asked.

"You wouldn't like it," I said. "What's farther in?" I pointed through the back of the house toward the forest that crowded close upon her place.

"I don't know," she said. "There used to be a town of fifty thousand people—Gregory, Illinois—about ten miles down the road, there. But there's not even any road, now. I don't know."

I looked closely at her.

"You haven't moved from this place since the time storms first started?"

"That's right." She looked somber. "Wendy and I sat here and prayed, after the first time change came close. At first we prayed for Tim—for my husband to come back. But now for some time we've just prayed that the mistwalls will leave us alone."

"Two of them are right on top of you," I said. "Didn't you think of getting away from them?"

"To what?" she said, shrugging. "I've got half a year's supply of food in the basement here—had to, since we live out of town. If they move over us, then it's over, all at once. Meanwhile, we're safer here than someplace else. I ran a boarding kennel, so I had the dogs, here, to guard me. And there was—or we thought there was—always the chance my husband . . . ."

She shrugged again and stopped talking.

"All right," I hefted both rifles and turned toward the door. "Come on, Sunday, Girl. As for you, Mrs. Walcott, wait fifteen minutes and then follow us out. You'll find the .22 leaning against a tree, a little way into the woods, there."

I opened the door. The woman's voice spoke from behind me to the dogs, commandingly.

"Quiet! Down!" Then her tone changed. "We could go with you."

I turned around. My first, unthinking reaction was that she was joking. I saw she was not. Then, suddenly, I saw and understood a great many other things.

I had been assuming, without really looking at her, that she was housewifely middle-aged. She was wearing slacks

and a man's shirt, and of course she had on no makeup.
Her hair was cut short—rather clumsily cut short; and
there were dark circles of weariness under her eyes. By
contrast with the girl, the only human member of the
opposite sex I had seen since the first time storm, at first
glance, Marie Walcott had looked maturely-fleshed and
unremarkable. Now, suddenly I realized that she was
probably no older than I. In fact, given the conditions of
civilization once more she would have been damned attractive. She was full grown, someone my own age, with
the body of a woman rather than that of a half-grown
girl, with a sane adult mind and capability of speech.
Suddenly I remembered that it had been a long time since
I and any woman. . . .

I noticed all this in a moment; and in the same moment,
I realized that she had wanted me to notice—had set out
to make me notice. It changed the whole picture.

"Go with us?" I said, more to myself than to her.

"We'd all be safer, in one large group," she said. "You
could use another grown-up. And of course, there's the
dogs."

She was right about the dogs. A pack like that, properly trained, could really be valuable.

"There's your daughter," I said. "She's too young to be
making long marches every day."

"I've got a cart the dogs can pull her in—also, we'd be
running into roads, and some kind of transportation sooner or later, don't you think? Meanwhile, I . . . we'd both
feel better with a man around."

She was giving me all the practical reasons why our
teaming up would work, and I was countering with all the
practical arguments against it; and we both knew that
we were talking around the one real reason I should or
should not add her to my party, which was that I was
male and she was female.

"Why don't you think it over?" she said. "Stay here
overnight and think about it. Maybe we can talk about it
some more, later on."

"All right," I said. "We'll stay until tomorrow." I
glanced out the window.

"I'd better camp off by the edge of the trees, there," I
said. "Sunday isn't going to take to your dogs just like
that—or they to him."

"Sunday?" said the woman. "Is that what you call him?

I think you heard me say my name. I'm Marie Walcott and this is Wendy."

"I'm Marc Despard," I said.

"Marc, I'm pleased to meet you." She held out her hand and I took it. It was a strange feeling to shake hands after the last few weeks. Her hand was small but firm, and there were callouses at the base of her fingers. "Are you French?"

I laughed. "The name's French-Canadian."

She let go of my hand and looked at the girl.

"I didn't hear . . ."

"She's never told me her name," I said. I looked at the girl. "How about it? Do you want to tell us now?"

The girl was absolutely silent. I shrugged.

"I've just been calling her 'Girl.'" I said. "I guess you'll have to do the same."

"Maybe," Marie smiled at her, "she'll tell us her name —later on, when she feels like it."

The girl stood without a word.

"Don't count on it," I said to Marie.

10

I had rigged a backpack-style tent for the girl and myself from some of the canvas in the boatdock before we left the deserted lakeshore house. I set this up at the edge of the trees, upwind of the dogs. Sunday had already begun ignoring the dog pack; and Marie rode herd on them through the afternoon, commanding them to be quiet any time they started to get worked up about Sunday or the rest of us. Once the camp was made, I left the girl with Sunday and went to the house alone.

Marie took me around and introduced me individually to each of the dogs. I spoke to each and petted each one briefly while Marie stood sternly over them to make sure that they behaved. Occasionally I got a brief tail movement by the way of acknowledgment but most of them merely rolled their eyes up at me and only endured both my touch and my voice. I guessed that I smelled too much of cat for any of them to be really comfortable; and I mentioned this to Marie. But she shrugged it off.

"They'll get used to you," she said. The tone of her voice indicated that they had better.

She left me then, to get dinner ready. I spent a little time trying to make friends with her daughter. But Wendy was a quiet, shy child who—like the dogs—evidently found me too strange and potentially frightening to warm up to, on short acquaintance. She was obviously relieved when I left her at last and went back to camp.

Sunday was there, tied to the trunk of a large tree with a length of our heaviest rope, ending in a loop around his neck. He was lying down and, to my surprise, did not seem to mind being restricted this way. Since he was not objecting and it was convenient to have him anchored so, I left him the way he was. The girl must have tied him up so that she could wander off by herself, because she was nowhere to be seen.

She had not returned by the time Marie stuck her head out her door to call us to dinner. I waited a little while, but she still had not come back when Marie called a second time; and I decided not to worry about her. There was no counting on her, anyway. Sunday was still not objecting to being tied up—which was ideal from my point of view. He had dozed off kittenishly lying on his back with his paws in the air, as if there was no dog within a thousand miles. I got up and left; and all he did was open his eyes sleepily to look after me.

The good smell of cooking reached me before I opened the door and surrounded me as soon as I came in. Marie had produced a ham—it had to have been a canned one —heated and glazed it, and filled out the meal with what must have been home-grown tomatoes, potatoes and a salad made with some greens I didn't identify, but which, with a cheese dressing, tasted magnificent.

"She didn't come with you?" Marie asked, as she sat down at the table with Wendy and me.

"She's gone off somewhere. Sunday's tied up," I said.

She nodded, evidently reassured. She did not know that Sunday was capable of chewing through any rope that tied him in no seconds flat, if the notion occurred to him. But he was not likely to wander off; and he had sense enough not to start trouble with the dogs, but to pick his way among them, if he got the urge to free himself and join me in the house.

It was a marvelous dinner. Marie had gotten rid of the slacks and shirt. She was wearing a soft, yellow dress that went well with the color of her blond hair, which— while still short—was smoothed out somehow and looked less as if it had undergone home barbering. She had used a touch of lipstick too, and possibly a hint of other makeup. The total result was enough to bring back the past in a way that the scotch and sodas I had made in the lake-front home never had.

I had been regretting all afternoon that I had not had the sense to bring at least one bottle from the liquor stock of the lakeshore home. But as it turned out, Marie had her own supply. She had not produced any wine with the meal; but afterwards she came up with a bottle of rum, after everything was over and Wendy had gone off to bed. It was not great rum, but it went well with the coffee.

We sat on the couch in her living room and talked, about our situations—and a lot else. Under the influence of the rum, I remember telling her more about myself than I had intended to ever tell anyone. But in the warmth and privacy of the living room, I was lulled into a sense of security. I knew very well that Marie was only out after her own advantage. I knew what was going on with both of us; but I did not give a damn. In fact, I remember thinking that I deserved something like this, after wet-nursing an insane leopard and a wild girl all these weeks. Somewhere along there with the rum and the coffee, I put my arm around Marie; and only a little later we turned the lights out.

I don't know how late it was. It was certainly sometime after midnight when I left the house. Marie followed me naked to the door in the darkness to put her head out and hiss the dogs into silence when they roused on seeing me. I gave her a last kiss and went across the dark ground under a young moon to the camp.

Sunday was curled up under the tree to which he had been tied; and there was a lump on the ground beside him that was the girl, come back. The groundsheet out of our tent was a black pool under them on the semi-moonlighted ground; and some of our blankets were spread over both of them.

I shrugged, drunkenly. If the girl wanted to lie out there and get soaked through with the morning dew, that was up to her. I crawled into the tent and wrapped myself as well as I could in the remaining blankets. I was either not quite asleep and hallucinating, or else I was already asleep and dreamed the whole thing; but it seemed to me that just before I dropped into a deep well of unconsciousness, Sunday raised his head and looked me right in the eye, speaking to me.

"You stink!" he said distinctly, in the girl's voice.—And that was the last I remember.

When I woke, someone was standing over me. But it was neither Sunday nor the girl. It was Marie; and she handed me a cup of hot coffee.

"Sorry to wake you," she said. "But I can use your help if we're going to get off today."

"Get off today?" I echoed stupidly. She stood there, looking down at me for a long second.

"That's what we talked about last night, wasn't it?" she said. "Do you remember?"

I started to say I didn't. But then it came back to me. She was right, of course. That was, indeed, one of the things we had talked about last night. We had made plans to leave today—all of us, together.

"Yes," I said. I lay looking at her, part of me hating myself and filled with self-contempt at letting myself be bought so easily; and part of me remembering last night and looking forward to tonight. "I'll be along in a bit."

"Good," she said.

She went off. I got up and dressed. The girl and Sunday were not to be seen. During the period on the lizard raft, with no way to do anything about it, my beard had grown to a respectable length. But I had always liked the feel of being clean-shaven, and as soon as we found the lakeshore home, I had been happy to discover a razor and go back to being naked-faced once more. Normally, I liked shaving. It was part of the familiar ritual of coming awake in the morning—and I did not come awake in the morning easily. But this morning the habitual scraping actions did not clean off a layer of guilt left on me by the night before. In a sense, I had sold Sunday and the girl down the river for the selfish satisfaction of my own desires.

Sunday, of course, did not know what was going on. But he was not going to have the old freedom he was accustomed to, living with the dog-pack alongside him, whether he knew it or not. Also, he was going to have to share me with a couple of extra humans—and that was not going to make him happy, either. He had adjusted to the girl; but the girl loved him—Marie and Wendy did not, and there was no guarantee that they ever would. As for the girl, she had already made it plain how she felt about the situation.

I washed the last of the soap off my face and began to pump myself up with counter-arguments. We had been bound eventually to bump into other people with whom we would want and need to associate. Sunday had been destined to have to learn to share me with other people, finally. The girl, likewise. The three of us could not go on forever being exclusively insane together, as we had been until I faced the freshwater sea and the fact that Swannee was gone for good.

It was not going to be easy adapting, for me either, I told myself. But I was going to have to do it. So were the girl and Sunday. That was life—you could not always have what you wanted.

By the time I went over to get some breakfast from Marie and help her prepare to move out, I had the top layer of my mind—if nothing beyond that—thoroughly convinced that I was not only doing the best thing for all concerned, but being considerably self-sacrificing to boot.

It took us most of the day to get ready. Marie had two carts fitted with bicycle wheels, which she had trained certain of her dogs to pull. The carts themselves were obviously homemade, but remarkably well put together. Marie, apparently, had a definite mechanical talent. They were light and rolled easily. But they had one real drawback—no springs except the bicycle parts that supported the wheels. They would be all right on road surfaces, but I could not see them lasting more than a few days loaded and going cross-country, as we were going to be doing sooner or later. However, since we had nothing in the way of materials and tools around to provide them with springs, I decided not to say anything. There was no point in borrowing trouble.

We started out shortly after noon. The girl—she had showed up in time for breakfast, after all—Sunday, and I made up the advance guard, about fifty yards ahead of the rest. Behind us came Marie, walking, and the two carts, with Wendy riding one and the other loaded with food, water and gear for all of us, plus the .22, which I had given to Marie. Three dogs pulled each cart; and all the rest moved in a tight and disciplined patrol around the carts and Marie.

The others travelled at a fair walking speed for cross-country; but they did not make as good time as Sunday, the girl and I would have by ourselves, because they stopped more often for one reason or another—and often, the reason was Wendy. The original three of us, up in front of them all, however, could pretty well ignore the problems of these others. It was almost like being off on our own again. Sunday, of course, did not mind the slow-er pace at all. It gave him that much more time to explore things. He and the dogs, I noticed, had already solved the problem of coexistence in typical animal fashion—by ignoring each other. Once, when Sunday lagged behind, one of the forward dogs trotted past him at a distance of less than ten feet, and neither one so much as glanced at the other.

Several times I took advantage of being alone with the girl to try getting her to talk some more. But she was not in the mood, evidently. Nor would she look at me.

"All right," I told her, at last. "You work it out by yourself, then."

I stepped out ahead, putting her from my mind and concentrating on scouting for our whole group. A few hours after we had left Marie's place, I ran across something like a logging road, or a farmer's tractor path among the trees, and followed it up until I could see through a thinning screen of forest to what was obviously a small town, down in a small cup-shaped valley area surrounded by open fields. It was about three hundred yards from the edge of the forest to the nearest buildings.

I turned about and headed back to contact Marie. Just in case there was anyone in that town, I did not want us to come strolling in followed by a leopard and a pack of dogs. Some nervous citizen was liable to take a shot—at Sunday, in particular. The rest were a fair distance behind me. Evidently, I had gained on them more than I had thought. At any rate, we got together once more and together came up to the edge of the woods to take a look at the town through some binoculars Marie had brought.

Through the binoculars, the town seemed deserted. There was no sign of movement, human or animal. I handed the binoculars to Marie, who was beside me.

"Take a look," I said.

She did.

"That's Gregory, I take it?" I said, when she put the binoculars down.

"Yes," she said. But she was frowning. After a short pause she added, but slowly and still frowning, "It's got to be."

"Got to be?" I asked. "What do you mean?"

"I mean it *is* Gregory—I recognize it," she said. "But I don't know . . . there's something different about it."

"Nobody in sight," I suggested.

"That, too," she said. "But something else. It looks changed, somehow. Only I can't say how."

I took the binoculars back from her and studied the buildings I could see. Aside from their stillness in the late afternoon sun, there was nothing that struck me immediately as unusual about the town. Then I noticed a house with the blinds down on all of its windows.

I looked at the other houses. Those nearby did not have their blinds drawn. If all had, of course, it could simply have meant that a time change had come through the area at night and caught the inhabitants after they had settled to sleep. But the houses close to the one with the blinds drawn had theirs up—then, moving the glasses about, I found first one, and then four more houses where all the shades seemed to be down.

It could mean nothing, of course.

"Do they know you in Gregory?" I asked Marie.

"Oh, yes," she said. "We did all our shopping here."

I turned to the girl.

"Hang on to Sunday. Keep him with you," I said. "Marie, you and I can take a walk in with a couple of the dogs—just a couple—and see if there's anyone there."

I left my rifle behind, and made Marie leave hers. We stepped out into the sunlight and walked toward the buildings. It was all so ordinary that I felt a little ridiculous; and then, when we were about fifty feet out in the open, a figure came shambling around the corner of the house with the blinds down and faced us.

I did not get a good look at it. It was very big, either an unusually large man or woman all bundled up in loose furs, or something else. Even its face was furry, or hidden by a beard. But it came around the corner of the building and lifted one arm. There was a wink of light from the end of the arm; and the dog furthest in front of us—leading the rest of us by perhaps fifteen feet—leaped into the air with a howl that broke off abruptly as it fell back on its side in the grass, to lie there still.

I dove to the ground, pulling Marie down with me; and something sizzled over our heads as we lay there. A second later, there were sounds like rifle shots from the town and the singing of bullets over our heads.

"Back!" I said to Marie. "Crawl! Back to the woods!"

We turned and went on our bellies. The shots continued, and once or twice I heard the sizzle overhead again; but nothing touched us. It seemed a long, long crawl. We were almost back when we came across the second dog we had taken with us, a lean German shepherd-type that had been named Buster, lying dead. In his case, it was a bullet from behind that had gone in at the back of his head and taken off half of his lower jaw when it came out. Flies were already buzzing around the corpse.

We crawled on, Marie and I, until the shadows of the trees were about us. Even then, we continued on hands and knees a little further before we risked standing up. Then we turned and went back to join the girl and Wendy for a look at the town.

But there was nothing to see. The fur-covered figure was no longer in sight; and the shooting had stopped.

"What was it?" said Marie. She was shaking and her voice was tight.

"I don't know," I said. I turned to the girl. "Did you get a look at it through the binoculars?"

The girl nodded.

"Was it a man or a woman?"

The girl shook her head.

"Why won't you talk?" Marie suddenly screamed at her.

"Easy," I said to Marie. "Easy." I spoke to the girl again. "Not a man or a woman either? You mean you couldn't tell?"

The girl nodded.

"You could tell?"

She nodded again.

"You could tell it wasn't a man or a woman?" I said. "What was it then?"

"I don't know," said the girl, unexpectedly. "A thing."

She turned and walked off. I went after her, but she would not even stand still to be questioned, let alone answer, after that. Defeated, I went back to Marie.

"Maybe something out of the future that wandered through its own mistwall into Gregory, here," I said to her. "Anyway, whatever it is, it doesn't seem to want to come after us—just seems to want us to leave it alone. I think we'd better go around this town. What's the next one up the line called? And how far is it?"

"Elton," said Marie. "And it's about five miles."

"That's where we'll head, then," I told her.

We stayed within the cover of the woods and made a circuit of Gregory. By the time we were around the town, the afternoon was fairly well advanced; but we pushed on, hoping to reach Elton. We never did, though. After nearly three more hours of travelling without a sight of a road or a town, we came to bluffs overlooking a river. A big river; easily a quarter of a mile across.

There was obviously no going farther that day. We set up camp on the bluff, and in the morning I went down to the river's edge to take a look at the situation.

The water was fresh and cold. The edge where I stood was overgrown with willows and seemed to drop off deeply; but a little farther downstream the river made a bend, and there was a sandy beach and shallow water. I explored that far, accompanied by Sunday and the girl. The current of the water seemed to slow, going around the curve, and there was plenty of driftwood on the beach to make into a raft. I went back to Marie on the bluff. She was making coffee and she gave me a cup.

"So you want to cross the river," she said; after I had told her what it was like, there.

I shrugged.

"We don't have to," I answered. "We can go upriver, or downriver, and we may even run into a bridge, somewhere, crossing it. But summer isn't going to last forever; and the more I think about it, the more it seems to me that we ought to keep heading due east. It's our best chance to find some large civilized group that's survived the time storms."

So it was settled—more or less. I did some planning, out loud, with Marie and the girl listening. The dogs could swim, of course. So could Sunday and we adults— or, rather, we two adults and the one near-adult, who was the girl. Wendy, the equipment and the supplies could be rafted over. Reducing the raft load to Wendy and our possessions meant we would need only a relatively small raft. Luckily we had a hammer and even some nails along, although, actually, I had decided to save the nails and chain the logs of the raft together with the dog chains, for maximum safety.

As I mentioned earlier, I had been looking forward to the evening—and Marie. However, it developed that Wendy was either coming down sick with something, or upset by the travel; Marie gave me to understand that, as far as that night went, she would be tied up with family matters. So as not to waste time, I took advantage of the long twilight to go down on the beach and make a start gathering the logs for the raft, then chopping them to length with Marie's axe.

Sunday and the girl went down there with me; and as things turned out, I built a fire and went on working by that, even after the sunset left us; so that we ended up making a separate camp down there. Just before I turned in for the night, something occurred to me.

"You know," I said to the girl, looking across the fire to where she sat with Sunday, "we left that raft of the lizards in one hell of a hurry, that night. I remember pulling you through the water; but I don't really remember how well you can swim—or even if you can really swim. Can you? Do you think you can make it across the river?"

I expected a nod or a shake of the head at the most. But to my surprise, she answered in words.

"I'm not going."

I stared at her.

"What do you mean—you're not going?" I exploded. "Do you think you can stay here on this side of the river, alone? Get that thought out of your mind. You're going."

She shook her head, looking not at me, but at the fire.

I sat, staring at her, too angry for words. Then I took hold of my anger with both hands, figuratively speaking, and tried to talk calmly.

"Look," I said, as reasonably as I knew how. "We've been together for some time, you and I and Sunday. But nothing lasts forever. You must have known that sooner or later we were going to be meeting other people and joining them, or they'd be joining us . . . ."

I went on talking, calmly and persuasively, using all the arguments I had used to myself the day before, and doing, I thought, a good job of it. It was only common sense I was telling her; and I pointed this out to the girl. Aside from her youth and sex, any single person stood a much reduced chance of survival. What would she do with herself? Practical matters aside, Sunday would miss her. For that matter I would miss her, myself . . . .

I was talking away quite earnestly, and even beginning to think that I was getting through to her, when she got up suddenly and walked away out of the circle of firelight, leaving me in mid-sentence.

I stared after her into the darkness. Something cold came in out of the night and sat down on my chest. For the first time, it occurred to me that she could actually be meaning to do what she had just said she would.

11

An hour after sunrise, Marie, Wendy, our equipment, supplies, dogs and all were down on the beach watching me finish off the raft. Watching and helping, as much as they could. It was Marie who brought up the subject of the girl.

"I think," said Marie, looking over to where the girl sat on a log, stroking Sunday at her feet, "everybody should do their share."

"She's not going," I said.

Marie stared at me.

"She's not going?" Marie said. There was an odd note in her voice—a note which could have meant anything. I could not interpret it at all. "You don't mean that?"

"I don't mean it," I said. "She does."

"Oh?" said Marie. She looked over at the girl again. "It's her idea?"

"That's right."

Marie stood for a moment, watching the girl.

"No," Marie said, finally. "She'll go."

I did not say anything more, myself. I concentrated on finishing the raft. When I was done, we launched it and loaded it with the contents of the two bicycle carts and the carts themselves. It floated well, a square of good-sized logs almost ten feet by ten feet in area; and there was plenty of room on it for Wendy—though the little girl was pale as moonlight and clearly frightened to death of riding across the river on the rocking log surface.

While Marie coaxed and soothed the child, I took six of the dog-leash chains I had set aside while I was making the raft. Three of these I put around Sunday's neck to make a choke-collar for him. I fastened the second three to the first and looped them around a log too big for the leopard to drag. Then I went to the raft and picked up the .22 rifle and its box of shells.

"What are you doing?" Marie interrupted her efforts with Wendy to stare at me. "That's mine. You gave it to me."

"I'm taking it back," I said.

I walked away, not listening to what else she said. The girl had come to stand concernedly over Sunday and examine his chains—Sunday, himself, had hardly blinked when I had put them on him. He lay basking in the sun. I walked up to the girl and shoved both rifle and shells into her hands.

"You can learn to shoot this," I said. "Keep the shells dry and use them up only when you really need to. Whatever you do, make sure they're not dirty when you put them in the rifle. And make sure no dirt gets in the barrel of the rifle. If it does, take some string from your pack, and tie a clean patch of cloth on the end of it. Drop the string through the barrel and keep pulling the cloth through the barrel until it looks shiny from end to end, when you hold it up and look at the light through it, the way you've seen me do. Have you got that?"

She took the box and gun from me without a word.

"I'm leaving Sunday with you," I said. "Don't unchain him until we've been gone at least a day and a night. If I'm not around, I think he'll stick with you; and he'll be even more protection to you than the gun. Remember, winter's coming on in a few months. Try to find some place where you can settle in and be protected until it warms up again."

She looked at me.

"Well," I said. "Goodby."

She did not move or speak. I turned and went back to Marie.

Marie had Wendy on the raft and was already stripped down to a yellow one-piece swimsuit. She looked good in it, as I would have expected since the night before last. I had not stopped to think about such niceties myself. Now, out of tribute to her own bathing dress, I left my shorts on—a foolish bit of male modesty which I had not planned on, earlier. But I had spare underclothing in my backpack, and I could hang the wet shorts outside the backpack to dry as I travelled, after we reached the other side.

I looked back once more at the girl and Sunday, and waved. Neither one responded, of course. I got into the cold river water, holding on to the raft along with Marie. The dogs took to the water on their own, after us; and we began the swim across.

As I said, the water was cold, in spite of it being midsummer. The current swept us farther downriver than even I had expected by the time we made the crossing; and by that time, in spite of considering myself a fairly strong swimmer, I was grateful to have the raft to cling to, and sympathetic to the dogs who had no such thing. One of them, indeed, got the idea at one point to try and climb up on the raft; but a sharp command from Marie made him drop back off it. All in all, though, we must have been in the water more than half an hour by the time we finally struggled ashore on a small sandy spot backed up by a space, about two house-lots in size, of sand and grass reaching back to the edge of a fairly thick woods.

I had gotten out, hauled the raft in close and lifted Wendy ashore, and was beginning to unload the raft when a tense word from Marie made me straighten up and turn around.

Five men had come out of the trees—about half-way out between trees and water. They stood perhaps twenty yards or so from us in a semi-circle, hemming us in against the river's edge. They were all well-dressed— dressed for the outdoors, that is. Each of them wore thick-soled country-style boots, with high tops disappearing up inside heavy trousers; and above the waist they all wore leather or firm-cloth jackets, with the collars of winter-weight shirts showing at the neck; and all but one of them wore some kind of hat. Every one of them had at least one handgun belted around his waist as well as a rifle in his hands.

The one without a hat stood a little forward of the rest and seemed to be the leader, though he was younger than any of the others, and even looked to be a good half-dozen years younger than I was. But he was as tall as I, and wider of shoulder, in his jacket. His face was heavy-boned; and like mine, it was clean-shaven—all the rest wore beards of varying lengths. He grinned at me as I reached for the rifle on the raft.

"Leave it lay," he said. I stopped reaching.

"Guard!" snapped Marie. "Point!"

Swiftly, the dogs fanned out around us, each facing one or more of the men, which in most cases meant that there were a couple of dogs on each; and each canine form went into its own version of a tense on-the-mark position, like a trained bird dog pointing quail. The rifles of the men came up.

"Hold it!" said the young man. "Keep your dogs there if you don't want them shot!"

Marie said nothing, but the dogs stood still. The young man dropped the butt of his rifle to the ground and leaned on the gun in friendly fashion—though I noticed the rest of them kept their weapons ready to use. He smiled at us again.

"Well," he said. "What's it like on the other side of the river?"

"There's nothing much there," I said. I was freezing to death, standing mid-thigh deep in the water, but I did not want to move out of arm's reach of the rifle on the raft. "What's it like on this side?"

"Nothing much on this side, either," the young man said. "Couple of empty towns . . . ."

He was answering me, but he was watching Marie. They were all watching Marie. It was that yellow swimsuit. I had not been unaware that she had put it on with at least part of her mind on what it would do to me. Now, it was doing the same thing to these men; only with them it was, I thought, turning out to be a bit too much of a good thing. But yet, instead of doing something sensible, like taking a jacket or blanket from the raft to cover herself, and in spite of the fact that, like me, she had to be both wet and cold, she continued to stand where she was, deliberately inviting their stares. Not only that, but now she had to start talking, to draw that much more attention on herself.

"What do you think you're doing?" she cried, pulling Wendy to her. "As if my child wasn't frightened enough, you have to come charging out of the woods like this with guns—"

She had begun to rub the little girl down with the towel Wendy had worn around her neck, as a seal to keep water spray from getting under the blanket in which she had been wrapped during the raft voyage. The activity may have been purely motherly, but it was almost as effective as if Marie had begun to do the dance of the seven veils in front of our visitors. A couple of them were grinning slightly.

"Well now, I'm sorry," said the young leader. "Awfully sorry." His men grinned a little more widely.

"You ought to be!" said Marie, towelling away. "Just because something's happened to the world doesn't mean the people can't be decent! Anybody with any brains would offer to help, instead of bursting out like that, like thugs—"

"We'll be glad to help," said the young man. "You don't understand us, that's why we came over, to help you—"

"I should think so!" snapped Marie. "That's more like it. Here, when there's hardly any people left in the world, those that are left need to stick together. Well, maybe I shouldn't jump down your throat like that—" She was still continuing to towel Wendy vigorously in her almost-dance, in spite of the fact that Wendy now, plainly, wanted only to be released. "But if you'd just had to swim an icy river like that, you'd be a little upset too, when a bunch of men with guns—"

"Mommy, I'm dry now!" Wendy was protesting, squirming in Marie's grasp.

"Hold still, dear!" said Marie. "As I was saying, a bunch of men with guns—"

I caught it then, out of the corner of my eye; just a flicker of movement. Suddenly, I saw what was happening, and why Marie had been standing there, chattering and bouncing about to hold their attention.

While she had been putting on her little show, the dogs had been about their own business. Apparently she had trained them well. As long as the eyes of the man it watched was upon it, the dog guarding him stood tensely still, at point. But the moment that attention moved elsewhere for even a fraction of a second, the dog stole forward—one step, two steps, even half a step, as if it was stalking a rabbit lying still and hidden in a cornfield. To begin with, the dogs had been almost as far away from the men as Marie and I were. Now, they had halved the distance between them and our welcoming committee.

Now, it was no longer a case of the men being able to kill all the dogs before the dogs could reach them. They might kill a good half of the dogs, but the other half

stood an almost equal chance of reaching them while
they were doing that.

In the same moment that I saw the flicker of movement, the man with the gun, at which the movement had
been directed, saw it too. Evidently the dog had gotten
too far inside our fields of vision to move without being
noticed.

"Tek—" shouted the man. "The dogs! Look!" The
young leader jerked his eyes from Marie and swept them
around the semicircle of half-crouching canines. At the
same time the others started to jerk their guns up. But I
had already taken advantage of the fact that their attention was off me to sweep up the rifle off the raft into
my own hands.

"Hold it!" I shouted.

I had the rifle to my shoulder, aimed at Tek's belt. The
dogs were ready.

"Hold it—just like he says!" barked Tek—if that was
the young leader's full name. He himself stood perfectly
still.

His men froze.

"That's better," he said, in a calmer voice. He looked
once more at Marie and me and smiled; but I could see a
little shininess of sweat on his face. A 30.06 slug through
the intestines is not a happy prospect; and I was close
enough so that even if I was a poor shot, I shouldn't miss.
"That's much better. You don't want to waste any of
these good dogs, now do you, ma'am? We'll just back out
of here and let you folks go your own way, since that's
what you seem to want. If we can't be friends"—and he
was smiling at Marie alone, now—"then that's just how
it'll have to be. Sorry, though. It'd have been nice to know
you. Now, we'll just start backing up . . . ."

And he did start backing up. His men imitated him.
The dogs immediately followed, step for step, as if invisible threads connected each of them to the man on
which the dog focused.

"Hold!" said Marie. The dogs stopped; and the men
kept backing, each holding his rifle in one hand, down by
his side and out of the way. I kept my own rifle steady
at my shoulder.

The men reached the edge of the trees and slipped
back into their shadow, all but Tek, who stopped briefly.

"Keep going," said Marie.

"Sure. See you sometime," called Tek.

"Only if we don't see you first!" answered Marie, grimly.

Tek waved. He paused for a second and looked directly at me. He made a little gesture like tipping a non-existent hat.

"You're a lucky man!" he called to me. "Don't anyone ever tell you you're not!"

There was no sneer in his voice. There did not have to be. His message was clear enough. I was negligible—it was Marie and her dogs who were driving him off. For a second I flared into a rage—and for a second I almost charged out of the water after him, to call him a liar to his face—then that answer-seeking reflex in the back of my mind pounced on his clear intent like Sunday pouncing on a scuttling fieldmouse. He was trying to get me to charge after him in just that fashion. The dogs were not dangerous from a distance without my rifle covering them from behind. If I got out in front they could shoot me, then kill the dogs safely from a distance they had now regained between themselves and the canines.

So I did not rush out, after all. Instead, I laughed. I laughed loudly, hoping he would hear me—but he was already gone into the shadows of the trees, and I could not tell if he was still within earshot or not.

I came out of the water then, but slowly, and handed the rifle to Marie.

"Watch the woods," I said.

I turned back to haul the raft, safely, far enough out of the water so that the river current could not pull it away until we had unloaded it. Then I took the rifle back from Marie while she rubbed some life back into my body and towelled herself dry. Meanwhile, there had been no further sign of Tek and his men. Marie posted a couple of dogs at the very edge of the woods, on watch; and we turned to unloading the raft.

Once we were unloaded, I built a fire to warm us up. It was only after the fire was going well and Marie had some soup heating on its flames, that I thought to look back across the river to see if the girl and Sunday had witnessed our encounter with Tek and his men. But a glance showed me that we had drifted so far down river in our crossing, that the beach where I had left girl and leopard was now around the bend of the further shoreline, out of sight. I turned back to the soup, grateful for its filling heat, but feeling a little empty inside all the same.

After I dressed, I scouted with Marie and a few of the dogs to see if the neighborhood was really clear of Tek and his compañeros. We found that the woods into which they had gone was actually only a narrow fringe of trees, perhaps a couple of hundred yards in width, paralleling the river. The woods were clear of human life and beyond them rose a small slope to a sort of shallow river bluff, from which we could see over a fairly wide, open, grassy area. There was no sign of Tek and company there, either, and no sign of mistwalls, or anything else, moving. We went back and made camp by the river, where we had landed. Marie and I both figured we deserved a little holiday.

The next day we pushed on east, with me scouting well ahead. A few of the dogs were beginning to take to me, finally—perhaps the water had washed off enough of Sunday's smell to make me socially acceptable to them—and there were a couple I could trust to obey a few simple commands. Marie drilled them with me; and they responded well. One was a bitch—a sort of large cocker spaniel mix and the more intelligent of the two. The other was a lean, nervous, German shepherd type, male and looking half-starved. The bitch was called Merry and the German shepherd was Cox. They would heel, stand, guard and scout for me in a circle, at a sweep of my arm —and that was pretty good, considering our limited acquaintance.

So, they and I got along pretty well, moving perhaps four hundred yards or so in front of Marie, Wendy and the rest. I was off by myself, as I liked it; but travelling with two dogs was not like travelling with Sunday. They would obey commands; Sunday almost never had—except by accident. They travelled at my pace; I had been used to travelling more or less at Sunday's. They were deadly weapons I could control. Sunday had been almost uncontrollable and absolutely unpredictable.

But there was one great point of difference that outweighed all their virtues. The crazy cat had loved me— loved me for myself alone. It was a love induced by accident and the time change effect, but nonetheless it was there. And I—I had gotten used to it. Merry and Cox could have been as cheerfully working for Tek at this moment, if Marie had drilled them into obeying him instead of me.

So I put thoughts of Sunday out of my mind—I had not dared to think of the girl from the first. Now I allowed myself the thought that it was lucky she was on the far side of the river, and Tek with his men, on this. Hopefully she would run into some decent people on her side. People being naturally spread out over the spectrum of human character as they were, she had as good a chance of finding good people as she had of finding bad ones. I put her out of my mind, too. No man—and no girl—could have the world just the way they wanted it, always.

By noon of the second day after we had crossed the river, we moved out of the relatively open area beyond the river bluff on this side and began to come on rolling country covered by what was obviously farmland, scattered with deserted-looking farm houses. The change was gradual enough so that it was impossible for us to tell whether the change from open country to cultivated earth was natural or the result of a time change. But in any case, the appearance of the area did not jibe exactly with Tek's words about only a "couple of empty towns" on this side of the river. We passed by the deserted-looking farmhouses at a healthy distance; and at no time did the dogs give any kind of alarm.

So three days of travel went by quietly with no sign of Tek and his group, or any other humans, and no sign of trouble. Then, on the morning of the fourth day we spotted a mistwall standing off to our right, and I changed our line of march to angle toward it.

12

Marie objected to the whole idea. Her own instinct was to head away from the mistwall; and I could not blame her.

"All right," I said, turning away. "You go on. I should catch up to you in a couple of days. If not, you'd better not wait for me."

I took perhaps a half dozen steps away from her before she made a sound; and then I heard her behind me.

"What can I do? *What can I do?*"

It was an aching, tearing sort of cry. I turned around and saw her, her eyes squeezed shut, her face white, her fists clenched at her sides, and all her body rigid. I went back to her.

Suddenly, I understood how it was with her. From her point of view, she had contributed to our partnership everything she had to contribute. She had abandoned what little security she still had left, following the time storm, to go with me—more for Wendy's sake, I suspected, than for her own. She had been adjustable, faithful and hardworking, a good partner by day and night. She had trusted her dogs, herself—and even her daughter—to me. And still, here on some reasonless whim, as it seemed to her, I was going to risk everything on a chance that could just as easily be avoided.

I put my arms around her and tried to get her to soften up; but she was as rigid as ever the girl had been in one of her states of shock. But I simply stood there and kept holding her, as I had kept holding the girl in those instances, and after a while, I thought I felt some yielding in her. She shuddered and began to cry, in great, inward, throaty, tearing sobs that were almost tearless.

However, after a while, even these began to quiet

down; and I began to talk, quietly, into her ear while I held her.

"Listen to me," I said, "There only were three things I might not have gone along with you on; and now that Sunday and the girl are gone, there's only one. But that's something I've been stuck with all my life. Now that I've taken on the question of figuring out the time storm, I don't have any choice. I've got to go through any mist-walls I find and see what's on the other side of them—I've got to, you understand? There's no choice for me when I come to something like this. There never has been."

"I know you don't love me," she said into my chest. "I never asked for that. But where will we go if you don't come back? What will we do?"

"You'll do just fine," I said. "All you have to do is sit down for half an hour and wait, while I step through the mistwall and take a look at what's beyond it before I come back out."

"All!" she said.

"That's right. All," I told her. "You'll have to take my word for it; but with most of the mistwalls I've seen, the two sides of them were pretty much the same, front and back. The odds are against anything being there that's either very good or very bad. If it's bad, I'll duck back right away. If it's good, it could mean a new, safe future for all of us. You ought to be pushing me to go and look, not holding me back!"

"Oh, you'll do what you want," she said and pulled away from me. But evidently it was settled; we set off for the mistwall.

At the point where we came up to it, the mistwall crossed a little hollow crowned by trees on both sides, so that there was a sort of natural trough some sixty yards wide and perhaps a hundred long leading to it. I had picked this point as one where Marie, Wendy and the dogs could stay more or less hidden from anyone observing from the higher level of land surrounding them. We had spotted the mistwall early, and we reached the trough, or hollow, perhaps an hour before noon. The mistwall itself was completely unmoving—now that I thought of it, I had never seen a motionless mistwall begin to travel, or a moving one stop. It could be that there were two different varieties of time lines involved . . . now that was a new thought.

I got everyone down in the hollow and climbed back out to the surrounding level to make sure they were invisible from anyone looking across the outside plain. They were, and using the binoculars reassured me that there was no sign of movement between the clumps of trees on the plain itself. They should be perfectly safe for an hour or so while I was on the other side of the mist-wall—certainly they would be safe for the time it would take me to go, turn around and come back, if I found something on the other side I did not like.

Going back down into the hollow, I found myself trying to remember if I had ever seen anyone or anything alive moving voluntarily through one of the mistwalls. But I could remember none.

Marie held me tightly for a long moment before she would let me leave them for the mistwall itself—and even Wendy clung to me. The little girl had been getting over her shyness where I was concerned, these last few days since the girl and Sunday had been gone. I felt a sudden touch of discomfort at the realization that I had not reacted to the small overtures the child had been making in my direction. It came to me suddenly and heavily that it was some obscure connection between her presence and the absence of the other two, the girl and Sunday, that had kept me cool to her. Now, suddenly, I felt guilty. It was not Wendy's fault that things were happening as they were.

At any rate, I broke away from Marie and her at last and walked into the dust and the mist, as tense as one of the dogs walking into a strange backyard. The physical and emotional feeling of upset took me before I had a chance to close my eyes against the dust—but again, as on that earlier time I had gone through the mistwall to find Marie's place, the sensations were less than I had felt before. I found myself wondering if it was possible either to build up an immunity to going through the walls, or else simply to get used to the reactions they triggered in living bodies.

I pushed ahead blindly, the ground becoming a little rough and uneven under my feet, until the lessening of the dust-sting against the skin of my face told me I must be coming out on the other side of the time change line. I opened my eyes.

I stood now in rugged territory. If I was not among

mountains, then certainly I was in the midst of some steep hills. Directly ahead of me was some sort of massive concrete structure, too large for me to see in its entirety. The part I was able to see was a mass of ruins, with new grass sprouting at odd points among the tumbled blocks of what had evidently been walls and ceilings.

What had smashed it up so thoroughly was hard to imagine. It didn't look so much as if it had been bombed as if it had been picked up and *twisted,* the way you might twist a wet towel to wring it dry. About it, the steep slopes, covered with gravel and a few fir and spruce trees, looked deserted under the cloudless, midday sky. The air temperature was perceptibly cooler than it had been on the other side of the mistwall, as if I was now at a noticeably higher altitude—though I had not felt the elevator-sort of inner ear sensations that would suggest a sudden change to a lower air pressure. There were no birds visible and no sounds of insects. Of course, if this new land was high enough it could be above the flight zone of most insects.

However, whatever the structure before me had been at one time, now it was a ruin only. There was no sign of life anywhere. It was far-fetched to think that there could be anyone in that pile of rubble who might have a greater understanding of the time storm than I did, let alone ideas on how to live with it or deal with it. I might as well go back through the mistwall to Marie, Wendy and the dogs.

But I hesitated. There was a reluctance in me to cut short this business of being off on my own—almost as much reluctance as there was in me to face Marie and admit the whole experiment of going through the mistwall had been profitless. I compromised with myself finally; it would do no harm to go around the ruin and a little farther into this new territory, until I could see the whole extent of it and perhaps make some guess as to what it had once been. The concrete of what was left of it appeared as modern, or more so, than anything in my native time—it might even have come from a few years beyond my original present.

It was an odd feeling that was pushing me to explore farther—a small feeling, but a powerful one. There was something about that jumble of concrete that plucked at my problem-solving mental machinery and beckoned it.

I swung to the right, approaching the ruin and circling it at the same time. As I got closer, the building turned out to be larger even than it had looked at first, and it was not possible to see it all at once. After a while, however, I got to where I could get a sight down one long side line of it. I still could not really see it as a whole, because it curved away from me, following the contours of the hill on which it was built; but it seemed to become progressively less of a ruin as its structure receded from me, and its interest to me grew. It reminded me a little of my own life, beginning as a wreck and developing into something with a shape, purposeful, but too big to see and know as a whole. I felt almost as if the building was something familiar, like an old friend built out of concrete; and I prowled further on alongside it.

It continued to sprawl out and curve away from me as I went; and after I had gone perhaps a quarter of a mile, I realized that I never would be able to see the thing as a whole. It was simply too big, and it spread out in too many directions.

I might have turned back then; but I noticed that the building was relatively undamaged in the further area of it I had now reached. Facing me were some windows that were whole, in sections of gray concrete wall that looked untouched. Farther on, there was even a door that looked slightly ajar—as if it needed only to be pushed open to let anyone into the interior.

I went toward the door. It was a heavy, fire-door type; and when I put my weight into it and pulled, it swung outward slowly. Inside was a flight of bare concrete stairs with black iron pipe railing, leading upward. I mounted the stairs slowly and quietly, the rifle balanced in my hands, ready to use, even while the sensible front of my mind told me that this was ridiculous. I was wasting my time on a deserted and destroyed artifact; and it was high time I was heading back to Marie and Wendy, who would be worrying about me by now.

Reaching the top of the stairs, I let myself through another door into a long corridor, with only a bare white wall and window to my left, windows through which the sun was now striking brilliantly, but aglitter with glass doors and interior windows to my right, through which I could see what seemed to be row on row of offices and laboratories.

I took a step down the corridor, and something plucked lightly at the cuff of my left pantleg. I looked down. What appeared to be a small black thread had been fastened to the wall of each side of the corridor and now lay broken on the floor where my leg had snapped it.

"Who's there?" asked a voice over my head.

I looked up and saw the grille of a speaker—obviously of some public address system that had been built into this corridor when the whole structure had been put up.

"Hello?" said the voice. It was tenor-weight, a young man's voice. "Who is it? Just speak up. I can hear you."

Cautiously, I took a step backward. I was as careful as I could be in picking up my foot and putting it down again. But still, when the sole of my boot touched the corridor surface, there was a faint, gritting noise.

"If you're thinking of going back out the way you came in," said the voice, "don't bother. The doors are locked now. It's part of the original security system of this installation; and I've still got power to run it."

I took two more quick, quiet steps back and tried the door to the stairway. The door handle was immovable and the door itself stood motionless against my strongest push.

"You see?" said the voice. "Now, I don't mean to keep you prisoner against your will. If you want to leave, I can let you out. I just thought we might talk."

"Can you see me?" I asked.

"No," he answered. "But I've got instruments. Let's see . . . you're about one hundred and ninety centimeters tall and weigh eighty-two point five three plus kilos. On the basis of voice tone and body odors, you're male, blood temperature approximately half a degree above normal, heartbeat fifty-eight—cool-headed customer, plainly— blood pressure a hundred and eight over eighty-seven. You're wearing some synthetics, but mostly wool and leather by weight—outdoor clothes. My mechanical nose also reports you as carrying a combination of metal, wood, oil and other odors that imply a rifle of some kind, plus some other metal that may be a knife; and according to the other scents you carry, you've been outside this building only a little while after coming from some place with a lot of grass, few trees and a warmer, moister climate."

He stopped talking.

"I'm impressed," I said, to start him up again. I did not trust his promise to let me go just for the asking; and I was looking around for some way out besides the locked door. There were the windows—how many stairs had I climbed on the way up? If I could break through a window, and the drop was not far to the ground . . .

"Thank you," said the voice. "But it's no credit to me. It's the equipment. At any rate, reading from what I have here, you're out exploring rather than looking for trouble. You aren't carrying equipment or supplies for living outdoors, even though the odors on you say that's how you've been living. That means such equipment and supplies you have must be elsewhere. You wouldn't be likely to leave them unattended—some animal might chew them up to get at whatever food you were carrying, so you probably have others with you. They aren't in view anywhere around the area outside the building, or I'd know about them, and you're the only one inside, besides me; so that means you just about had to come through that stationary line of temporal discontinuity, out there."

I stopped looking for windows. Now I actually was impressed. The equipment had been remarkable enough in what it could tell him about me; but any idiot could sit and read results from gauges and dials, if he had been trained well enough. This kind of hard, conscious reasoning from evidence, on the other hand, was something else again.

"What did you call it—a temporal discontinuity?" I asked.

"That's right. Have you got another name for it?" said the voice. "It really doesn't matter what it's called. We both know what we're talking about."

"What do you call it when it moves?" I asked.

There was a long second of silence.

"Moves?" said the voice.

I damn near grinned.

"All right," I said, "now I'll do a little deducing. I'll deduce you haven't left this building since the time storm struck."

"Time storm?"

"The overall pattern of your temporal discontinuities," I said. "I call that a time storm. I call individual discontinuities like the one out there, time lines. I call the haze in the air where one is, a mistwall."

There was a pause.

"I see," he said.

"And you haven't left this building since that mist-wall appeared out there, or since whatever it was, first happened to this building?"

"That's not quite the way it's been," he answered. "I've gone outside a few times. But you're right, essentially. I've been here since the first wave of disruption hit, studying that discontinuity you came through. But you—you've been moving around. And you say there're discontinuities that move?"

"Some of them travel across country," I said. "Where they've gone by, the land's changed. It's either changed into what it's going to be sometime in the future, or into what it was, once, in the past."

"Very interesting . . ." the voice was thoughtful. "Tell me, are there many people out there, where the moving dis——time lines are?"

"No," I said. "It's been some weeks and I've covered a lot of ground. But I've only found a handful. The Hawaiian Islands seem to have come through pretty well. You can hear broadcasting regularly from there on shortwave and other stations on the radio, now and then—"

"Yes, I know," the voice was still thoughtful. "I thought it was the discontinuities cutting off most of the reception."

"I doubt it," I said. "I think there just aren't many people still left in the world. What was this place?"

"A federal installation. Research and testing," said the voice, absently. "What's it like out there?"

"It's like a world-sized crazy quilt, cut up into all sorts of different time areas, marked off one from each other by the mistwalls—by the time lines or discontinuities. The big problem is the situation's still changing. Every moving time line changes everything where it passes."

I stopped talking. His voice did not pick up the conversation. I was busy thinking about the words "research and testing."

"You said you'd been studying the time line, there," I said. "What have you learned so far?"

"Not much," his voice was more distant now, as if he had moved away from the microphone over which he had been speaking, or was caught up in some other activity, so that he was giving me only a part of his attention. "What you call the mistwall appearance seems to be a matter of conflicting air currents and temperature differentials between the two zones. But there doesn't seem to be any material barrier . . . you say they sometimes move?"

"That's right," I said. "Any reason why they shouldn't?"

"No, I suppose . . . yes," he said. "There's a reason. As far as I've been able to measure, these lines of discontinuity stretch out beyond the reach of any instruments I have. In other words, they go right off into space. You'd assume any network of forces that massive would have to be in balance. But if certain of the lines are moving, then it has to be a dynamic, not a static, balance; and that means . . . ."

"What?"

"I don't know," he said. "Maybe I'm just letting my human ideas of size and distance influence me. But I've got trouble imagining something that big, shifting around internally."

He stopped talking. I waited for him to start up again. But he did not.

"Look," I said. "I just sort of ran from this overall situation, the way you'd run for shelter from a thunderstorm, for the first few weeks. But now I'm trying to find out if there isn't some way to get on top of the situation— to control it—"

"Control?"

I waited a second; but he did not say any more.

"What's the matter?" I asked. "Did I say some kind of dirty word?"

"You don't understand," he said. "If the whole disturbance is bigger than our planet, possibly system-wide— and in some sort of dynamic balance, the idea of controlling it is . . . ." He hesitated. For the first time there was something like emotion in his voice. "Don't you realize we never have been able to control even a hurricane—no, not even a thunderstorm like the one you were talking about—when this first hit us. Have you any idea of the magnitude of the forces involved in something like this, if it's stretching all over the solar system?"

"What makes you think it is?" I asked.

He did not answer.

"All right," I said, after a moment. "If you're not going to talk, let me out of here and we'll say goodby. I was going to invite you to come along with me—out where you can study the moving lines as well as this static one. But I gather that's not the way you like to work."

I turned on my heel, went back to the stairway door and pushed. But it was still locked.

"Wait," he said. "Do you have other people with you?"

"Yes," I told him. "How about you? Are you alone here?"

"That's right," he said. "There were a couple of hundred people in the installation here, when the disruption first hit. When I got my senses back, I was the only one left. I was in the hyperbaric chamber at the time—not that I can figure out why that should have made a difference."

"I've got an idea about that," I said. "I think some of us are just naturally immune—statistical survivors."

"Survivors."

"Of the time changes. It's only a thought. Don't ask me for details."

"An interesting thought. . . ."

The voice trailed off. Down the long inner wall of the corridor, one of the doors opened, and a short, lightly boned figure in white slacks and white shirt stepped out and came toward me. He was so small that my first thought was that he could not be more than twelve or fourteen years old in spite of his adult voice; but when he got closer, I saw that his face was the face of a man in his late teens or early twenties. He came up to me and offered me his hand.

"Bill Gault," he said. It was a strong name for someone that light.

I shook hands with him.

"Marc Despard," I answered.

"I think I'd like to go with you, after all," he said.

I studied him. He was in no way frail or abnormal, just light and small. At the same time, his lack of size and the spurious air of being half-grown about him, made me hesitate now at the thought of adding him to our party. I had just not expected anyone so . . . so physically insignificant, to be the person behind the voice I had been talking with. For a moment I felt a touch of exasperation. All my life, until I had run into the girl and the crazy cat, I had gotten by nicely with no responsibility for anyone but myself. But since this damned time storm started, it seemed I had done nothing else but play guardian and protector—to girls, leopards, women and children—and from the look of Bill Gault, I now had another responsibility on my hands. I could imagine what would happen if this featherweight should try to stand up alone to one of Tek's men, for example.

"Well, you can't just walk out there like that," I said. "Haven't you got some heavier clothes and some hiking boots? And if you've got a gun of any kind around, bring that along, too, with whatever in the way of a pack and extra clothing you can scrape up."

"Oh, I'm all prepared," Bill Gault said. "I've had things ready for some time, in case I did decide to leave."

And you know—he had. He took me down the corridor to a room where he outfitted himself in synthetic wool and leather gear that filled me with envy. Evidently, this installation had been testing, among other things, various kinds of special-duty outerwear for the armed services. When he was done, he looked like an officer in the ski troops, lacking only the skis. The well-stuffed backpack he wore was a marvel; and he had both a revolver and the latest in army lightweight, automatic rifles.

I looked at the rifle particularly.

"You don't have another one like that lying around, do you?" I asked.

"This is the only one," he said. "But there's a machine pistol, if you'd like it."

I looked at him. He had looked so ready in his outdoor garb, it had been hard for me to remember that he had been boxed up here since the time storm had started. But one good innocent sentence like that brought back the realization in a hurry.

"You've got ammunition for it?"

"Lots of ammunition," he said.

"And," I said, "you were actually going to let us walk off without it? You were going to leave it behind?"

"Well, you've already got a rifle," he said, nodding at the 30.06. "And a machine pistol's not very practical for hunting."

I shook my head.

"Get it," I said, "and as much ammunition for it as you think I can reasonably carry."

He did. It was an Uzi. And the damn fool would have left it behind.

"Let's go," I said, loading my pockets and belt with the spare clips he had brought, until I felt heavy enough to walk bow-legged. "That is, unless you've got some other useful surprises to spring on me."

"Nothing I can think of," he said. "Food—"

"Food's no real problem," I said. "There seems to be canned goods enough to last the few of us who're left for the rest of our lifetimes. Come on."

He led me out. The door opened this time when I pushed on it. We went down the stairs and out of the building; and I led him back to the mistwall.

"What should I expect?" he asked, as we came up to it.

His tone was so casual that, for a second, I did not understand. Then I looked at him and saw that his face was pale. Calm, but pale.

"You're thinking of how it was when the time storm first caught you?" I said. He nodded. "It won't be that bad. It seems to get easier with experience. Hang on to my belt, though, if you want; and if I feel you let go, I'll put down the rifle and lug you through myself. But try and stay on your feet if you can, because we can use both these guns if we can get them out."

He nodded again and reached out to hook fingers in my belt.

"You'll have to close your eyes against the dust when we get close," I said. "Just concentrate on keeping on your feet, and staying with me."

We went into the mistwall then. It was not bad at all for me, this time; but I could imagine how it might be for him. I was so undisturbed by the passage through that I had attention to spare when I heard Marie's voice on the far side of the mistwall, as we started to come out of the far side of it.

". . . shoot it!" Marie was crying, almost hysterically.

"No," said another voice. "If you make them hurt him at all, I'll shoot *you!*"

It was the girl talking and making the longest speech I had ever heard her utter.

13

I took a few more steps forward out of the dust and opened my eyes. There was a regular convention in session in the hollow where I had left just Marie, Wendy and the dogs. They, of course, were still there; and all the dogs were on guard position, not making a sound. Wendy was holding tight to her mother, and Marie was facing away from me.

Beyond Marie were the girl and Sunday. The girl sat crosslegged on the ground, with the .22 rifle aimed at Marie. The girl's back was against the back of Sunday. He also was seated, on his haunches, and looking bored —but the tip of his tail was twitching ominously. He faced outward at a half-ring of figures, all with their rifles facing in Sunday's direction but looking momentarily baffled. Tek and his gang had come visiting us again and, apparently, encountered a problem.

The appearance of myself and Bill Gault out of the mistwall did nothing to make their problem any easier. In fact, clearly it came as a severe jolt. They stared at us as if Bill and I were ghosts materializing before their eyes; and a sudden intuitive conclusion clicked into place in the back of my mind. Just as I once had, obviously they were in the habit of avoiding mistwalls. No doubt, everybody still on the face of the earth today avoided them, instinctively, remembering the emotional upset and discomfort of their first experience with any part of the time storm. And here were Bill and I, strolling out of this particular mistwall as casually as walking from one room into another.

Hard on the heels of that bit of understanding came another. The scrap of overheard conversation I had heard suddenly resolved itself. Clearly, the "it" Marie had been telling Tek and his men to shoot had been Sunday; and, just as clearly, Sunday and the girl had come here hunting me—which meant that Tek and company had probably been following them, as well as the dogs and us, all this time.

I had gotten this far with my thoughts, when the frozen moment in which the girl and Tek's gang stared at me was abruptly and joyously smashed asunder by Sunday. Plainly, he heard, smelled, or otherwise recognized me in spite of his back being turned. He jumped to his feet, turned about, and came bounding at me like a kitten, purring like an outboard motor and stropping himself up against me with unrestrained enthusiasm.

I had a second to brace myself, but being braced did not help much. When a hundred and forty pound leopard throws an affectionate shoulder block into your midsection, you realize the advantages of four legs over two. At least when one cat makes loving demonstrations to another, the recipient has a couple of spare feet to prop himself upright with. I staggered and nearly went down. Meanwhile, Marie had turned around to see what was going on and saw me.

"Marc!" she cried.

There was so much desperate relief in her voice, I was almost ready to forget that she had seemed on the verge of entering into partnership with the enemy to get rid of Sunday and the girl. But our difficulties were not at an end, because now she also came to throw her arms around me.

"You've been gone for hours!" she said.

I had no time to point out that I had not even been gone one hour, at the most; because Sunday, seeing her coming, had already classed her as a potential attacker and finally decided to do something about her. I fended her off with one arm, while just managing to slap Sunday hard on the nose to check the lethal paw-swipe with which he would have turned our little reunion into a very real tragedy.

I succeeded—but of course, success left me with a rebuffed woman and a rebuffed leopard at once, on my hands. Marie was hurt that I should shove her off. Sunday was destroyed. I tried to soothe the leopard with my hands and the woman with my voice at the same time.

"Marie—no!" I said. "Bless you! I love you—but stand back, will you? Sunday's likely to claw you in half."

"Then what are you doing petting the animal?" cried Marie.

"So he won't get loose and claw somebody else! For Christ's sake—" I yelled at her, "stand back, will you? Keep Wendy back—"

I was running out of breath. Sunday had forgiven me and was once more trying to throw frantic, affectionate shoulder blocks into me.

"Down, Sunday!" I managed, finally, to wrestle the leopard to the ground and lie on him while he licked cheerfully and lovingly at any part of my person that was within tongue-reach. I looked up and glared at the girl.

"What are you doing on this side of the river?" I snarled.

"He pulled himself loose!" she said.

I went on glaring at her. She was an absolute, bare-faced liar. Sunday would have choked himself to death on those chains I had used to restrain him, before he would have been able to pull himself free. Of course, the girl had turned him loose herself, deliberately, so that they could both follow me. I knew it, and she knew I knew it; and I could see she didn't care a hoot that I knew it.

Girl, leopard and woman—I could not do a thing with any of them. I looked around for something in my own class to tie into; and my gaze lighted on Tek. The man was two axe-handles across the shoulders and besides being six years or more younger than I, had that easy, muscular balance of movement that signals the natural athlete. He could, almost undoubtedly, have held me off with one hand while beating me to death with the other; but just at that moment, if I had not been occupied with the absolute necessity of keeping Sunday flattened out, I would have picked a fight with Tek for the simple joy of having something legitimate to hit.

I had dropped both the machine pistol and the rifle, necessarily, needing both hands to handle Sunday and Marie. But the pistol was only a short arm's length from me. I scooped it up, now, pointing it at Tek, and noticed that Bill Gault had maintained enough presence of mind to lift his army automatic rifle into firing position under his arm. In terms of sheer firepower, we two more than matched up to the hunting rifles carried by Tek and his men, and the dogs could mop up any other difference that existed. But then, Tek took me completely by surprise.

"Hold it!" he shouted, before I could say anything more. "Hold it—I'm with you!"

To my astonishment, he threw his rifle toward Marie and walked unarmed up to us and turned around to face his former crew. He grinned at Marie and nodded pleasantly to me.

"Just give the orders," he said to me. "I won't pick up my gun unless you say so."

There had been a moment of frozen disbelief on the part of his men when he had switched sides. But now there was a general outcry from them.

"Tek!"

"Tek, you bastard—what are you doing to us?"

"Tek, damn it!"

"Tek , . . ."

"Sorry," he said, shrugging his shoulders and smiling at them. "I can tell when I've run into a better team, that's all. If you're bright, you'll come over on their side, too. If you're not, don't blame me."

Three of the five of them began to argue with him all at once. He said nothing, though, and gradually their voices died down. One of the two men who had not tried to argue him out of it finally spoke. He was a narrow-bodied balding man in his late thirties or early forties, with a sharp, hard face.

"That was all pretty quick and easy," he said. "Almost like it was planned, the quick way he went over to them. Come on, the rest of you. Let's clear out and leave Tek with them, if that's what he wants."

The men shifted uneasily. I looked at Tek, but he was staring off at the horizon, ignoring the whole matter with an indifference as sublime as Sunday's could be on occasion. But the other man who had not argued with Tek now spoke up.

"Sure, Garney," he said. "Let's all go off and let you run things instead of Tek—is that it? I'm sticking with him. Come on, everybody."

He walked across to us and laid his rifle down beside Tek's. But I noticed he laid it down carefully. It was a bolt action, and he had the bolt uppermost; and when he stepped back from it, he was only a couple of feet away from a quick grab to regain it.

Slowly, one by one, the others came over. All except the man called Garney, who had suggested they leave Tek behind. When at last they were all standing with us, leaving Garney alone, Tek took his eyes off the horizon slowly and gazed at him.

"Well," he said, gently. "So long then, Garney. Maybe you better head off in a different direction from where we're going."

"All right, Tek," said Garney, "that's all right. I wouldn't want to have anything more to do with any of you."

He backed up a few steps, watching us. Then, evidently deciding that it was simply not practical to back the long distance it would take to get him out of our rifles' range, he turned his back and walked swiftly away. He went off, up over the lip of the hollow and disappeared.

Tek's men who had joined us moved to pick up their rifles.

"Leave them lay!" said Tek.

They stopped, staring at him; and he nodded in my direction. "Leave them, until the chief here tells us what to do."

I became suddenly conscious of the fact that they were all staring at me; and that I was still lying sprawled out on Sunday, trying to control him with one hand, while I clung to the Uki and attempted to keep it pointed, with the other. Sunday had quieted down somewhat by this time; so I scrambled to my feet, cuffed him lightly when he tried to recommence his greetings to me and faced Tek with his men.

"All right," I said. "Let's talk about this. I don't remember hanging out any sign asking for volunteers."

Tek shrugged.

"All I can do is try," he said.

"Marc!" said Marie, sharply. She looked at me for a second as if she was going to say something then and there, then closed her mouth and crossed the little distance between us. This time, I was glad to see, she made it a point to approach me on the opposite side from Sunday. She came up to me and took hold of my arm, whispering in my ear.

"Marc, are you crazy?" she demanded. "Isn't it better to have these men as friends, instead of enemies?"

I was about to answer sharply, when I thought better of it. I nodded to Tek.

"Ask him how he'd answer that," I said out loud. "Go ahead."

Something like a dark shadow seemed to pass across Marie's face; and she looked at me oddly. But she stepped back from me without a word and turned to face Tek.

"I asked Marc if it wasn't better to have you as friends instead of enemies," she said, loudly and clearly. "He said to ask you how you'd answer that."

"Sure," said Tek, "if I was him, I'd want to know how you'd know you could trust us."

She stared at him. He smiled back.

"You see, now," he said, "I'm not trying to put anything over on anybody. I volunteered to join you all on my own. It's up to the chief there—what did you say his name was? Marc? It's up to Marc."

"And up to me, too!" said Marie, sharply.

"And you, too, of course, ma'am," said Tek. "But—no offense to you and your dogs—but I'd worry a bit more about Marc, here, if it came right down to picking one of you over the other to have trouble with. Him, his pet leopard, and his friend there."

He nodded to Bill Gault. I had almost forgotten Bill. Now, I called him over and introduced him to Marie, Wendy, and the girl, while still keeping a cautious eye on Tek and the others. All the time, the back of my mind was working. The truth of the matter was, if Bill and I were to dig into this business of the time storm seriously, we would need troops to take the ordinary work and fighting off our hands. Plus the fact that we might well be adventuring through a mistwall into a situation where a number of people with guns were needed. —

Also, something Tek had just said had sparked off a notion in the back of my mind. While listing the things that might worry him about having me for an enemy, Tek had specified Sunday as one of them. I had grown so used to Sunday that I had almost forgotten how unnatural it was to other people to see a full grown leopard tagging after me like a kitten. The tendency was for the watchers to assume I had a lot more control over him than I actually did—as well as to assume that he was a great deal brighter and more responsive than his cat brain would ordinarily allow. There was a bluff I could run.

"All right," I said, "I'll tell you what we can do. We can take all of you on a probation, and see how you'll do. Leave your guns piled where they are; and if any of you have to go someplace away from the camp, where you might run into trouble, one or two of the dogs can go with you. Meanwhile, I'll set the leopard to watch you. He may not be able to tell me what you talk about; but if any of you make any move that looks as if you mean to hurt one of us, he can tear you apart before you'll know what hit you."

I looked them over.

"Well?" I said. "How about it? Want to join us on those terms?"

They looked at me hesitantly—all but Tek. Then they looked at Tek.

"Marc—" began Marie, and then checked herself.

"What?" I looked at her.

"Nothing," she said. I looked back at the men.

"How about it?"

"Speaking, just for myself, of course," said Tek, "I think that's fine—real fine. I've got no intentions of being anything but a good friend to you all anyway, so your leopard doesn't worry me a bit. But that's just me. The others are going to make their deals with you on their own."

"All right," I said. "Suppose the seven of you find a place to sit down together over there about ten yards away from your guns and the rest of us. I've got some things to do."

Tek led off agreeably. He sat down, and the rest followed.

I turned my attention to the girl, who was now getting to her feet. She had been holding her rifle grimly aimed at Marie, all the while, but now she lowered it.

"Are you all right?" I asked her. "You haven't been hurt or anything? Have you been getting enough to eat?"

She looked at me with a very strange expression. For a moment I swore she was going to answer me. But habit took over. She turned without a word and walked away from me to where Sunday was, a few steps away, and began petting him, with her back to me.

"I take it that means 'yes'!" I called after her. She did not reply, of course. The voice of Marie spoke in low, but tight, tones in my ear.

"Marc, she's not staying, she or that leopard, either."

I turned to stare at her. She looked ready to fight.

"Of course they're staying," I said.

"Then I'm leaving, with Wendy and the dogs."

"And Tek and his men right behind you," I said. I had not meant to put it that bluntly; but I was just about out of patience. "Go ahead."

She glared at me fiercely for a moment, then turned and went to Wendy. But she made no move to begin a departure.

I looked around for Bill Gault, saw him standing waiting a little distance away and beckoned him over to me. He came and I led him off out of low-voiced earshot of the rest.

"I didn't mean to lead you into a touchy situation like this," I said. "You can go back to your installation, if you feel like it, and I won't blame you."

"No," he said. "You were right. I couldn't really learn anything more, shut up there. The only way to study the situation is to look at as many of the discontinuities as I can find. We ought to keep on the move and, every time we get near one, have a look at it."

"Good," I told him. "By the way, you never did tell me what your field is. Were you a research scientist, a lab man, or what?"

"Well, no," he said. "I do have a degree in physics . . . but actually, I was just technical editor for the installation."

He gazed at me uncomfortably.

"Technical editor!" I said.

"That's right."

"Well, what the hell can you do, then?" I demanded. I was about at the end of my temper, anyway; and this last disappointment threatened to cut me loose. I had taken it for granted he was some sort of scientific expert, at least.

"I can do a lot!" Bill said, swiftly. "I can observe, make tests and record—and I know something about physics, as

I said. Also, I've been up to my eyebrows in everything
we worked on at the installation for the five years I've
been there. I'm not helpless."

"All right," I answered. "But you're going to have to
show me."

He did. During the two weeks that followed, my opinion of him, starting from the sub-basement level of that
moment, went steadily up. He had brought with him in
his backpack some remarkably small, but durable instruments to measure temperature, air pressure, wind velocity
and humidity, plus a few less common things like electro-
static levels and magnetic flows. He also designed a
number of long rods for pushing these into and through
a mistwall, while we stood safely outside.

This is not to say we did not enter the walls. In the
final essential, it was necessary to go through them. As
we moved across country in the days following the addition of Tek and his men to our group—to say nothing
of Bill himself, and the rejoining of the girl and Sunday—
we ran into at least one, and sometimes more, mistwalls a
day. We would make all the tests on them that Bill could
think of; but once he had the results noted down, it was a
matter of he and I going through them, that is, unless it
were a moving mistwall we were investigating, in which
case we spotted them early through binoculars and moved
to outflank and see behind them.

We did not go into them as blindly as I had gone into
earlier ones. Among other designs of Bill's were rod or
rope devices to be thrown through the mistwall and
dragged back, to give us an idea of the ground situation
and atmosphere beyond. The third time we used them,
what we learned kept us from walking off a cliff on the
far side of the mistwall, before we would have had a
chance to open our eyes. But, in the end, in almost every
instance, we still had to go through personally.

We found a number of different situations, from raw
desert to empty city, on the far sides of these walls; and
we profited from what we found. Fourteen days after our
group had come to its full size, we were riding in a sort
of motorcade, all of us, including the dogs. Our vehicles
consisted of a couple of brand new motor homes for
sleeping and living quarters, preceded by a couple of jeep
carryalls and followed by a pickup truck, all three smaller vehicles with four-wheel drive, carrying the armed

members of the party while we were on the move. With wheels under us, outflanking the moving mistwalls became not only easier, but more certain.

There were four of us who carried weapons to start with—myself, Marie, Bill, and also the girl. She had become attached to that .22 of hers. In fact, she refused to give it up, and when I had her fire it for me, I found that she had not merely kept it in good condition, she was developing into a good shot. At short to medium range in rough country, a light gun like a .22 could be as effective as an elephant gun, in every way but impact, if the person shooting it was accurate enough; and I was glad to have her able to use it.

By the end of the first week we added a fifth gunner—Tek. The man had worked hard to do anything that was asked of him; until he had begun finally to make a believer even out of me. The conclusion I came to at last was that whatever it was he wanted, for the moment, at least, it included cooperation with the rest of us. I walked him off a short distance from our night camp on the end of our seventh day together and asked him a lot of questions about himself.

The answers were unhesitating and interesting. His full name was Techner, pronounced "Tek-ner," Wilson Ambervoy—he had been named for a couple of grandparents. He had been good enough as a high school football player to get a scholarship to the University of Indiana—and Indiana had fielded a Big Ten team which did not play mediocre football. However, he had not taken the study end of college seriously and had flunked out midway through his sophomore year. Luckily—he was usually lucky, Tek told me frankly—he got a job immediately with an uncle who owned a paint store. The uncle was in poor health and inside of half a year, Tek was managing the store. About that time, he got into real estate. With the cosignature of his paint store uncle, Tek swung a mortgage and bought a twelve-unit apartment building. To run it, he brought in a friend named Ricky, a drinking buddy the same age as himself, who had a knack for card games and was in the habit of having a poker session in his former bachelor apartment every night after the bars closed.

He and Tek remodeled two of the apartment units of their building into one large one to make, as Tek put it, "a pretty impressive-looking cave"; and the after-hours card games expanded. Meanwhile, they made it a point to rent the rest of the units to girl friends of Tek's; and a number of these would also drop in on the card game after hours to make sandwiches, pour drinks and watch the game. If the supply of these girls ran short, Tek went out prospecting and found some more.

The result was that there were always a number of good-looking girls around the card game, and young male strangers began dropping in for a hand or two, just to meet them. Tek's buddy did well with his cards. He paid Tek a percentage of his winnings as rent for the apartment; and the other units became very much in demand among Tek's girl friends, so that he was able to raise the rent several times and still keep every unit filled.

". . . You understand," Tek said to me. "Nobody cheated in the card games. There was nothing professional about the girls. Just everybody had a good time, and Ricky and me had it for free—well, maybe we came out a little bit ahead, but when we did, we just spent it on more good stuff . . . ."

And then the time storm had come along; Tek had been taking a nap. When he woke, he was alone in the apartment building. Alone in an empty town. He ended up going out adventuring, and one by one, he ran into the other men of his gang, whom he recruited out of a sort of pack-instinct for leadership.

"But that wasn't really what I was after," Tek said to me as we walked together, with the camp and the fire we always built for it distant in the twilight before the small town on the outskirts of which we had stopped for the night. "You know, even before this time storm, or whatever you call it, came along, I was beginning to get a little filled up on the apartment, the fun and games, and all the rest of it. I was beginning to want to do something —I don't know what. I still don't know. But just roaming around, living off the country, isn't it either."

Tek stopped and looked at me in the growing dimness.

"They're not bright, you know," he said, "those five back there I picked up. Garney was the brightest of them all; and he was nothing you could build on. Now, little old Bill Gault there, he's bright; and you are, too. Someday maybe you'll tell me what you did before this happened and where you came from; and I'll bet it'll be interesting. And this business of yours with the mistwalls—it might lead to something. That's what I want. Something."

He stopped talking.

"All right," I said. "Let's head back."

Halfway back to the camp, I came to a conclusion.

"You can start carrying a rifle tomorrow," I told him. "But don't forget you're still under orders. Mine."

"Right," he said. "But I'd be on your side anyway."

"For now, you would," I said dryly.

He laughed.

"Come on, man," he said. "Anything can happen if you look far enough into the future. If anything comes along to change the situation that much, you'll know about it as soon as I will."

So we moved on with five gunners instead of four, and things went almost suspiciously well. The plan Bill and I had evolved was based on our theory that our best chance to get on top of the time storm was to keep looking for the most advanced future segment we could find. Hopefully the more advanced an area we could hit, the more likely we were to find the equipment or the people to help us deal with the time storm. If we were going to be able to do something about it, that was where we were most likely to find the means. If we were going to be forced to live with it—perhaps we could find the techniques and patterns we needed in something beyond our present time slot.

As I had discovered earlier, however, the time changes seemed to be weighed toward the past, rather than toward the future. We found three futuristic-looking segments behind mistwalls; but they were either apparently stripped of anything or anyone useful, or else their very futureness was in doubt. It was two weeks and two days before we found a segment that was undeniably part of a city belonging to a time yet to come—a far future time, we thought at first. Though of course, there was no way we might tell how much time would have been necessary to make changes.

This particular segment was behind the second mistwall we had encountered that day. The first had showed us nothing but unrelieved forest, stretched out over descending hills to a horizon that was lost in haze, but which must have been many miles off. Such a landscape might be part of a future segment, but it was not passable by our wheeled vehicles, and it promised nothing. We pulled back through the mistwall—it was then about ten in the morning—paused for an early lunch and went on.

About 2:30 P.M., we saw a second, stationary mistwall and moved up to it. We were travelling along a gravel road at the time, through what seemed like an area of small farms. The mistwall sliced across a cornfield and obliterated the corner of what had once been a tall, white and severely narrow farmhouse—an American Gothic among farmhouses.

We left our motorcade in the road, and Bill and I walked up the farm road into the farmyard, carrying most of the instruments. The rest straggled along behind us but stayed back, as I had repeatedly warned them to, a good twenty yards from where we were working.

I said the rest stayed back—I should have said all the rest but Sunday. The leopard had put up with seeing me go through mistwalls for about two days after he and the girl had rejoined us and had contented himself with overwhelming me with pleased greetings when I returned. Like all our humans, he obviously had a powerfully remembered fear of the time lines, in spite of having crossed one at Marie's place. But after Bill and I had penetrated through the third wall we had encountered, I had heard something odd behind me and looked to see Sunday coming through the mistwall behind us, tossing his head, his eyes closed and mewling like a lost kitten. He broke out and came to me—still with his eyes closed and evidently depending on nose alone—and it had taken me fifteen minutes to soothe him back to quietness. However, going back through the mistwall later, he had been much less upset; and two days later he was accompanying us with the indifference of a veteran. Of course, as soon as he started coming through the mistwalls after us, the girl did too. But it was possible to order her not to; Sunday could not be kept back.

So, in this case, as had become his habit, Sunday followed Bill and me up to the mistwall and waited while we made our measurements and tests. These showed it to be little different from the many other walls we had tested. But when we finally went through this time, we found a difference.

We came out in a—what? A courtyard, a square, a plaza . . . take your pick. It was an oval of pure white

surface and behind, all about it, rose a city of equal whiteness. Not the whiteness of new concrete, but the whiteness of veinless, milk-colored marble. And there was no
sound about it. Not even the cries of birds or insects. No
sound at all.

14

". . . We were the first," wrote Samuel Taylor Coleridge
in his *Rhyme of the Ancient Mariner*—
  "Who ever burst,
  Into that silent sea. . . ."

If you know that bit of poetry, if you love poetry the
way I do, you will be able to feel something like the feeling that hit Bill and me when we emerged from the
mistwall into that city. Those lines give it to you. It was
with us and that city beyond our time, as it had been with
that sea and Coleridge's Mariner. It was a city of silence,
silence such as neither of us had ever heard, and such as
we had never suspected could exist—until that moment.
We were trapped by that silence, held by it, suddenly
motionless and fixed, for fear of intruding one tiny noise
into that vast, encompassing and majestic void of sound-
lessness, like flower petals suddenly encased in plastic. It
held us both, frozen; and the fear of being the first to
break it was like a sudden hypnotic clutch on our minds,
too great for us to resist.

We were locked in place; and perhaps we might have
stood there until we dropped, if it had been left to our
own wills alone to save us.

But we were rescued. Shatteringly and suddenly, echoing and reechoing off to infinity among the white towers
and ways before us, came the loud scrape of claws on a
hard surface; and a broad, warm, hard, leopard-head
butted me in the ribs, knocking me off my frozen balance
to fall with a deafening clatter to the pavement, as my
gun and my equipment went spilling all around me.

With that, the spell was smashed. It had only been that
first, perfect silence that operated so powerfully on our
emotions, and that, once destroyed, could never be re-

created. It was an awesome, echoing place, that city, like some vast, magnificent tomb. But it was just a place once its first grip on us had been loosed. I picked myself up.

"Let's have a look around," I said to Bill.

He nodded. He was not, as I was, a razor addict; and over the two weeks or more since I had met him, he had been letting his beard go with only occasional scrapings. Now a faint soft fuzz darkened his lower face. Back beyond the mistwall, with his young features, this had looked more ridiculous than anything else; but here against the pure whiteness all around us and under a cloudless, windless sky, the beard, his outdoor clothing, his rifle and instruments, all combined to give him a savage intruder's look. And if he looked so, just from being unshaved, I could only guess how I might appear, here in this unnaturally perfect place.

We went forward, across the level floor of the plaza, or whatever, on which we had entered. At its far side were paths leading on into the city; and as we stepped on one, it began to move, carrying us along with it. Sunday went straight up in the air, cat-fashion, the moment he felt it stir under his feet, and hopped back off it. But when he saw it carrying me away from him, he leaped back on and came forward to press hard against me as we rode—it was the way he had pressed against me on the raft during the storm, before he, the girl and I had had to swim for shore.

The walkway carried us in among the buildings, and we were completely surrounded by milky whiteness. I had thought at first that the buildings had no windows; but apparently they had—only of a different sort than anything I had ever imagined. Seeing the windows was apparently all a matter of angle. One moment it seemed I would be looking at a blank wall—the next I would have a glimpse of some shadowed or oddly angled interior. It was exactly the same sort of glimpse that you get of the mercury line in a fever thermometer when you rotate the thermometer to just the proper position. But there was no indication of life, anywhere.

Around us, over us, the city was lifeless. This was more than a fact of visual observation. We could feel the lack of anything living in all the structures around us like an empty ache in the mind. It was not a painful or an ugly feeling, but it was an unpleasant feeling just for the reason that it was not a natural one. That much massive construction, empty, ready and waiting, was an anomaly that ground against the human spirit. The animal spirit as well, for that matter; because Sunday continued to press against me for reassurance as we went. We stepped off the walkway at last—it stopped at once as we did so— and looked around at a solid mass of white walls, all without visible windows or doors.

"Nothing here," said Bill Gault after a while. "Let's go back now."

"No," I said. "Not yet."

I could not have explained to him just why I did not want to give up. It was the old reflex at the back of my head, working and working away at something, and feeling that it was almost on top of that missing clue for which it searched. There had to be something here in this empty city that tied in with our search to make reason out of the time storm, the time lines, and all the business of trying to handle them or live with them. I could feel it.

"There's no one here," Bill said.

I shook my head.

"Let's get inside," I said. "Any one of these buildings will do."

"Get inside? How?" He looked around us at the marble-white, unbroken walls.

"Smash our way in somehow," I said. I was looking around myself for something to use as a tool. "If nothing else, the machine pistol ought to make a hole we can enlarge—"

"Never mind," he said, in a sort of sigh. I turned back to look at him and saw him already rummaging in his pack. He came out with what looked like a grey cardboard package, about ten inches long and two wide, two deep. He opened one end and pulled out part of a whitish cylinder wrapped in what looked like wax paper.

The cylinder of stuff was, evidently, about the same consistency as modelling clay. With its wax paper covering off, it turned out to be marked in sections, each about two inches long. Bill pulled off a couple of sections, rewrapped the rest and put it away, back in his pack. The two sections he had pulled out squeezed between his hands into a sort of thin pancake, which he stepped over and pressed against one of the white walls. It clung there, about three feet above the ground.

"What is it?" I asked.

"Explosive," he said. "A form of plastic—" He pronounced it plas-*teek,* with the emphasis on the second syllable—"but improved. It doesn't need any fuse. You can do anything with it safely, even shoot a bullet into it. Nothing happens until it's spread out like that, thin enough so that sufficient area can react to the oxygen in the air."

He moved back from the wall where he had spread out the pancake, beckoning me along with him. I came, without hesitating.

We stood about thirty feet off, waiting. For several minutes nothing happened. Then there was an insignificant little *poof* that would hardly have done credit to a one-inch firecracker; but an area of the white wall at least six feet in diameter seemed to suck itself inward and disappear. Beyond, there was a momentary patch of blackness; and then we were looking into a brightly lit chamber or room of some sort, with several large solid-looking shapes sitting on its floor area, shapes too awkwardly formed to be furniture and too purposelessly angular to seem as if they were machinery.

Like the room, like the walls, they were milky white in color. But that appearance did not last long.

Without warning, the damaged wall blushed. I don't know how else to describe it. From white it turned blood-red, the reddishness most intense around the edges of the hole blown in the wall and toning down from there as it spread outward. And it spread with unbelievable speed. In a moment, the color change had swept over all the walls and pavement around us and raced on to turn the city, the whole city, to red.

Far off among the buildings, a faint, siren sound began. It was uncomfortably as if the city was a living thing we had wounded, and now it was not only bleeding internally but crying.

But this was just the beginning of the change.

"Look!" said Bill.

I turned back from gaping at the city to see Bill pointing once more at the hole in the wall. The red around the ragged rim of broken material had darkened and deepened until it was almost black—a thick and angry color of red. But now, as I watched, that dark-red edge began to develop a hairline of white—glowing white-hot-looking brightness beyond the edge of darkest red. And this tiny edge of white thickened and widened, tinged with pink where it came up against the dark red, but continuing to thicken in whiteness on its other, broken edge that touched only air.

"It's healing itself," said Bill.

I had not realized it until he put it into words, but that was exactly what was happening. The white that was appearing was new wall surface, growing down and inward, beginning to fill the hole that we had blown in the wall.

I took a step forward as soon as I realized this, then stopped. The hole was already too small for me to go through, easily; and those white-glowing edges did not look like anything I would want to brush up against on my way past.

"All right," I said to Bill, "let's try it someplace else, and next time be a little quicker about going through, once we've opened it up."

"No. Wait," he said, catching hold of my arm as I started off to a further section of the wall. "Listen!"

I stopped and listened. The distant, wailing, siren-sound had been continuing steadily, but without any indication of coming any closer to us and the scene of the action. But now that Bill had my attention, I heard another sound superimposed on the first. It was the noise of a faint, dull-toned but regular clanking. The sort of thing you might hear from a large toy tractor, if it had been constructed with its movable parts, out of plastic rather than metal. And this sound was coming toward us.

I had the machine pistol up and aimed without thinking; and Bill had his gun also pointed, when the source of the noise came around the corner of the same building where we had blown the opening in the wall. It came toward us, apparently either not understanding, or understanding but ignoring, the menace of our guns. I stared at it, unbelievingly, because I had a hard time making up my mind whether it was creature or machine.

By the time I had reluctantly concluded it was a creature, it was less than a dozen feet from us and it stopped. A machine I might have risked pumping a few slugs into. A creature was another matter entirely. Aside from the fact that killing another living thing has some emotional overtones to it, there were a great many more dangerous possibilities involved for us if it was alive, and our hostile response was not successful. So we simply stood and looked it over, and it looked us over.

It looked—it's hard to say how it looked in that first minute. Something like a Saint Bernard-sized, very short-limbed, very heavy-headed, bulldog shape, with a clump of three tails or tentacles, about two feet in length, sprouting from each shoulder. The whole body was covered with rectangular bony plates about a couple of inches at their widest, which flexed at their jointures with the plates surrounding them to allow the body beneath them to move. Smaller plates even covered most of the massive head. The two eyes were brown and large.

"Don't shoot!" I said to Bill, without taking my eyes off the creature.

I don't know what movement of his, if any, triggered off that reaction in me. At the moment, I only know two things. I had been searching from the very beginning, for an x-factor, a Game Warden, a missing piece to the puzzle of the time storm; and the old reliable search-reflex in the back of my mind now was practically shouting at me that this might be it. And—second, but no less important —the whole improbable being radiated an impression of non-enmity. That impressive armor, that ferocious head, somehow added up, not so much to something threatening, as to something rather clumsy and comic—even lovable, like the bulldog it faintly resembled.

Still, I would have had trouble convincing Bill of any of that alone—but luckily, just at that moment, I got corroborative testimony from a completely unexpected source—Sunday. Up until now the leopard had not moved; but now, suddenly, he strolled past me, right up to the creature, and proceeded to strop himself in a friendly manner up one side of it and down the other. He then sniffed it over a few times and gravely returned to me. That did it. Bill lowered his gun.

"Hello," I said to the creature. The word sounded almost ridiculous in the context of our confrontation, here in this silent, strange place. The creature said nothing.

"I'm Marc Despard," I said. "This is Bill Gault."

Still no answer.

"Marc," said Bill, in a strained, thin voice. "Let's start backing up, slowly. If it lets us go, we can back right into the mistwall, and maybe it won't follow us—"

He broke off because some sounds were finally begin-

ning to come from the creature. Sounds that were something like a cross between the internal rumblings of in-
digestion and the creaking of machinery that had not
been used in a long time.

"Due . . . ." said the creature, in a deep-tone, grating
voice. "Yanglish."

It fell silent. We waited for more sounds, but none
came.

"Start backing if you want," I answered Bill, still keeping my gaze, however, on the creature. "I'm going to stay
and see if I can't find out something about this."

"I . . . ." said the creature, loudly, before Bill could
answer me. There was a pause while we waited for more.

"I am . . . ." it said, after a second. Another pause.
Then it continued, in jerks, almost as if it were holding a
conversation with itself, except that the pauses between
bits of conversation became shorter and shorter until
they approached ordinary sentence-length human speech.

"I am . . . ." said the creature again.

" . . . Porniarsk."

"Porniarsk. I am . . . an of . . . ."

"I am Porniarsk Prime Three . . . of . . . an . . . ."

"I am Porniarsk Prime Three, an . . . avatar . . . of
Porniarsk . . . ."

" . . . Expert in Temporals General. I am the . . . third
. . . avatar of Porniarsk . . . who is an . . . expert on the
Temporal Question."

"It's a robot of some sort," said Bill, staring at
Porniarsk's avatar.

"No," it said. "I *am* Porniarsk. Avatar, secondarily
only. I am living— . . . alive. As you are."

"Do we call you Porniarsk?" I asked.

There was a pause, then a new sort of creaking, un-
used machinery noise; and the heavy head was nodding
up and down, so slowly, awkwardly and deliberately that
the creature called Porniarsk looked even more comic
than before. It broke off its head-movements abruptly
at the top of a nod.

"Yes," it said. "Porniarsk Prime Three is . . . a full
name. Call me Porniarsk. Also, *he.* I am . . . male."

"We'll do that," I said. "Porniarsk, I'm sorry about
damaging your city here. We didn't think there was anyone still around."

"It is not . . . it isn't my city," said Porniarsk. "I mean

it's neither mine as avatar, nor is it something that belongs to me as Porniarsk. I come from . . . ."

He had been going great guns, but all at once he was blocked again. We waited, while he struggled with his verbal problem.

"I come from many . . . stellar distances away," he said, finally. "Also from a large temporal . . . time . . . distance. But I should say also that, in another measure, I am . . . from close to here."

"Close to this world?" Bill asked.

"Not . . ." Porniarsk broke off in order to work at the process of shaking his head this time, "to this world, generally. Just to . . . here, this place, and a few other places on your Earth."

"Is this place—this city or whatever it is . . ." asked Bill, "from the same time as the time you come from?"

"No," said Porniarsk. "No two times can be alike—no more than two grains of sand be identical."

"We aren't stupid, you know," said Bill. For the first time I'd known him, there was an edge in his voice. "If you can tell us that much, you can do a better job of explaining things than you're doing."

"Not stupid . . . ignorant," said Porniarsk. "Later, perhaps? I am from far off, spatially; from far off, temporally; but from close, distance-wise. When you broke the wall here, this city signalled; I had been for a long period of my own time on the watch for some such happening at any one of the many spots I could monitor; and when the city signalled, I came."

"Why is the city so important?" I asked.

"It isn't," said Porniarsk, swinging his heavy head to look at me. "You are important. I believe. I'll go with you now unless you reject me; and at last, perhaps we can be of use to ourselves and to the universe."

I looked at Bill. Bill looked at me.

"Just a minute," I said. "I want to look this place over. It's from out of our future, if my guess is right. There may be a lot of things here we can use."

"Nothing," said Porniarsk. "It is only a museum—with all its exhibits taken away long since."

He made no visible move that my eyes could catch, but suddenly, all the walls about us seemed to suck themselves in and produce circular doorways.

"If you would like to look, do so," Porniarsk said. He

folded his short legs inward under him and went down like a large coffee table with its four supports chopped away by four axemen at once. "I will wait. Use-time is subjective."

I was half-ready to take him at his words that the "city" was no use to us; but Bill was beckoning me away. I followed him away and around a corner, with Sunday trailing along after me, out of sight of Porniarsk. Bill stopped, then, and I stopped. Sunday went on to sniff at an open doorway.

"Listen," whispered Bill, "I don't trust it."

"Him," I said, absently. "Porniarsk—he said he was male."

"He also said he was an avatar," said Bill. "The incarnation of a deity."

Bill's carping pricked me the wrong way.

"—Or the incarnation of an idea, or a philosophy, or an attitude!" I said. "Why don't you read all of the entry in the dictionary next time?" Abruptly, I realized that he was scared; and my jumping on him was the last sort of move likely to help matters. "Look, he's just the sort of thing we've been hunting for. Someone out of the future who might be able to help us handle this time storm business."

"I don't trust . . . him," said Bill stubbornly. "I think he's just planning to use us."

"He can't," I said, without thinking.

"Why not?" Bill stared at me.

He had me, of course. I had responded out of my feelings rather than out of my head—or, to be truthful, out of my reflex for pattern-hunting, which was still yelling that I might have found the missing piece necessary to complete the jigsaw puzzle. I did not know why I was so unthinkingly sure of the fact that while we might be able to use Porniarsk, he could not use us. I had thought that the end result of my certainty about Swannee's survival had taught me some healthy self-doubt. But here I was, certain as hell, all over again.

"I've just got a hunch," I said to Bill then. "But in any case, we can't pass him up. We've got to, at least, try to get the information we need out of him. Now, you can see the sense of that, can't you?"

He hesitated in answering. I had hit him on his weak

side—the side that believed in scientific question and experimentation.

"Of course you can," I went on. "There's no point to anything if we throw away the first good lead we've found to making sense out of things. Let's go back now and take Porniarsk along with us to the rest of them. There'll be plenty of time to find out what he's after personally, once we've got him back in camp. Whatever he's got, I'll feel a lot safer when he's got the dogs, Sunday and the rest of our guns all around him—don't you agree?"

Bill nodded reluctantly.

"All right," he said. "But I want to look into a few of these buildings, anyway."

"We'll do that, then." I could afford to give in on a small point, now that he'd yielded on the large one. "But I've got a hunch Porniarsk's right, and there's nothing to find."

So, accompanied by Sunday, we searched through a couple of the now-open buildings. But it was just as I'd thought. Porniarsk had not been lying so far as we could discover. The buildings were nothing but a lot of empty rooms—in immaculate condition, without a trace of dust or damage—but empty. Echo-empty.

In the end we went back and collected Porniarsk. He clattered to his feet as we came up and fell in step with us when I told him we were headed back through the mistwall to the rest of our people. However, I stopped when we came to the nearer edge of the wall.

"I'd like you to wait here, Porniarsk," I told him, "while Bill and I go through first. Give us a chance to tell the rest of our people about you and tone down the surprise when you show up. Is that all right with you?"

"All right," said Porniarsk, clunking down into lying position again. "Call when you want me to come after you."

"We will," I said.

I led Bill and Sunday back through the mist. When we opened our eyes on the other side, it was to find a deserted, if cozy-looking, farmyard. The cooktent had been set up in the yard and Marie had both charcoal grilles going, but no one was on duty except the dogs. Clearly, the others were all inside the farmhouse—the very sort of place I had ordered them never to go into unless I told them it was safe, and only after a couple of us had done

a room-by-room search with guns, first. There were too
many nasty surprises, from booby traps to ambushes, that
could be set up in a place like an abandoned building.

"Get out here!" I shouted. "Get out here, all of you!"

I had the satisfaction of seeing them come scrambling out
of the door and even out of a couple of windows, white-
faced, possibly thinking we were under attack from somewhere, or perhaps another mistwall was bearing down on
us. It was not the best of all possible times to rub a lesson
in; but I took a few minutes once they were outside to
read them out for what they had done.

"Well, it's ridiculous!" said Marie. "It isn't as if we
walked in there blind. Tek and the girl took their guns
and checked it out first."

Of course that put a different face on the matter, but I
was hardly in a position to admit so at the moment. I
looked over at Tek and the girl. He, of course, had been
too smart from the beginning to make his own excuses;
while the girl, of course, was simply following her usual
practice of not talking. But I met her eyes now; and grim,
angry eyes they were.

"They did, did they?" I said. "And who ordered them to
do that?"

"I asked them to," said Marie.

"You did?"

"Yes, I did!" said Marie. "For God's sake, Marc, the
rest of us have to start doing things on our own, sooner or
later, don't we?"

I was finding myself slipping into a public argument
with my people—not the best thing for a leader, if he
wants to hold his position.

"Right! And I'll tell you when. Meanwhile—" I went on
before she, or any of the rest of them could say something
more, "Bill and I brought back someone for you all to
meet. Brace yourself—he's not human. Bill, do you want
to call him?"

"Porniarsk!" shouted Bill, turning to the mistwall.

Marie and the rest also turned toward the mistwall,
with a swiftness that cheered me up somewhat. I had
meant what I had said to Porniarsk about preparing them
for the shock of meeting him. Now the thought in my
mind was that a little shock might have a salutary effect
on them. We were not an army of world-conquerers, after
all. Half a dozen determined adults with decent rifles

could wipe us out, or make slaves of us at a moment's notice, if we took no precautions.

Porniarsk came clanking through the mistwall into view and stopped before us.

"I am Porniarsk Prime Three," he announced, in exactly the same tones in which he had introduced himself to Bill and me. "The third avatar of Porniarsk, an expert in temporal science. I hope to work together with you so that we all may benefit the universe."

"Yes," said Bill dryly. "Only, of course we've a little more interest in helping ourselves first."

Porniarsk swiveled his heavy head to look at Bill.

"It is the same thing," Porniarsk said.

"Is it?" said Bill.

Porniarsk creaked off a nod.

"What you've observed as local phenomena," he said, "are essentially micro-echoes of the larger disturbance, which began roughly half a billion years ago, according to your original time pattern."

"Oh?" said Bill. He was trying to be indifferent, but I could catch the ring of interest in his voice that he was trying to hide. "Well, just as long as it can be fixed."

"It cannot be fixed," said Porniarsk. "The knowledge is not available to fix it."

"It isn't?" I said. "Then what's all this about helping the universe?"

"The whole problem is beyond my time pattern and any other time pattern I know," said Porniarsk. "Yet, our responsibility remains. Though we cannot solve, we can attack the problem, each of us like the ants of which you know, trying to level a mountain such as you are familiar with. With each micro-echo, each infinitesimal node attacked, we approach a solution, even if it is not for us to reach it."

"Wait a minute—" began Tek.

He had not liked my blowup over their going into the house without my orders, even though he had said nothing. And now, the note of potential rebellion was clear in his voice.

"Hold it!" I said, hastily. "Let me get to the bottom of this first. Porniarsk, just how far does the whole problem extend—this problem of which our troubles here are a micro-echo?"

"I thought," said Porniarsk, "I had made clear the

answer to that question. The temporal maladjustments are symptoms of the destruction of an entropic balance which has become omnipresent. The chaos in temporal patterns is universal."

None of us said anything. Porniarsk stood waiting for a moment and then realized he had not yet reached our basic levels of understanding.

"More simply put," he said, "all time and space are affected. The universe has been fragmented from one order into a wild pattern of smaller orders, each with its own direction and rate of creation or decay. We can't cure that situation, but we can work against it. We *must* work against it; otherwise, the process will continue and the fragmentation will increase, tending toward smaller and smaller orders, until each individual particle becomes a universe unto itself."

. . . And that's all of what he said then that I remember, because about at that point my mind seemed to explode with what it had just discovered—go into overdrive with the possibilities developing from that—on a scale that made any past mental work I had ever done seem like kindergarten-level playtime, by comparison. At last, my hungry rat's teeth had found something they could tear into.

15

They tell me that, after a while, I came to and gave everybody, including Porniarsk, orders to pack up and move on; and I kept the avatar and all of us moving steadily for the better part of the next three weeks. Just moving, not stopping to investigate what was beyond the mistwall, or in any of the buildings or communities we passed. Pushing forward, as if I was on a trek to some far distant land of great promise.

Moments of that trek, I dimly remember. But only moments. I was too full of the end result of all the speculations I had been making about the time storm— now paying off all at once. I did have flashes of awareness of what I was doing, and of what was going on around me. But it was all background, unimportant scenery, for the real place I was in and the real thing I was doing, which was The Dream.

In The Dream I was the equivalent of a spider. I say "the equivalent of" because I was still myself; I was just operating like a spider. If that doesn't make sense, I'm sorry, but it's the best I can do by way of explanation. As description, it hardly makes sense to me either; but I've never found another way to describe what that particular brain-hurricane was like.

In The Dream, then, I was spider-like; and I was clambering furiously and endlessly about a confusion of strands that stretched from one end of infinity to the other. The strands had a pattern, though it would have taken someone infinite in size to stand back enough to perceive it as a whole. Still, in a way I can't describe, I was aware of that pattern. My work was with it; and that work filled me with such a wild, terrible and singing joy that it was only a hairline away from being an agony. The

141

joy of working with the pattern, of handling it, sent me scrambling inconceivable distances, at unimaginable speeds, across the strands that filled the universe, with every ounce of strength, every brain cell engaged in what I was doing, every nerve stretched to the breaking-point. It was a berserk explosion of energy that did not care if it destroyed its source, that was myself, as long as things were done to the pattern that needed doing; and somehow this was all associated with my memories of my first determination to put my brand on the world about me; so that the energy sprang from deep sources within me.

Actually, what I was experiencing was beyond ordinary description. The pattern was nameless. My work with it was outside definitions. But at the same time, I knew inside me that it was the most important work that ever had been and ever would be. It carried an adrenalin-like drunkenness that was far beyond any familiar self-intoxication. People talk, or used to talk, about drug highs. This high was not a matter of chemistry but of physics. Every molecule of my body was charged and set vibrating in resonance with the pattern and the work I was doing upon it.

Meanwhile, I continued, with some detached part of my consciousness, to lead and direct my small band of pilgrims; effectively enough, at least, so that they did not depose me as a madman and set up some new leader in my place. Not—as I found out later—that they did not all notice a difference in me and individually react to, or use, that difference to their own purposes. When I returned wholly to myself, I found that a number of things were changed.

It may have been sheer accident that I was able to return at all, but I don't think so. I think I was ready to back off from the pattern, at least for a while; and what triggered my return was only a coincidence, or the first summons able to reach over the long distance to that part of me that was out there on the web-strands of the universe.

It was Sunday—I almost said, "of course"—who brought me back. Apparently, he had been sticking to me like a paid attendant all through this three week period. I would guess he had sensed enough of the fact that a major part of my mind was missing, to make him worried. Most of the time I must have paid him no attention. But during my brief flashes of awareness of those about me, I remember being annoyed by the fact that I was literally tripping over him every time I turned around.

In this instance, I was momentarily partway back in my full senses, and I had deliberately left the others, gone off out of sight and sound of the others to find a place where I could sit on a rock and be alone for a bit. Sunday had followed me; and he pushed himself on me after I was seated, almost crawling into my lap. I shouted at him to go away; and in exasperation, when he paid no attention, I cuffed at him with my open hand.

It was not a hard blow. I had never hit Sunday hard; but sometimes, swinging at him was the only way to get across the idea that I was serious about what I wanted. Still, as I struck at him, that little part of my mind that was back, apart from the pattern, was beginning to feel a twinge of guilt for hitting him. Only, abruptly, that guilt was lost in a much deeper feeling of shock, and suddenly, I was stone-cold sober, free of the web-pattern for the first time in three weeks.

Because I missed him. My hand swung through nothing but empty air, and I almost fell off the stone.

Sunday had dodged—and that was all wrong. I don't mean wrong, physically, of course. Naturally, his cat reflexes made my human ones look silly. If he had wished, at any time in all the while we had been together, he could have seen to it that no finger of mine ever came close to him. But he never had. He had never dodged before. It was one of the effects of the time storm upon him. When I would lose my temper and slap him, he only closed his eyes, flattened his ears, and crouched down like a kitten before an annoyed mama leopard.

But this time, he had dodged. And he sat now, just out of arms' length, gazing at me with an expression that, for the first time in our months of being together, I could not read.

"Sunday?" I said wonderingly.

He came to me then, with a bound, pushing against me, licking at my hands and face and purring like a motorboat. Just as he evidently had known I was gone, now he knew I was back. Indeed, indeed I was back—and it was wonderful from my point of view as well. I hugged the old son of a bitch and came close to crying over him, in return.

It was at this moment that a shadow fell across us both; and I looked up to see the girl. Where she had come from—whether she had been standing off at a distance, watching Sunday and me—I don't know. But there she was; and the look on her face was like the look now on Sunday's. I almost reached out my arms to her also, as naturally and instinctively as I was hugging and punching Sunday; but just as I was about to do so, the back of my mind said, *"Hold it! What're you doing? She's no crazy leopard!"* And I hesitated.

It was only a second's hesitation, but apparently it was enough. The look went out of her face, and the next thing I knew, she was gone. For a wild moment I thought of going after her; then I told myself there was no point in it until she got over whatever had made her leave.

Her going like that had left me with an empty place inside me and just above my belt buckle, though. I sat where I was, fondling Sunday until I felt normal again, then got to my feet; and the two of us headed back toward the others, who were at a noon camp just over a rise to our left. I joined them; and nobody seemed to notice anything different about me.

However, beginning at once, and through the three days that followed, I quickly began to discover differences in them. It dawned on me that those in my inner circle of people had been as aware of my abnormal mental state as had Sunday and the girl and had gone on pretending to everybody else that I was perfectly normal, for reasons of their own.

The reason in Marie's case was obvious. As the consort of the leader of our little band, she had a self-interest in seeing that I was not deposed for reasons of mental incompetence. Tek, apparently, liked the position of follower for some strong reason of his own. I got the impression that he was waiting for something, and the time was not yet ripe for whatever it was. Bill volunteered *his* reason.

"Thank God you're all right again," he said to me, the first time we were off together out of earshot of the others, on an advance patrol in the pickup. "If you'd gone on that way, with your mind a thousand miles off most of the time, for another week, this outfit would have fallen apart."

"Oh, I don't think so," I said. "Tek and Marie would

probably have worked out some kind of agreement to keep the tribe together."

He looked at me, I thought, a little oddly.

"Even if they had," he said, "that'd be as bad as falling apart. We're not out here just to survive. We're out here to find out what makes the temporal discontinuities operate. With you not in charge, any hope of that'd be lost."

"Not necessarily," I said.

"Necessarily. I can't control them, and you're the only other intelligent person here." He was serious.

"Don't underestimate Tek," I said.

"He's smart," said Bill grimly. "He's not intelligent. He can't appreciate the value of going after knowledge for its own sake. If he ever tries to take over from you, I'll kill him. I told him so."

I stared at Bill. Evidently, he meant what he had said.

"There's no danger," I said. "Anyway, you'd better wait until I call for help, before you go thinking of killing anyone. We don't want anybody shot by mistake."

"All right," said Bill. Exactly as if he was agreeing not to pass the salt at breakfast until I asked for it.

"Good," I said. "Now everything's just the way it has been. Let's forget it."

Only it wasn't—just the way it had been, I mean. For one thing, Marie had gone away from me in a manner that's hard to describe. She acted no differently than she ever had, but it was almost as if she had given up hope that there could be anything more than an alliance of convenience between us. Put that way, it doesn't sound like anything too important. But it left me feeling guilty in spite of the fact that I was fully convinced that I owed her nothing; and, in addition, I was helpless to do anything to mend the situation.

Tek had also changed. He was as much at my orders as ever, but I found him taking charge of the other men whenever there was a vacuum of command, quite as if I had appointed him my lieutenant. And finally, there was the girl . . . .

For one thing, she had evidently acquired a name while my mind was off on the web. It sounded like "Elly" when the others used it; but Marie, when I asked her, told me that it was actually Ellen and that Tek had given it to the girl. Well, at least, that made more sense. It was unlikely she had suddenly remembered her name, when she had gone this long time without remembering anything else. But when I asked Tek what made him think he could name her, he denied he had.

"I had to call her something," he said. "I asked her what she wanted for a name, and that's the one she picked for herself."

Ellen was a pretty enough name in its own way; I wondered where she had gotten it. But "Elly," or however they might have spelled its contraction, was ugly, I thought. I could not bring myself to use it. As far as I was concerned she was still "the girl"; but I was plainly a minority of one in that.

Tek was paying a good deal of attention to her, and she was spending most of her time in his company. For no particular reason, I found I didn't approve of that either. She had developed more than I had noticed—I now noticed—since those first days when the only things that looked human on her were a shirt and jeans. She wore dresses now that, possibly with Marie's help, had been altered to fit her; and her hair was always clean, tied in a ponytail at the back of her head. She was even starting to develop a few curves.

All this was to her credit, of course. She was as sparing with words as ever, but the change in her made her seem a good deal older; and possibly that was what had attracted Tek's interest in her. As I say, I found that I didn't approve—although there seemed no specific reason I could nail down for going to him and telling him to leave her alone.

In the first place, even if he agreed, I knew her better than to think *she* would leave him alone, particularly if I was the one who ordered it. In the second place, I had been ready to abandon her behind me on the bank of that river, so who was I to assume any responsibility for her? Finally, what did I have against Tek, anyway? Since he had been with us, he had been a model of propriety and obedience to orders; and she was only somebody born yesterday. So why make it any of my business?

I still didn't like it. I was stuck with the irrational feeling that he was nowhere near good enough for her. Unfortunately, I couldn't even get her alone to tell her so. I had been wrong about thinking she would get over what had put her off when I had hesitated in reacting to her, back on the rock where Sunday had returned me to my complete self. As far as she seemed to be concerned, I was invisible and inaudible.

To hell with her, I thought, and put my mind to deciding what our tribe should aim for next. We had evidently been travelling with no goal at all, being kept moving by my half-minded, but compulsive, determination. The evening of the day I made up my mind to put the whole question of the girl and Tek out of my mind for good, I waited until after dinner and then got Porniarsk and Bill together.

"Come along with me in one of the jeeps," I said. "It's time we had some discussion about this whole business of the time storms. I want to talk to the two of you, alone."

"No," said Porniarsk. "You want to talk to me, alone."

Bill looked startled and then bleak. He was not much at giving away his feelings through his expressions, but I had learned to read him fairly well by this time; and what I now read was that Porniarsk's words were like a slap in the face to him.

"Sorry, Porniarsk," I said. "I'm the one who decides how many of us are going to talk, and when."

"No," said Bill. "You talk to him alone. It may be important."

He turned around and walked off.

I opened my mouth to call him back and then closed it again. Inside that boy-sized body and behind that innocent face was the identity of a mature and intelligent man; and he had just shown himself capable of thinking in larger terms than I, in my reaction against Porniarsk's words.

I turned to look at the alien. It was still early evening and the whole landscape around us was softened and gentled by the pinkening light. Amidst all that softness, the bony-plated, uncouth form of Porniarsk looked like a miniature dinosaur out of a brutal and prehistoric age. Porniarsk said nothing now, merely stood looking at me and waiting. There was no way I could guess whether he had understood my reaction and Bill's and was simply unconcerned with our human feelings, or whether he had understood neither of us at all.

I had been pretty well ignoring Porniarsk during the last few weeks of my involvement with The Dream; and in fact, there seemed little to be learned from him unless he chose to inform us. His speech by this time was as

human as that of the rest of us; but the thoughts behind
his words, when he did speak, remained indecipherable.
He moved from one statement to another by a logic
mostly invisible to our human thinking.

And yet—he was not without some kind of emotion,
even some kind of warmth. There was no more sentiment
to be read in the tones of his voice, or in his actions,
than in those of a robot; but he seemed . . . likeable. I
don't know what other word to use. He seemed to radiate
a sort of warmth that we all, including the men we had
acquired along with Tek, felt and responded to. Even the
animals seemed to feel it. I had seen how Sunday had
taken to him at first sight. The dogs also, in their rare
free moments when they were not under command or
tied up, would seek him out, wagging their tails and
sniffing him all over each time as if this was a first meeting, before ending by licking at his armor-plated hide.
Porniarsk paid them no more attention than he did Sunday or one of us humans when he was not exchanging
specific information on some point or other. He seemed
not to need to eat. Whenever he had no place in particular
to move to, he would fold up and drop into a lying
position with a clatter like that of a dumped load of
bricks. But whether he ever slept in this position, I had
never been able to find out. Certainly, I had never caught
him with his eyes closed.

So—Porniarsk was a conundrum. He usually left us
no choice but to accept him pretty much as he was. And
now, with Bill having walked off, I found myself about to
do just that, one more time.

"All right, Porniarsk," I said. "It's you and me then.
Come on."

I climbed into the jeep beside which we had been
standing as we talked. Porniarsk made one of the as-
tounding leaps he seemed to be capable of with only a
slight flexing of his post-like legs, and crashed down into
the seat beside me, on his haunches. The jeep rocked
sideways on its springs—I had estimated before this that
if Porniarsk weighed an ounce, he must weigh well over
three hundred pounds—but recovered. I started the vehicle up and we drove off.

I did not go more than a few hundred yards, just
enough to put us out of earshot of the rest of the camp.
Then I killed the motor and turned to Porniarsk. It was

an odd feeling to find myself almost nose to nose with that massive, bulldog-like head. For the first time I noticed his eyes were not just brown in color, but so deep a brown as to be almost black. This close, I could see their pupils contract and expand in cat-fashion, while we talked.

"All right, Porniarsk," I said. "I need your help. You evidently know a lot more about the time storm effects than we do. I want to stop this random moving around just in hopes we'll run into a piece of country that's future enough for us to be able to do something about the mistwalls and the rest of it. I need you to help me figure out where to head."

"No," said Porniarsk.

"No?" I said.

"You do not need me to help you find a trigger area," said Porniarsk.

"What's that supposed to mean?" I said. This, coming on top of his rejection of Bill, was enough to stir my temper again.

"It's supposed to mean that my assistance is not required to set you on the road to the destination you wish. You've already set yourself on that road."

I took rein on my emotions. I reminded myself that I had to stop anthropomorphizing him. He was probably only trying to tell me something, and the fact that he was not built to think like a human was getting in the way.

"Since when?" I asked, as calmly as I could.

"Since your temporary abstraction, and during your partial involvement with the overall problem, ever since the moment in which my words caused you to visualize the magnitude of it. Am I making myself—" Porniarsk broke off uncharacteristically in mid-sentence. "Am I talking sense?"

"I don't know," I said. "How'd you know why I collapsed, or about how I've been since?"

"I've been watching you," he said, "and drawing conclusions from what you do. The conclusions are those I just stated."

"What've I been doing, then?"

"Going," he repeated, with no hint of impatience in his voice, "toward a trigger area."

I felt a sort of delicate feeling—an instinct to caution.

There was no way he could have known what had been
working in the back of my mind with The Dream, these
last few weeks; but he was talking one hell of a lot as if
he had read my mind.

"That could be an accident," I said. "What makes you
think it's anything more than an accident?"

"You withdrew," he said. "But then you recovered
enough to guide your party, if not in a straight line, in a
consistent direction by the most travellable route, toward
the location of an area I know to contain devices of assistance at a technological level, which might achieve a
first step of halting the moving lines of temporal alteration—temporal discontinuities, as Bill calls them, or mistwalls, as you say."

I stared at him.

"If you know about a place like that," I said, "why
haven't you done something about the temporal—oh, hell,
whatever you want to call them—before now?"

"The devices are devices of assistance, but not of a
design which will assist me. I'm a avatar, as I told you, an
avatar of Porniarsk Prime Three. The devices would be
of assistance to Porniarsk himself, but he's otherwise engaged."

"Tell him to drop whatever's otherwise engaging him
then, and get over here."

"He wouldn't come," said the avatar. "This planet is
your problem. The problem of Porniarsk is a larger one.
It involves many planets like this. Therefore, he has such
as I who am his avatar, so he can have several manipula-
tive sets of himself at work. But all I am is an avatar.
Alone, I can't manipulate the forces involved here, no
matter how competent the device of assistance available
to me."

I shook my head.

"All right, then, Porniarsk—or Porniarsk's avatar—" I
began.

"Porniarsk is fine," he interrupted. "You'll never meet
Porniarsk himself, or any of his other avatars, so there's
no danger of confusion."

"I don't know about that," I said. "You've got me pretty confused right now. I don't understand any of this."

"Of course," said Porniarsk, agreeably. "You're unedu-
cated."

"Oh? Is that it?"

"How could you be otherwise? You've never had the chance to learn about these forces and their effects. I can't educate you, but I can explain specific elements of the situation as you run across them. Trying to explain them before you encounter them won't work because you don't have either the vocabulary or the concepts behind the vocabulary."

"But I will when I run into these elements?" I said. "Is that it?"

"On encountering the experience, you'll see the need for the appropriate terms, with which you might then be able to understand enough of the underlying concepts to work with."

"Oh?" I didn't mean to sound sarcastic, but this kind of conversation with Porniarsk had a habit of driving me to it. "My understanding's not guaranteed then?"

"Be reasonable," said Porniarsk; and this kind of appeal in colloquial, uninflected English from the genial gargoyle sitting next to me, had to be experienced to be believed. "How can *I* guarantee *your* understanding?"

How, indeed? He had a point, there.

"I give up," I said, and I meant it. "Just tell me one thing. How did I happen to know enough to head in the right direction?"

"I don't know," Porniarsk answered. "I'd expected that, sooner or later, you'd ask me if there were any future areas containing the means to do something about the time storm effects locally, that is, here on this world. Then I could have directed you to such an area. However, you've directed yourself to one without me. I don't understand how. Porniarsk himself wouldn't understand how, though perhaps he could find the answer. I'm only an avatar. I can't."

"All right, tell me what to do now, then," I said.

Porniarsk's head creaked in a negative shaking.

"There's nothing I can advise you on until you've experienced the immediate future area of the assistance device technology," he said. "Now that I've seen you do this much by yourself, I'd be cautious about advising you in any case. It might be that you'll learn more, and faster, on your own."

"I see," I said. "That's fine. That's just fine. Then tell me, why did you stop Bill from coming out here with us, if you weren't going to tell me anything anyway?"

"Bill wouldn't believe me," said Porniarsk. "He doesn't trust me."

"And I do?"

The gargoyle head leaned slightly, almost confidentially, toward mine.

"You've learned something you shouldn't have been able to learn by yourself," said Porniarsk. "You've touched the greater universe. Of course, you don't trust me, either. You're too primitive to trust an avatar of another kind, like myself. But in your case, trust isn't necessary."

"Oh?" I said. "Why?"

"Because you want to believe me," said Porniarsk. "If what I'm saying is true, then you're headed toward something you want very much. That's not the same thing as trust; but trust can come later. For now, your wanting to believe will do."

16

So we drove back to camp in the last of the twilight and in silence. I only asked him one question on the way back.

"Do you really give a damn about any of us?" I said. "Or are you just interested in the time storm?"

"Porniarsk cares for all life," his steady voice answered. "If he didn't, he'd have no concern with the time storm. And I am Porniarsk, only in an additional body."

It was a cold comfort. I believed him; but at the same time, I got the feeling that there was something more he was withholding from me.

In any case, there was nothing to do now but keep going. Oddly, I trusted him. Something had happened to me since The Dream; and that was that, in a strange way, I had come to feel an affection and responsibility for him, along with all the others. It was as if a corner of my soul's house had put up a blind on one window to let in a little sunshine. I did take Bill aside the next day and give him a rough briefing on my conversation with Porniarsk. Bill fulfilled Porniarsk's prediction by being highly skeptical of the avatar's motives and implications.

"It sounds to me like a con game," he said. "It's part of a con game to flatter your mark. Did you feel you were headed any place in particular, these last three weeks?"

I hesitated. Somehow, I didn't get the feeling that Bill was ripe right now for hearing an account of The Dream, and how it had been with me. But there was no way to answer his questions fully without telling him about my back-of-the-brain spiderwork.

"I had a feeling I was tied into something important," I said. "That's as far as it went."

153

"Hmm," said Bill, half to himself. "I wonder if Porniarsk's telepathic?"

"That's as far-fetched as me supposed to be knowing where we're going, when I didn't know where we're going," I said.

Bill shrugged.

"If we hit this trigger area place soon, you'll have known where we're going," he said. "No reason there shouldn't be as much truth to telepathy. When did Porniarsk say we'd reach the area?"

Of course, wound up as I had been by what he'd had to say about me personally, I'd forgotten to ask him.

"I'll find out," I said and went off to look for the avatar.

Porniarsk politely informed me that we should hit the trigger area in about a day and a half the way we were travelling; and, yes, it would be behind a mistwall like all the other mistwalls we'd seen. As to what was inside, it was best I experienced that for myself first, before Porniarsk did any explaining.

He was not wrong. Late in the afternoon of the following day, we spotted a stationary mistwall dead ahead; and two hours later we set up evening camp a couple of hundred yards from it.

The countryside here was open pastureland, rolling hills with only an occasional tree but small strands of brush and marshy ponds. Here and there a farmer's fence straggled across the landscape; and the two-lane blacktop road we had been following, since its sudden appearance out of nowhere ten miles before, ran at an angle into the mistwall and disappeared. The day had been cool. Our campfires felt good. Autumn would be along before long, I thought, and with that began to turn over ideas for the winter; whether to find secure shelter in this climate or head south.

I made one more attempt to get Porniarsk to tell me what lay on the other side of the mistwall; but he was still not being helpful.

"You could at least tell us if we're liable to fall off a cliff before we come out of the wall, or step into a few hundred feet of deep water," I growled at him.

"You won't encounter any cliffs, lakes, or rivers before you have a chance to see them," Porniarsk said. "As far as the terrain goes, it's not that dissimilar from the land around us here."

"Then why not tell us about it?"

"The gestalt will be of importance to you later."

That was all I could get out of him. After dinner, I called a meeting. Porniarsk attended. I told the others that Porniarsk believed that, beyond this particular mist-wall, there was an area different from any we'd run into so far. We might find equipment there that would let us do something about the time storm and the moving mist-walls. Bill and I, in particular, were interested in the chance of doing so, as they all knew. For one thing, if we could somehow stop the mistwalls from moving, we could feel safe setting down someplace permanently. Perhaps we could start rebuilding a civilization.

It was quite a little speech. When I was done, they all looked at me, looked at Porniarsk, who had neither moved nor spoken, and then looked back at me again. None of them said anything. But looking back at them, I got the clear impression that there were as many different reactions to what I had just said as there were heads there to contain the reactions.

"All right then," I said, after a reasonable wait to give anyone else a chance to speak. "We'll be going in, in the morning. The ones going will be Bill, me, and three others, all with rifles and shotguns both, in one of the jeeps. Anybody particularly want to be in on the expedition, or shall I pick out the ones to go?"

"I'll go," said Tek.

"No," I said. "I want you to stay here."

I looked around the firelit circle of faces, but there were no other volunteers.

"All right then," I said. "It'll be Richie, Alan, and Waite. Starting with the best shot and working down the list."

The fourth man, Hector Monsanto, whom everybody called "Zig," did not look too unhappy at being left out. He was the oldest of the four men we had acquired along with Tek, a short, wiry, leathery-featured individual in his late thirties, who looked as if most of his life had been spent outdoors. Actually, according to Tek, he had grown up in a small town and had been a barber who spent most of his time in the local bars.

He was the oldest of the four and the least agile. The other three were in their early to mid-twenties and could move fast if they needed to.

So, the following morning we tried it. It took about an hour or so for Bill to satisfy himself, by throwing a weighted line through the mistwall and pushing pipe lengths screwed together to beyond the mistwall's far edge, that the terrain beyond was both level and safe. Then we brought the jeep we were going to use up to the wall and got in with our weapons. I climbed in behind the wheel with Bill on the other front seat. Alan, Richie, and Waite got into the back. We made a pretty full load.

Then Sunday, purring loudly, as if congratulating us all on a permission no one had given him, leaped up into Bill's lap and settled down for the ride; and, before I could shove him out, the girl began to climb into the back seat holding a rifle.

"Hold it!" I roared. "Everybody out!"

We off-loaded, everybody except the girl and Sunday, who took advantage of the available empty space to settle down that much more firmly.

"Now, look—" I began to the girl.

"I'm going," she said. Sunday purred loudly and cleaned the fur on top of one of his forepaws. It was a double declaration of insubordination.

Of course, there was no way I could stop them. I could put them out of the vehicle, but they could walk in right behind us. Sunday had proved that, unlimited times. In fact, I had known—everybody had known—that he would be coming along. I had not counted on the girl.

I glared around me. This particular expedition was sorting itself out in exactly the wrong way. I don't know what made me so convinced that there might be danger beyond this mistwall. I'd gone into a number of others confidently enough. Perhaps it was Porniarsk's refusal to tell me exactly what was beyond the wall. At any rate, I felt the way I felt; and for that type of feeling, I was taking all the wrong people and leaving all the wrong people behind.

An ideal expeditionary group would have been myself, Tek, and a couple of the men, none of whom meant a great deal to me—except myself; and I was too much of an egotist to think that I couldn't survive whatever mystery lay in front of me. Sunday, the girl, Bill, even to a certain extent, Marie and little Wendy, were people I cared about to one degree or another and would just as soon have kept safely in the rear area.

But Bill could not be left behind, in justice. The quest to understand the time storm was as much his as mine. Sunday could not be kept out, in practice; and now the girl had proclaimed her intention to go in with us whether I wanted her to or not. Meanwhile Tek, who outside of myself was the one person fit to take charge of those left behind, if enemies of some kind suddenly appeared over the horizon behind us, could, by no stretch of common sense, be taken. Ever since Marie, Wendy, and I had run into him and his group, I had been half-expecting that any day, we might bump into another such armed and predatory gang.

"All right!" I said. "If everybody's going to go, we'll have to use the pickup. Let's get it cleared out!"

The pickup was our main transport. In the back, it had all our camping equipment, food, fuel, and other supplies. We had unloaded part of what it contained to set up camp the night before; but if it was to be used as a battle wagon, the rest of the box had to be cleared. We moved back and went to work.

Twenty minutes later, we once more approached the mistwall; this time in the pickup, in low gear. The girl and Bill and I were in the front seat with the windows rolled up, with me as driver. In the open box behind were Alan and Waite and Richie, holding a disgruntled Sunday on a leash. I'd shut the leopard out of the cab by main force and snapped his leash around his neck when he tried to join the three of us in the cab. As I pushed the nose of the pickup slowly into the first dust of the mistwall, there was a heavy thud on the roof of the cab. I stopped, rolled down the window and stuck my head out to glimpse Sunday, now lying on the cab top. I rolled the window back up and went on.

The mist surrounded us. The dust hissed on the metal of the pickup's body, as the motor of the truck grumbled in low gear. We were surrounded by an undeviating whiteness in which it was impossible to tell if we were moving. Then the whiteness lightened, thinned, and suddenly we rolled out into sunlight again. I stopped the truck.

We were in a rocky, hilly section of country. The thin, clear air that made everything stand out with sudden sharpness signalled that we were at a higher altitude, and the sparseness of vegetation—no trees and only an occasional green, spiny bush—suggested a high, desert country, like the *altiplano* of inland Mexico. The landscape was mainly rock, from hard dirt and gravel, to boulders of all sizes. Rough, but not too rough for the jeeps to get through; and, if a clear route could be found between the boulders, probably even the pickup could be nursed along.

The ground before us was fairly clear and level, but boulder-strewn slopes rose sharply to the right and left of us. Directly ahead, the level space dipped down into a cup-shaped depression holding what appeared to be a small village. The buildings in the village were odd; dome-shaped, with floorless, front porch extensions, consisting simply of projecting roofs upheld at each end by supporting poles. Under those roofs, out in the open, there seemed to be a few machines or equipment—mechanical constructs of some kind. No human beings were visible. Beyond the village, the ground rose sharply into a small mountain—it was too steep to be called a hill—wearing a belt of trees halfway up its several hundred feet of height. On one side of the mountain, the bare peak sloped at an angle the jeeps could possibly manage. But the other slopes were all boulder-strewn and climbable only by someone on foot.

On top, crowning the peak, was a large, solid, circular building, looking as if it had been poured out of fresh white concrete ten seconds before we appeared on the scene. That was as much as I had a chance to notice, because then everything started to happen.

A number of objects hit loudly on the body and cab of the truck, one shattering the window next to Bill. At the same time, there was a yowl of rage from Sunday and I caught sight, fleetingly, of the leopard leaping off the roof of the cab to the right, with his leash trailing in the air behind him. Suddenly the rocks around us were speckled by the visages of dark-furred, ape-like creatures.

The guns of the men in the box were firing. The girl, who had been seated between Bill and myself, scrambled over Bill crying out Sunday's name, opened the door of the pickup on that side, and disappeared. Bill exited after her; and I heard the machine pistol yammering. I jerked open the door on my side, rolled out on to the hard-pebbled earth, and began firing from a prone position at any furry head I could see.

There was a timeless moment of noise and confusion—and then without warning, it was over. There were no longer any creatures visible to shoot at, except for perhaps four or five who lay still, or barely stirring, on the ground. I fired a few more rounds out of reflex and then quit. The other guns fell silent.

I got to my feet. Sunday stalked back into my line of vision, his tail high in self-congratulation. He headed for one of the two furry figures that still moved. I opened my mouth to call him back; but before he could have reached the creature, a rifle in the box behind me began to sound again, and both the moving bodies went motionless.

"Quit that!" I shouted, spinning around. "I want one alive—"

I broke off, suddenly realizing I was talking to a man who wasn't listening. Richie, his round face contorted, was kneeling behind the metal side of the pickup box, firing steadily at the dark-furred shapes; and he kept at it until his rifle was empty.

I climbed into the box and took the gun away from him as he tried to reload it.

"Simmer down!" I said.

He looked at me glassy-eyed, but sat without moving. There wasn't a mark on him.

But the other two were hit. Alan had one side of his face streaming blood from what seemed to be a scalp wound. He was holding up Waite, who was breathing in an ugly, rattling way with his face as white as the building on the peak. His right hand was trapped behind Alan; but he kept trying to bring his left hand up to his chest, and Alan kept holding it away.

My head cleared. I remembered now that the barrage that had come at us had contained not only thrown rocks but a few leaf-shaped, hiltless knives. One of the knives was now sticking in Waite's chest low on the left side. It was in perhaps a third the length of its blade; and evidently it had slid in horizontally between two ribs.

Waite coughed, and a little pink froth came out the corners of his mouth.

"He wants to get the knife out," said Alan, pleadingly to me. "Should we just pull it out, do you think?"

I looked down at Waite. It did not matter, clearly, whether we took the knife out or not. The blade had gone into his lungs and now they were filling up with blood. Waite looked back up at me with panic in his eyes. He was the quiet one of Tek's four men and possibly the youngest. I had never been sure if he was really like the others, or whether he had simply gotten swept up and tried to be like them.

There was nothing I or anyone else in our group could do for him. I stood looking down at him, feeling my helplessness, like something in my own chest being raggedly cut. This was one of the people I had been thinking meant little or nothing to me and would be easily expendable. I had not stopped to realize how close a group like ours could come to be, living together like a family, moving together, facing a possibly dangerous world together. Maybe he would die more quickly without the knife blade in him and removing it would be the kindest thing we could do for him.

"If he wants it out, he might as well have it out," I said.

Alan let go of Waite's arm. The arm came up, and its hand grasped the handle of the knife but could not pull it out. Alan half-reached for the knife himself, hesitated, tried again, hesitated, and looked appealingly at me.

I reached down and took hold of the handle. The blade stuck at first, then slid out easily. Waite yelled—or rather, he tried to yell, but it was a sound that ended in a sort of gargle. He pulled away a little from Alan and leaned over forward, face tilted down intently toward the bed of the box, as if he was going to be sick. But he was not. He merely hung there sagging against the grip of Alan's arms, his gaze calm and intent on the metal flooring; and then, as we watched, he began to die.

It was like watching him dwindle away from us. His face relaxed and relaxed, and the focus in his eyes became more and more general, until all at once there was no focus at all and he was dead. Alan let him down quickly but softly on the bed of the box.

I turned and climbed out of the box back on to the ground. I saw Bill standing on this side of the truck now and Sunday nosing curiously at one of the bodies. Suddenly, it struck me.

"Girl!" I shouted at Bill. "The girl! Where is she?"

"I don't know," said Bill.

I ran around the front of the truck and the bouldered slope on the side I'd seen her disappear.

"Girl!" I kept shouting. *"Girl!"*

I couldn't find her. I found one of the dead ape-creatures, but I couldn't find her. I started threading back and forth among the rocks as I worked up the slope; and then, suddenly, I almost fell over her. She was in a little open space, half-sitting up with her back against a boulder and a torn-off strip of her shirt tied around one leg above the knee.

For a moment I thought she was already dead, like Waite—and I couldn't take it. It was like being cut in half. Then she turned her head to look at me, and I saw she was alive.

"Oh, my God!" I said.

I knelt down beside her and wrapped her up in my arms, telling myself I would never let go of her again. Never. But she was as stiff and unresponsive in my grasp as a wild animal caught in a trap. She did not move; but she did not relax either, and finally, this brought me more or less back to my senses; I didn't want to let her go, but I stopped holding her quite so tightly.

"Are you all right?" I said. "Why didn't you answer me?"

"My name's Ellen," she said.

"Is that all!" I hugged her again. "All right! You'll be Ellen from now on. I won't ever call you anything else!"

"It doesn't matter what you call me," she said. "I'm not going to be here anyway."

She was still stiff and cold. I let go of her and sat back on my knees so that I could see her face; and it was as unyielding as the rest of her.

"What do you mean, you aren't going to be here?" She was talking nonsense. She had evidently been hurt or wounded in the leg, but that could hardly be serious.

"Tek and I are going away by ourselves. It's already decided," she said. "We were just waiting to make sure you got through this last mistwall all right. You can keep Sunday. He only gets in the way all the time anyway."

She turned, grabbed hold of the boulder against which she had been leaning, and pulled herself up on one leg.

"Help me back to the pickup," she said.

My head was whirling with that crazy announcement of hers. I stared down at her bandaged leg.

"What happened to you?" I said, automatically.

"I got hit by a rock, that's all. It scraped the skin off and bled a little, so I wrapped it up; but it's only a bruise."

"Try putting your weight on it." Something automatic in me was doing the talking. "Maybe it's broken."

"It's not broken. I already tried." She took hold of my arm with both her hands. "It just hurts to walk on it. Help me."

I put an arm around her, and she hopped back down the slope on one leg, by my side, until we reached the cab of the pickup, and I helped her up on to the seat. I was operating on reflex. I could not believe what she had said; particularly, just now, when I had just realized how important she was to me. It was the way I had found myself feeling about Waite, multiplied something like a million times. But there were things demanding decisions from me.

Richie and Alan were still in the back of the truck with the body of Waite. I looked at them. Somebody had to take the pickup back through the mistwall with the girl and Waite. Richie was the unhurt one, but his eyes still did not look right.

"How badly are you hurt?" I asked Alan.

"Hurt?" he said. "I didn't get hurt."

"You could fool me," I said dryly. He didn't seem to get it. "Your head! How bad's the damage to your head?"

"My head?"

He put up a hand and brought it down covered with blood. His face whitened.

"What is it?" he said. "How bad . . . ." His bloody hand was fluttering up toward the head wound, wanting to touch it, but afraid of what it might feel.

"That's what I want to know," I said.

I climbed into the cab and bent over him, gingerly parting the hair over the bloody scalp. It was such a mess I couldn't see anything.

"Feel anything?" I asked, probing with my fingertips.

"No . . . no . . yes!" he yelped.

I pulled my hands away.

"How bad did that feel?" I asked him. He looked embarrassed.

"Not too bad—I guess," he said. "But I felt it, where you touched it."

"All right," I told him. "Hang on, because I'm going to have to touch it some more."

I probed around with my fingers, wishing I'd had the sense to bring bandages and water with us. He said nothing to indicate that I was giving him any important amount of pain; and all my fingers could find was a swelling and a relatively small cut.

"It's really not bad at all," he said sheepishly, when I'd finished. "I think I just got hit by a rock, come to think of it."

"All right," I said. My own hands were a mess now. I wiped them as best I could on the levis I was wearing. "Looks like a bump and a scratch, only. It just put out a lot of blood. If you're up to it, I want you to stay."

"I can stay," he said.

"All right, then. Richie!"

Richie looked at me slowly as if I was someone calling him from a distance.

"Richie! I want you to drive the pickup back through the mistwall. You're to take the girl and Waite back, then pick up some bandages, some antibiotics and a jerry can of drinking water and bring it back to us. Understand me?"

"Yeah . . . ." said Richie, thickly.

"Come on, then," I said.

I climbed out of the box of the pickup and he came after me. I saw him into the cab and behind the wheel.

"He'll take you back to the camp," I told the girl and closed the door on the driver's side before she could answer—assuming, that is, that she had intended to answer. The pickup's motor, which had been idling all this time, growled into gear. Richie swung it about and drove out of sight into the mistwall, headed back.

I looked around. Bill was standing about twenty yards ahead of me. Beside him was Porniarsk, who must have followed us through the mistwall at some time when I wasn't looking. They seemed to be talking together, looking down into the village, the machine pistol hanging by its strap, carelessly, from Bill's right arm. It was incautious of him to be so relaxed, I thought. We had driven off one attack, but there was no way of knowing we might not have another at any minute.

I went toward them. As I did, I had to detour around

the body of one of the attackers, who had apparently been trying to rush the pickup. It lay face-down, the ape-like features hidden, and it reminded me of Waite, somehow. For a moment I wondered if there were others among its fellows that were feeling the impact of this one's death, as I had felt that of Waite. My mind—it was not quite under control right then, my mind—skittered off to think of the girl again. Of Ellen—I must remember to think of her as Ellen from now on.

It was so strange. She was small and skinny and cantankerous. How could I love her like this? Where did it come from, what I was feeling? Somehow, when I wasn't paying any attention, she had grown inside me, and now, she took up all the available space there. Another thought came by, blown on the wandering breeze of my not-quite-in-control mind. What about Marie? I couldn't just kick her out. But maybe there was no need for worry. All Marie had ever seemed to want was the protection inherent in our partnership. It might be she would be completely satisfied with the name of consort alone. After all, there were no laws now, no reason that I couldn't apparently have two wives instead of one. No one but us three need know Marie was a wife in name only . . . of course, the girl would have to agree . . . .

I stopped thinking, having reached Bill and Porniarsk. They were still looking down at the village. I looked down, too, and, to my surprise, saw it populated and busy. Black, furry, ape-like figures were visible all through its streets and moving in and out of the dome-shaped houses. Most, in fact, seemed to be busy with whatever objects they had under the porch-like roofs before the entrances of their buildings. But a fair number were visible simply sitting in the dust, singly or in pairs, doing nothing; and a small group were in transit from one spot to another.

They were within easy rifle shot of where we stood, and the three of us must have been plainly visible to them; but they paid us no attention whatsoever.

"What the hell?" I said. "Is that the same tribe that hit us just now?"

"Yes," said Bill.

I looked at him and waited for him to go on, but he nodded at Porniarsk instead.

"Let him tell you."

Porniarsk creaked his head around to look sideways and up at me.

"They're experimental animals," Porniarsk said, "from a time less than a hundred years ahead of that you were in originally when the time storm reached you."

"You knew about them?" The thought of Waite made my throat tight. "You knew about them waiting to kill us, and you didn't warn us?"

"I knew only they were experimental animals," said Porniarsk. "Apparently part of their conditioning is to attack. But if the attack fails, they go back to other activities."

"It could be . . ." said Bill slowly and thoughtfully, "it could be their attack reflex was established to be used against animals, instead of the people of the time that set them up here; and they just didn't recognize us as belonging to the people level, as they'd been trained to recognize it."

"It's possible," said Porniarsk. "And then, if they attacked and failed, they might be conditioned to stop attacking, as a fail-safe reflex."

"That's damned cool of the both of you," I said, my throat free again. "Waite's dead and you're holding a parlor discussion on the reasons."

Bill looked at me, concerned.

"All right, all right," I said. "Forget I said that. I'm still a little shook up from all this. So, they're experimental animals down there, are they?"

"Yes," said Porniarsk, "experimental animals, created by genetic engineering to test certain patterns of behavior. Up there on the height behind their community is the laboratory building from which they were observed and studied. The equipment in that structure that was designed for working with this problem is equipment that, with some changes and improvements, may be able to aid in controlling the effects of the time storm, locally."

Bill was staring straight at me. His face was calm, but I could hear the excitement under the level note he tried to speak in.

"Let's take a look, Marc."

"All right," I said. "As soon as the pickup comes back, we'll go get a jeep and try that long slope on the right of the peak."

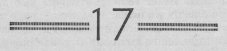

17

The only vehicle-possible route to the peak led down through the main street of the village. When Alan got back with a jeep, we left him there; and Porniarsk, Bill and I drove down the slope and in between the buildings. We had perhaps twenty feet to spare on either side of us as we went through the village, for the central street—if you could call it that—was twice the width of the other lanes between buildings. The furry faces we passed did not bother to look at us, with a single exception. A slightly grizzled, large, and obviously male individual—none of them wore anything but a sort of Sam Browne belt, to which were clipped the sheaths that held their knives and some things which looked like small hand tools —sat in front of one building and stared from under thick tufts of hair where his brows should be, his long fingers playing with the knife he held on his knees. But he made no threatening moves, with the knife or anything else.

"Look at that old man," said Bill, pointing with the muzzle of his machine pistol at the watcher.

"I see him," I said. "What do you want me to do about him?"

"Nothing, I'd suggest," said Porniarsk. My question had not really called for an answer, but perhaps he had not understood that. "That one's the Alpha Prime of the males' community. The name 'Old Man' fits him very well. As Alpha Prime, his reflexes, or conditioning, dictate a somewhat different pattern of action for him alone. But I don't think he or the others will act inimically again, unless you deliberately trigger some antagonistic reaction."

"What are they all doing?" Bill asked.

I looked in the direction he was staring. There were a number of porches along the left side of the street, each

166

with one or two of the experimentals under them. I picked out one who was operating what was clearly a spinning wheel. Another was cutting up a large sheet of the leathery material their harnesses were made out of, plainly engaged in constructing Sam Brown belts. But the rest were working with machines I did not recognize and either getting no visible results, or results that made no sense to me. One, in particular, was typing away energetically at a sort of double keyboard, with no noticeable effect, except for a small red tab that the machine spat out at odd intervals into a wire basket. The worker paid no attention to the tabs he was accumulating, seeming to be completely wound up in the typing process itself.

"They're self-supporting, after a fashion," said Porniarsk. "Some of what they do provides them with what they need to live. Other specific activities are merely for study purposes—for the studies of the people who put them here."

"Where are those people?" I asked. "Can we get in touch with them?"

"No." Porniarsk swiveled his neck once more to look at me from the seat beside me. "They are not here."

"Where did they go?"

"They no longer exist," said Porniarsk. "No more than all the people you knew before your first experience with the time storm. You and Bill and the rest of you here, including these experimental creatures, are the ones who have gone places."

I took my attention off the street for a second to stare at him.

"What do you mean?"

"I mean you, and those with you, are people the time storm has moved, rather than eliminated," Porniarsk answered. "I'm sorry, that can't be explained properly to you yet, by someone like me, not until you understand more fully what has been involved and is involved in the temporal displacements. Remember, I told you that this disturbance began roughly half a billion years in your past?"

I remembered. But it had only been a figure to me at the time. Who can imagine a time-span of a half a billion years?

"Yes," I said.

"It also began several million years in your future," said

Porniarsk. "Perhaps it might help you to think, provisionally, of the time storm as a wave-front intersecting the linear time you know—the time you imagine stretching from past to future—at an angle, so that your past, present and future are all affected at once by the same action."

"Why didn't you tell us this before?" demanded Bill.

"Unfortunately, the image I just gave you isn't really a true one," said Porniarsk. "You forget the matter of scale. If the time storm is like a wave-front on a beach, we and our worlds are less than individual atoms in the grains of sand that make up that beach. What we experience as local effects appear as phenomena having very little resemblance to the true picture of the wave-front as a whole. I only mention this because it's now become important for Marc to be able to imagine something of the forces at work here."

The front wheels of the jeep jolted and shuddered over some small rocks. We were moving beyond the end of the village street and up over open ground again. I gave my attention back to my driving.

The drive up even the easy side of the peak was rough enough, but the jeep was equal to it. With enough foresight, it was possible to pick a route among the really heavy boulders that would otherwise have barred our way. A little more than halfway up, we hit a relatively level area of hard earth, surrounding the basin of a natural spring coming out of the cliff; and we stopped to rest and taste the water, which was cold enough to set our teeth on edge. I had not been conscious of being thirsty, except for a fleeting moment when I told Richie to bring back a jerry can of water with the other things. He had; and I had forgotten to get a drink then. Now I felt a thirst like that of someone lost in the desert for two days. I drank until my jaws ached, paused, drank, paused, and drank again.

After a bit we went the rest of the way up to the top of the peak, where the building was. Seen up close, it turned out to be a structure maybe sixty feet in diameter, with only one entrance and no windows. Like a blockhouse at a firing range, only larger.

The entrance had a door, which slid aside as we came within a stride of it. We had a glimpse of darkness beyond, then lighting awoke within, and we stepped into a brightly illuminated, circular interior, with a raised platform in the center and open cubicles all around the exterior wall, each cubicle with a padded chair, its back toward the center of the room and its cushions facing a sort of console fixed to the wall.

"What is it?" asked Bill, almost in a whisper. He was standing with Porniarsk and me on the raised platform but, unlike us, turning continually on his heel as if he wanted to get a view of all hundred and eighty degrees of the room at once.

"It is," said Porniarsk, "something you might think of as a computer, in your terms. It's a multiple facility for the use of observers who'd wish to draw conclusions from their observations of the inhabitants in the village."

"Computer?" Bill's voice was louder and sharper. "That's all?"

"Its working principle isn't that of the computers you're familiar with," said Porniarsk. "This uses the same principle that's found in constructs from the further future, those I've referred to as devices-of-assistance. You'll have to trust me to put this construct into that future mode so it'll be useful in the way we need."

"How'll we use it?" Bill asked.

"You won't use it," said Porniarsk. "Marc will use it."

They both turned their heads toward me.

"And you'll teach me how?" I said to Porniarsk.

"No. You'll have to teach yourself," Porniarsk answered. "If you can't, then there's nothing anyone can do."

"If he can't, I'll try," said Bill tightly.

"I don't think the device will work for you if it fails for Marc," said Porniarsk to him. "Tell me, do you feel anything at this moment? Anything unusual at all?"

"Feel?" Bill stared at him.

"You don't feel anything, then," said Porniarsk. "I was right. Marc should be much more attuned. Marc, what do you feel?"

"Feel? Me?" I said, echoing Bill. But I already knew what he was talking about.

I had thought, at first, I must be feeling a hangover from the fight with the inhabitants of the village. Then I'd thought the feeling was my curiosity about what was inside this building, until I saw what was there. Now, standing on the platform in the center of the structure, I knew it was something else—something like a massive excitement from everywhere, that was surrounding me, pressing in on me.

"I feel geared-up," I said.

"More than just geared-up, I think," Porniarsk said. "It was a guess I made only on the basis of Marc's heading for this area; but I was right. Porniarsk hoped only that a small oasis of stability might be established on the surface of this world, in this immediate locality. With anyone else, such as you, Bill, that'd be all we could do. But with Marc, maybe we can try something more. There's a chance he has an aptitude for using a device-of-assistance."

"Can't you come up with a better name for it than that?" said Bill. His voice was tight—tight enough to shake just a little.

"What would you suggest?" asked Porniarsk.

I turned and walked away from them, out of the building through the door that opened before me and shut after me. I walked into the solitude of the thin, clean air and the high sunlight. There was something working in me; and for the moment, it had driven everything else, even Ellen, out of my mind. It was like a burning, but beneficent, fever, like a great hunger about to be satisfied, like the feeling of standing on the threshold of a cavern filled with treasure beyond counting.

It was all this, and still it was indescribable. I did not yet have it, but I could almost touch it and taste it; and I knew that it was only a matter of time now until my grasp closed on it. Knowing that was everything, I could wait now. I could work. I could do anything. The keys of my kingdom were at hand.

18

Then began a bittersweet time for me, the several weeks that Porniarsk worked on the equipment in what we were now calling the "roundhouse." It was sweet because, day by day, I felt the device-of-assistance coming to life under the touch of those three tentacle-fingers Porniarsk had growing out of his shoulders. The avatar had been right about me. The original Porniarsk had not suspected there would be anyone on our Earth who could use the device without being physically connected to it. But evidently I was a freak. I had already had some kind of mental connection with this place, if only subconsciously, during the days of The Dream in which I had pushed us all in this direction and to this location. I said as much to Porniarsk one day.

"No," he shook his head, "before that, I'd think. You must have felt its existence, here, and been searching for it from the time you woke to find your world changed."

"I was looking," I said. "But I didn't have any idea what for."

"Perhaps," said Porniarsk. "But you might find, after the device is ready and you can look back over all you've done, that you unconsciously directed each step along the way toward this place and this moment, from the beginning."

I shook my head. There was no use trying to explain to him, I thought, how I had never been able to let a problem alone. But I did not argue the point any further.

I was too intensely wrapped up in what I could feel growing about me—the assistance of the device. It was only partly mechanical. Porniarsk would not, or could not, explain its workings to me, although I could watch him as he worked with the small colored cubes that made

171

up the inner parts of seven of the consoles. The cubes were about a quarter the size of children's blocks and seemed to be made of some hard, translucent material. They clung together naturally in the arrangement in which they occurred behind the face of the console; and Porniarsk's work, apparently, was to rearrange their order and get them to cling together again. Apparently, the rearrangement was different with each console; and Porniarsk had to try any number of combinations before he found it. It looked like a random procedure but, evidently, was not; and when I asked about that, Porniarsk relaxed his no-information rule enough to tell me that what he was doing was checking arrangements of the cubes in accordance with "sets" he already carried in his memory center, to find patterns that would resonate with the monad that was me. It was not the cubes that were the working parts, evidently, but the patterns.

Whatever he was doing, and however it was effective, when he got a collection of cubes to hang together in a different order, I felt the effect immediately. It was as if another psychic generator had come on-line in my mind. With each addition of power, or strength, or whatever you want to call it, I saw more clearly and more deeply into all things around me.

—Including the people. And from this came the bitter to join with the sweet of my life. For as, step by step, my perceptions increased, I came to perceive that Ellen was indeed intending to leave with Tek as soon as my work with the device had been achieved. She was staying for the moment and had talked Tek into staying, only so that he and she could hold down two of the consoles, as Porniarsk had said all of the adults in our party would need to do when I made my effort to do something about the time storm. After that, they would go; and nothing I could say would stop her.

The reasons why she had turned to Tek as she had, I could not read in her. Her personal feelings were beyond the reach of my perception. Something shut me out. Porniarsk told me, when I finally asked him, that the reason I could not know how she felt was because my own emotions were involved with her. Had I been able to force myself to see, I would have seen not what was, but what I wanted to see. I would have perceived falsely; and since the perception and understanding I was gaining with the help of the device were part of a true reflection of the universe, the device could give only accurate information; consequently, it gave nothing where only inaccuracy was possible.

So, I was split down the middle; and the division between the triumph and the despair in me grew sharper with the activation of each new console. After the fourth one, the avatar warned me that there was a limit to the step-up I could endure from the device.

"If you feel you're being pushed too hard," he said, "tell me quickly. Too much stimulus, and you could destroy yourself before you had a chance to use the device properly."

"It's all right," I said. "I know what you're talking about." And I did. I could feel myself being stretched daily, closer and closer toward a snapping point. But that point was still not reached; and I wanted to go to the limit no matter what would happen afterwards.

It was the pain of Ellen's imminent leaving that drove me more than anything else. With the device beginning to work, I was partly out of the ordinary world already. I did not have to test myself by sticking burning splinters in my flesh to know that the physical side of me was much dwindled in importance lately. It was easy to forget that I had a body. But the awareness of my immaterial self was correspondingly amplified to several times its normal sensitivity; and it was in this immaterial area that I was feeling the loss of Ellen more keenly than the amputation of an arm and a leg together.

There was no relief from that feeling of loss except to concentrate on the expansion of my awareness. So, psychically, I pushed out and out, running from what I could not bear to face—and then, without warning, came rescue from an unexpected direction.

It was late afternoon, the sunlight slanting in at a low angle through the door to the roundhouse, which we had propped open while Porniarsk worked on the last console. Bill and I were the only other ones there. We had opened the door to let a little of the natural breeze and outer sunwarmth into the perfectly controlled climate of the interior; and in my case, this had brought the thought of my outside concerns with it, so that for a moment my mind had wandered again to thinking of Ellen.

I came back to awareness of the roundhouse, to see

Bill and Porniarsk both looking at me. Porniarsk had just said something. I could hear the echo of it still in my ear, but without, its meaning had vanished.

"What?" I asked.

"It's ready," said Porniarsk. "How do you feel—able to take this seventh assistance? You'll remember what I told you about the past increases not being limited? They each enlarge again with each new adaptation you make to the device. If you're near your limit of tolerance now, the effect of this last increase could be many times greater than what it is presently; and you might find yourself crippled in this vital, non-physical area before you had time to pull yourself back from it."

"I know, I know," I said. "Go ahead."

"I will, then," said Porniarsk. He reached with one of his shoulder tentacles to the console half behind him and touched a colored square.

For a second there was nothing. Then things began to expand dramatically. I mean that literally. It was as if the sides of my head were rushing out and out, enclosing everything about me . . . the roundhouse, the peak, the village, the whole area between the mistwalls that now enclosed me, all the other areas touching that area, the continent, the planet . . . there was no end. In addition, not only was I encompassing these things, but all of them were also growing and expanding. Not physically, but with meaning—acquiring many and many times their original aspects, properties, and values. So that I understood all of them in three dimensions, as it were, where I before had never seen more than a single facet of their true shape. Now, seen this way, all of them—all things, including me—were interconnected.

So I found my way back. With the thought of interconnection, I was once more in The Dream, back in the spider web spanning the universe. Only now there were patterns to its strands. I read those patterns clearly; and they brought me an inner peace for the first time. Because, at last, I saw what I could do, and how to do it, to still the storm locally. Not just in this little section of the earth around me, but all around our planet and moon and out into space for a distance beyond us, into the general temporal holocaust. I saw clearly that I would need more strength than I presently had; and the pattern I read showed that success would carry a price. A death-price.

The uncaring laws of the philosophical universe, in this situation, could balance gain against loss in only one unique equation. And that equation involved a cost of life.

But I was not afraid of death, I told myself, if the results could be achieved. After all, in a sense, I had been living on borrowed time since that first heart attack. I turned away from the patterns I was studying and looked deeper into the structure of the web itself, reaching for understanding of the laws by which it operated.

Gradually, that understanding came. Porniarsk had used the word "gestalt" in referring to that which he hoped I would perceive if I came to the situation here with a free and unprejudiced mind; and the word had jarred on me at the time. The avatar, we had all assumed, came from a race more advanced than ours—whether it was advanced in time or otherwise. I had taken it for granted that any twentieth-century human terms would be inadequate to explain whatever Porniarsk dealt with, and that he would avoid them for fear of creating misunderstandings.

—Besides, "gestalt" came close to having been one of the cant words of twentieth-century psychology; the sort of word that had been used and misused by people I knew, who wanted to sound knowledgable about a highly specialized subject they would never take the time to study properly and understand. Granted, the avatar was probably using the human word nearest in meaning to what he wanted to say, I had still felt he could have explained himself in more hard-edged technical or scientific terms.

But then, later, he had also used the word "monad"; and, remembering that, I now began to comprehend one important fact. The forces of the time storm and the device he was building so I could come to grips with them, belonged not so much to a physical, or even a psychological, but to a *philosphical* universe. I was far from understanding why this should be. In fact, with regard to the whole business, I was still like a child in kindergarten, learning about traffic lights without really comprehending the social and legal machinery behind the fact of their existence. But with the aid of the device, I had finally begun, at least, to get into the proper arena of perception.

Briefly and clumsily, in the area in which I would have to deal with the time storm, the only monads—that is, the

only basic, indestructible, building blocks or operators—
were individual minds. Each monad was capable of reflecting or expressing the whole universe from its individual
point of view. In fact, each monad had always potentially expressed—it; but the ability to do so had always
been a possible function, unless the individual monad-mind
had possessed something like a device-of-assistance to im-
plement or execute changes in what it expressed.

Of course, expressing a change in the universe, and
causing that change to take place, was not quite as simple
as wishing and making it so. For one thing, all monads involved in a particular expression of some part of the
universe at a particular moment were also involved with
each other and had to be in agreement on any change
they wished to express. For another, the change had to
originate in the point of view of a monad capable of reflecting all the physical—not just the philosophical—universe as plastic and controllable.

The time storm itself was a phenomenon of the physical
universe. In the limited terms to which Porniarsk was
restricted by our language, he had explained to me that it
was the result of entropic anarchy. The expanding universe had continued its expansion until a point of in-
tolerable strain on the network of forces that made up
the space-time fabric had been reached and passed. Then,
a breakdown had occurred. In effect, the space-time bubble had begun to disintegrate. Some of the galaxies that
had been moving outward, away from each other and the
universal center, producing a state of diminishing entropy,
began, in spot fashion, to fall back, contracting the universe and creating isolated states of increasing entropy.

The conflict between opposed entropic states had
spawned the time storm. As Porniarsk had said, the storm
as a whole was too massive for control by action of the
monads belonging to our original time, or even to his.
But a delaying action could be fought. The forces set
loose by the entropic conflict could be balanced against
each other here and there, thereby slowing down the
general anarchies enough to buy some breathing time, until the minds of those concerned with the struggle could
develop more powerful forces to put in play across the
connection between the philosophical and physical universes.

I was a single monad (though, of course, reinforced

with the other seven at their altered consoles), and not a particularly capable one basically. But I was also something of a freak, a lucky freak in that my freakiness apparently fitted the necessity of the moment. That was why I could think, as I was privately doing now, of creating an enclave in the time storm that would include the whole earth and its natural satellite, instead of merely an enclave containing just the few square miles surrounding us, which had been Porniarsk's hope.

"I'll need one more console adapted," I said to Porniarsk. "Don't worry, now. I can handle it."

"But there's no one to sit at it," said Bill.

"That's correct," said Porniarsk patiently. "There are only seven other adults in your party. I haven't any effectiveness as a monad. Neither has the little girl."

"She hasn't?" I looked hard at the avatar.

"Not . . . in effect," he said, with a rare second of hesitation. "A monad is required to have more than just a living intelligence and a personality. It has to have the capability of reflecting the universe. Wendy hasn't matured enough to do that. If you could ask her about it, and she could answer you, she'd say something to the effect that to her the universe isn't a defined entity. It's amorphous, unpredictable, capable of changing and surprising her at any moment. For her, the universe as she now sees it is more like a god or devil than a mechanism of natural laws—something she's got no hope of understanding or controlling."

"All right," I said. "I'll settle for the fact she's at least partially a monad."

"There's no such thing," said Porniarsk. "A monad either is, or is not. In any case, even if she was a partial monad, a partial monad is incapable of helping you."

"What about when it's combined with another partial monad?"

"What other partial monad?" Bill asked.

"The Old Man, down at the village."

"This is even worse than your idea of using Wendy," said Porniarsk. For the first time since we'd met him, the tone of his voice came close to betraying irritation with one of us. "The experimentals down below us are artificially created animals. The very concept of 'universe' is beyond them. They're only bundles of reflexes, conditioned and trained."

"All but one of them," I said. "Porniarsk, don't forget there're a lot of things I can see now with the help of the seven sets you've already produced, even if they don't have monads in connection with them yet. One of those things is that the Old Man may have been bred in a test tube—or whatever they all came from—but he's got some kind of concept of 'universe,' even if it's limited to his village and a mile or so of the rock around it. When we first came in here and passed the initial test of their attack, all the rest of them immediately took us for granted. Not the Old Man. By design or chance, he's got something individual to measure new things against, plus whatever it takes to make new decisions on the basis of that measurement. And you can't deny he's adult."

No one said anything for a moment.

"I don't think," said Bill at last, "that Marie's going to like Wendy being hooked up to something like the Old Man."

"Wendy won't be. They'll both just be hooked in with all the rest of us. Anyway, I'll explain it to Marie."

"How'll you get the Old Man to cooperate?"

"He doesn't have to cooperate," I said. "I'll bring him up here, connect him to one of the consoles and chain him to it with Sunday's chain. Then give him a day or two to get used to the feel of assistance, and his being in connection with my mind. Once he feels the advantages these things give him, my bet is he'll get over being scared and become interested."

"If you use force to bring him up here," said Porniarsk, "you'll undoubtedly trigger off the antagonisms of his fellow experimentals."

"I think I can do it without," I said. "I've got an idea."

With that, I left the two of them and went back down to our camp, which was set up at the foot of the peak. I unchained Sunday and went looking for Marie. Sunday could only be trusted to stick around the camp when I was there. He had shown no particularly strong hunting instincts before in all the time I had known him; but for some reason the experimentals seemed to fascinate him. Since the first day of our camp at the foot of the hill, when I had caught him stalking one of the village inhabitants who was out hunting among the rocks, we had kept him chained up when I was up on the peak. It was possible he might not have hurt the experimental, but the sight I had had of him, creeping softly along, belly almost dragging the ground and tail a-twitch, was too vivid to forget.

At any rate, now I let him loose, and he butted his head against me and rubbed himself against my legs all the time I was looking for Marie. I found her, with Wendy, down at the creek by the foot of the peak, doing some washing.

It was not the time to mention that I wanted Wendy at one of the consoles. The little girl had come to trust me; and—I don't care how male and solitary you are—if a small child decides to take to you, you have to carry your own instincts somewhere outside the normal spectrum not to feel some sort of emotional response. Anything unexpected or new tended to frighten Wendy; and any concern or doubt about it by her mother made the fright certain. The idea would have to be presented to Wendy gently, and with Marie's cooperation. I spoke to Marie now, instead, about the other matter I had in mind.

"Have you got any of that brandy left?" I asked.

She put down in a roaster pan some jeans of Wendy's she was wringing out and shook her hands to get the excess water off. She had her own slacks rolled up above her knees and her legs and feet bare so that she could wade into the creek. The work had pinkened her face and tousled her hair. She looked, not exactly younger, but more relaxed and happy than usual; and for a second I felt sad that I had not been able to love her after all, instead of Ellen.

"What's the occasion?" she asked.

"No occasion," I said. "I'm hoping to bait the Old Man in the village down there, so I can get him up to the roundhouse. We want to try him with the consoles. You do have some brandy left?"

"Yes," she said. "How much do you want?"

"One full bottle ought to be plenty," I said. "Is there that much?"

"I've got several full bottles," she said. "Do you want it right away, or can I finish up here first?"

"I'd like to get down to the village before dark."

"I'll be done in five minutes."

"Fine, then," I said and sat down on a boulder to wait. It took her closer to fifteen than five minutes, as it turned out, but there was still at least an hour or so of sunset left. We went back to the camper; she got me an un-

opened bottle of brandy, and I walked down to the village
with it.

The whole thing was a gamble. I had no idea what kind
of body chemistry the experimentals had. From what
Porniarsk had said, they had evidently been developed by
future humans from ape stock; chimpanzee at a guess.
The larger part of their diet seemed to be some sort of
artificially prepared eatable in a cube form that came
from inside one of the dome-shaped buildings. But since
the building was small, and the supply of the cubes seemed
to be inexhaustible, I had guessed that there was some
kind of underground warehouse to which the building
was merely an entrance. However, in addition to the
cubes, the experimentals were at least partly carnivorous.
They went out into the rocks around the village in the
daytime to hunt small rodent-like animals with their
throwing knives; and these they either ate raw on the spot
or carried back into their buildings at the village to be
eaten at leisure.

All these things seemed to add up to the strong possibility that they had digestive systems and metabolisms
pretty similar to a human's. But there was no way of
being sure. All I could do was try.

The Old Man was not out in the open when I first
walked into the village, but before I was half a dozen steps
down the main street, he had emerged from his dwelling
to hunker down in front of his doorway and stare at me
steadily as I approached. I detoured along the way to
pick up a couple of handleless cups or small bowls that
one of the local workmen was turning out on his machine.
I'd thought earlier of bringing a couple of containers from
our camp, then decided the Old Man would be more
likely to trust utensils that were familiar to him. I came
up to within ten feet of him, sat down cross-legged on
the hard-packed, stony dirt of the street, and got my bottle from the inner jacket pocket in which I had been carrying it.

I put both cups down, poured a little brandy into both
of them, picked up one, sipped from it and started staring
back at him.

It was not the most lively cocktail hour on record. I
pretended to drink, pouring as little as possible into my
cup each time, and putting somewhat more into the other
cup, which slowly began to fill. The Old Man kept staring

at me; apparently, he was capable of keeping it up without blinking as long as the daylight lasted. Eventually, even the small amounts of liquor with which I was wetting my tongue began to make themselves felt. I found myself talking. I told the Old Man what fine stuff it was I was drinking, and I invited him to help himself. I speculated on the interesting discoveries he would make if he only joined me and became friendly.

He continued to stare.

Eventually, the other cup was as full as it could safely be, and the sun was almost down. There was nothing more I could do. I left the cups and the bottle with the top off and got to my feet.

"Pleasant dreams," I said to him, and left. Back once more in the rocks a safe distance from the village, I got out my field glasses and peered down in the direction of his building. It was almost dark, and one thing the experimentals did not have was artificial lighting. They all disappeared into their buildings at dusk and only reappeared with the dawn. But by straining my vision now, I was able to make out a dim figure still in front of the Old Man's building. I squinted through the binoculars, my eyes beginning to water; and, just as I was about to give up, I caught a tiny glint of light on something moving.

It was the bottle, being upended in the general area of the Old Man's head. I gave an inward, silent whoop of joy. Unless he had decided to use the brandy for a shampoo, or unless he turned out to have a body that reacted to alcohol as if it was so much branch water, I had him.

I waited until the moon came up, then got the pickup and drove by moonlight down through the main street of the village to the Old Man's building. I took an unlit flashlight and went in the building entrance. Inside, I turned the flashlight on and found the Old Man. He was curled up in the corner of the single room that was the building's interior on a sort of thick rug. He reeked of brandy, and was dead drunk.

He was also no lightweight. I had not thought it to look at him, for all the experimentals looked small and skinny by human standards; but apparently they were nothing but bone and muscle. Still, I managed to carry him out to the pickup and get him inside the cab. Then I drove back out of the village to the camp.

At the camp, I took him out of the pickup, unchained Sunday and put him in the pickup, put the chain and collar on the Old Man and lifted him, still snoozing, into one of the jeeps. By this time, I was surrounded by people wanting to know what I was doing.

"I want to try him out on the equipment up at the roundhouse," I said. "He drank almost a full bottle of brandy, and he ought to sleep until morning, but with all this noise he may just wake up. Now, will you let me get him put away up there? Then I'll come down and tell you all about it."

"We already had dinner," said Wendy.

"Hush," said Marie to her, "Marc'll have his dinner when he gets back. You're coming right back down?"

"In twenty minutes at the outside," I said.

I turned on the lights of the jeep and growled up the hillside in low gear. The partitions between the consoles had supports that were anchored in the concrete floor of the roundhouse; and I chained the sleeping Old Man to one of these. As an afterthought, I took from the jeep the canteen of drinking water we always kept with each of the vehicles and left it beside him. If he got drunk like a human, he was likely to have a hangover like a human.

Then I growled my way back down again to the camp to turn Sunday loose, answer questions, and have my dinner.

To everybody except Porniarsk and Bill, who already knew what I had in mind, I explained my capture of the Old Man with a half-truth, saying I wanted to see if he could be useful as a partial monad when we tried to use the equipment in the roundhouse, the day after tomorrow. It was not until later that evening, in the privacy of the camper, after Wendy was asleep, that I talked to Marie about using the little girl at one of the consoles. Surprisingly, Marie thought it was a very good idea. She said Wendy had no one to play with but the dogs, and she had been wanting badly to get in on what the adults were doing.

19

I slept that night, but I did not rest. As soon as I closed my eyes I was off among the strands of the spider web, riding the shifting forces of the time storm about our world. I scuttled about, studying them. I already knew what I would have to do. Every so often, for a transitory moment, the forces in this area I had chosen came close to a situation of internal balance. If, at just the right moment, I could throw all the force controlled by the eight other monads and myself against the tangle of conflicting forces that was the storm, hopefully I could nudge this tiny corner of the storm into a state of dynamic balance.

Why do I say "hopefully"? I knew I could do it—if only Wendy and the Old Man, under the assistance of the device, would give me amplification enough to act as an eighth monad. For it was not power I needed but understanding. As clearly as I could see the forces now, I needed to see them many times more clearly, in much finer detail. Close in, focused down to the local area which was all that Porniarsk had envisioned me bringing into balance, my vision was sharp enough. But on wider focus, when I looked further out into the time storm, the fine detail was lost. One more monad and I could bring those distant, fuzzy forces into clarity.

It was merely a matter of waiting until morning, I told myself, finally, and made myself put the whole problem out of my head. At my bidding, it went; which was something such a problem would never have done a week before. But then another thought came to perch on my mind like a black crow.

I was aware I had never been what the world used to call a kind or moral man, a "good" man, as my grand-

father would have said. I had always let myself do pretty
much what I wanted, within practical limits; and I had
never been particularly caring, or concerned for other
people. But ethical laws are a part of any philosophical
universe; they have to be. And was it entirely in agreement with those laws, now, my carrying these eight other
people—nine, if you counted the Old Man as being in the
people category—into a joust with something as monstrous as the time storm, only because of my own hunger
to know and do?

Granted, I could not see any way in which they could
be hurt. The only one I was putting on the line, as far as I
knew, was myself. But there are always understandings
beyond understandings. Perhaps there was some vital bit
of information I did not have.

On the other hand, perhaps that was not really what
was bothering me. I looked a little deeper into myself
and found the real fishhook in my conscience; the un-
answered question of whether, even if I knew there was
real danger to the others, I would let that be reason
enough to stop me. Perhaps I would go ahead anyway,
prepared to sacrifice them to my own desires, my own
will.

This question was harder to put out of my mind than
the time storm problem, but in the end, I managed. I lay,
open-eyed and without moving, until the dawn whitened
the shade drawn over the window on the side of the
camper across from the bunk on which I lay with Marie.

I got up and dressed quietly. Marie slept on, but Wendy
opened her eyes and looked at me.

"Go back to sleep," I told her. She closed her eyes
again without argument. (Probably only humoring me, I
thought.)

Dressed, I glanced at Marie, half-tempted to wake
her and say a few words to her. But there was no good
reason for that, I realized, unless I only wanted to leave
her with some enigmatic, but portentous, statement she
could remember afterwards and worry over, wondering if
she could have done something more for me in some way;
and things might have been different. I was a little
ashamed of myself and let myself out of the camper as
softly as I could.

Outside, the morning air was dry and cold. I shivered,

even under the leather jacket I was wearing, and fired up
the coleman stove to make a pot of coffee. All the time I
was making it, I could feel the Old Man's presence in the
back of my mind. He was connected to the console, which
meant he was in connection with me. I could feel that he
was awake now and suffering from the hangover I had
anticipated. The discomfort was making him savage—I
could tell that, too. But underneath the savagery he was
beginning to wonder a little at what his mind could now
sense of me, and through me, of the larger universe.

I made my coffee, drank it, and drove one of the jeeps
to the roundhouse. Inside, around where the Old Man
had been, it was a mess. He had been sick—I should have
thought of the possibility of that. In addition, he had
urinated copiously.

I cleaned up, cautiously. Now that he was awake, I
had enough respect for those ape-like arms of his not to
let him get a grip on me. But he let me work on until I
was right next to him, without making any move in my
direction. He was still staring at me all the time, but now
there was a speculative gleam in his brown eyes. He had
now realized who it was his mind connected to. I could
feel him in my head, exploring the connection and the
situation. I had guessed right. Now, he was interested.
But his mind was still alien to me, much more alien than
Porniarsk's.

I took a chance, disconnected him from the console,
unhooked his chain from the stanchion, and led him outside, to ensure that any further eliminations he was moved
to would take place somewhere else than in the roundhouse. I found a boulder too heavy for him to move and
with a lower half that was narrower than the top, so that
the loop of chain I locked around it could not be pulled
off over the top. I rechained him to this. The boulder was
on the far side of the roundhouse, so that he could neither
see his village nor be seen from it, assuming that his fellows down there had distance vision good enough to pick
him out. Then I left him with some bread, an opened can
of corned beef and a refilled canteen of water, and went
down to my own breakfast. He let me go without a sound,
but his eyes followed me with their speculative look as
long as I was in sight. All the way down the mountain, I
could feel his mind trying to explore mine.

Once back at the camp, I got out the binoculars and looked over the village. Its inhabitants were out of their homes and about their daily activities. None of them seemed to be missing the Old Man or showing any curiosity about the lack of his presence. That much was all right, then. I went back, put the binoculars away and ate breakfast. All the others were up and also breakfasting; but there was a tension, a taut feeling in the very air of the camp.

I did not feel like talking to anyone; and the rest seemed to understand this. They left me alone while I was eating—all but Sunday, who clearly sensed that something unusual was up. He did not rub against me in his usual fashion, but prowled around and around me, his tail twitching as if his nerves were on fire. He made such an ominous demonstration that I was alarmed for Bill, when at last, he started to come toward me.

But Sunday drew back just enough to let him get close, although he circled the two of us, eyeing Bill steadily and making little occasional singing noises in his throat.

"I don't want to bother you," Bill said. His voice was hardly more than a murmur, too low for any of the others to overhear.

"It's all right," I said. "What is it?"

"I just wanted you to know," he said, "you can count on me."

"Well," I said, "thanks."

"No, I really mean *count* on me," he insisted.

"I hear you," I said. "Thanks. But all you'll have to do today is sit at that console and let me use you."

He looked back at me for a second in a way that was almost as keyed-up and strange as Sunday's present behavior.

"Right," he said and went off.

I had no time to puzzle over him. There was Sunday to get into the cab of the pickup and the doors safely closed on him; and the leopard was just not agreeable to going in this morning. In the end I had to haul him in as a dead weight, swearing at him, with one fist closed on the scruff of his neck and my other arm around his wedge-shaped cat chest below his forelegs. I didn't dare have any of the others help me in the mood the leopard was in —even the girl. Though, in fact, she was busy at the moment, doing something in the motor home with Marie

—and she probably would not have come anyway if I'd
called.

I finally got Sunday in and the door closed. Immediately he found himself trapped, he began to thrash around
and call to me. I closed my ears to the sounds he was
making and got my party into the jeeps and headed up
the side of the peak. I was already at work with the back
of my head, monitoring the present interplay of the forces
in the storm, as far as I could pick them out. A real
picture of the pattern out as far as the Moon's orbit
would have to wait until the others were all at their
consoles and connected with me. I thought I was gaining
some advantage from them already, which was a very
good sign. Either I had been building psychic muscle since
the last two consoles had been finished, or the Old Man
was proving to be even more useful than I had hoped.
Actually, in one way, he had already exceeded expectations; because I was still as strongly linked to him as I
had been when he had been connected to the console and
chained inside the roundhouse.

Wendy, who had been chattering away merry and
bright in the back of the jeep I was driving, fell into
dubious silence as we pulled up to the level spot where
the roundhouse stood and she saw the Old Man staring at
us. But he only gave her and the others a single surveying
glance and then came back to concentrate on me as I got
out of the jeep and came back toward him.

He knew where I was going to take him. He came
along almost eagerly when I unlocked the chain and led
him to the roundhouse door. It slid aside automatically as
we got within arm's length of it, and he went over the
threshold ahead of me with a bound, headed toward his
console. I took him to it and chained him on a short
length of the chain, so that he could not reach around the
partition to whoever would be at the console next to him.

Bill followed me in and blocked the door open to the
outer air, as we had got in the habit of doing. The others
followed him. They began to take their places under
Porniarsk's direction and let themselves be connected to
their consoles. The dark material clung to itself when one
end of it was loosely wrapped around the throat. The
further end of it reached through the face of the console
to touch the pattern of blocks inside. It was so simple as
to seem unbelievable, except for the fact that the strap

had a mild, built-in warmth to it. It was a semi-living thing, Porniarsk had told me. All the connections in the roundhouse were made with such semi-living objects. They operated like psychic channels. If you imagine the tube through which a blood transfusion is being given, as being alive and capable of making its own connection with the blood systems of the two people involved in the transfusion, you have an analogous picture.

The straps were vaguely comforting to wear, like a security blanket. I noticed Wendy brighten up for the first time since seeing the Old Man, when hers was wrapped around her throat by Bill. There was one waiting for me at the monitoring station in the middle of the room; but I wanted to try seeing what kind of connection I could have with the other monads without it, before I strapped myself in.

Bill and Porniarsk strapped in the others, then Bill strapped himself in, and Porniarsk went to the monitoring station. He reached with one tentacle for the colored square on the console there that activated all connections. His tentacle flicked down to touch the square, and the connection already established between myself and the Old Man suddenly came alive with our mutual understanding of what would happen when activation took place.

The Old Man howled.

His vocal capabilities were tremendous. All of us in the roundhouse were half-deafened by the sound, which rang like a fire siren in our ears, and broadcast itself outward from the propped-open door. In that same second, Porniarsk's tentacle touched the surface of the square, and the connections were activated. Full contact with all the other monads there erupted around me; and full perception of the time storm forces out of Moon orbit distance smashed down on me like a massive wall of water. The Old Man's howl was cut off in mid-utterance. I found my body running for the roundhouse door.

For with contact had come full understanding of what the Alpha Prime had done, and what he had been trying to do. I burst out of the roundhouse and looked down the steep, bouldered face of the peak that fell toward the village. The lower edge of it was alive with black, climbing bodies.

How the Old Man had contacted them, I did not
know. His connection with me and the console had made
it possible, that was obvious; but he had used channels of
identity with his own people that were not part of my
own, human machinery. The most I could understand was
that he had not actually called them, in a true sense. He
had only been able to provoke an uneasiness in them that
had sent most of them out hunting among the lower rocks,
in the direction of the peak.

But now they had heard him. Lost somewhere in the
gestalt of the monad group of which he and I were a
part—Porniarsk had been right in his use of that word,
for the group, myself and this place were all integrated
into a whole now—the Old Man's mind was triumphant.
He knew that he had called in time, that his people had
heard and were coming.

I whirled around and stared back into the roundhouse
through the open door, though I already knew what I
would see. Inside, all the figures were motionless and
silent. There was not even a chest-movement of breathing
to be seen in any of them, for they were caught in a
timeless moment—the moment in which we had contacted
the storm and I had paused to examine the pattern of its
forces. Even Porniarsk was frozen into immobility with
his tentacle-tip touching his activation square on the monitor console. The square itself glowed now, with a soft,
pink light.

I was still unconnected and mobile. But the Old Man's
people would be here in twenty minutes; and all our weapons were down at the camp.

I watched my body turn and run for the nearest jeep,
leap into it, start it, turn it, and get it going down the
slope toward camp. I had the advantage of a vehicle, but
the distance was twice as much, down to camp, than it
was up the slope the experimentals were climbing, and
twice as far back up again. The jeep bounced and slid
down the shallower slope on this side of the peak, skidding
and slewing around the larger boulders in the way. My
body drove it; but my mind could not stay with it, because I had already seen enough of the present moment's
pattern to locate the upcoming pressure point I searched
for. That pressure point would be coming into existence
in no more time than it would take the villagers to climb

to the roundhouse, possibly, even in less time. I had that long only to study all the force lines involved and make sure that my one chance to produce a state of balance was taken exactly on the mark.

20

It was not the pattern of forces in the time storm itself I studied; but the image of this pattern in the philosophical universe during that fractional, timeless moment when I had first tapped the abilities of our full monad-gestalt. That image was like a three-dimensional picture taken by a camera with a shutter speed beyond imagination. Already, of course, the configuration of the forces in the storm had developed, through a whole series of changes, into totally different patterns, and they were continuing to change. But with the gestalt and the device to back me up, I could study the configuration that had been and calculate how the later patterns would be at any other moment in the future.

In any such pattern—past, present, or future—the time storm forces of any given area had to have the potential of developing into a further state of dynamic balance. The potential alone, however, was not good enough. To begin with, the forces had to be very close to balance, within a very small tolerance indeed; otherwise, the relatively feeble strength of my gestalt would not be able to push them into balance.

But first, the imbalances to be corrected must be understood in detail. Balance was an ideal state; and the chances of it occurring naturally were as small as the total time storm itself was large. The only reason it was barely possible to achieve it artificially lay in a characteristic of the time storm itself; the storm's tendency to break up progressively into smaller and smaller patterns and for these to break up in turn, and so on. This was the same characteristic that Porniarsk had mentioned as presenting the greatest danger of the storm if it was not fought and opposed. The continuing disintegration would continue to

191

produce smaller and smaller temporal anomalies until, at
last, any single atomic particle would be existing at a different temporal moment than its neighbor. But in this
case, it offered an advantage in that the disintegration
process produced smaller temporal anomalies within larger ones, like miniature hurricanes in the calms that were
the eyes of larger ones; and so, by choosing the right
moment to act, it was possible to balance the forces of a
small, contained anomaly, without having to deal with the
continuing imbalanced forces of a larger disturbance containing it.

Of course, the word "hurricane" did not really convey
the correct image of a temporal anomaly. In its largest
manifestation, such an anomaly represented the enormous
forces released in intergalactic space along the face of
contact between an expanding galaxy and a contracting
one. Here on earth, in its smallest—so far—manifestation,
it was an area such as the one we and the experimentals
were inhabiting now, with the conflicting forces existing
where the mistwalls marked their presence. Temporally,
the mistwalls were areas of tremendous activity. Physically, as we had discovered, they were no more than bands
of lightly disturbed air and suspended dust, stretching up
from the surface of the earth until they came into conflict
with other forces of their same "hurricane."

In my philosophical image of the apparent walls that
were time storm force-lines, I saw them in cross-section,
so that they seemed like a web of true lines filling a three-
dimensional space, the interstices between lines being the
chunks of four-dimensional space they enclosed. Seen
close up, the lines looked less like threads than like rods of
lightning frozen in the act of striking. Whatever this appearance represented of their real properties in the physical universe, the fact was clear that they moved and were
moved by the other force-lines with which they interacted;
so that they developed continually from one pattern to another, in constant rearrangement, under the push of the
current imbalance.

I already knew in what general direction the patterns
in the area I was concerned with were developing. But
now I projected these developments, studying the parade
of succeeding configurations for specific details, looking
for one that would give me a possibility of forcing a

balanced pattern into existence before the experimentals arrived at the roundhouse. I could not do this until I had returned with weapons and driven off the figures now climbing the peak, for the good reason that the pattern showed me the development of affairs here, as well as the larger picture. I alone, even with guns, would not be able to drive off those who were coming. There were more than a hundred of them; and this time they would not give up as easily as they had before. They had been conditioned to ignore the roundhouse. Now, somehow, the Old Man had managed to break that conditioning. The only thing that would stop them would be fright at some great natural event. A volcanic eruption, an earthquake—or the meteorological reaction when the mistwall through which we had entered went out of existence, and the atmosphere of the area on its far side suddenly mixed with the atmosphere on this.

I must get down, get weapons, get back up, and hold them off long enough to use the gestalt successfully to produce balance in the pattern. My mind galloped past the developing patterns, checking, checking, checking; and as it went, the jeep under me was skidding and plunging down the slope to our camp.

I slid in between our tents, at last, in a cloud of dust and stopped. I jumped out of the jeep, unlocked the door of the motor home, and plunged inside.

Warm from the hot, still atmosphere within, the guns were where we always kept them, in the broom closet, with the ammunition on a shelf above. I grabbed two shotguns and the two heaviest rifles, with ammo. But when I reached for the machine pistol, it was not there.

I spent, perhaps, a couple of frantic minutes looking for it in improbable places about the motorhome, before I finally admitted to myself that it was gone. Who could have managed to get into the vehicle, which Marie and I kept locked religiously except when one of us was in it, was something there was no time to puzzle about now. With its extendable stock collapsed, the weapon was light and small enough to be carried under a heavy piece of outer clothing by either man or woman—and most of us going up to the roundhouse this morning had worn either a jacket or a bulky sweater. I got out of the motorhome in a hurry, not even bothering to lock it behind me. I made the driver's seat of the jeep in one jump, gunned the still-running motor and headed back up the slope of the peak.

I was perhaps a hundred and fifty yards from the camp when the dead silence that had existed there registered. Sunday had been back there all the time I was getting the guns, locked up in the cab of the pickup. But I had not heard a sound from him, in spite of the fact that he must have heard the jeep arrive, and seen, heard, and possibly even smelled me. He should have been putting up as much racket as he could, in an effort to make me come and let him out. But there had been no noise at all.

I drove another twenty yards or so before I gave in to the suddenly empty, sick feeling inside me. Then, I wrenched the jeep around and roared back down to the camp to the pickup.

I did not need to get out of the jeep to look at it. I did not even need to get close. From twenty feet away, I could see the windshield of the pickup lying on the hood of the vehicle like a giant's lost spectacle lens. Somehow, Sunday had managed to pop it completely out of its frame. And he was gone.

I knew where he was gone. I got the field glasses and looked off up the steep slope leading directly to the round-house, where the tiny black figures of the experimentals could now be seen more than halfway up. Down below them, I saw nothing for a moment—and then there was a flash of movement. It was Sunday, headed to join me on top, where he must have believed me to be, not travelling by the roundabout, easy slope I had come down in the jeep, but directly up the mountainside on a converging route with those from the village below.

He would keep coming. If the experimentals did not get in his way, he would simply pass them up. But if they tried to stop him, he would kill as long as he could until he was killed himself. But he would keep coming.

The idiotic, loving beast! There was nothing but death for him where he was headed; but even if he had known that, it would not have stopped him. There was nothing I could do for him now. I could not even take time out to think of him. There were eight people and a world to think of.

I ripped the jeep around and headed up the slope. The best I could do; the longer distance before me would make it a tossup whether I could get back to the round-house before the experimentals arrived.

I had the upcoming patterns of the time storm in my head now. I could see the one I wanted developing. It was not an absolutely sure thing, so far; but it was as close to a sure thing as I could wish for in limited time, such as we had now. It would form within seconds after I made the top of the peak and the roundhouse.

There was nothing more I could do now but drive. In the roundhouse the others were still immobile—even the Old Man—caught up in the gestalt. I gave most of my attention to the ground ahead.

It was the best driving I had ever done. I was tearing hell out the jeep, but if it lasted to the top of the peak that was all I asked of it. I did not lose any time, but what I gained—the best I could gain—was only seconds. When I did reach the level top and the roundhouse at last, the experimentals were not yet there.

I skidded the jeep to a stop beside the door of the roundhouse and tossed one rifle, one shotgun, and most of the ammunition inside. Then I pulled the block that was holding the door open—and all this time, the storm pattern I was waiting for was coming up in my mind—stepped back, and the door closed automatically. The experimentals did not have doors to buildings. Perhaps they did not know what a door was and would think, see-ing this one closed, that there was no entrance into the roundhouse. If they did by accident trigger the door to opening, those inside would have the other two guns which, one way or the other, they would be awake and ready to use; for in a moment I would either win or lose, and the gestalt would be set free again.

I watched the door close and turned just in time to see the first round, ape-like head come over the edge of the cliff-edge, some forty yards away. I snatched up the rifle and had it halfway to my shoulder when I realized I would never fire it. There was no time now. The moment and the pattern I waited for were rushing down upon me. I had no more mind to spare for killing. Still standing with the rifle half-raised, I went back into the pattern; meanwhile, as if through the wrong end of a telescope, I was seeing the black figure come all the way up into view and advance, and other black figures appear one by one behind him, until there were four of them coming steadily toward me, not poising the knives they held to throw, but holding them purposely by the hilt, as if they wanted to make sure of finishing me off.

It was the final moment. I saw the pattern I had waited for ready to be born. I felt the strength of my monad gestalt; and at last, I knew certainly that what I was about to try would work. The four experimentals were more than halfway to me; and now I could understand clearly how the indications I had read had been correct. I would be able to do what I had wanted; and with the windstorm that would follow the disappearance of the mistwalls, the experimentals would panic and retreat. But the cost of all this would be my life. I had expected it to be so.

I stood waiting for the experimentals, the pattern rushing down upon me. In the last seconds, a different head poked itself over the edge of the cliff, and a different body came leaping toward me. It was Sunday, too late.

The pattern I awaited exploded into existence. I thrust, with the whole gestalt behind me. The fabric of the time storm about me staggered, trembled and fell together—locked into a balance of forces. And awareness of all things vanished from me, like the light of a blown-out lamp.

21

The world came back to me, little by little. I was conscious of a warm wind blowing across me. I could feel it on my face and hands; I could feel it tugging at my clothes. It was stiff, but no hurricane. I opened my eyes and saw streamers of cloud torn to bits scudding across the canvas of a blue sky, moving visibly as I watched. I felt the hard and pebbled ground under my body and head; and a pressure, like a weight, on the upper part of my right thigh.

I sat up. I was alive—and unhurt. Before me, out beyond the cliff-edge where the experimentals had appeared, there was no more mistwall—only sky and distant, very distant landscape. I looked down and saw the four black bodies on the ground, strung out almost in a line. None of them moved; and when I looked closer I saw clearly how badly they had been torn by teeth and claws. I looked further down, yet, at the weight on my thigh, and saw Sunday.

He lay with his head stretched forward to rest on my leg, and one of the leaf-shaped knives was stuck, half-buried in the big muscle behind his left shoulder. Behind him, there was perhaps fifteen feet of bloody trail where he had half-crawled, half-dragged himself to me. His jaws were partly open, the teeth and gums red-stained with blood that was not his own. His eyes were closed. The lids did not stir, nor his jaws move. He lay still.

"Sunday?" I said. But he was not there to hear me.

There was nothing I could do. I picked up his torn head, somehow, in my arms and held it to me. There was just nothing I could do. I closed my own eyes and sat there holding him for quite a while. Finally, there were sounds around me; I opened my eyes again and looked up

to see that the others, released now that the gestalt was
ended, had come out of the roundhouse and were standing
around looking at the new world. Marie was standing
over me.

Tek and Ellen were off by themselves some thirty
yards from the roundhouse. He had turned the jeep
around and evidently pulled it off a short distance in a
start back down the side of the peak. But for some
reason he had stopped again and was getting back out
of the driver's seat, holding one of the rifles, probably
the one I had thrown into the roundhouse, tucked loosely
in the crook of his right elbow, barrel down. Ellen was
already out of the jeep and standing facing him a few
steps off.

"You go," she was saying to him. "I can't now. He
doesn't even have Sunday now."

I remembered how much Sunday had meant to her in
those first days after I had found her. And how he had put
up with her more than I ever would have expected. But
she had always been fond of him. And I—I had taken
him for granted. Because he was mad. Crazy, crazy, insane cat. But what difference does it make why the love's
there, as long as it is? Only I'd never known how much of
my own heart I'd given back to him until this day and
hour.

Ellen was walking away from Tek and the jeep now.

"Come back," Tek said to her.

She did not answer. She walked past me and into the
roundhouse through the door that was once more propped
open. In the relative shadow of the artificially lit interior,
she seemed to vanish.

Tek's face twisted and went savage.

"Don't try anything," said Bill's voice, tightly.

I looked to the other side of me and saw him there. He
was pale-faced, but steady, holding one of the shotguns.
The range was a little long for accuracy with a shotgun;
but Bill held it purposefully.

"Get out if you want," he told Tek. "But don't try anything."

Tek seemed to sag all over. His shoulders drooped; the
rifle barrel sagged downward. All the savageness leaked
out of him, leaving him looking defenseless.

"All right," he said, in an empty voice.

He started to turn away toward the jeep. Bill sighed

and let the shotgun drop butt-downward to the earth; so that he held it, almost leaning on the barrel of it, wearily. Tek turned back, suddenly, the rifle barrel coming up to point at me.

Bill snatched up the shotgun, too slowly. But in the same second, there was the yammer of the machine pistol from inside the roundhouse, and Ellen walked out again holding the weapon and firing as she advanced. Tek, flung backward by the impact of the slugs, bounced off the side of the jeep and slid to the ground, the rifle tumbling from his hands.

Ellen walked a good dozen steps beyond me. But then she slowed and stopped. Tek was plainly dead. She dropped the machine pistol as if her hands had forgotten they held it; and she turned to come back to me.

Marie had been standing unmoving, close to me all this time. But when Ellen was only a step or two away, Marie moved back and away out of my line of vision. Ellen knelt beside me and put her arms around both me and the silent head I was still holding.

"It'll be all right," she said. "It's all going to be all right. You wait and see."

22

We had won. In fact, the world had won, for the freezing of the movement of the time lines into a state of dynamic balance was complete for the immediate area of our planet. But for me, personally, after that there followed a strange time, the first part of which I was not really all there in my head and the second part of which, I was most earnestly trying to get out of my head.

It was left to the others to pick up the pieces and deal with the period of adjustment to the new physical state of affairs, which they did by themselves. Of the months immediately following the moment of change at the station, I have no clear memory. It was a period of time in which days and nights shuttered about me, light and dark, light and dark, like frames on a film strip. Spring ran into summer, summer into fall, and fall into winter, without any real meaning for me. When the cold months came, I would have still sat outside in jeans and a tank top if the girl or Marie had not dressed me to suit the temperature; and I would probably have starved to death if they had not put food in front of me and stood over me to see that I ate it.

My reality during that time was all inside my skull, in a universe where the grey fog of indifference only lifted to a sharp awareness of psychic pain and guilt. Sunday had loved me—the only thing in the world that ever had—and I had killed him.

Porniarsk had worked a piece of technological magic almost immediately, out of knowledge from the time and place of his original avatar; but it did not help the way I felt. He had created some kind of force-field enclosure, in which Sunday's stabbed and slain body was held in stasis —a sort of non-cryogenic preserving chamber. He could

not bring Sunday back to life, Porniarsk told me; but as
long as time had become a variable for us, there was
always the chance that, eventually, we would contact
someone with the knowledge to do it. He told me this
many times, repeating himself patiently to get the information through the fog about me. But I did not believe
him; and, after the first time, I refused to go anywhere
near the black-furred body lying still, inside its glass-like
energy shell.

The core of my guilt, though none of the rest suspected
it, lay in the knowledge of my responsibility for Sunday's
death—and something more. The further element was
part of the knowledge that I had always failed with any
person or thing who had tried to get close to me. It was a
fact of my experience; and, buried behind it all this time,
had been the darker suspicion that when I could not turn
love away from me, I would always at least manage to
destroy its vehicle. Now, in my awareness of my own
responsibility for the death of Sunday, I had confirmed
that suspicion.

The confirmation was my own private purgatory. No
one, not even Porniarsk, seemed to suspect that I might
have, subconsciously, used the moment of coming to grips
with the time storm to rid myself of the one creature who
embarrassed me with an affection I lacked the personal
machinery to return. But I myself knew the truth. I knew
—and I woke fresh to the knowledge every morning. I
sat with it through days of the months that followed and
went to sleep with it at night.

As I saw it, my sin was not one of simple, but of
calculated, omission. Which made it one of commission instead. It printed itself as a damning question on the clouds
above me in the daytime and glowed, invisible to all eyes
but mine, on the darkness of the ceiling above me, at
night. If I could read the factors of the time storm, the
question ran—and I had been able—then why hadn't I
also taken a moment to puzzle out the factors of human
and animal interaction that had led to the deaths of Tek
and Sunday?

I had not done so, the whisper inside me repeated night
and day, because I had wanted them dead. Particularly, I
had wanted Sunday dead; for if he continued to exist and
follow me about, eventually the other humans would discover that there was an emptiness in me where a heart

ought to be. Then it would strike them that I could never care two cents for them either; and they would turn on me because who could be safe with someone like me around?

So, I told myself all this through something like a year and a half following the time storm; and in the telling I skirted the grey edge of insanity, because I could not stand myself as I now knew myself to be. It was a grim trick of fate that had sent me into life lacking the one necessary, invisible part that would have made me human, rather than some flesh and blood robot. Inside my mind, I pounded on walls, screaming at the unfairness of circumstances, that had taken me out of a situation where I had not known what an emotional cripple I was and brought me face to face with the fact of it.

For that was what had happened. Beginning with my mental explosion, when I had found out that Swannee was gone—dead and gone, gone forever—there had been a string of small confrontations. A series of little turns which gradually turned me about one hundred and eighty degrees, until at last I saw myself full-on in the mirror of my mind and stared at the metal bones shining through my plastic skin, the glow of the light bulbs artificially illuminating the polished caverns of my eyesockets. It was then I realized what had been going on in my unconscious all along.

Only Swannee had known me for the essentially nonhuman I was. Her reaction to that had been a sort of proof that I was human; but with all hope of finding her gone, I ran the risk of being recognized. At first, I had believed that the two with me—the crazy girl and the insane cat—were no threat to my secret. No one could expect me to have to prove myself to them. But then had come Marie and the unrecognized, but nagging, suspicion that she sensed the lack in me. Then Bill, another real person to watch me and draw conclusions. Then Porniarsk, who, perhaps, was too alienly knowledgeable; and after him, the experimentals, who, by definition, must also be creatures without souls, so that at any moment any one of the other people, the real people, might say to themselves—*look at the way he acts with Sunday! Doesn't that strike you as being like the way you'd expect the experimentals to respond to any affection or kindness?*

But the greatest danger had come from the girl outgrowing her craziness after all. She had known me too long; and she had known Sunday. There had been signs in her to show that she knew me better than I had thought she did. I wanted to keep her around; but unless I did something, she would be the very one who would watch me with Sunday and put two and two together—after which she would have no use for me, and I would lose her forever.

Of course, Tek had threatened to take her away anyway, which would have solved things in a way I did not want. But deep inside me, I knew Tek was no match for me. He had never really been a threat. There were a dozen ways in which I could have eliminated him from the situation, right down to following him and the girl, killing him and bringing her back by force. No, Sunday had been the one to eliminate, and now I had taken care of him. Sitting around by myself as the days and nights went past, I mourned—not for him, but for the bitterness of having to face what I was, when I had been so successful at hiding it from myself before.

The others were very patient with me. I would have shot me, dug a grave, tumbled myself in and got rid of the extra mouth to feed, the extra clothes to wash. But they were different. So they endured me, letting me roam around as I liked, only coming to collect me when it was time for a meal or bedtime; and I had the privacy I wanted.

Or at least, I had it for a long time. But then my isolation began to be invaded. I don't know when I first became conscious of it; perhaps I had been seeing his dark, lean figure around, but ignoring it for some time. But the day came when I noticed the Old Man sitting watching me, hunkered down in the shade of a boulder (it was summer again by that time) about thirty yards off along the hillside where I sat by myself.

I remember wondering then how he had gotten loose. In the back of my mind, he had been still chained up, all this time, in the station. Possibly, I thought, they had turned him loose some time since to go back down with his fellow experimentals. I did not want to come out of my grey fog to the effort of asking any of the others about him, so I decided to ignore him. He was simply sitting, watching me; and his limited mind, I thought, should get tired of that after a while, and I would be rid of him.

I decided to ignore him.

But he did not grow tired of watching and go away. Gradually, I began to be aware that he would always be around somewhere close, even if he was not plainly visible. Not only would he be there, but after some weeks, it became obvious that he was gradually lessening the distance at which he sat from me.

I had no idea what he was after; but I wanted him gone. I wanted to be left alone, even by imitation sub-humans. One day—he was now in the habit of sitting less than twenty feet from me—I let one hand that was hidden from him by my body drop casually on a stone about the size of a medium hen's egg, gathered it in, and waited. Some time later, when I thought I saw his attention distracted for a moment—as it turned out I was wrong—I scooped it up and threw it at him as hard as I could.

He lifted a hand and caught it before it reached him.

The catch he made was so effortless that I never tried to throw another thing at him. Nothing except his arm had moved, not even his shoulder. His long, skinny arm had simply lifted and let the stone fly into the palm of it. Then he had dropped it, discarding it with a disinterested opening of his fingers; and all the while, his eyes had stayed unmoving on mine.

Sour fury boiled in me at that; and it was enough to bring me partway back to life. My first reaction was that I would tell Bill or one of the others to take him away and chain him up again. But then, it struck me that if I betrayed the fact that I was no longer pretty much out of things, the others would want me to come back to being human with them again—which would put me once more on the way to having my secret discovered.

I decided I would have to get rid of the Old Man myself; and I began to plot how to do it. Eventually, I worked out a simple, but effective, plan. I would take one of the handguns when no one was looking and hide it in my shirt until I had a shot at him that a blind man could not miss. Then when the others came to find out who had fired, I would tell them he had made threats of attacking me for some time now; and finally, I had been forced to kill him in self-defense.

The business of getting the gun was simple enough. The handguns and most of the rifles were still kept in the motor home where I lived with the girl, Marie and little

Wendy. I helped myself to a snub-nosed .32 revolver the morning after I had concocted my scheme and tucked it inside my shirt into the waistband of my slacks. The shirt was loose enough so that it hid any outlines that might have shown through. Then I went about my daily business of leaving the others as soon as I had eaten breakfast and going off to sit among the rocks of the hillside about half a mile from camp.

I had been tempted to go even farther than usual from the camp—far enough so that the sound of my shot could not be heard. But, now that I had made up my mind to kill the Old Man, I was afraid of doing anything out of the ordinary that might make him suspicious. Therefore, I went to my usual place and sat down in the morning sunlight. Shortly I spotted him, squatting less than thirty yards off in a patch of shadow.

I sat where I was, ostensibly ignoring him. After a little while, I made an excuse to glance in his direction and saw that he was a good deal closer than before—perhaps half the distance. It was curious, but I had never been able to actually catch him in the process of moving. Whenever I looked, he was always seated and still, as if he had been there for several hours.

The morning wore on. He came close—but close was still not close enough. He was less than fifteen feet from me at last and would come no closer, but he was off to my left side behind me, so that I would have to turn about to face him and pull the gun at the same time—two movements that, I was sure, would startle him into leaping for protection behind one of the large boulders that were all around us.

That particular day ended with nothing happening. I sat. He sat. The only difference from the many days we had spent, together but apart, before was that for the first time, my mind was not concentrated on my inner fog, but on stealthily observing him and calculating the possibility of luring him within certain range of my weapon.

However, he did not cooperate. The next day, it was the same thing. The next day, again the same. I finally realized that he was either too wary or too diffident to approach me except from an oblique angle. I would have to resign myself to waiting until he came almost close enough to be touched, or otherwise put himself in some other completely vulnerable position.

I consoled myself with the fact that all I needed was patience. He would be bound to come close eventually, since every day he inched a little nearer. In fact, it took him nearly three weeks before he did come near enough to provide the target I wanted; and in those three weeks, something strange began to happen to me. I found myself actually enjoying the situation we were both in. I was still trapped in my own miseries like a fly in a forest of flypaper, but at the moment, I was navigating between the sticky strands under the impetus of the excitement of the hunt. I was reminded one day of a poem I had not thought of for years, or read since I was a boy, by Rudyard Kipling and called "The Ballad Of Boh Da Thon." It was about a bandit who had been chased by an English army unit weeks on end, and it had a pair of lines that applied nicely to the Old Man and me:

> *And sure if pursuit in possession ends,*
> *the Boh and his trackers were best of friends . . . .*

For the first time I found myself beginning to like the Old Man, if for no other reason than that he was giving me something to want.

However, the day finally came in which—glancing out of the corners of my eyes—I felt, rather than saw, him squatting almost within the reach of one of my arms and certainly within the reach of one of his.

There was no way I could miss with the revolver or he could dodge, at this distance. But, strangely enough, now that I had him exactly where I wanted him, I was more than ever fearful of frightening him off, of missing him somehow. I was as shy as a kid on his first date. I wanted to turn and look at him; but it took all my will to do so. For a long time I could not manage to turn my head toward him at all. Then, as the sun began to climb higher in the sky, I began to swivel my head on my neck so slowly that it felt like the movement a stone statue might make over centuries. When the sun was directly over our heads, I was still not looking squarely at him, although now I was conscious of his dark shape as a sort of cloud, or presence, at the corner of my left eye.

All this time I had been sliding my hand gradually in between the two lowest buttons of my shirt. I slid it in until my cold fingers lay flat on the warm skin of my belly, and the tips of those same fingers touched the hard curve of the polished butt of the revolver.

It was now noon, lunchtime; but I was afraid of breaking the spell. So I continued to sit without going back to camp, and the Old Man continued to sit, and the sun moved on while the slow, agonizing, almost involuntary turning of my neck continued. I was like someone under a spell or curse. I began to be afraid that the day would end, and I would have not turned enough to catch his eyes with my own, to hold his attention for the seconds I would need to draw the gun and shoot him. Strangely, in this moment, I had finally lost all connection with my reason for killing him. It was simply something to which I was committed, as a tightrope walker might be committed to cross a narrow wire stretched from one cliff to another.

Then—I don't know why—but there was an abrupt snapping of the tension. Suddenly, I was free to turn my head as swiftly as I wanted.

I turned and looked directly at him.

It was a shock. I had completely forgotten that I had never looked closely into his features before. The black-haired anthropoid face, with something of the immutable sadness of the gorilla, looked back at me. It looked back at me from as close a distance as the features of some human companion might face me across a table in a restaurant. But the Old Man's face was all black fur, red nostrils, yellow teeth and yellower eyes—eyes as yellow as Sunday's had been.

For a moment, those eyes froze me. They placed a new paralysis upon my soul, one that, for a moment, I did not believe I could throw off. Then, with a fierce effort, I told myself that this was not Sunday or anything like him; and I felt my hand reaching automatically for the revolver.

My fingers closed upon the butt. I pulled it loose from the pressure of the waistband of my pants—and all the time I was looking directly into his face, which did not alter its expression, but gazed steadily back at me.

It was a moment outside of time. We were caught together in a tableau, flies in amber both of us, frozen and incapable of movement—except for that gun-hand of mine which continued to move with a life of its own, closing about the gun butt and lifting it to clear the muz-

zle toward the face before me. There was something
inevitable about its movements. I could have felt no more
trapped by circumstances if I had been tied down in the
path of a juggernaut.

In a second it would have been over—but in that
second, the Old Man reached out and placed a hand on
both my shirt and the hand holding the gun, arresting my
movement.

The pressure of his hand was a calm, almost a gentle
touch. I could feel the unexerted strength behind his
fingers; but he was not gripping my hand, merely laying
his own on top of it, just as, once, I might have stopped
some business guest reaching for the check of a lunch to
which I had just taken him. It was not the kind of touch
that could have checked me from continuing to draw the
gun and shoot him if I had decided to. But somehow, I
was stopped.

For the first time I looked directly into—deeply into—
those eyes of his.

I had gone to zoos once and looked into the eyes of
some of the animals there. There were no more zoos
now, nor was it likely that there would ever be again. But
once there had been; and in their cages, particularly in
the cages of the big cats, the apes, and bears and the
wolves, I had looked into wild animal eyes from only a
few feet of distance. And there had seen something in
those eyes that was not to be found in the eyes of my fellow humans. There were eyes that looked at me from the
other side of the universe. Perhaps they could be loving,
perhaps, under stress, they could be filled with fury and
anger; but now, to me, a human, they were remote—
separated from me by a gulf neither man nor beast could
cross. They looked at me, without judgment and without
hope.

If they lived and it was their fate to encounter me in
the open, they would deal with me as best their strength
allowed. If I died they would watch me die, simply because there was nothing else they could do, whether I
was their deepest enemy or their dearest friend. Their
eyes were the eyes of creatures locked up alone in their
own individual skulls all the hours and minutes of their
life. As animals, they neither knew nor expected the communication every human takes for granted, even if he or
she is surrounded by mortal foes.

The eyes of the Old Man were like that—they were the fettered eyes of an animal. But mixed in with that, there was something more—for me alone. It was not love such as Sunday had had for me. But it was something in its own way, perhaps, as strong. I recognized it without being able to put a name to it—although suddenly, I knew what it was.

The Old Man and his tribe, who had been born from test tubes, had been created on the brink of humanity. They teetered on the nice edge of having souls. Of these, the most aware was the Alpha Prime, Old Man himself, because he was the most intelligent, the strongest and the most questioning. Also, he had shared the monad with me in that moment in which we had brought the local effects of the time storm to a halt. In fact, he had shared it alone with me, before any of the other humans had joined in. He had been exposed then to communication for the first time in his life; and it must have awakened a terrible hunger in him. I realized that, all this time, he had been trying to get back into communication with me.

So, that is why as soon as he had been let free again— whenever that was—he had begun to search me out, to approach me little by little, day by day, until now, at last, he sat an arm's length from me. He not only sat at arm's length from me, but with his hand in a gesture that was almost pleading, arresting the gun with which he must know I had planned to kill him.

My own soul turned over in me. Because I suddenly understood what he had understood. From the beginning, because of what we had shared in the moment of the taming of the time storm, he had been much more understanding of me than I had suspected. He had known that I did not want him near me. He had known that my desire to be free of him could be murderous. And he had known what I was doing when my hand went inside my shirt.

I had had enough experience with him to know that my strength was like a baby's compared to his—for all that we probably weighed about the same. It would have been no effort for him to have taken the gun from me. He could have easily broken the arm that held it or throttled me with one hand. But he had done none of these. Instead he had merely come as close as he ever must have come in his life to pleading with someone to spare him, to accept him, to be his fellow, if not his friend.

In that same moment I realized that he—strange as it seemed and incredible as it was that he should have the capability, just from that solitary shared moment in the monad—understood better than any of them how Sunday had felt about me, and how I had felt about Sunday. In his animal-human eyes I read it, how I had *really* felt about Sunday; and at last—at last—I fell apart.

I had been right both ways. I had been right in that I was someone who did not know how to love. But I had been wrong, in spite of this, when I told myself I had not loved the crazy cat. All this I understood suddenly, at last, in the moment in which the Old Man squatted before me, with one long hand still laid flat against my shirt, over the spot where my fist and the revolver that was to have killed him were concealed. The floodgates within me went down suddenly and I was washed halfway back again once more to the shores of humanity. Only halfway, but this was farther than I had ever been before.

23

I sat there and cried for a long time; and the Old Man waited me out as he might have waited out a storm, squatting in a cave in the hills. When it was over, I was sane again; or at least as close to sanity as I could expect to be, under the circumstances. Together we went back to the camp, and from then on, he was openly at my side most of the daylight hours.

What he had done, of course, was to crack the protective shell I had grown about myself in reaction to the massive internal effort of controlled power that had been involved in using the monad. In doing that, I had discovered muscles of the inner self that I had not known I owned, and I had also tuned myself up emotionally with a vengeance. In self-defense, with Sunday's death, my mind had closed itself off until it could heal the psychic tearings these stresses had created. Now that I was back in my skull, however, these things were suddenly very obvious to me; and some other things as well. Chief of these was that there was a great deal I needed to do with myself if I wanted to continue my joust with the time storm and the universe.

Meanwhile, I was faced with reentering the world of the living. To my pleasure and to the feeding of a new humbleness inside me, the others had been doing very well without my guiding hand. I found that I was now ruler of what might well be called a small kingdom—and that was only the beginning of the discoveries awaiting me.

A great deal had happened in the year and a half that I had been obsessed with myself. For one thing, the world was a world again. With the interference from the moving time lines ended, shortwave radio communication had tied the continents back together, resulting in the mutual

211

discovery of all us survivors that there were more of us than we had suspected. The North American continent was now a patchwork of relatively small kingdoms, like my own, with the exception of the west coast, from Baja California northward halfway into British Columbia, Canada. That west coast strip, as far east as Denver and in some cases beyond, was now a single sovereignty under a woman who called herself the Empress. The Empress was from the Hawaiian Islands—which appeared to have suffered less than any other part of the world from the moving mistwalls and the time changes of the time storm. The islands had lost no more than two-thirds of their population, as opposed to a figure that must be much closer to ninety-eight or ninety-nine per cent for most of the rest of the world. The Empress was a woman from the island of Hawaii itself, who had seized control there with a ragtag, impromptu army, and then gone on to take over the other islands and the west coast of North America.

England and Ireland, apparently, were nearly deserted. Most of northern Europe also was a wasteland because of a brief ice age that had come with some of the time changes and covered most of that continent with an ice sheet from the Arctic Circle as far south as the middle of France. This ice sheet was now gone; but the human life that was left was now all below the former ice line. Stretching around the Mediterranean and into the north of Africa were essentially nothing more than scattered, single family households. The rest of Africa, like South America, was largely noncommunicating, from which Bill assumed that those areas had been pretty well depopulated by the time storm also.

Russia, India and the whole Oriental area had also been hard hit. As a result they appeared to have fallen back into a sort of peaceful medieval, agricultural condition, with small villages scattered sparsely across the immensity of land. Australia and New Zealand had lost almost all of their cities, but had a surprising number of families surviving pretty much as they always had in the interior and on the rest of that island continent. However, these people, although articulate and largely supplied with their own radios, were so widely scattered that they were also, in effect, no more than individual families living in isolation.

Bill had made a large map on one wall of the rambling,

continually building structure that my group had come to call the summer palace. The place was a strange construction, being composed partly of lumber, partly of native rocks cemented together, and partly of cement blocks trucked in from a half-obliterated town thirty miles away, that had owned a cement block factory. The palace had poured-concrete floors and bare walls for the most part; but Bill had been a good enough architect to see that it was adequately wired and equipped with ductwork, not only for heating, but for summer air conditioning. I think that I had been conscious of the existence of his map in it, during my non-participating period; but I had never looked at the map with any degree of interest until the Old Man cracked me out of my shell. Now that I did, I found myself marveling that what was left of the world could have gotten its scattered parts back into contact with each other in such a short time.

I discovered something else, as a byproduct of re-awakening to what was going on around me. This was that our new world was a world hungry for news, and I myself was a piece of that news. By this time, all the people on earth who had radio receivers knew who it was who had brought the local effects of the time storm into balance. They knew what I looked like, who my lieutenants were, and what our local situation here was. I was, I discovered, regarded as a sort of combination of Einstein and Napoleon—and the planet's number one celebrity. This attention might ordinarily have given me a large opinion of myself. However, under the circumstances, it had a hollow ring to it. It was rather like being crowned King of the Earth on the stage of the empty Hollywood Bowl, while an audience of five sat in the middle of the front row seats and applauded energetically. After discovering what it was like, I put my position in the world-wide, public eye out of my mind and concentrated on matters close to home.

It was curious that I, who had once believed that I could never endure to be married, now had two wives. Of course, legally, I was married to neither one of them; but wives they were in every practical sense of the word, and particularly in the eyes of the community surrounding us. Marie and Ellen—I would have bet anyone that if there were ever two women likely not to get on with each other at all, it would be those two. Marie was talkative,

conventional and probably—she had never told me her
age—older than I was. The girl was certainly still well
under twenty, close-mouthed to an almost abnormal degree, and recognized no convention or rules but her own.
What the two of them could have in common was beyond
me. I puzzled over it from time to time but never succeeded in getting an answer.

But they joined forces magnificently when it came to
lining up in opposition to me. One of the typical examples
of this appeared directly after I had come back to my
senses and rejoined the world of the living. All the time
that I had been more or less out of my head, they had
taken care of me as if I had been three years old. Now
that I had my ordinary wits back, rather than just getting
back to normal ways, they both apparently decided, without a word, that I should get it through my head that my
days of being waited upon were over.

This would have been all right if they had merely returned to the normal pattern of affairs that had existed
before we got the time storm forced into balance. But
they now moved as far in the direction of leaving me to
my own devices as they had gone previously in watching
over me. In fact, the whole matter went to what I considered ridiculous limits.

For example, during the time I had been obsessed with
my inner problems, I had been, except for rare intervals,
as sexless as a eunuch. When I came back to myself, of
course, that changed. The day the Old Man helped me
break loose, I found myself waiting for the evening and
the hours of privacy in the motor home. I had never
been one to want more than one woman in my bed at a
time; and I was not at all sure whether it was the girl or
Marie I wanted that night. But I definitely knew that I
wanted one or the other. I gave them time to get settled
first; but when I came to the motorhome, Ellen was nowhere to be seen and Marie was a mound under covers on
her own bed, her back toward me.

I blew gently into her ear to wake her up and get her
to turn toward me. She came to, but not satisfactorily.

"Not tonight," she murmured sleepily, and pulled the
blanket up to where it almost covered her head.

Annoyed, I left the motorhome and went out to look
for Ellen. I found her after some search, in a sleeping bag
at the foot of a tree, with her rifle leaning up against it

in arm's reach. The rebuff from Marie had taken some of the rosy glow off my feelings. I poked the sleeping bag and her eyes opened.

"What are you doing out here?" I said.

"Sleeping," she said. "Goodnight."

She closed her eyes and pulled her head down into the sleeping bag.

Angry, and not a little hurt, I wandered off. Was this all the two of them cared for me after all? Here I was back to normalcy and neither one seemed to give a damn. It was almost as if they had preferred me as the mindless near-idiot I had been for the past eighteen months.

I went back into the motor home, opened the cupboards that held our bottled goods and took out a bottle of sour mash bourbon. I made myself a solitary campfire off into the woods, at the edge of the clearing holding the motor-home and the half-finished shape of the summer palace, and set out to get myself drunk by way of solitary celebration. But it did not work. I got thickheaded without feeling any better and finally gave up, going back to the motor home and falling into my own lonely bunk without bothering to do much more than take off my boots.

If that was all they cared for how it had been with me this past year and a half, I thought resentfully as I dropped off.

It was not until late the next morning, when I woke up to a dry mouth, a headache and the sunlight streaming through the windows of the motor home, that it occurred to me to think how it might have been for them too. If I had been essentially without a woman all that time, they had been essentially without a man. Or had they? That was a question I found I really didn't want to consider, although I made a mental note to find the answer sometime later. (I never did find out as a matter of fact.) I got up, washed, shaved, changed clothes and went out.

Not only had they forsaken my bed, there was no sign of any breakfast made for me. Not that I was incapable of cooking for myself, but I had gotten used to having the spoon all but put in my mouth, and I felt the transition to the present state of neglect to be unnecessarily harsh and abrupt. However, the motor home refrigerator, run from the standby oil generator outside it, had cold juice, eggs and canned sausage. I made myself a pretty decent meal, scrupulously washed up after myself—just to rub

their noses in the fact that I could be independent too—
and went outside to see what was going on.

There was no one around outside the summer palace,
not the girl or Marie—not even Wendy. Now that I began to think of it, I had a vague impression from the past
months that Wendy was ceasing to be the timid little
creature she had been when I first saw her and was beginning to develop into a lively young girl, busy every hour
of the day all over the place.

I went into the summer palace, prowled through its
rooms and discovered Bill busily at work at a large drafts-
man's table in the same room that had the map on the
wall. Besides those two items, the room had three large
filing cabinets, a regular desk covered with papers, and
one wall entirely in bookcases.

"Hello," I said to Bill.

He glanced at me over the top of whatever it was he
was drawing, put down his pen and ruler and got off the
high stool he had been sitting on. We shook hands with
awkward formality.

"How are you?" he asked.

"Fine," I said. "Just fine."

I glanced around the room.

"You've all been pretty busy," I said.

"Oh well," answered Bill, "there's always a lot to do."

"And you've been doing most of it, I'd guess," I said.

"Oh, no," he shook his head, "I couldn't have carried
most of the responsibility here if I'd wanted to. Actually,
all I've been doing is handling the instruction, the main-
tenance and supply, and things like that. Marie and Ellen
have been doing most of the everyday work of running
things. Marie's a natural manager, and Ellen—"

He paused.

"Go on," I said, interested. "You're about to say that
Ellen is—"

"Well, I was going to say—sort of a natural general,"
he said awkwardly. "Maybe I ought to say, a natural war
leader. She's been the one who's been making sure that all
our people know how to use their guns and that none of
our neighbors think they can walk in here and help themselves to anything we've got."

"Neighbors? What neighbors?" I asked.

"Well," he said, "to the north and northwest of us it's
the Ryans, and the TvLostChord. To the west, it's Wal-

linstadt. South and moving around to the east, it's Billy Projec and his tribe. Not that we've anything really to worry about, even if they all took it into their heads to combine against us."

He shot me a quick glance.

"We've now got over six hundred people," he said.

"Six hundred people!"

I was rocked back on my heels. I had vaguely gathered during the last year and a half that the numbers of my small community were growing; but I had guessed that, at the most, we would have somewhere between thirty and fifty people. Six hundred under these conditions was a small nation.

"Where did they all come from?" I asked.

"Some of them knew about us back when the mistwalls were still operating," said Bill. "Or they heard about us from others they ran into. We were a pretty good-sized party—and a well-equipped party—to be moving around back then. After the time changes stopped locally, they began gradually to drift in, either out of curiosity or because they'd always wanted to join us."

He waved a hand at the filing cabinets.

"I've got each one down on the census rolls," he said. "In fact, if you'd like, you can read each one's life history up to the time they've joined us. About nine months ago, I made everybody fill out a complete file on themselves; and now we make every new person do that before we accept them here. I've got not only the facts of the life, but bloodtype, medical history, occupational skills and everything else that might be useful information for us."

I shook my head. His mind and mine were two different constructs. The last thing I would have thought about with a group that size would be getting into their former occupations and bloodtypes. It had probably been the first thing that Bill had thought of. He had an orderly brain.

"You don't need me," I said. "From what I can see you've all been doing fine on your own."

Now he shook his head.

"All we've been doing is keeping the machinery running, idling, waiting for you to do something with it," he said. "Do you want to look around at things?"

"Yes," I said.

He led me out of the room and down a corridor of the summer palace that I had not been in before—or if I

had, I didn't remember having been through it—and out
another door. A jeep and a station wagon were parked
there. He got in behind the wheel of the jeep and I
climbed in beside him.

"Porniarsk's got his working area back here behind the
summer palace," Bill said as he started up the motor of
the jeep and backed it away from the building, to swing
it around to head down the hillside. "But I thought we'd
end up with him. Let me show you the rest of it first."

We drove down through the belt of trees into the lower
area where the village of the experimentals had stood. I
had not been down here since we had halted the effects of
the time storm, and what I saw was startling. The village
of the experimentals was still there; although it was now
enclosed in cyclone fencing and the gates wide enough to
drive a truck through were standing ajar. Sprawling out on
the open space beyond and slightly downhill from the village was what could only be described as a town—a new
town of everything from prefab houses to tents.

"Eventually," Bill spoke in my ear over the noise of the
motor as we negotiated the now clearly marked, if unsur-
faced, road downward from the tree belt, "we'll set up
some uniform construction. For the present, however,
we've been giving anyone who's accepted here a free hand,
provided their housing and their habits conform with
our sanitary regulations and local laws."

"Who enforces our local laws?" I asked, bemused.

"Everybody belongs to the militia, and everybody who
belongs to the militia pulls police duty on a regular rota-
tion," said Bill. "That's Ellen's department. You should
ask her about it. She's on top of it all the time; and she
makes it work without a hitch. From what I can gather,
we've got a much more organized community here than
they have almost anyplace else in the world. Of course,
the people who are here badly want to be here. They all
think that you're going to go on pulling miracles out of
your hat and that they'll end up, either on top of things,
or with all the luxuries of former civilization back again."

"All that, just because we managed to stop the time
storm?" I said.

"It's a function of the situation," Bill said, with his
precise pronunciation of each word. "Think of it this
way. You're the sorcerer. Porniarsk's your demon assistant."

"You're my Grand Vizier, Ellen's General of the Armies and Marie's the Number One Queen—is that it?" I asked.

Bill laughed.

"Yup," he said.

24

By this time we were almost down level with the gates of the experimentals' village.

"How come you've got them penned up?" I said.

"They're not penned," Bill answered. "That fence is there for their own protection, in case some of our newcomers don't have the sense to leave them alone. Or in case there's a sudden surprise attack on us from somewhere. They can lock their gates and have a certain amount of protection until we drive the attackers off. They seem to understand that perfectly well."

He looked at me briefly.

"I think the Old Man can communicate with them all right," he said. "Anyway, things have gone pretty smoothly with all of them since we stopped the effects of the time storm."

There were a few of the experimentals out in front of their buildings; and these watched us solemnly as we passed, but made no move either to come toward us or to retreat inside. The jeep roared on and we drove down what seemed to be a sort of center street between the heterogeneous buildings of the human community. Eight or nine young children were flying kites in a clearing half-surrounded by trees, just beyond the village. The picture they made was so normal and so pre-time storm that it jolted me.

"Where did all the kids come from?" I asked.

"Some of the people coming in had them," Bill said, braking the jeep to a halt before one large quonset hut. "And we've had several babies born here during the past year. Of course, those are too young to play yet. Still, the proportion of children to adults isn't that large. I don't think we've got more than twenty of them."

I shaded my eyes and tried to make out a familiar figure among the darting young bodies.

"Is that Wendy out there?" I said.

"I don't think so," said Bill without turning around. "She's probably out with the dogs somewhere. She handles them now most of the time, instead of Marie; and they've gotten so that they follow her wherever she goes. Generally, Marie thinks it's a good thing; and I agree. The dogs are good protection for her. This is our government building here. Come on in."

He got out of the jeep. I followed him and we went up three wooden steps and in the front door of the quonset. It was like stepping into any busy office. Behind a low barrier of wooden fencing, there were five desks at which three men and two women were sitting, typing or engaged in other paperwork. File cabinets occupied one wall and there was a large copying machine in a corner.

"Where are you getting the power to run all this?" I asked Bill. For the typewriters were all electric, and the copier looked as if it had to require at least a 220 volt line.

"We put in a much larger gas generator," said Bill, leading me through a gate in the wooden fence. "Before fall, we ought to finish a dam on the river and have a waterpowered generator that'll take care of all our needs for the next five years."

He led me into a corridor with two doors on each side and opened the first one on the right briefly.

"Supplies," he said.

I looked in. It was, as he had said, a supply room. Most of the supplies were clerical; but I saw some stacks of blankets and other material for household living. A chained and locked gunrack against the far wall of the room held rifles, and there was a rack of handguns below it, also chained and locked. I shut the door again and turned to open the door across the way.

"Communications," he said briefly, and led me into a radio room containing two women, one young and one middle-aged. It was filled with radio equipment that even to my amateur eye seemed impressive.

"Bebe, Jill," Bill said, "this is Marc Despard."

The two looked up from their panels, smiled and nodded to me. Bill led me out of the room again.

"Now," said Bill, moving down to knock on the second door on the left, "this is—"

"Come in," said Marie's voice.

Bill smiled at me and led me in. Marie was seated behind a large desk in a very businesslike office, with papers in front of her. She was looking over the papers at a lean, big-boned man who must have stood about six feet six when he was on his feet. Right now he was sitting down, dressed in a white shirt and what seemed to be white duck pants.

"I'll be right with you, Marc," she said, and picked up what was apparently an interrupted conversation with the man in white.

"What you've got to make them understand, Abe, is that if they want to draw supplies and cook their own meals, they have to do it according to our rules. At our convenience, not theirs. I'm not going to put up with anyone either wasting food or not eating adequately—any more than I'd put up with their breaking any of the other laws. That means they submit their menu for the week in advance to you, you approve it, and then—only then —you authorize one of your own people to give them supplies for just exactly what they've planned to serve. You understand?"

"Sure," said Abe, in a deep slow voice. He had a touch of some Eastern European accent.

Marie looked away from him over to me again.

"Marc," she said, "this is Abe Budner, our Director of Food Services and chef for the community kitchen. I'm hoping we can train people to take the chef's job off his hands before long."

Abe Budner got up as slowly and solemnly as he had spoken, shook hands with me and sat down again.

"We're just looking around," Bill said.

"Good," said Marie briskly. "Because I really don't have time to stop and talk now. I can tell you all about this work this evening, Marc."

We were dismissed. Bill and I left.

"And this," said Bill, knocking on the remaining door in the corridor, "is Ellen's."

We waited, but there was no answer to his knock.

The door at the far end of the corridor opened behind us.

"Something?" said a voice. We turned and I saw what

looked like a boy of about eighteen, wearing dark pants and a khaki shirt with two brass buttons pinned on the left side of his shirt collar.

"Ellen's out checking the Ryan boundary," this individual said. "Is there anything I can do for you?"

He looked questioningly at me.

"This is Marc Despard, Doc," said Bill.

"Marc Despard? I'm really glad to meet you, sir," said Doc flusteredly and energetically, shaking my hand. "I've looked forward to meeting you."

"Well, now you have," I said. I was not exactly taken with him.

"Doc is Ellen's second in command," said Bill. "His full name's Kurt Dockwiler, but we all call him Doc. His militia rank is captain."

"Oh?" I said.

"I was just going to show Marc Ellen's office," Bill added.

"You bet. Come in," said Doc, stepping past us, throwing open the door and leading us in. I followed him and Bill brought up the rear.

I don't know what I had expected; but Ellen's office was simply a tidy, utilitarian place with the usual filing cabinets, a perfectly clean desk and a few extra chairs facing the desk as if she had been holding a conference recently.

"If you'd like to wait," said Doc, "she ought to be back in about twenty minutes. I can send over to the kitchen for coffee—or anything else."

"No, I'm just looking around," I said. "I'll see her tonight."

"Of course!" Doc followed Bill and myself back down the corridor and out through the outer office. "If I can ever be useful in any way, Mr. Despard, the message center can reach me at any time."

"I'll remember that," I said getting in the jeep.

Bill started up and we drove off.

"How old is he, anyway?" I said.

"I don't know exactly," answered Bill. "Twenty or twenty-one, I think."

"He looks more like Ellen's age."

"Nothing wrong with that," Bill said.

I looked at him. But his face was perfectly innocent of any particular expression.

"I'm just surprised there aren't any older men around to hold down a job like that," I told him. "That's all."

"We've got older men, of course," said Bill. He was heading the jeep back up into the trees in the direction of the summer palace. "Most of them have families, or at least somebody, who make them a bad choice for a high risk occupation. Then again, none of them have Doc's qualifications."

"Qualifications?"

"His father was career army," Bill said. "He absorbed a lot of the military art, just by growing up in various bases. That and other things. He's a black belt in judo and he's taught survival classes. Also he's a mountain climber."

There was not much to say to that. I sat quiet during most of the ride back up to the summer palace, and in that time I came around to feeling that I might have been a little unfair to Doc.

"We'll go see Porniarsk now," Bill said, stopping the jeep once more at the palace. "I didn't take you to him right away because I thought either Marie or Ellen might have things they'd want to show you in their areas; and their schedule is pretty well tied in with other things. Porniarsk, you can see any time."

I felt a warmth of old affection at the thought of the alien avatar. Porniarsk, with his ugly bull-dog shape and unemotional responses, was a particularly stable point in my pyrotechnic and shifting universe. I followed Bill into the palace, thinking with surprise that, in all the last year and a half, I had not sought out Porniarsk once and had seen him in total perhaps no more than half a dozen times.

The room in the summer palace that Bill led me into, eventually, must have had as much floor space as the quonset hut down in the village we had just left. It was a rectangular room with floor, walls and ceiling painted white and a row of windows all down one side. The other walls were occupied mainly by equipment that had once been in the station. Apparently, Porniarsk had had it all transported down here.

However, what caught my eye immediately was not this, nor even the friendly sight of Porniarsk himself, but a box shape with transparent sides perhaps twenty feet long by six wide and three deep, almost filled with some greyish-blue substance. When I got closer, I saw that whatever it was seemed to be a liquid. There was a noticeable *meniscus,* and a black tube running over the edge of one of the sides and down into the box showed the apparent angular distortion at the surface that a stick does, poked down into water. Porniarsk had been doing something with the tank; but he turned and came to meet us as we entered.

"How are you, Marc?" he said as we met, his easy speech at odds, as always, with the curious mechanical sound of his voice, and his manner of speaking.

"I'm fine—now," I said. "How've you been?"

"There's been no reason for me to be other than I always am," Porniarsk said.

"Of course," I said. "Well, then, how have things been going?"

"I've been getting a few things done," Porniarsk said. "But nothing with any great success. But then, real progress isn't often dramatic, being a matter of small steps taken daily that add up to a total accomplishment over a period of time."

"Yes," I said. I thought of the experience it had taken me a year and a half to come to terms with. "There's a lot of things I'd like to talk to you about."

"I'm glad to hear it," said Porniarsk. "On my part, I've been looking forward to talking to you. I can progress much more rapidly if I've got a primary mind to work with; and the only primary mind we've produced so far is you."

"Only me?" I said. It jarred me slightly to hear it—at the same time I felt a small ego-pleasure.

"Primary minds can only be developed or uncovered by monad activity," he said. "All the other minds involved in the gestalt only resonated and amplified yours, without developing. So I've been restricted to doing what I can with the resonating minds. In fact, I've been restricted to the one resonating mind that had no other duties to occupy it."

He turned his head and nodded ponderously toward a corner. I looked and saw the Old Man, perched on the seat before one of the consoles taken from the station, the helmet on his head.

"The Alpha Prime," said Porniarsk. "He's been my main subject. Happily, he seems eager for the experience of being connected with the equipment here. Daytimes, he's generally unavailable. I understand he's been with you most of the time. But at night, he often comes here on his own initiative to work with me."

I gazed at the Old Man. He squatted utterly still on the chair before the console, with a curious assurance—almost as if it was a throne and he was a king.

"What could you learn from him?" I asked.

"It's not what I can learn *from* him," said Porniarsk deliberately, "but what I could learn *through* him. Just as I want to learn and discover matters through you—though since you're a primary mind, I'd expect that you'd also learn, and be able to add the knowledge you personally gain to what I can gain."

He stopped speaking for a second, then started again.

"In fact," he said, "I ought to point out that what I can learn is limited by the kind of instrument I am, myself—personally. As an avatar of Porniarsk I've got only so much conceptual range. On the other hand, Marc, your conceptual range is something I don't know. It could be less than Porniarsk's—that is to say, mine—or it might be a great deal greater. It could be limitless, in that you might be able to go on increasing it, as long as you want to make the effor to extend its grasp. Which brings me to an important point."

He stopped again. But this time he did not continue immediately.

"What point?" asked Bill, finally.

"The point," said Porniarsk is his unvarying accent, "of whether Marc, after his one experience with the monad, really wants to explore further into an area where mind becomes reality and where it's impossible to draw a line where the definitive change occurs."

"I'll answer that," I said.

It came to me suddenly, that while I'd never really come to doubt that I wanted to dig deeper into the time storm and everything connected with it, for the last year and a half, I'd been hiding from the fact that I'd eventually have to get back to that work.

"I don't have any reverse gear." I said. "The only way for me to go is straight ahead. Even standing still doesn't work."

"In that case," said Porniarsk, "you and I have a big job ahead of us."

"Fine with me," I said.

"I guessed so from the beginning," said Porniarsk. "So,

in that case, maybe we might talk right now about the basic principles involved here, and how you can be involved also."

"Absolutely," I said. I meant every word I said. "This all ties in with something I want to do—something I'm going to do."

"If you'll forgive me," said Porniarsk, "I felt that about you from the first time we met. However, it's a lot bigger universe than you, or the entities of your time, seem to realize. If you were anything else than a rather unusual individual, I'd have to say you're presumptuous to have the ambition I think you're entertaining."

"I told you I've got something to do," I said. "In any case, we both want the same thing, don't we? To control this runaway situation with time?"

"Quite correct. But remember what I said—if you weren't an unusual individual, I wouldn't be devoting this much energy to you. Not because I wasn't interested; but because it'd be a waste of time. By your own standards, Marc, you're arrogant. Partly, this is simply because you recognize your own ability. Part of it is a prickliness, what you'd call a chip on the shoulder, because other people don't see what you see. I can sympathize with this. But it's still something you'll have to overcome, if you're going to achieve the full primary identity you'll need."

"We'll see," I said.

I had been looking forward to talking to him. I had a great deal, I had thought, to tell him. What I most wanted to talk about was how it could be that, just as it had been back in the days when I had been playing the stock market, I could almost taste—almost *feel*—what it was I wanted to take hold of in the time storm. But his sudden criticism put me off.

"You said this was some sort of representation of the storm?" I said, turning to the tank.

"Yes," he answered.

"I don't see anything."

"It's not operating right now," said Porniarsk. "But I can turn it on for you."

He went to a control panel on the far wall and touched several studs and dials there with the tips of his shoulder tentacles.

"What you'll see," he said, coming back to Bill and

me, "isn't actually a view of the time storm. What it is, is
a representation produced by the same equipment that
was in the station. Look into the tank. Not at it, into it."

I'd already been looking—but now I realized my error.
I had been staring the same way you might stare at a fish
tank from entirely outside it. But what this piece of equipment apparently required—and require it did, for it was
evidently already warming up, and I could feel it drawing
my attention psychically the way a rope might have pulled
me physically—was for an observer to put his point of
view completely inside it.

There was nothing remarkable about the first signs of its
activation. All I saw were little flickerings like miniature
lighting, or, even less, like the small jitterings of light that
register on the optic nerves when you close your eyes and
press your fingers against the outside of the eyelids. These
small lights will-o'-the-wisped here and there through the
blueness of whatever filled the tank; and I suddenly
woke to the fact that what I had taken to be a sort of
blue-grey liquid was not liquid at all. It was something
entirely different, a heavy gas perhaps. Actually, I realized,
it had no color at all. It was any shade the subjective attitude of the viewer thought it was. For me, now, it had
become almost purely black, the black of lightless space;
and I was abruptly, completely lost in it, as if it was
actually the total universe and I stood invisible at the center of it.

The little flickerings were the forces of the time storm
at work. They had been multiplying to my eye as my
point of view moved their centerpoint; and now they
filled the tank in every direction, their number finite, but
so large as to baffle my perception of them. I understood
then that I was watching all the vectors of the full time
storm at work at once; and, as I watched, I began slowly
to sort their movements into patterns.

It was like watching, with the eyes of a Stone Age savage, a message printing itself on a wall in front of you; and
gradually, as you watched, you acquired the skill of reading and the understanding of the language in which the
message was set down, so that random marks began to ori-
ent themselves into information-bearing code. So, as I
watched, the time storm began to make sense to me—but
too much sense, too large a sense for my mind to handle.

It was as if I could now read the message, but what it told was of things too vast for my understanding and experience.

Two things, I saw, were happening. Two separate movements were characteristic of the patterns of the still-expanding storm. One was a wave-front sort of motion, like the spreading of ripples created by a stone dropped in a pond, interacting and spreading; and the other was like the spreading of cracks in some crystalline matrix. Both these patterns of development were taking place at the same time and both were complex. The wave-fronts were multiple and occurring at several levels and intensities. They created eddies at points along their own line of advance where they encountered solid matter, and particularly, when they encountered gravitational bodies like stars. Earth had had its own eddy, and it had been only the forces within that eddy that we had been able to bring into dynamic balance.

The crystalline cracking effect also intensified itself around gravity wells. It was this effect that threatened the final result of the storm that Porniarsk had first warned us about—a situation in which each particle would finally be at timal variance with the particles surrounding it. The cracking extended and divided the universe into patterns of greater and greater complexities until all matter eventually would be reduced to indivisible elements. . . .

So much I saw and understood of what the tank showed. But in the process of understanding so much, my comprehension stretched, stretched, and finally broke. I had a brief confused sensation of a universe on fire, whirling about me faster than I could see . . . and I woke up on the floor of the room, feeling as if I had just been levelled by an iron bar in the hands of a giant. The heavy, gargoyle head of Porniarsk hung above me, inches from my eyes.

"You see why you need to develop yourself?" he asked.

I started to get up.

"Lie still," said the voice of Bill, urgently; and I looked to see him on the other side of me. "We've got a real doctor, now. I can get him on the radio from the communications room here and have him up here in twenty minutes—"

"I'm all right," I said.

I finished climbing to my feet. Looking beyond Porniarsk, I saw a huddled mass of black fur at the base of the console, a helmet still on its head.

"Hey—the Old Man!" I said, leading the way to him. Porniarsk and Bill followed.

He was still on the floor by the time I reached him and took the helmet off; but apparently he, too, was coming out of it. His brown eyes were open and looked up into mine.

"Yes," said Porniarsk, "of course. He'll have been in monad with you just now."

The Old Man was all right. He continued to stare at me for a second after I took his helmet off; then he got to his feet as if nothing had happened. I thought that if he really felt as little jarred as he looked, by what had decked us both, he was made of stronger stuff than I. My knees were trembling.

"I just want to sit down," I said.

"This way," Bill answered.

He led me out of the room and down a corridor, the Old Man tagging after us. We came to a solid, heavy-looking door I had never seen before in the palace. He produced a key, looked at me for a second with a shyness I'd never seen in him before, then unlocked the door and pushed it open.

"Come in," he said.

I stepped through, feeling the Old Man crowding close behind me—and stopped.

The room Bill had opened for us was narrow and long; and one of its lengthier walls was all windows. They were double windows, one row above the other so that, in effect, that wall of the room was almost all glass; and the view through them was breathtaking. I had seen what was to be seen through them, but not from this particular viewpoint.

From where I stood in the room, my gaze went out and down the open slope just below the palace, over the tops of the tree belt below to a familiar view, the village of the experimentals and the human town beyond. But then it went further—for the angle of this room looked out, between a gap in the lower vegetation, to the open land beyond, stretching to the horizon and divided by a road that had not been there a year and a half ago. Now this road stretched like a brown line to where earth and sky met, with some small vehicle on it a mile or so out, moving toward us with its dust plume, like a squirrel's tail in the air behind it.

"How do you like it?" I heard Bill asking.

"Wonderful!" I said—and meant it.

I turned to talk to him, and for the first time focused in on the interior of the room itself. There was a rug underfoot and a half a dozen armchairs—overstuffed armchairs, comfortable armchairs. I had not realized until now that I had not seen a comfortable piece of furniture in months. The kind of furniture that we tended to accumulate was that which was most portable, utilitarian straight chairs and tables of wood or metal. Those in this room were massive, opulent things meant for hours of comfortable sitting.

But there was more than furniture here. Most of the available floorspace was stacked with books and boxes containing books. All in all, there must have been several thousand of them, stacked around us. The piles of them stretched between the armchairs and right up to a massive stone fireplace set in the middle of the wall opposite the windows. There was no fire in the fireplace at the moment, but kindling and logs had been laid ready for one. At the far end of the wall in which the fireplace was set, I saw what the ultimate destination of the books would be, for the first two vertical floor-to-ceiling shelves of built-in bookcases were completed and filled with volumes, and framing for the rest of the shelves stretched toward me what would eventually be three solid walls of reading matter.

"Sit down," said Bill.

I took one of the armchairs, one that faced the windows, so that I could gaze at the view. The small vehicle I had seen—a pickup truck—was now close to the town. Without warning, the music of The Great Gate of Kiev from Moussorgsky's *Pictures At An Exhibition* poured forth around me into the room.

"I thought," said Bill from behind me, "that we ought to have some place just for sitting. . . ."

He was still being shy. The tones of his voice carried half an apology, half an entreaty to me to like what I saw around me.

"It's really magnificent, Bill," I told him and turning, saw him standing at one end of the windows, looking out himself. "Who's been building all this for you?"

"I've been doing it myself," he said.

I took a long look at him. I had known he was a good man in many ways; but I had never thought of him as a carpenter, mason, or general man of his hands. He looked back at me stiffly.

"I wanted to surprise people," he said. "Only just now you seemed jolted by what happened, so . . . I actually wasn't going to tell anyone until I had it all finished, the books on the shelves, and all that."

"Look. This room's the best idea you could have had," I told him.

I meant it. God knows, if anyone ever loved reading, it was me. I was no longer looking at the view now, I was looking at the books, beginning to feel in me a stirring of excitement that I would not have guessed was still possible. The books were suggesting a million things to me, calling to me with a million voices. Maybe only a handful of those voices had anything to tell me about the things I really needed to know; but the possible smallness of their number did not matter. It was me against the time storn and I was humankind; and what was humankind was locked up in those codes of black marks on white paper that had once filled libraries all over the earth.

Suddenly, I wanted to know a million things, very strongly. There was the dry ache in my throat and the fever in my head of someone athirst and lost in a desert.

25

I was reading the last paragraph of Joyce's short story "The Dead" in his collection *Dubliners:*

"Snow was general all over Ireland. It was falling on every part of the dark central plain, on the treeless hills, falling softly upon the Bog of Allen and, farther westward, softly falling into the dark, mutinous Shannon waves. It was falling, too, upon every part of the lonely churchyard on the hill where Michael Furey lay buried. It lay thickly drifted on the crooked crosses and headstones, on the spears of the little gate, on the barren thorns. His soul swooned slowly as he heard the snow falling faintly through the universe and faintly falling, like the descent of their last end upon all the living and the dead."

There was something there I told myself, tight with certainty. There was something there. A certain part of humankind and the All. A tiny something; but something.

I put down that book and went to find the words of Ernest Hemingway, in the first paragraph of *A Farewell to Arms:*

"In the late summer of that year we lived in a house in a village that looked across the river and the plain to the mountains. In the bed of the river there were pebbles and boulders, dry and white in the sun and the water was clear and swiftly moving and blue in the channels. Troops went by the house and down the road and the dust they raised powdered the leaves of the trees. The trunks of the trees too were dusty and the leaves fell early that year. . . ."

Something . . . I went looking further.

Hui-Nan Tzu, in the second century before Christ, had written:

"Before Heaven and Earth had taken form all was vague and amorphous. Therefore it was called the Great

Beginning. The Great Beginning produced emptiness and emptiness produced the universe. . . . The combined essences of heaven and earth became the yin and yang . . ."

Sigmund Freud:

"No one who, like me, conjures up the most evil of those half-tamed demons that inhabit the human breast . . ."

Tennyson, in *The Passing of Arthur:*

> *Last, as by some one deathbed after wail*
> *Of suffering silence follows, or thro' death*
> *Or deathlike swoon, thus over all that shore,*
> *Save for some whisper of the seething seas,*
> *A dead hush fell; but when the dolorous day*
> *Grew drearier toward twilight falling, came*
> *A bitter wind, clear from the North, and blew*
> *The mist aside, and with that wind the tide*
> *Rose, and the pale King glanced across the field*
> *Of battle, but no man was moving there . . . .*

Einstein, *What I Believe:*

"It is not enough that you should understand about applied science in order that your work may increase man's blessings. Concern for man himself and his fate must always form the chief interest of all technical endeavors . . . that the creations of our mind shall be a blessing and not a curse to mankind. Never forget this in the midst of your diagrams and equations . . ."

"Do you feel it?" I asked, looking at the Old Man as the two of us sat alone in Bill's library. "Do you feel it, too, there—someplace?"

He looked back at me out of his fathomless, savage brown eyes without answering. He was not my companion in the search for what I sought. Only a sort of trailer or rider who hoped I would carry him to the place which would satisfy his own hunger for understanding—that hunger which being part of the monad had awakened in him. It was his curse not to be quite human—but still not to be simply a beast, like Sunday, who could love, suffer and even die, unquestioningly. It was something I could see, like a heavy load on him; how he knew he was dependent on me. After a second, he put a long hand lightly on my knee, in a nearly beseeching gesture that had become habitual with him lately and stirred my guts each time he did it.

So we continued; he with me, and I poring over the books in the library, along with many more Bill had since brought me from the surrounding territory. What I was after was still undefined, only a feeling in me of something that must be there, hidden in the vast warehouse of human philosophy and literature. But I kept finding clues, bits and pieces of thought that were like gold dust and stray gems spilled from the caravan of knowledge I tracked.

I had not concerned myself about it during the first few days of this. But after a week or two, it occurred to me to wonder that no one, not Marie, or Bill, or even Ellen, had been after me to take charge of our community, once more. The wonder brought with it both a touch of annoyance and a sneaking feeling of relief. I was bothered that they did not miss my help more; but at the same time, I felt in my guts that what I was doing was by all measures more important than being an administrator. So, the summer colors outside the window dried and brightened to fall ones, then faded to the drab brown of winter grass and the occasional white of snow, with only the different hues of evergreen to relieve the scene; and I came to understand that my presence was required, so to speak, only on state occasions.

One of these was called Thanksgiving, although for convenience it was held on the tenth of December and began three weeks of general celebration that ended with New Year's Day. At Thanksgiving dinner that year we had as guests in the summer palace the leaders and chieftains of the surrounding communities Bill had listed for me.

The leaders themselves were a mixed bunch. Merry Water of the TvLostChord was in his early twenties, thin, stooped, black, and intense. He had the look of someone about to fly into a rage at a word; and in fact, the three wives and five children he brought with him walked around him, so to speak, on tiptoes. He was the only really young man among the leaders present, and the rest of his semi-communal group, Bill told me, were about the same age.

Bill Projec was in his late thirties. He claimed to be pure-blooded Sioux from the Rosebud Reservation in South Dakota; but he did not have the look of the Sioux I had seen around Minnesota, although otherwise he looked undeniably Indian. He had a face that looked as if he could walk through a steel wall without a change of expression. Actually, he was almost exclusively a political leader for his colony, of whom only a few were also Indian. Petr Wallinstadt was in his mid-fifties, a tall post of a man with iron grey hair, large hands and a heavy-boned face. He was a limited-minded man whose quality of leadership lay in an utter steadfastness of attitude and purpose. Whatever Wallinstadt said he would do, he would do, Bill had told me in the briefing he had given me on the leaders before their arrival, and calling him stubborn was a weak way to describe him. Once he had made up his mind, it was not merely no use to try to argue further with him, he literally did not hear you if you tried to talk about it.

Old Ryan—otherwise called Gramps—was the patriarch among the leaders, and the patriarch of his own group as well. He may have been only a few years older than Wallinstadt, or he may have been as much as twenty years older. He was white-haired, as wide as a wall, bright, tricky, domineering, and explosive. He and Merry Water did not hide their intentions about steering clear of each other; and there had been bets made in the other communities for some time now as to when the two would hit head on and over what. One possible reason why this had been avoided so far may have been the fact that the young Ryans (anyone in Gramps' group was labelled a Ryan, whether he or she was one by blood or not) sneakingly admired the more esoteric freedoms of the TV-LostChord people; and there was a good deal of fraternization—and sororization, to coin a word—going on. Meanwhile, the two leaders stayed close to home and ran into each other in person only on occasions such as this Thanksgiving bash at our place.

There had been considerable jockeying by the four leaders from the moment they showed up to see who could get the most of my attention. Not surprisingly, Old Man Ryan was the clear winner. He could not monopolize my time, but he could and did get half again as much of it as anyone else. I found myself with a sneaking liking for the old bastard, a title he came by honestly both in the ancestral and moral sense and was, if anything, rather proud of. For one thing, he had both brains and experience; and he was not the monomaniac that Merry was, the taciturn farmer that Petr Wallinstadt was and had been before the time storm, or the suspicious chip-on-the-shoulder character that Billy was. Ryan could talk about many things and did, and his sense of humor was well-developed, though raunchy to the point of unbelievability.

It was he who brought up the matter of The Empress, after about a week or so of celebrating. We were standing in the library, brandy snifters half-full of beer in our hands, looking down the slope in the late-winter afternoon sunlight to the river, where a skating party was in progress on the ice that stretched out from the banks to the black, open water of midchannel.

"What'll you do if she comes?" Ryan asked, without warning, in the midst of a talk about spring planting.

"Who?" I asked, absently.

My attention and my mind were only partly on the discussion we had been having about storing root vegetables; and it seemed to me I had missed something he had said. Actually, I had been concentrating on the skaters. In the early twilight, some of them had put on hard hats with miner's lamps attached to them and these, now lit, were glinting like fireflies in the approach of the early twilight. The little lights circled and wove figures above the gray of the ice. Patterns of all kinds had been a fascination to me from my beginning. It had been the patterns I saw in the movements of the stock market that had been the basis of my success there. Similarly, with the management of my snowmobile company and everything else right up to our duel with the time storm, in which my ability to see the force-patterns was crucial. Now, I was beginning to make out a pattern in the encircling lights. It was a fragile, creative pattern, built as it developed, but determined by the available space of ice, the social patterns of the occasion, and the affections or dislikes of the individuals involved. I felt that if I could just study the swirl of lights long enough, I would finally be able to identify, by his or her movements, each invisible individual beneath a light source.

"Who?" I asked again.

"Who? The Empress! Beer getting to you, Despard? I said, what'll you do if she comes this way? And she'll be coming, all right, if she lives that long; because she's out to take over the world. You've got a pretty good little part-time combat force but you can't fight three hundred full-

time soldier-kids, equipped with transports, planes, helicopters and all sorts of weapons right up to fly-in light
artillery."

"What'll *you* do if she comes?" I asked, still not really
with him.

"Christ! Me? I'll wheel and deal with her, of course,"
he grunted into his glass, drinking deeply from it. "I
know I can't fight her. But you might be sucker enough to
try."

He tickled me. I finally pulled my attention entirely
from the skater patterns on the ice.

"So?" I said, mimicking his own trick of argument.
When he got serious like this, he talked with the explosive-
ness of a nineteen-twenties car backfiring. "I better not
plan to ask you for help if I'm crazy enough to take her
on, then? That it?"

"Damnright!" He stopped backfiring suddenly, turned
full on to face me, and switched to purring like an
asthmatic alley cat. "But you're smart. You know well as
I do how many ways there are to peel a grape like that.
Now, if you'd just let old Gramps do the talking—for
your bunch and mine only—I tell you I can deal with
someone like her. . . ."

"Sure you can," I said. "And with you dealing with her
for your people and mine, all the other groups would be
forced into joining us, in their own self-defense. Which
would leave her with the idea—particularly since you
could help it along while you were doing the dealing—that
you were the real power in this area, the man to settle
with; and, like all the rest, I was in your pocket."

"Screw you!" He swung away from me to stare out the
window at the skating party. The cold afternoon was dark-
ening fast; and his fat profile, against the dimming light,
showed panting and angry. "Let her take your balls then.
See if I make you a neighborly offer like that a second
time!"

I grinned. He could not help himself. It was simply in
him to push for an advantage as long as he had the
strength to do it. If I ever really needed an alliance with
him, I knew he would jump at the thinnest offer. From
what Bill had told me, we would have had very little
trouble conquering all our neighbors, including Gramps
and his clan, if we took the notion.

But all this did not alter the facts that the Empress was

nothing to grin about and that the old man had a head on his shoulders. I sobered.

"What's this about her having three hundred full-time soldiers, aircraft and artillery?" I asked. "Where'd you hear that?"

"One of my boys came back from the west coast," he said.

"*Back* from the west coast?" I said. "When did any one of your people go out there?"

"Ah, it's some time back," he said, taking a drink from his snifter. He was lying and I knew it, but I couldn't waste half an hour pinning him down to the truth. "The point is, he was in San Luis Obispo. There's an old army camp outside that town, and she's been using it as a training area. All the people in town know about the planes and the helicopters and the guns. And the soldiers came into San Luis Obispo every night to hit the bars. They've got four actual bars in there."

"She's got half the world to go after down to the top of South America, and the other half clear up to Alaska," I said. "What makes you think she'd be coming this way?"

"Don't be a jerk," grunted Ryan. "It's not country you take over nowadays. It's people. The important places. And this place is important enough. It's got you here."

Unfortunately, he was right. It had gradually begun to dawn on me, since I came from living exclusively inside my own skull, how much I was considered some sort of post-time storm wizard, not only among the people of our own community, but generally around the globe. Why they had settled on me and not on Porniarsk—or even on Bill, for that matter—puzzled me. Possibly Bill was not colorful enough to make good myth and legend; and Porniarsk could be considered too inhuman to be judged the wizard rather than the wizard's familiar. But it was a fact that this impression of me seemed to be spreading all over the world, according to the shortwave talk we heard, no doubt growing more wild and hairy the greater its distance from anyone who had ever seen me in person.

That being the case, it suddenly made sense why the Empress might mount an expedition in my direction. She could hardly lose. If I was as magical as rumor had it, she would be acquiring a valuable sort of Merlin. If I was not, she could still keep me close under wraps and maintain the legend, threatening people with my powers, and

gaining the sort of credit anyone acquires by owning a pet
sorcerer.

A corner of that situation suddenly opened up into innumerable corridors of possibilities; and the pattern-seek-
ing portion of my mind began to gallop along them to
map out the territory to my own advantage.

Ryan was still talking to me.

"What?" I asked.

"Got through to you with that, didn't I?" he said.

"That's right, Gramps," I told him, "you got through to
me."

I turned to face him.

"I want to talk to that boy of yours," I said. "I want to
hear him tell me about everything he saw."

"Well, now I don't know . . . ."

"We can dicker over your price for letting him talk to
me later. Is he here with the people you brought along?"

"No," said Ryan, frowning. "Now, where did he say he
was going? Seems to me he said something about going
east this time . . . ."

But, of course, this was only his way of making sure he
gave nothing away for nothing. I had to promise him I'd
send someone over to do welding for him on a windmill
generator he was putting up—none of his group could
weld for sour apples; and then of course, it turned out
that the relative who'd been on the west coast was out on
the ice right now, together with the others we were watching from the window.

I had the boy in—he was only eighteen—and with
Ryan, Bill, and Ellen standing by, we shook him down for
everything he could remember about the Empress and her
armed forces. He was a little reticent about why he had
gone away to the Pacific coast in the first place. I got the
impression he had had a fight with Gramps and run off
before the old man could have him beaten up by some of
the more loyal sons and daughters of the clan. He kept
moving because he ran into no one who particularly
wanted him to stay; and so he had ended up somewhere
around San Bernardino, where he found work as a wagon-
driver (the west coast was short of petroleum products,
and horse breeding was becoming a way of life). As a
teamster he had eventually driven a load of freight north
to San Luis Obispo and spent a week or so in the town
before selling his freight goods to someone other than the

person he was supposed to deliver them to, and cutting and running with the sale price.

Once safely away from San Luis Obispo, he had decided to head home. Not only because San Bernardino was now an unhealthy place for him, but because he thought he could probably buy his way back into Gramps' favor with the stories he had to tell, if not with his newly acquired possessions. For he had used the value of the goods he had stolen to buy himself the best horse, saddle and rifle he could find. Besides, as he told us, he was more than a little homesick by that time.

It turned out, however, he did not have that much more of value to add to what Gramps had already told me, except that his description of the planes used to transport the Empress' troops revealed them to me to be VTOL's, vertical-take-off-and-landing craft. That bit of information explained how the Empress could plan to airlift her soldiers into potential battlefields around a world where airports and landing strips were either no longer in existence or in bad states of repair. With VTOL's, she would be able to land just about anywhere.

But—there was a joker in the deck at the same time. My mind went *click* and put the matter of the petroleum shortages and the horse breeding together, in a military context. Her aircraft would need fuel to operate. That meant that to come as far east as we were, she either had to be sure of finding refueling spots along the way—the remains of cities with fuel still in storage somewhere—or carry her fuel along. To carry it along in the aircraft themselves would leave no room for the troops. It was an equation in supply that had only one sensible solution. Before she went anywhere, she would need to send the fuel ahead of her overland, for which horse-drawn wagons were the only answer. Not only that, but her soldiers must necessarily hoof it to within a few miles of their objective. Meanwhile, the pilots of the aircraft would undoubtedly fly them empty, except perhaps for the Empress herself and her immediate staff, to a rendezvous with the soldiers on foot, when those were at last within striking distance of their objective.

I sent Gramps and his wandering relative away and laid the matter, as I saw it, before Bill and Ellen.

"What it means," I told them, "is that we've got a cushion of a few months between the time when she decides to come this way and when she actually gets here. Not only that, but we ought to be able to set up some sort of agreement with communities west of us to warn us when her soldiers and wagons start to come through. Is there someone around here we could send off to do that for us?"

Bill looked at Ellen.

"There's Doc. He'd be good at it," Bill said, "if you could spare him for a couple of weeks."

"Doc?" I echoed; and then I saw them looking at me. "All right, all right. I just can't get over how young he is."

That was not the right thing to say. Ellen's face did not change an inch, but I could feel her reaction.

"Once they get to know him," Bill said, "Doc can command a lot of respect. And it isn't exactly like taking a stroll in the park, travelling around like that these days. The number of things that still might have kept somebody like young Ryan from coming back alive might surprise you, Marc. With Doc, we'd have the best possible chance of getting our envoy back."

"All right," I said. It was a time for giving in. "I was just thinking how he'd strike other people who'd see him the way I see him. But you know better than I do. I suppose I ought to get to know him better myself."

Ellen grinned, a thing she did rarely.

"You'll learn," she said.

I was left with the feeling that while I was forgiven, I had lost a point to her, nonetheless.

Well, as I told myself after they left, all that was mainly in her, Bill and Marie's department. My department, right now, was tracking down that something I searched for in the library and in my own head. I had not been able to do much while the holiday season was still on, with the guests around; but as soon as all that nonsense was over, I went back to work.

The search I returned to kept producing the same results as it had before, only more of them. I kept picking up clues, bits, indications, twingles—call them what you like. What they all really added up to was evidence that what I searched for was not just in my imagination. At the same time, they were no more than evidence. I began to lie awake nights, listening to the breathing of the woman-body beside me, staring at the moon-shadowed ceiling over the bed and trying to stretch my mind to form an image of what I was after. But all I could come up with was that whatever its nature, it was something of a kind with the time storm. Not *akin* to the time storm, but something belonging to the same aspect of the universe.

What I searched for had to deal with the total universe, no matter what else it did. If nothing else, the track of its footsteps was undeniably there, like the track of some giant's passing, all through the thought and creativity of the literary world.

I became avaricious, impatient to close on the quarry I hunted. My reading speed, which had been fast to begin with, increased four or five times over. I galloped through books furiously, swallowing their information in huge gulps, making a pile of unread volumes at the right of my chair in the library every morning, mentally ripping out the information they contained in chunks, and dropping the empty to the left of the same chair, in the same second that I was picking up the next book. As the winter wore on toward spring, I became like an ogre in a cave —I turned into a blind Polyphemus, made drunk by Ulysses, bellowing for books, more books.

Nonetheless, I did not lose myself in this, the way I had lost myself after Sunday's death. I continued to dress, shower, shave, and eat my meals on time. I even pulled myself out of my search now and then when there was an administrative or social matter that needed the attention of Marc Despard. But, essentially, the winter snows and the waking year that took place around me this year were like some scene painted fresh daily on a wall at which I barely looked; and it came as a shock to me one morning to look out on the fields of April and see that the snow was gone and there was a fuzz of new green everywhere.

I had made a fresh stack of books at the end of the previous day on the right side of my chair; but the morning I first noticed the new green of the landscape, I did not reach out, as usual, to pick up the top volume and start devouring it. For some reason the Old Man was not keeping me company that day. Lately the sun, through the wall of windows, had been so warm that I had gotten out of the habit of making the fire in the fireplace. That morning a curious stillness and peace seemed to hold all the room, piled and cluttered and jumbled as it now was with the books I had demanded and discarded until it looked like a warehouse.

But out beyond the window was warm yellow sunlight; and where I sat was like a small bubble of timelessness, a moment out of eternity where anyone could catch his breath, without the moment wasted being charged against his life. Instead of reading, I found myself just sitting, looking out down the slope and over the town and the plain beyond.

I had been reading a great deal of writing on religion in the past few weeks, on yoga and Zen and all the martial arts, trying to pin down what the Chinese called *Ch'i* and the Japanese *Ki,* and which was usually translated by the English word "spirit." As I sat staring out the window, a male cardinal flew down and perched on a feeding platform for birds which Bill had set up during the winter with my hardly noticing it. I stared at the cardinal; and it came to me that I had never seen such a beautiful color in my life as the rich red of his body feathers leading up to the black ones at his throat. He balanced on the feeder, pecked at some seeds Bill had put there, then lifted his head and was perfectly still against the high blue sky of spring.

Something happened.

Without warning, the timeless moment that enclosed me also reached out through the glass pane of the window to encompass the cardinal as well. It was not a physical thing happening, it was a moment of perception on my part—but all the same it was real. Suddenly I and the cardinal were together. We were the same, we were identical.

I reached down and picked up not one of the unread books, but the last volume that had been in my hands the evening before. It fell open near the beginning, where I had laid it face down, open, for a minute yesterday; and under the influence of the timeless moment, the words I had read before stood forward to speak to me with a voice as large as the world. They were the words of the opening paragraph of Chapter 2: THE VALUE OF OUR EXISTENCE, in the book *Aikido in Daily Life* by Koichi Tohei, who had founded Ki Society International, and who had himself studied under Master Morihei Ueshiba, the founder and creator of the art of Aikido.

"Our lives are a part of the life of the universal. If we understand that our life came from the universal and that we have come to exist in this world, we must then ask

ourselves why the universal gave us life. In Japanese we use the phrase suisei-mushi, *which means to be born drunk and to die while still dreaming, to describe the state of being born without understanding the meaning of it and to die still not understanding . . . ."*

With that it all came together; not suddenly, but at once, so that it was as if it had always been together. I had been like someone born drunk, doomed to die drunk—and now I was sober. The cardinal was still on the feeder; the timeless moment still held the library; but it was as if a strange golden light had come out to flow over everything. All at once I understood that what I had been after was not just in the scraps of lines I had read in the books that had passed so hotly through my hands. It was not the fragments of ideas, the shards of wisdoms I had studied that alone were precious bits of what I sought; but that everything I had read, everything I had experienced, the world and all in it—all time and all space— were what I hunted and needed to grasp. And now I could grasp it, not by making my hands big enough to cup the universe in my palms, but by taking hold anywhere, in anything as small as a moment, a sentence, or the sight of a bird on a feeder.

With that understanding, it seemed to me that the golden light was suddenly everywhere; and I was abruptly aware of life around me as far as my mind could stretch to picture it. I could feel the rapid beating of the heart of the cardinal on the feeder. I could feel the beating hearts of the experimentals and the humans at the foot of the slope. I could feel the slow, true life in the firs and the oaks and the grasses and flowers. I could feel the blind stirring of the earthworms in the newly warmed earth. My new sensitivity ranged on and out without limit, beyond the horizons and over the whole world. I could feel life stirring everywhere, from the shark cruising the hot tropical seas, to the Weddell seal sun-bathing on the south Polar ice. The whole globe beat to the rhythms of existence, and below the beat were the quieter, more massive rhythms of the inanimate, of the soil, rock, water, wind, and sunlight. Gravity pulled. The Coriolis force spun, clockwise to the north, counterclockwise to the south. The intermixing patterns of weather sounded together like the disciplined instruments of an orchestra rendering a symphony.

I do not remember the golden light leaving and the sensitivity it had brought me. Just, after a while, it was gone and the cardinal had vanished from the feeder. I was back to feeling with merely the ordinary sensitivities of my body and mind; but within those I felt alive as I never had before. Everything seemed as if seen under a very bright light, clear and sharp. My mind was racing. I seethed with energy. I could not wait to put what I had just found to practical use. I bolted from the chair and went out of the summer palace by the entrance where the vehicles stood. There was a jeep sitting in the parking area. I climbed behind its wheel and sent it bouncing down the slope toward the town. I did not quite know where or how I was going to take hold of the universe in the new way of doing so that had just become clear to me; but now it seemed impossible that I could not find a place and a means.

But oddly, as I got close to the flat ground and the houses, a strange shyness came over me. I had been down there only briefly before on half a dozen separate occasions, and each time I had gone directly to City Hall to see Ellen, Marie, or someone else, then left again in less than an hour. It came home to me that I really had never met those who lived in the town; and I was abruptly as conscious of my stranger status as a grade school child on a first day at a new school.

I parked the jeep in some bushes that hid it several hundred yards from the closest of the buildings, got out and went ahead on foot.

The first building I found myself heading for was a temporary one with a platform floor, plank walls and a canvas tent roof. To this was being added a more permanent structure of cement block walls and gable roof, already shingled. There was no glazing as yet in the window opening, and outside the door aperture, a white pickup truck was parked, from which a man in blue jeans and sweater was carrying in various lengths of lumber.

I reached the pickup while he was still inside and waited by it until he came out again. He was a lean, black-haired type in his late twenties or early thirties with a long, straight nose.

"Hi," I said.

He glanced at me indifferently.

"Hullo," he said, went to the truck, and began pulling off some twelve-foot lengths of two by four.

"Can I give you a hand?"

He looked at me again, not quite so indifferently.

"All right," he said. "Thanks."

I went over to the truck as he backed off from it with his two by fours, picked up several of my own and followed him through into the building.

There was no light inside except what came through the window openings, but this was enough to see that the building would be illuminated well enough with natural light, even on dark days, once it was finished. The two by fours were apparently for wall studs, for he had several partitions already framed up.

I carried my load over to where he was piling his. A cement floor had been poured, but not professionally finished, and the footing was both gritty and a little uneven. But it, like the wall framing and the block laying of the outer shell was good enough for security and use. We worked together at unloading the truck for some time without saying anything to each other.

I found myself getting an odd pleasure out of being useful in this ordinary way. The feeling was above and in addition to the pleasure of the physical exertion which, once I warmed up to it, was body-enjoyable, the way such efforts usually are. I was conscious of the housebuilder eyeing me as we worked, but that was as much reaction as he showed until we had finished getting all the two by fours into the building. I came out from carrying in the last two lengths of lumber and found him standing, considering what was left on the truck—mostly nails and odds and ends of hardware.

"What next?" I asked him.

"I forgot to pick up conduit for the wiring," he said, without looking at me. "Well, let's get the rest of it in. You and I better take the nail cartons together, one by one. They're heavy."

We pulled a nail carton to the open tailgate, took it each on a side and carried it in. As we went toward the door opening, he spoke.

"You're Marc Despard, aren't you?"

"Yes," I said.

He stared hard at me for a second.

"No, you're not," he said, as we stepped into the semigloom of the interior.

"I'm afraid I am."

"You can't be."

"I'm afraid I am."

"Look, he's got a long beard and he's six inches taller than you are."

We laid the carton of nails down and went out after another.

"I tell you," he said, as we went in carrying the second carton, "you can't be. I know. I know what Despard looks like."

I grinned. I couldn't help myself.

"So do I," I said.

"Then you admit you aren't him."

"No," I said. "I'm him. What makes you think I've got a beard and I'm six inches taller?"

"Everybody knows that. Besides, you never come down from that mountain."

"I do now."

"Shit!"

We carried in the other cartons without words. It occurred to me suddenly that he might think I had been laughing at him and that all this was some sort of practical joke on my part. I was distressed.

"If I don't look like Marc Despard," I asked him, "why'd you ask me if that's who I was?"

He did not answer me immediately. It was not until we had made one more delivery inside and were back out in the sunlight that he spoke again, without looking directly into my face.

"I don't know why you'd want to help me."

"You had this truck here to be unloaded," I said. "It goes faster with two people than with one."

"There's got to be more to it than that." He stopped dead and faced me. "What's up? What is it? What's going on? Is there some kind of law here or something like that I've broken?"

"Man—" I began, and then broke off. "Look, I don't even know your name."

"Orrin Elscher."

"Orrin—" I held out my hand. "Marc Despard. Glad to meet you."

He stared at my hand as if it had a mousetrap in it, then slowly put out his own hand and we shook.

"Orrin," I said, "it was just such a fine day I thought I'd come down, and when I got here I saw you unloading the truck, so I thought I'd offer you a hand. That's all there is to it."

He said nothing, only took his hand back.

We finished unloading the truck. It was strange, but once upon a time it would have bothered me that he was bothered. I would have geared up emotionally in response to his emotions. But now all I could think of was what a nice day it was and the enjoyment of using my body to some practical and useful purpose. I was getting the same sort of pleasure from unloading that truck that I might have gotten from engaging in a favorite sport; and I was grateful to Orrin Elscher for providing me with the opportunity for that pleasure. As far as his puzzle about me went, I felt no pressure to explain it. In his own time he would understand; and if that time never came, it would not make any real difference to the world. All that really mattered was that his truck was unloaded, he had been saved some work, and I had enjoyed myself.

I had gotten this far in my thinking when I remembered I had left the summer palace intending to put my new insight to work; and here I had forgotten about it completely.

But of course I hadn't. I saw the connection now between the insight and what I was presently doing. I had set out to take hold of the universe; and I had done that. There was no such thing as an unrelated action; and the act of my helping Orrin to unload his truck connected with the necessary completion of his house, the development of the whole town, the future of the people here, plus their effect and interrelation with all the rest of the people in the world. In fact, it connected with the whole future pattern in a way I could see building and stretching out until it became part of the great spider web of interacting forces that contained the time storm itself. As for me, in enunciating that connection by being part of it and recognizing it, I had expanded my own awareness that I needed to stretch before I could take the next step against the storm.

We finished unloading the truck.

"Well, take care of yourself," I said to Orrin and turned away.

I was perhaps five steps from him, headed back toward where I had hidden the jeep, when I heard him call me.

"Mr. Despard—"

I turned to find him right behind me.

"I—thank you," he said.

"Nothing to thank me for," I answered. "I enjoyed the workout. I suppose I'll be seeing you around?"

"Sure," he said—and then, more strongly, added, "Sure. You will!"

"Good."

I turned and went. I had gotten a good echo from him, like the unblurred ring of uncracked metal when you tap a bronze vase with a fingernail. I went back to the jeep, got behind the wheel, and after a moment's thought headed on into City Hall.

But there was no one around when I got there. Even the typists were not at their desks. I looked at my watch and saw it was just after ten in the morning. Coffee break time, perhaps. I went out, got back in the jeep and headed back up toward the summer palace, enjoying the bright day, the sight of the buildings and people I passed, as if the whole world was something marvelous invented yesterday that I had never seen before.

When I got to the summer palace there were eight vehicles of various kinds parked in the parking area. As I climbed out of the jeep, Bill came out of the door with a rush.

"There you are," he said. "We've been looking all over for you. The Empress is on her way. We just got word."

26

We were not surprised to see the helicopters ignore the town and head directly toward the summer palace. There were three of them, all the size of aircraft I had flown in between airports like LaGuardia and Kennedy in New York. They could each hold at least thirty people comfortably.

We stood in the parking area and watched them come —a baker's dozen of us, including the Old Man and Porniarsk. There was nothing much else we could do. Our advance warnings from the communities farther west had earlier confirmed the fact that Paula Mirador, the Empress, was indeed moving toward us with at least five hundred armed bodies (about one-third of them women) plus three .155 millimeter howitzers. She had apparently merely passed through these other communities, pausing just long enough to accept their formal submissions on her way. Wisely, no one had tried to oppose her, and we ourselves were hardly in a position to do so, even though we were probably the strongest single social unit between our territory and the Rockies.

According to her usual battle plan, which our scouts had confirmed, she had the main body of her troops standing off just over the horizon, with the VTOL transports ready and waiting. The howitzers were with them, ready to be moved in close to pound flat any property we owned before the troops followed to mop up any still-living defenders. It was a strong military argument she proposed.

We had not given in to it—yet. Our town was evacuated, except for a half-dozen fortified positions with .50 caliber machine guns, hidden among the buildings. These, if they survived the artillery, could make it something less than a picnic for the troops advancing on the wreckage.

251

Whether the Empress knew about our machine guns was a question. She apparently knew a good deal about us, but possibly not the full extent of our weapons and supplies.

The rest of our noncombatants were scattered, back in the hills, with a light force to guard them and weapons of their own, as well as enough food and other basic supplies to last a year. She could not hunt them all down, even if she wished to spend the time trying. Aside from all this, there were three more heavy machine guns and gun crews camouflaged and dug in to cover this parking area from the surrounding rocks and trees—and one other machine-gun nest hidden inside the palace. Even if she were bringing as many as sixty or eighty soldiers in her helicopters, it would not be a wise idea for her to simply try and make the thirteen of us prisoners by head-on force.

But of course all this was beside the point. She did not really want to waste trained people and ammunition on us, any more than we wanted to fight a small war with her. She and we were both lining up our resources face-to-face for a bargaining session. The helicopters sidled in, looking very dramatic against the blue sky with its few patches of high clouds, and settled to earth with a good deal of noise and raised dust.

The doors of the two furthest from us opened, and uniformed men with rifles and mortars and a couple of light machine guns jumped out and set up a sort of perimeter, facing the surrounding country. They did not, however, move too far away from their planes and seemed to be making the point that they were there to protect the helicopters and themselves primarily.

After they had settled down, there was a wait of two or three more minutes then the door to the helicopter closest to us opened, the steps were run down, and a dozen men and women in civilian clothes came out to range themselves like an honor guard in a double line ending at the foot of the steps.

Another brief wait, and a single figure came out. There was no doubt that this was Paula Mirador, even if the rest of the proceedings had been designed to leave any doubt. I stared, myself. I had not seen anything like this since before the time storm; nor had any of us, I was willing to bet. We had grown so used to living and dressing with practicality and utility in mind that we had forgotten how people had used to wear clothes, and what sort of clothes they might wear.

Paula Mirador was a page out of some ghostly fashion magazine, from her dainty, high-heeled, cream-colored boots to an elaborately casual coiffure. She looked like she had just walked out of a beauty shop. In between was a tall, slim woman who only missed being very beautiful by virtue of a nose that was a little short and a little sharp. Besides the boots and the warm brown hair of her coiffure, she wore a carefully tailored white pants suit over an open-throated polka-dotted blouse, with the wide collar of the blouse lying over the collar of the suit. A grey suede shoulderbag with an elaborately worked silver clasp hung from one shoulder.

She took my breath away—and not by virtue of her band-box perfection alone. Her hair was not that blonde, her face was not that perfect, but something about her rang an echo of Swannee in my mind.

She walked down the steps, not looking at us yokels, and gazed around at the general scenery, then said something to one of her civies-dressed attendants, who popped to and turned away to peel off an escort of eight armed troopers to come toward us.

Once upon a time, I would have credited the attendant with a prior knowledge of what I looked like, seeing him come directly toward me, alone. Lately, however, I had begun to realize how much the way in which human beings instinctively position themselves gives out signals. The group pattern of those standing around me amounted to a sign with an arrow pointing to me and the words *here is our leader*.

At any rate, the envoy, a round-faced young man in his mid-twenties, who looked something like a taller version of Bill, came up within a dozen feet of me and stopped. His troopers stopped with him.

"Mr. Despard?" he said. "You are Mr. Despard, aren't you, sir? I'm Yneho Johnson. The Empress would like to speak to you. Will you follow me, please?"

I did not move.

"That makes two of us," I said. "I'd like to talk to her. I'd like to know what the hell she's doing here on my property without my invitation. I'll wait here five minutes. If she hasn't come personally to explain by that time, I'll blow the whole batch of you apart. You're parked on top of enough buried industrial dynamite to leave nothing but dust."

He blinked. Whether because of my tone and attitude, or because of the information about the dynamite, was hard to tell. Probably both. The dynamite, of course, was a bluff. It would have taken twenty truckloads of that explosive to mine the whole parking area even sparsely. But there was no way he and the rest of Paula's party could be sure we did not have that much; and in any case, I had nothing to lose by bluffing since they outgunned us anyway.

He hesitated. I turned away.

"Bill," I said, "see he doesn't waste time."

I walked back a few steps toward the palace, hearing Bill's voice behind me.

"You've lost fifteen seconds already," Bill was saying. "Do you want to try for more?"

I turned around and saw Johnson, with his escort, retreating at a fair pace toward his mistress. He rejoined her and spoke animatedly. She, on the other hand, as far as we could tell from this distance, was the picture of cool indifference. She waved a hand gracefully on the end of one slim wrist, and he came back to us with his bodyguards.

"Mr. Despard," he said. "The Empress warns you. If you're bluffing, you'll be shot down by our escort troops as soon as the five minutes are up. If you're not bluffing, whether you kill us or not, her troops, who love her, will catch you and roast you over a slow fire. She, herself, never bluffs."

I turned toward Doc.

"Doc," I said, "shoot him."

Doc unslung the machine pistol he had hanging from his right shoulder.

"Stop. Stop—" shouted Yneho Johnson. "Don't! Wait a minute. I'll be right back."

"Just under two minutes left," I reminded him, and watched him gallop back across to his Empress.

They were still talking a minute later.

"Four minutes up," said Bill, behind me.

"Let it get down to thirty seconds," I told him.

We waited.

"Coming up on four and a half minutes," Bill said.

I stepped out in front of the others and made an elaborate show of looking at my watch.

"Now," I said to Bill, under my breath.

He had a small detonator switch in his pocket, with a wire running from it back into the palace and from there out again to a spot in the parking area near its west edge. He reached into the pocket, pressed the detonator button; and a fountain of dirt exploded very satisfactorily to about thirty feet in the air, thereby cleaning us out of dynamite almost completely—and not industrial dynamite at that, but the sort of explosive that used to be available in hardware stores in mining areas. I made a large show of looking at my watch again.

"Maybe they won't realize it's a warning," said Marie, tightly.

"They'll realize," Ellen said.

They had. The Empress was at last on the move toward me—not by herself, but with her whole entourage surrounding her. Mentally, I docked her a couple of points for not coming sooner. It should have been obvious to her that if there was one patch of ground in the parking area not likely to be mined, it would be the space where I and my own people were standing. She came on until her group merged with mine, and she walked up to stand face to face with me, smiling.

"Marc," she said, "you and I have to have a private talk."

"I can talk out here," I said.

"*You* probably can." She was very pleasant. "I find it works better for me if I don't take my own staff into my confidence exclusively. But don't you think we could both be a little more relaxed and free if it was just the two of us chatting?"

It was not an unreasonable argument; and I had already made my point—which was that I was not about to make any deal behind the back of my associates. I could afford to give in gracefully.

"All right. Come inside," I said.

I took her into the palace. On the still air indoors, I could catch a hint of perfume about her that had not been noticeable outside. I was suddenly very conscious of her physically—both of her female presence and her bandbox costuming. The ghost of Swannee moved momentarily between us, once more. On impulse I took her to the library, cleared the books off one of the other chairs for her, and we sat down facing each other.

"You must have somebody around who cares about preserving information," she said, looking about the room.

"Yes," I said. "What did you want to talk about?"

She crossed one leg over the other.

"I need your help, Marc."

"You could have written me a letter, Paula."

She laughed.

"Of course—if it'd just been a matter of you and me. But I'm the Empress and you're Marc Despard, the man who controls the time storm. When two people like us get together, it has to be a state visit."

"Aside from the fact that I don't begin to control the time storm," I said, "what about this state visit of yours? A state visit with an army and three howitzers?"

"Don't pretend to be something other than the intelligent man I know you are," she answered. "All this show of force is an excuse for you, Marc—an excuse for you to agree to work with me because that's the only way you can keep the people you have around you now from being hurt."

"I'm that valuable?"

"I said, don't pretend to be less bright than you are. Of course you're that valuable."

"All right. But why should I take advantage of your excuse? Why should I want to work with you, in any case?"

"Wouldn't you rather have the resources of the whole world at your fingertips, than just what you can reach here, locally?"

"I don't need any more than I have here," I said.

She leaned forward. There was an intensity, a vibrancy about her that was very real, unique. She had to know I knew she was using it deliberately to influence me.

"Marc, this world still has got a lot of people in it who need putting back together into a single working community. Don't tell me you don't want to have a hand in that. You're a natural leader. That's obvious, aside from the time storm and what you've done with it. Can you really tell me you'd turn your back on the chance to set the world right?"

She either had a touch of the occult about her, or she was capable of reading patterns from behavior almost as accurately as I might have myself. My deep drive to defeat the time storm reached out with its left hand to touch the basic human hunger to conquer and rule. Mentally, I gave her back the two points I had docked her earlier—and a couple more besides. But I did not answer her right away; like a good salesman, she knew when to close.

"Say you'll at least talk it over with me in the next few days," she added.

"I suppose I can do that," I told her.

So it turned out that her appearance became a state visit in reality. The main body of her troops and the how-itzers stayed out of sight over the horizon, although none of us, including me, ever forgot they were there; and she, with her immediate official family, slipped into the role of guests, as old Ryan and the others had been over the Thanksgiving holidays.

She was a good deal more entertaining than my neighbors had been, and much more persuasive. She had a mind like a skinning knife. But the most effective argument she brought to bear on me in the next five days was the pretense that she was putting her military strength aside and trying to convince me by argument alone. I knew better, of course. As I just said, none of us could forget those troops and the artillery just beyond field glass range. But her refusal to bring her military muscle directly into the discussion left me to argue silently with my own conscience over whether it was not just personal pride or stubbornness on my part that made me so willing to expose my wives and friends to death or maiming rather than join forces with her.

She had another lever to use on me, although at the time I did not rate its effectiveness with that of the argument-only ploy. She was reputed to have the kind of legendary sexiness that made her troops dream of her at night and consider all other women as watered-down sub-stitutes; but I got no such signals from her at all. Except for the odd moments in which she reminded me of Swannee, she was good company and interesting, that was all. At the same time, by contrast, she did seem to make Marie look limited and unworldly, and Ellen juvenile.

Of course, she and I had very little time out of each

other's company. We were the two heads of state and if she was to be entertained by us, I usually had to be on stage myself. The time I had with my own people was what was left over, usually either the early hours in the morning, before Paula had put in an appearance from the several rooms—suite was too pretentious a word for them—we had turned over to her and her several personal attendants—or late at night after she had tired out.

It was a situation that put both Ellen and Marie, particularly, at some distance from Paula and myself, but perhaps this was not a bad arrangement. It developed that neither of them liked her or saw anything but serious trouble coming from any extended association with her.

"She really doesn't like you, either, you know," Marie told me, the evening of the third day Paula had spent with us. "She doesn't like anyone."

"She can't afford to," I said. "She's a ruler. She's got to keep her head clear of likes and dislikes for individuals so she can make her decisions strictly on the basis of whether something is a good thing for her people, or not."

"A good thing for her or not, you mean," said Marie.

That was unusually outspoken for Marie. But the more I thought over what I had said to her, the more I liked the ring of my own words. I went to Ellen's room and tried the same speech on her.

Ellen snorted.

"Is that supposed to be an answer?" I said. "All right, tell me. Exactly what is it that's wrong with Paula?"

"Nothing's wrong with her," said Ellen.

"Well, you must think something's wrong or you wouldn't be acting this way. What is it?"

"You."

"Me?"

"You want to be a damn fool, go ahead and be one."

I lost my temper.

"How can I be a damn fool? I've got to find some way to deal with her and do it with gloves on. She can wipe us all off the map if I don't!"

Ellen got up out of bed, put on her clothes and went for a walk—at three in the morning. Nobody but she could have done something like that with such finality and emphasis. Her back was an exclamation mark going out the door.

Bill did not like her either. Neither did Doc. For that matter, neither did the Old Man, who always disappeared when Paula came on the scene. I began to feel like the tragic hero in a Greek play with the chorus in unison warning me of disaster at every step. I did not mention any of this to Paula; but she evidently sensed some of it at least, because along about the end of the week she got off on a subject that was particularly timely in view of the situation.

". . . It *is* a lonely life," she said, apropos of something I had said. We were taking a stroll through the woods below the summer palace early in the morning. "Rank does more than isolate you socially. Do you realize, Marc, you're essentially the only person in the world I can talk to on the level, so to speak? With everyone else, I have to remember I'm the Empress. But it's not even *that* so much as having to put myself in the balance sometimes against everyone around me when it comes to making decisions. Every so often, all the advice I get is one-sided; and sometimes I have to brace myself to turn it all down and go just the opposite way, because when it gets down to it I have to trust my own decision more than all of theirs or else I'm not a fit ruler."

"I know what you mean," I said.

"Sure you do." She glanced at me for a moment, then looked ahead the way we were walking. "You can't take on responsibility without taking on everything else that goes with it."

She stopped and turned to face me. I stopped also, necessarily, and turned toward her.

"That's why it would mean so much to have you with me, Marc," she said. "I know you've got your own work with the time storm. I've only just begun to realize these last few days how important that is. But what you're needed more for, now, is to help me unify this torn-up Earth we've got and put it on a single, working community basis. That's your higher responsibility, at the moment."

"And if I'm not with you, I'm against you?"

"Oh, Marc!" she said, sadly. "I'm not a monster."

I felt slightly ashamed of myself. It was a fact that, so far, I had seen nothing in her that was not reasonable to the point of being admirable. The only evidence I had ever had that contradicted this was contained in the large body of rumor about her; and I had some experience with rumors, having heard some of the ones that circulated about me.

"Well," I said, "how much time are you asking me to invest?"

"A couple of years at the most." She looked sideways at me as we walked. "Certainly no more than that."

"You think you can take over the world in two years? That's better than Alexander's record, and he was only thinking about the Asian continent."

"There aren't that many people nowadays. You know that as well as I do," she said. "And it's a matter of contacting just the large population centers. Once those are organized, the small communities in each area and the individuals will want to adjust to the situation on their own."

"Two years . . ." I said. All at once, it seemed like a long time away from here, away from the library and Porni-arsk's workroom.

"Look," she said, stopping again. Once more we faced each other and, for the first time since I had known her, she touched me, putting a hand lightly on my arm. "Let's forget about it for today. Why don't we do something different? You let me entertain you for a change."

"How?"

"We'll fly to my base camp and have lunch there. You can see for yourself what my regular soldiers are like and why I think it won't take even two years to bring order to the world."

"I don't know," I said. "The others may worry. . . ."

"Even if they do, it'll do them good," she said. "When they see you coming back safe and sound after going off alone with me, they'll understand I'm no one to be afraid of."

"All right."

We went back up to the palace. I did not quite feel like telling Ellen or Marie I was taking a solo jaunt into Paula's armed camp, so I looked for Bill or Doc. Doc was the one I found first; and he took the idea of my going calmly enough. In fact, it seemed to me his eyes even lit up a bit at the idea.

"Want me to come?" he asked.

"It's not necessary—" I checked myself. "Come to

think of it, why not? You may be able to see some things there I won't."

I sent him to tell Bill we were both going and went back to explain to Paula that there would be two of us, feeling somewhat smug with the notion that I had taken some of the force out of the objections the others would have to my going entirely alone.

"Of course, bring him," said Paula graciously, when I mentioned that I couldn't come after all, unless I had someone like Doc along with me. It had occurred to me that, just as I had, she might be underestimating Doc because of his youth. I had learned better during the past few months; but if she was making the same initial error, it could do us no harm and might turn out to our advantage. On the helicopter ride to her camp, accordingly, I watched her closely for any sign that this was the case, but saw no clear signals either way. She was friendly but a little condescending to him, which could mean that she did not, in fact, recognize his worth, or simply that she lumped him in with all those human bodies she looked down on from her status as Empress.

The camp, when we got there, was impressive enough. Paula's soldiers might or might not love her, as rumor had it, but they were well-uniformed, well-armed, and under good discipline. Their field tents were pitched in a hollow square with Paula's clump of larger tents at the center, so that these were protected on all sides. The helicopter that brought us put us down in the open space outside this interior clump of tents and within the camp area. If Paula had been intending to make me prisoner once she had me here, she would have had no difficulty once we had landed. There were armed guards ten deep around me in all directions.

But as it was, our visit was nothing but pleasant. Paula evidently travelled with a full complement of personal servants—I estimated at least two full helicopter-loads worth, which meant that she might not have needed to be so saving of fuel as I had guessed—including a number of younger women, none of them quite as good-looking as she was, but close enough. These were dressed as impractically as she was, with an eye to appearance rather than practicality; and this puzzled me until I began to realize that their primary job, or at least their highly important

secondary job, was to act as ornaments and geishas. They
were all over Doc and me while we were having cocktails
before lunch, and they both served and joined us at the
meal itself.

I did not at all mind being fussed over by these attendants; and I could all but see Doc's ears wiggling. I say, I
could all but see his ears wiggling. What I saw, of course,
was that they did not wiggle at all, and he was so poker-
faced and determinedly indifferent to the attentions he was
getting that it was almost painful to watch. Being a little
more case-hardened by years than Doc, I had a corner of
my mind free to note that it was a shrewd move of Paula's
to provide herself with such courtiers. Not only did they
act as a setting to show her off and emphasize her authority, they added an extra level between her and ordinary
female humanity. Perhaps her troops did worship her, after all, seeing her set off this way, in the same way that
they might worship a god or a demigod.

After lunch, Paula called in the commander of her soldiers, a small, lean, grey-haired man named Aruba with
three stars on each shoulder strap of his impeccable uniform. General Aruba and Paula together took us out to
look over the camp and observe her troops. Those in
uniform were all young. I saw some boys and girls I could
swear were no more than fourteen or fifteen years old.
They were all cheerful, bright-looking and had the air of
individuals aware of themselves as members of an elite
group. There was a curious uniformity among them, too,
which puzzled me for a while before I realized that I saw
no tall bodies among them, either female or male. Like the
general, they were short, and most tended to a squareness
of body.

Aside from their size, though, they were impressive.
They were apparently spending their time in active training while awaiting the results of Paula's negotiations with
us. They had set up an obstacle course outside their camp,
and we watched as some thirty or forty of them ran
through it, looking like trained athletes. They were, as
Gramps Ryan had hinted, a far cry from my part-time
militia.

After the inspection tour, we stepped into Paula's largest tent once more for drinks and then were flown back
to the summer palace. I was itching to know what Doc's
reaction was to everything we had seen; but I was back in

host position again and could not abandon Paula to plunge immediately into conference with one of my staff. So it was nine that night before I had a chance to get together with him and the others. We held a staff meeting down in the City Hall, safely away from the summer palace and the view or hearing of any of Paula's attendants.

"Well," I said to Doc, when we were at last gathered over the coffee cups in Ellen's office—he and I, Ellen, Marie, and Bill—"how about it? What did you think of those soldiers of hers?"

"Well," Doc scratched his right ear, "they're in good shape physically. They're well-trained. They're young and bouncy and they've learned to obey orders. I'd guess they know their jobs—"

"Tough as we've heard they are, then," said Ellen.

"Maybe," said Doc.

"Why maybe?" I demanded.

"Well," said Doc, "they're not veterans. My dad and the other officers used to talk a lot about that; and it was a fact. I mean, I could see it too. The ones who'd actually been shot at somewhere along the line knew what it was like; but there was no way the ones who hadn't been shot at could know what it was like. My dad and the others used to say there was no telling what a man who hadn't been shot at was going to do the first time he was."

"What makes you so sure the ones we saw haven't been shot at?" Bill asked.

Doc shrugged.

"They just look like they haven't. I mean, it shows."

"How?" I said. "For example?"

"Well . . ." he frowned into his coffee cup for a second, then looked back at me. "They're too bright-eyed and bushy-tailed. Too gung ho. You understand? If they were veterans, they wouldn't be wasting energy except when they had to. For example, when they were off duty, you'd see them off their feet, setting or lying down somewhere. That sort of thing."

We thought about it for a moment.

"You try to remember," Doc said, "when it was you last heard of the Empress actually fighting anyone. Maybe on the Islands, where she started, there was some fighting. But ever since she landed on the west coast, it seems she just shows up with all those guns and whoever she's dealing with surrenders."

"Then you think we might have a chance, fighting her?" Bill asked. "Is that it?"

"We might have a chance," Doc said. "One thing for sure, the people we've got carrying guns are going to use them and keep on using them when the fighting starts."

There was another short silence, full of thought.

"I don't like it," said Marie finally. "There's still too many of them compared to us."

"I think so too," I said. "Even if we were sure of winning, I don't want our town wrecked and even one of our people killed. Now, Paula's been after me to join her for the next year or two while she brings the rest of the world under control—"

They all started to talk at once.

"All right, now just hang on there for a moment!" I told them. "If I do decide to go with her, it doesn't necessarily mean I'm going to stay for two years, or even one year. But if that's the best way, or the only way, to get her to leave everybody else alone here, then my spending some time with her is a cheap way to buy her off."

"But what sort of a place will this be without you?" said Marie fiercely.

"Come on, now," I said. "The rest of you run everything here. All I've been doing is sitting around and reading books. You can spare me, all right."

"Marc," said Bill, "you aren't needed here because you've got duties. You're needed here because you're the pivot point of the whole settlement."

"Let him go," said Ellen. "It's what he wants to do."

Bill looked at her quickly.

"You don't mean that."

"All right, I don't," said Ellen. "But it gripes me."

She folded her arms and looked hard-eyed at me.

"And what about the time storm?" Bill said to me. "How can you keep on working toward a way to do something permanent about that, if you go off with Paula? What if the balance of temporal forces we set up breaks down sometime in the time you're gone? What if it breaks down tomorrow?"

"If it breaks down tomorrow, I can't do a thing more about it but try to reestablish the balance again, the way I did the first time."

"You can't do that if you're not here," Marie said.

"Don't talk nonsense, Marie," I said to her. "Paula

needs a stable Earth as much as we do. She'd send me back in a hurry to reestablish a balance of forces if that balance broke down and mistwalls started moving again."

"It might not be so easy to reestablish next time, Porniarsk says," Bill put in. "What about that?"

"If it's not as easy, it's not as easy," I told them all. "I tell you I'm not yet ready to take on the time storm again to produce any more permanent state of balance than I did before."

For a second, nobody said anything. The silence was as prickly as a fistful of needles.

"Anyway," said Ellen, "have you checked with Porniarsk? You owe him that much before you do anything like going off."

As a matter of fact, I had completely forgotten about Porniarsk. The avatar was never concerned or consulted in any of our purely human councils about community matters; and as a result, I had fallen out of the habit of thinking about him when decisions like this were to be made. Ellen was quite right. I could not do anything with the time storm if I lost the help of Porniarsk. If I simply went off with Paula and he should think I'd given up on the storm. . . .

"I haven't checked with him yet," I said. "Of course I will. I'll go talk to him now. I suppose he's in the lab?"

"I think so," said Bill.

"Yes, he is," said Ellen. "I was just in there."

That bit of information caught at my attention. As far back as I could remember, Ellen had never paid any particular attention to Porniarsk. I went out and down the corridors toward the lab. On the way, I passed the little interior courtyard where Sunday lay preserved; and on impulse I checked, turned, and went in to look at him.

I had not come to see him in months. It had been a painful thing even to think of him for a long time; and while now the pain was understood and largely gone, the habit of avoidance was still strong in me. But at this moment, there was a feeling in me almost as if I should let the crazy cat know that I was going—as if he was still alive and would worry when I did not come back immediately. The roofless courtyard was dark, except for starglow, when I stepped into it, and cold with the spring night. I closed the door by which I had come out and reached out to thumb on the light switch controlling the

floodlights around the walls. Suddenly the courtyard
was illuminated so brightly it hurt my eyes; there, to my
right, was the transparent box in which Sunday lay.

It was like a rectangular fish tank a little longer than
the leopard and perhaps three feet deep, set up on a
wooden support about coffee table height and dimensions.
Within, it held that same fluid-looking stuff that filled
Porniarsk's universe viewing tank and which he had given
me to understand was actually something like an altered
state of space—if you could picture nothingness as having
variable states. At any rate, what he told me it did was
to hold Sunday's body in a condition outside of the movement of time, any time. As a result, his body was even
now in exactly the same condition it had been in less than
two hours after his death, when Porniarsk had surrounded
it with a jury-rigged version of this non-temporal space
tank.

Nearly two hours, of course, was far too long for him
to have been dead if we had been hoping for any sort of
biological revival. If it had been possible to mend his
wounds and start his life processes in the present state of
his dead body, there would have been nothing to bring to
life. His brain cells had died within minutes without oxygen, and the information contained in them was lost. A
body in perpetual coma would have been all we could have
achieved.

But what Porniarsk had hopes of was something entirely
different. It was his expectation that, if we could learn
to control the time storm even a little, we might be able
to either acquire the knowledge directly, or contact others
farther up the temporal line who had it, so that we could
return the temporal moment of Sunday's body back to a
few seconds before he had been wounded. It was a far-
fetched hope and one that I, myself, had never really
been able to hold. But if Porniarsk could believe in it, I
was willing to go along with him as far as his faith could
take us.

Perhaps at that, I thought to myself as I stood looking
at Sunday's silent form lying there with its eyes closed
and its wounds hidden under bandages, I had indeed had
some secret and sneaking hope of my own, after all. I
needed to hope. Because Sunday was still there in my
mind like a chunk of jagged ice that would not melt. He
represented unfinished business on my part. He had died

before I could show him that I appreciated what he had given me—and the fact that the gift was an unthinking animal's one did nothing to lessen the obligation. What I owed to the others, to Ellen, to Marie perhaps, and Bill—or even to Porniarsk himself—I still had time to pay, because they were still alive and around. But the invoice for Sunday's love, and his death, which had come about because he had rushed to rescue and protect me, still hung pinned to the wall of my soul with the dagger of my late-born conscience.

No—it was not because of how he had died that I was in debt to him, I thought now, watching his motionless body in the floodlights. It was what he had done for me while he was alive. He had cracked open the hard shell that cased my emotions, so that now I walked through the world feeling things whether I wanted to or not; which was sometimes painful, but which was also a part of living. No, regardless of what happened with Paula, I could never be diverted permanently from work with the time storm, if only for my hope of seeing Sunday alive again, so that I could let him know how I felt about him.

I turned off the lights. Suddenly, in the dark and the starlight, I began to shiver, great shuddering, racking shivers. I had become chilled, standing there in the raw spring night in my shirtsleeves. I went back to the warmth inside and down the hall a little farther to Porniarsk's lab.

He was there when I stepped through its door and the Old Man was with him, squatting silently against one of the walls and watching, as the avatar stood gazing into the universe tank. They both turned to me as I came toward them.

"I thought I'd drop by," I said; and the social words sounded foolish in this working room, spoken to the alien avatar and the experimental, near-human animal. I hurried to say something more to cover up the fatuous sound of it. "Have you found out anything new?"

"I've made no great gain in knowledge or perception," Porniarsk said, quite as if I had last spoken to him only an hour or two before, instead of something like months since.

"Do you think you will?" I said.

"I have doubts I will," he said. "I'm self-limited by what I am, as this one here—" he pointed to the Old Man, who turned to gaze at him for a second before looking back at me, "is self-limited by what he is. Porniarsk himself might do a great deal more. Or you might."

"You're sure there's no hope of getting Porniarsk here?" I asked. I had asked that before; but I could not help trying it again, in the hope that this time the answer would be different.

"I'm sure. There's a chance of something large being accomplished here. But there's a certainty of something not so large, but nonetheless important, being accomplished where Porniarsk is now. He will never leave that certainty for this possibility."

"And you can't tell me where he is, even?"

"Not," said the avatar, "in terms that would make any sense to you."

"What if things change? Could you then?"

"If things change, anything is possible."

"Yes," I said. I was suddenly very aware that we were at the end of a long and full day. I would have sat down just then if there had been a chair nearby; but since neither Porniarsk nor the Old Man used chairs, the nearest one at the moment was at a far end of the room, and it was not worth my going and bringing it back.

"I haven't been getting anywhere myself, I'm afraid," I said—and immediately, having said it, remembered that this was not quite true. I hesitated, wondering if my experience of several days past with the cardinal that had come to perch on the bird feeder, and all that had followed, would mean anything to the avatar. "Well, there has been something."

He waited. The Old Man waited. If they had been two humans, at least one of them would have asked me what that something had been.

"I've been doing a lot of reading for some time now . . ." I went on after a moment; and I proceeded to tell Porniarsk how the Old Man had cracked me loose from the mental fog I'd been in ever since Sunday's death, and how I had started on my search through everything I could lay my hands on between book covers. I had never told him this before; and, hearing the words coming from my mouth now, I found myself wondering why I had not.

Porniarsk listened in silence, and the Old Man also listened. How much the Old Man comprehended I had no way of telling. He certainly understood a fair amount of what we humans said to each other, apparently being limited, not so much by vocabulary, as by what was within his conceptual abilities. Certainly he knew I was talking about him part of the time, and almost certainly, he must have understood when I was talking about that moment on the mountainside when I was ready to kill him and the touch of his hand stopped me.

Porniarsk let me go through the whole thing, right down to the description of the golden light and my helping Orrin Elscher unload his pickup truck. When I was finally done, I waited for him to say something, but still he did not.

"Well," I said, at last. "What do you think? Did I really break through to something, or didn't I?"

"I've no way to answer that question," Porniarsk said. "Any discovery can be valuable. Whether it's valuable in the way we need it to be, valuable toward learning how to control the time storm, I've no way of knowing. Basically, I'd say that anything that expands your awareness would have to be useful."

I found myself less than happy with him. It had been a great thing to me, that episode with the cardinal and the golden light and the passage with Elscher; and the avatar's treating it so calmly rubbed me the wrong way. I was on the edge of snapping at him; then it came to me that I was having one of the suspect emotions—anger.

So—why was I angry? I asked myself that, and the answer came back quickly and clearly. I was angry because I had been expecting to be patted on the back. Subconsciously, I had been cooking in the back of my head all this time a neat little argument for him, to the effect that I had made this large step forward, working on my own; so going off with Paula would not waste any time, since I could continue working toward more large steps while I was away. But now Porniarsk had shot the whole scheme down by not showing the proper astonishment and awe at my accomplishment; and I was left without the necessary springboard for my argument.

All right. So it was a case of going back and starting over again—with honesty this time.

"We're up against a situation," I said. "I may have to leave here for a time. I don't know how long."

"Leave?" Porniarsk asked.

I told him about Paula.

"You see?" I said, when I was done. "The only safe

way for the people here—and for that matter, for what you have in this room and any work with the time storm— is for me to go along with her, for a while anyway. But it's temporary. I'll only be gone for a while. I want you to know that."

"I can understand your intentions," said Porniarsk. "Can I ask if you've weighed the importance of what you want to protect here against the importance of what you may be able to do eventually in combatting the time storm? If nothing else, an accident could destroy you while you're away from here."

"Accident could destroy me here."

"It's much less likely to do so here, however; isn't that so? With this Paula, you'll be moving into an area of higher physical risk?"

"Yes, I guess so," I said. "No. No guess about it. You're right, of course."

"Then perhaps you shouldn't go."

"God help me, Porniarsk!" I said. "I've got to! Don't you understand? We can't fight her and survive. And we've got to survive first and get our work with the time storm done after, because there's no way to do it the other way around."

"You're sure we couldn't survive if you stayed?"

"As sure as I am of anything."

He stood, the heavy mask of his features facing me silently for a second.

"Do one thing, please," he said. "It's been some time since you looked into the viewer here. Will you look again now, and tell me if there's any difference in what you see?"

"Of course," I told him.

I stepped up to the tank and looked into it. Now that I focused in on the space contained by it, I once more saw the myriad of tiny lights moving about in it. I looked at them, feeling a strange disappointment; and it took me a second or two to realize the reason. I had unconsciously bought my own story about having accomplished some breakthrough in understanding, the moment with the cardinal. I had really expected to see something more than I ever had, the next time I looked into this device; and now came disappointment.

Identified, the disappointment grew to a sharp pang. It was against all reason. I did not want to discover evidence that would be against my going with Paula. I wanted evidence that I should go, and it was exactly that sort of evidence that I was getting. But I realized that this was not what I really wanted—it was not what my heart wanted.

I reached into my memory to recapture the moment with the cardinal and the golden light that had been everywhere. But it slipped away from my imagination. I could not evoke it. A bitter anger began to rise in me. My mind beat against the iron bars of its own inability, and what I reached for went further and further from me.

I may have said something. I may have snarled, or sworn, or made some sound. I think I remember doing something like that, though I am not sure. But suddenly, there was a touch on my left hand. My mind cleared. I looked down and saw the Old Man beside me. He had taken hold of my fingers, and he was looking up at me.

My mind cleared. Suddenly, Sunday and the cardinal and all things at once came back together again. All the angry emotion washed out of me and I remembered that it was not by pushing out, but by taking in, that I had finally found the common pattern that connected me with all things else. I let go then, opened up my mind to anything and everything, and looked into the universe tank once more.

There were the lights again. But now, as I watched, I began to pick up rhythms in their movements, and identify patterns. Forces were at work to shift them about, and those forces were revealed in the patterns I saw. As I identified more and more of them, their number grew until they began to interact, until larger and larger clusters of lights were locking together in interrelated movements. There was no golden illumination around me this time; but there was an intensity—not a tension, but an intensity —that mounted like music rising in volume until it reached a certain peak, and I broke through. All at once, I was there.

I was no longer standing looking into a viewing device. I was afloat in the actual universe. I was a point of view great enough to see from one end of the universe to the other and, at the same time, able to focus in on single stars, single worlds. Now I observed not the representation, but the reality; and for the first time I perceived it as a single, working whole. From particle to atom, to star, to galaxy, to the full universe itself, I saw all the parts working together like one massive living organism moving in response to the pressure of entropy. . . .

"My God!" I said—and I heard my own voice through the bones of my skull, very small and far away, for I was still out there in the universe. "My God, it's collapsing! It's contracting!"

For it was. What I looked at were the patterns of a universe that had been uniformly expanding, all its galaxies spreading out from each other, creating an entropy that was running down at a uniform rate. But now the pattern had been expanded too far. It had been stretched too thin, and now it was beginning to break down in places. Here and there, galaxies were beginning to fall back into the pattern, to reapproach each other; and where this was happening, entropy had reversed itself. In those places, entropy was increasing, side by side and conflicting with those still-expanding patterns in which entropy continued to decrease.

The result was stress, a chaos of laws in conflict, spreading like a network of cracks fracturing a crystal, spreading through the universal space, riding the tides of movement of the solid bodies through space. It was stress that concentrated and generated new fractures at the points of greatest mass, primarily at the center of the galaxies; and where the fracture lines ran, time states changed, forward or back, one way or another.

Four billion years ago, the first stress crack had touched our galaxy. My point of view turned time back to that point and I saw it happen. An accumulation of entropic conflict near the galaxy center. A massive star that went nova—but unnaturally, *implosion* nova.

There was a collapse of great mass. A collapse of space and time, followed by an outburst of radiating time faults, riding the wave patterns of the stellar and planetary movements within the galaxy, until at last the time storm reached far out into the galactic arms and touched our own solar system.

What had gone wrong was everything. What was falling apart was not merely this galaxy, but the universe itself. There was nothing to tie to, no place to stand while the process could be halted, the damage checked and mended. It was too big. It was everything, all interconnected, from the particles within my own body to the all-encompassing universe. There was no way I or anyone else could stop something like that. It was beyond mending by me, by humanity, beyond mending by all living intelligent beings. Facing it, we were less than transitory motes of dust caught up in a tornado, helpless to even dream of controlling what hurled us about and would destroy us at its whim. . . .

27

I woke in my own bed and with the féeling that I had
been through this once before. For a moment, I could not
remember when; then I recalled my earlier experience
with the universe tank and how I had passed out after
getting caught up in what I saw there. I felt a momentary
quirk of annoyance. If I was going to fold up every time I
tried to see things in that tank. . . .

But the annoyance faded as I remembered what I had
seen. Here, lying in the familiar bed in the familiar room
with everything simple and usual about me, the memory
seemed impossible, like nothing more than some bad
dream. But it was not a bad dream. It was reality; and in
spite of the comfortable appearance of everyday security
that surrounded me, the fact of the time storm as I had
seen it loomed over us all like some giant, indifferent
mountain that might crumble and bury us at any moment,
or might let us live a thousand years in peace.

But still . . . for all that I could feel the shadow of
the storm still dark on me, I was not quite as destroyed
by it as I had been when I had first seen it in its full dimensions, imaged in the tank. A reaction had taken place
inside me, a stubborn reflex against utter despair and hope-
lessness. There was no way I could even begin to dream,
as I had for so long, of controlling the storm. And still
. . . and still . . . something inside me was refusing to give
up. Some strange and snorky part of my being was insisting
that the situation could still be fought and perhaps overcome.

It was impossible. Perhaps a thousand more individuals
like myself, armed with powers beyond the powers of
gods, might have stood a chance of achieving control, but

I was alone and had no such powers. Only, there it was. I could not let go. Something in me refused to do it.

Ellen came in, carrying a glass of water.

"How are you?" she asked.

"I'm all right," I said.

The shade was pulled down on the bedroom's one window and a light was on. But now that I looked, I saw the paler, but brighter, gleam of daylight around the edge and bottom of the shade.

"How long have I been here?" I asked, as she came over to me. She handed me the glass of water and also, two white pills.

"Take these," she said.

"What are they?" I asked, looking at the pills in my hand.

"She didn't tell me, but Marie said you should take them when you woke up."

"Now damn it, I'm not taking some medication I don't know about just because you say Marie says I should take them."

"I think they're only aspirin."

"Aspirin?"

I looked at them closely. Sure enough, they had the little cross stamped on one side that was the trademark of the brand we had been able to get our hands on locally; and when I held them close to my nose, I could catch a faint whiff of the acid smell that was the sign of aspirin when it was getting old. Overage drugs were one of our problems since we were restricted to stocks from time periods all antedating at least the time when we had balanced the forces of the time storm. These two tablets were really fresher than most of their kind that I had encountered in the last half year. Marie must have been hoarding these against some emergency. I felt ashamed of myself. I did not need the pills, but they would only keep on aging toward uselessness if I did not take them, while swallowing them would do me no harm and make Marie feel her efforts had not been wasted.

I took them.

"Porniarsk wants to talk to you if you're up to it."

"I'm up to it, all right." I threw the covers back and sat up on the edge of the bed. They had undressed me.

"Where are my pants?"

"Closet," said Ellen. "Maybe you'd better not get up."

"No, I'm fine," I said. She looked unconvinced and I decided to lie a little. "I had a headache but it seems to be getting better already."

"If you're sure," said Ellen. "I'll go tell him then."

She went out, and I had time to get dressed before Porniarsk trundled into the room.

"Are you well?" he asked me.

"Fine," I said. "No problems. I'm not even particularly tired."

"I'm glad to hear that. Do you remember what you said before you collapsed?"

"I'm not sure . . . ."

"You said 'My God . . .' and then you said 'It's impossible. I can't do it. It can't be done . . .' Can you tell me what you meant and what made you say that?"

"What I saw in the tank," I said.

I told him what that had been. When I was through he stood for a second, then creaked off one of his heavy-headed nods.

"So you believe now that further effort to control the storm is useless?" he asked.

"That's the way those patterns looked," I said. "But now . . . I'm not sure. I still don't see any hope in them, but at the same time, I don't seem to be able to bring myself to give up."

"I'm glad of that," said the avatar. "With no will to succeed, you'd fail even if there was good reason to expect success. But with will, there's always hope. Porniarsk himself has always believed that the apparent is only the possible. Therefore failure, like success, can always be only a possibility, never a certainty."

"Good," I said. "But what do we do now?"

"That's my question to you," said Porniarsk. "My earlier guess was right. Your capabilities are far beyond mine. It's up to you to find the answer."

For the next three days I tried, while holding Paula in play as well as I could. But the evening of the fourth day her impatience came out in the open.

"I'll need an answer tomorrow, Marc," she said, as she went back to her own rooms. "I've spent more time here now than I planned."

It was the eleventh hour, clearly. I thought of calling Porniarsk, Ellen, and Marie together for a brainstorming session and rejected the notion. There was nothing they could do to help me. As Porniarsk had said, it was up to me—alone.

I isolated myself in the library, paced the floor for a while, and came up with absolutely nothing. My mind kept sliding off the problem, like a beetle on a slope of oily glass. Finally, I gave up and went to bed alone, hoping that something might come to me in my sleep.

I woke about three hours later, still without a solution. My mind was spinning feverishly; but only with worries. What was to become of Ellen and Marie, and for that matter, our whole community, if I went off as Paula's captive-servant and either died or did not come back? What could help the world if the local forces of the storm broke out of balance again? There was no answer anywhere except the hope of doing something with the storm after all and using control of its forces to somehow break the hold that Paula's superior army gave her over us all.

And I could not find such a hope. Every possibility seemed bleak and dry and worn out. There was only one way to unlock the door confronting me—with some kind of a key; and there was no key. My thoughts had spun around in a circle so long they were exhausted. I threw on the topcoat that I used as a bathrobe and went back to the library to get away from my own circular idea-dance.

Under the artificial lights, the library was still and comfortless. I sat down in one of the overstuffed chairs and closed my eyes. My mind skittered off at all angles, throwing up pictures of everyone for whom I felt responsible . . . Marie, Wendy, Ellen, the avatar. . . .

Their images chased each other before the vision of my imagination, like movie film played on the inner surfaces of my closed eyelids. Even the shapes of people who were not around any more. I watched Tek, going down from the bullets of the machine pistol in Ellen's hands; Samuelson, waiting with his rocket launcher for the outsize toy-like attackers of his small town; Sunday, as I had first seen him; Sunday again, with Ellen, back when I had called her only "the girl"; Sunday. . . .

Sunday.

Suddenly, with the thought of him, it all came together. My mind opened up like a flower at sunrise, and life flowed back into me. The light and all things in the still room seemed to change. Once more, I felt my identity with all my people and the cat who slumbered; and I saw at once what could perhaps be done if there was time enough. I got to my feet with my idea still in me and went as quickly as I could to Porniarsk's lab.

Porniarsk was standing immobile beside the vision tank, his eyes fastened on nothing, when I turned the lights on in the dark room. It was impossible to tell whether he slept at times like this, or whether in fact he slept at all. We had all asked him about that at one time or another, and he had always answered that the question was meaningless in his terms and unanswerable in ours. Now, when the lights went on, he stayed as he was for a second, then turned his head to look at me.

"What is it, Marc?" he asked.

"I think I might have it!" I said. "It just came to me. Look, you can run this tank like a computer, can't you? I mean you can extrapolate the storm forward and back?"

"Yes."

"How far forward?"

"Until extrapolation's no longer possible," he said. "Until the time storm destroys the universe, or the capacity of the tank's logical sequencing is exceeded."

"Look," I said. My vocal chords were tight and my voice bounced loudly off the bare, white-painted concrete walls. "There's always been the chance we might be able to get help with the storm up forward, but I've never thought about that in terms of a really long way forward. I remember now, when I was seeing the patterns in the tank, I thought that if I could find a thousand like me something might, just might, be done. We'd never find anything like that in the reasonably near future. But, if we went as far forward as we could—maybe way up there there really are a thousand others like that. Away up there. As far into the future as we can reach."

"And if there were," said Porniarsk. "How could we contact them?"

"We might be able to go to them." The words were galloping out of me and my brain felt wrapped in flames. "If I could just see what the storm patterns were, up in that time—just the patterns affecting this immediate area, the area right around this house, maybe just even around this lab—I might be able to unbalance the present forces enough so they'd correspond. I might be able to produce a time change line; one single mistwall to move just us, far down the future-line to them."

He neither moved nor made a sound for five or six seconds, while my heart beat heavily inside me, shaking my chest.

"Perhaps," he said.

The breath I had not realized I was holding went out of me in something like a grunt.

"We can do it?"

"I can show you the ultimate pattern possible to this device—perhaps," he said. "Are you sure you can make use of it, if I do?"

"No," I said, "I can try, though."

"Yes," he said. His head went up, his head went down, in one of his nods. "I'll need time to work out the storm patterns that far forward."

"How much time?"

He looked at me steadily.

"I don't know. Maybe days. Maybe, some years."

"Years!" I said. But then the sense of what he was saying sank into me. The furthest pattern perceivable by the vision tank could only be reached by going through all preceding patterns.

"When I've reached the limits of the device's capacity," he said, "I can call you in to see it."

"Then we need to buy whatever time that takes," I said. "That settles it. I'll tell Paula I'll go with her."

"Probably that's best. But you'll have to be able to come back here when I've found the final pattern."

"I'll get back," I said. "Don't worry about that."

I felt wonderful. All my frustration had vanished in a burst of energy and certainty. I would not have gone back to bed even if I could have slept. I looked at my wristwatch, and it was five-thirty in the morning.

"I'll wake up everyone who needs to know and tell them," I said, "right now. Will you come along?"

"You don't need me," he said, "and any time wasted from now on delays the final moment of achievement."

"All right."

I went out and started waking up the others. A little under an hour later I had them all sitting around the dining room of the summer palace, drinking coffee to get their eyes open and waiting for an explanation. I had rung into the meeting all those whom I thought must know what would be going on, but nobody else. At the table were El-len, Marie, Bill, Doc, and Wendy—Wendy looking par-ticularly sullen. She was grown up enough now to have a fourteen-year-old boyfriend—or thought she was. I thought ten years old ridiculously young for anything like that, though it was a fact she was beginning to develop physically; and she had asked to have him take part in this council as well. Naturally, I had spiked the notion. It was merely the last in a series of efforts she had made recently to get her mother and the rest of us to adopt the boyfriend into our inner family.

For the rest, Doc looked unperturbed, as if he was the only person there, besides myself, who was wide awake. Ellen looked concerned, Marie looked drawn and older than I had ever seen her look, and Bill was still white-faced and shrunken-looking from interrupted slumber.

"I'm going to tell Paula today I'll go with her," I said, without preamble. "We'll probably take off later today."

I told them about my hope, my talk with Porniarsk and about what he was already at work on at this moment.

". . . The point is," I wound up, "Porniarsk and the rest of you are probably safe here as long as Paula still con-siders me a friend and coworker. If that changes, she might think of keeping me under control by picking up some of you as hostages for my good behavior. So, if things get prickly between the two of us I'll send you warning of it; and I want you all to clear out of here immediately and scatter. Scatter all over the place, each one by yourself—and don't let the rest of the community know you're going."

Wendy looked grim.

"I mean that," I said, looking her in the eye. "Nobody. Wendy, you can stay with your mother; but everybody else take off alone."

"Marc," said Marie, "do you really need the rest of us to go into the far future with you, if this works? Can't you just go alone, tell the people there what you want to tell them, and then come back?"

"How can I?" I said. "You know I need a monad ge-stalt to control the storm forces; and that'll take all of you. So, listen. What I'll do is take the Old Man with me. If I send him back to you or if he comes back under any conditions, that's your signal. Take off and scatter."

"Marc," said Doc, "you'll need some way of getting the

message from us in a hurry when Porniarsk finds what he's after. How's about I make regular runs to you, just to bring in letters from the home folks and a box of cookies and such, so Paula's people won't think anything of it when I pop in with the word?"

I looked over at him gratefully. It was nice to hear a sensible mind at work around the table that morning.

"Good," said Ellen. "Then if you need help getting away from wherever you are, Doc can help you."

Another sensible mind.

"Fine idea, Doc," I said. "You're right, Ellen. Anybody else have any suggestions?"

"How long will you be gone altogether?" Marie asked.

"I can't tell," I said. "It depends on how fast Porniarsk can reach the ultimate configuration in his tank. Why?"

I knew why. She was having more and more trouble controlling Wendy and leaning on me more and more for that task.

"Maybe Wendy could go with you. She could see something of the rest of the world that way."

"No!" said Wendy and I, simultaneously. That was all I needed, to have Wendy on my hands, while I was trying to keep Paula happy and unsuspecting. I thought quickly. "Too dangerous for her."

"I don't want to," whimpered Wendy, who was no slouch herself at picking up cues. Marie looked from the girl to me, helplessly. She knew she was being double-teamed, but she was helpless to do anything about it.

"All right," I said. "Then, if nobody's got any more suggestions, you can get busy putting together what I'll need to take with me and spreading the word that I'll be going. I'll break the news myself to Paula over breakfast in an hour or so."

28

Paula took the news coolly. Whether this was because some of her people had already picked up the word of it that was spreading rapidly through the ranks of our own people, or simply because it was a strategy on her part to act as if her enlisting me had never been in doubt, was impossible to tell. In either case, it made no difference to me, who was going with her for my own private reasons.

"All right," she said, over the breakfast table. "How soon can you be ready?"

"Six hours, maybe," I said.

"In that case, I'll wait for you and you can join my staff right here. If you hadn't been able to move quickly, I'd have needed to let you catch up with me. I'll send word to my officers. No offense to your kitchen help, Marc, but I'll be glad to get back to my own headquarters and have some decent coffee."

There was only one small incident of interest in our leaving. Paula's people had already climbed aboard the helicopters that had been sitting parked and waiting for them, and I was not yet aboard the one carrying Paula herself. The Old Man, as I said, had shown no liking for Paula; and now he had made himself scarce. Doc had found him, finally, about half a mile from the summer palace among the rocks of the hillside and literally held an automatic pistol at his head to get him to come along back to the takeoff point. The Old Man knew what human weapons were and came, but not happily.

When I finally saw him approaching, squatting ominously beside Doc in the front of the jeep, I changed my mind about taking him.

"Look," I said to Doc, under my breath, when the jeep drove up and stopped by the entrance ladder of the 'cop-

ter, "this isn't going to work. If he's going to bolt the
minute I take my eyes off him, this'll never work. Leave
him here and you come along instead while we figure
things out. Then I can send you back with word."

"All right," said Doc, climbing out of the jeep. "Do I
have time to pick up any gear, or—"

But at that point, the Old Man solved the problem for
us. He had been staring at the 'copter, and at me, all the
while the jeep was driving out to us on the open area.
He was not unintelligent and he must have finally realized
that I was actually going, with or without him. At any
rate, he took a sudden leap out of the jeep directly onto
the first step of the ladder, caught my hand and pulled me
toward him and the steps.

"That's all right, then," I said to Doc. "But why don't
you come along anyway, at least until I've had a chance
to settle down. No, you won't have time to bring anything. Got any kind of weapon with you?"

"Pistol."

"All right. I can shake down Paula's people for what
you'll need beyond that, and what you'll need to get back
here from wherever she's headed next. Let's get inside."

He followed me up the ladder, the Old Man preceding
us.

"What's this?" said Paula when we were inside and the
ladder was being taken in, the entry hatch being shut behind us. She looked from Doc to me.

"There's some unfinished business," I said. "I've got
some decisions yet to make. He can carry word back from
wherever we stop, a couple of days from now—if that's all
right with you?"

"Certainly. Why not?" She turned her attention to the
Old Man who still clung to my hand. "This is the creature? I thought I saw it around earlier. Is it housebro-
ken?"

"Since long before I met him," I said. "All his people
learn to live like human beings while they're growing up,
just as our children do."

"People?" She smiled. "Well, keep him out of the way.
Find your seats now."

She turned away.

Apparently, we were not to return to where her camp
had been when I had visited. Her orders had already gone
out, and her troops and wagons had been on the move

from an hour after I had broken the news to her over our breakfast table. We flew on eastward and put down by a river about twenty-five miles further on, where the motorized section of Paula's transport had already arrived and set up her personal tents. Later, that evening, the main body of her wagons and infantry arrived.

I kept Doc with me for four days, mainly so he could prowl around and get acquainted with the way Paula's people did things; then I sent him home before they saw through the bright-eyed, teenage image he had been careful to wear anywhere near her and them. The Old Man stayed close in the tent I had assigned to me for my exclusive use and was no problem. I found myself happy to have him there. He was, after all, a small touch of home.

We continued to move steadily eastward. In open country, between objectives, the pattern seemed to be for Paula's headquarters to stay comfortably put for three days while her army marched forward. Then her motorized division would move the headquarters tents and equipment forward one short day's trek in their jeeps and trucks. Meanwhile Paula, her general, and a handful of us who were at the top of the table of organization took it easy for most of the day, then struck the pavilion tent and made a half to three-quarters of an hour hop in a single 'copter to the new site, while the other two aircraft followed empty except for pilots and copilots.

It was a pleasant life, but monotonous; particularly when it began to be obvious that Paula had no real need for services from me, but was only carrying me along as a satellite to impress possible enemies and reluctant allies. I had a great deal of time on my hands; but it turned out this had been provided for by Paula's foresight. I discovered one of the main duties of her large staff of women clerks and attendants.

Briefly, they were there to keep everyone happy, from me down to the lowest officer in the army; and also to keep us out of Paula's way and off her mind, except when she had a need for us. A good share of this, I picked up from my own observation; but it was General Pierre de Coucy Aruba who dotted the i's and crossed the t's for me.

The general was a drinker. That is, he could not yet be called a drunk because he held his alcohol without visible sign and never seemed to prolong his drinking beyond three or four drinks. But those drinks came at every

lunch, dinner, cocktail hour and late supper at which I
ever saw him.

"You could call me a philosopher," he told me one
evening in his tent, after a post-dinner planning session
with his staff had concluded. His officers were gone and
he had invited me in for a private chat with just the
two of us.

"You might think that I could probably set up with my
own army and carve out a nice little empire for myself,"
he went on. "And I could—I could. But I'm not the kind
who wants an empire for himself. *'Everybody's a little
mad except thee and me, and I even have my doubts about
thee.'* People intrigue me. I like to be comfortable and
watch them. So I'm the perfect commander for our Empress. She knows she never needs to worry about a military coup as long as I'm in control."

"I can see she'd appreciate that," I said.

"Yes, indeed." He smiled at me—and it was a smile,
not a grin, with the sun-wrinkles deepening at the corners
of his eyes and the tidy, little grey mustache quirking upwards at the corners. "Wouldn't you, in her shoes?"

"I gather she makes a good boss?" I said.

"A good Empress, you mean." He waggled a forefinger
at me. "Always remember that. An Empress has to be an
Empress, at all times. That's why the young ladies."

"The young ladies?"

"Of course. Familiarity breeds contempt." He smiled
again. "And there's no familiarity like that in bed, eh?"

"That's true enough," I said soberly, thinking of my own
two women.

"Most queens had trouble out of getting laid," he
said. "Most empresses, too. Queen Elizabeth . . . Catherine
of Russia . . . notice none of the girls around here, though,
are quite as good-looking as the Empress?"

"I had," I told him.

"Obviously. The art of controlling a man with your female presence is to be just out of reach, but out of reach.
You understand?"

I did. Not only did I understand, but a certain near-
demonic impulse moved in me, and my trader's instinct
was challenged. During the days when Paula had been
talking to me about coming with her on her road of
conquest, she had sent up clear signals that she was attracted to me personally. I had taken for granted, that

part, if not all of this was calculated, to gain her own ends. But, as it turned out, she had wanted me neither for my services as a magician nor myself; she had simply bought herself a show piece at the cost of nothing more than promises, rather than having to spend her troops and material to get it. Again, it had been a case of "seller beware"; so I really had no kick coming if I had taken counterfeit currency for what I had sold. But for her to assume that, after having been sharped, I would cheerfully reconcile myself, given the equivalent of two cents on the dollar, was something of an insult.

Accordingly, I played the game with the female staff, so as not to arouse any suspicious; but privately, I set my sights on Paula after all. I was patient. I had my ability to see patterns working for me. Success would be along, down the line there, somewhere.

Meanwhile, in the patterns, I had found another hobby to occupy my time. Now I had broken through twice to the oneness of the universe, and there was no longer any doubt in my mind that such a state of mind existed; and if that was so, anything was possible, even the destruction of the time storm. I made it an invisible exercise to look around me for patterns constantly, and to develop my perception of them to the point where that perception and recognition and understanding of the patterns would be simultaneous.

The work paid off. The patterns were there, all about me all the time. They were there in the interactions of people, in their physical movements, their speech, their reactions, and their thinking; and in all else about fauna, flora, earth, and sky. Little by little, my knowledge of such patterns became deeper and surer, until it began to approach eerily close to the true magic of telepathy and second sight. I could have played chess now, better than anyone I had ever encountered; but the chess patterns, for all that they were fascinating and innumerable, were dead patterns. I preferred the live patterns created by my fellow men and women.

So I observed and learned; and, curiously, I could feel the Old Man learning through me.

Meanwhile, we were marching to the Atlantic seaboard. The points we searched out were sometimes the fragments of cities or towns that still held supplies or needed equipment; or sometimes they were population centers like my own community, which had not existed before the time storm forces had been balanced, but which had sprung up since around some acquired communication equipment or military force.

In every case, however, these places and the people in them were plainly inferior to the armed strength of the Empress. They sometimes bluffed for a day or two before yielding, but in the end they all acknowledged her as their overlady. Then, at last, we ran into opposition.

We had reached the ocean and a place that called itself Capitol, which once had been half Washington International Airport, and was now half that and half something else, because deep-water ocean lapped up against the base of cliffs that abruptly cut off the main road into the airport. On the ocean, moored out a little distance from a jerry-built wharf, were a number of small ocean-going craft. Still hangared about the airport were a number of 1980 commercial passenger jets and—on the land area of that part that now opened to the ocean—some light, five-passenger craft, that were like flying bubbles with stubby wings, and a tiny power plant that seemed permanently fueled with an inexhaustible, built-in supply of energy.

These were from some time later than the twentieth century; and these also were the real prize from Paula's point of view. The craft, in their own right, were almost as famous as I was in mine. For, although there were still large cruise ships and other massive watercraft to be found up and down the Atlantic coast, there was no way now to either maintain or operate them. It was still possible to cross the Atlantic in boats up to the size of small yachts. But the trip would be uncomfortable and a matter of some weeks. With these light aircraft out of the post-twentieth century, the ocean could be crossed in hours.

Once more, Paula moved in, going gutsily herself with a small guard to negotiate, while readying her armed forces and artillery behind her. But this time, the target did not yield; and she was forced to fight for what she wanted.

Not only that, but these people fought hard. It took nearly a week for Aruba and his soldiers to take the place and subdue its inhabitants; and it cost them over half of their strength in casualties. Replacements would have to be marched across the continent from the west

coast, since she could not trust any of the recently subjugated communities in between to furnish her with loyal
fighters. That meant months. Fall and winter would be
upon us before they were here and trained. Paula herself,
and her inner staff officers, could cross the ocean by air at
any time; but the small boats available could not ferry
her army across the Atlantic in bad weather. We were
stuck where we were until spring.

I saw the pattern of this situation evolving ten days
before the rest of them did. It solidified in my mind on
the first day of hard fighting in which they pounded the
enemy positions with artillery and confidently advanced
afterwards, only to be cut to pieces by machine-gun fire. I
saw it; and I raged inside at the inevitable delay it implied for Paula's plans of world conquest. Doc was overdue
for one of his periodic visits, and for the first time, I
found myself fearing, rather than hoping, that he would
bring me word that Porniarsk had found the ultimate
universe pattern possible to the viewing tank. If the
avatar had found it, I had no choice. I could not delay
going home, with the risk that, in the meantime, some
chance here might kill me, cripple me, or somehow pre-
vent me from returning at all.

On the other hand, I told myself, I did not want Paula
still on the North American continent when I left her,
without leave, and headed once more for my own territory. I wanted her on the other side of the world, by
preference; or at least across the Atlantic, so that the
trouble and expense of sending forces after me to bring me
back would be so great she would delay as long as possible in doing so. It was, I believed, a reasonable reason
for wishing her success. Therefore, as the week of fighting
went on and casualties mounted, I looked grim along with
everyone else in the Empress camp—but for my own
private reasons.

About Thursday, Doc finally arrived.

"Porniarsk's found it?" I said, the moment we could
get off someplace where we were safe from being overheard. In this daylight instance, that meant a training area
behind the field hospital, where we could see there was no
one else within earshot.

"No," he said. "Not yet."

"Good!" I said. He stared at me for a fraction of a
second.

"Never mind," I told him. "I'll explain later. What's the rest of the news?"

"I was going to say," he said, "Porniarsk doesn't have it yet, but he thinks he's close—"

"Hell's bloody buckets!"

This time he really did stare at me, his tanned young face stretched smooth-skinned with puzzlement.

"I've got a reason." I said. "Go on."

"I was saying, Porniarsk hasn't found the furthest possible future configuration the device can show; but he did find a sort of sticking point—some point where he got hung up for some reason. He's pretty sure he can get the tank to go beyond it, with a little more work; but he says to tell you he thinks this sticking point is some kind of sign he's close to the ultimate."

I took a deep breath.

"All right," I said. "If he has, he has. I'll talk to you about that in a minute. Anything else important? How's everybody? The community running the way it should?"

"Nothing else. I've got some letters for you, of course." He tapped the leather wallet that hung from one of his shoulders. He always brought me a bundle of personal mail, that being the ostensible reason for his coming. "But everyone's fine. And the place's running, like always, on the button."

"Fine. Let's go back to my tent."

We headed toward it. It was a matter of elementary caution not to talk to him for more than a few seconds as we were now, for fear of triggering off suspicions. Given the important and general news, we could do a fairly good job of discussing matters in hyperbole while I went through the home mail, even if there might be ears listening.

At the tent the Old Man leaped up to seize my hand, then turned to grasp one of Doc's as well. He walked with us to a pair of armchairs, still hanging on, and hunkered down between us. Since he and I had been away from home, he had become more dependent, not only on me, who had been the only human, originally, he would get close to, but on Doc during Doc's brief visits.

"Make yourself a drink," I said to Doc now, "while I go through these letters."

"Thanks," he said enthusiastically. He pried his hand loose from the Old Man's and went over to the table that did duty as my liquor cabinet. Doc was, in fact, a non-drinker as well as a nonsmoker. But he always carried cigarettes with him, and he was expert at making a show of both smoking and drinking, these being only two of a large number of casual acts he had perfected, apparently on the off-chance that the misdirection in them might prove useful someday. I ripped open my letters and read them.

They were perfectly ordinary, personal mail from home; and in spite of the fact that they were intended primarily as camouflage, I found myself going through them as eagerly as anyone else would, away from home and family against his will. Marie was still worried about Wendy, who herself had written me a few lines of pure prattle—under duress probably. Ellen had written almost as brief a note, saying that things were fine, just the way I'd left them, and there was no need to worry about anything. I read the last line as a hint to take Marie's motherly concern with a certain amount of advisement. Ellen's language could not have been any more spare and stiff if she herself had been a soldier in the field; so that the word "love" at the end looked incongruous. But I knew her.

Bill wrote he was pleased with the way things were going. From him, this would be a reference to Porniarsk's work. Also, he mentioned that he had finally refined the "emergency harvest plans," which would be a reference to my orders that they all split up and scatter if Paula suddenly decided to take some of them hostage as insurance against my noncooperation. Porniarsk sent no message.

"Good," I said to Doc, when the last letter had been read. "Things seem all right at home."

"They are," he answered. "Have you got letters for me to take back?"

"Over on the writing table, there," I said. He went to get them. "Were you planning on heading back right away?"

"Unless there's something to keep me here."

He tucked the letters I had written into his wallet, came back and sat down. The Old Man took his hand again.

"I was just thinking—why don't you stick around a day or so until we've taken this local area? They're putting up quite a fight, and if you stay you'll be able to go back and tell the women personally that I didn't get hurt in the process."

"Glad to," said Doc. "You've got a good life here. Far as I'm concerned, it's a vacation with all expenses paid."

He had a nice, light tone to his voice as he said it; but his eyes were sharp on mine, ready to read why I was asking him to stick around. I shook my head very slight, to tell him *not now*, and started to talk about the situation, saying nothing that wasn't highly complimentary to Paula and confident about her eventual achievements here, but filling him bit by bit with data on the actual state of affairs militarily. When I was done, he knew what the facts were, but not what the connection was between these and the reason I wanted him to stick around.

That was the third day of the battle for control of the area. It was not until Sunday that Paula's soldiers overran most of the strong points of the opposition and not until Monday afternoon that they finished mopping up.

"As long as you've stayed this long, you might as well stay for the victory celebration, too," I told Doc.

"Suits me," he said. His voice sounded a little thickly from one of the couches in my tent where he sprawled with a glass in his hand; but his eyes were as clear and steady as the eyes of a sniper looking along the sights of his rifle.

I was more glad to have him there than I had thought. I had seen the pattern of the battle's consequences building all week. Paula and Aruba, in particular, must be seeing the same thing themselves, now that the fight was over and the returns were in. So, while the rank and file survivors whooped it up in celebration, Paula herself and her immediate staff would now be biting into the bitter fruit of a win that had cost so highly. The way they would react, I had told myself, could tell me a lot more about their patterns; and part of what I might learn might be useful information to send home with Doc.

Paula had already had to face one particular ugly truth; that there was a point beyond which her well-trained soldiers would not obey her. From dressed-up recruits they had turned into veterans in the bloodbath of the last seven days; and commanders back to the dawn of history could have told her what would happen when such soldiers were finally allowed to overrun an enemy who had bled them heavily in preceding days. Her kids had turned into killers. They slaughtered right and left on that Monday afternoon as they subjugated the conquered people.

It was Paula's first setback. There were aircraft mechanics and boat mechanics, as well as other experts, among her former enemies that were worth regiments to her; but there was no way she could hold her blood-high soldiery back long enough to weed out such valuable individuals from the otherwise killable chaff of the local population. Monday cost her dearly.

Nonetheless, she had to put a good face on it and appear to encourage the wild celebration that ensued that night. It began at late afternoon and went on until dawn, by which time all but a few rarely tough individuals had collapsed. It was at dawn that Aruba came for me.

That he came himself for me, rather than sent for me, was an index of his upset. He stepped into my tent, peered for a second at the still form of Doc, who appeared to be asleep on one of the couches, and then looked back at me. In the early daylight coming through the plastic windows of the tent, his face was sallow, the shade of new liverwurst.

"She wants to see you," he said.

"Paula?" I asked.

He nodded. I got to my feet. I was still dressed. Anything could have happened in that night just past and I had not felt like trying to sleep.

"What about?" I asked, as I went with him out into the cool morning. A breeze was blowing from the ocean.

"She'll want to tell you herself," he said and licked his lips. He had been badly shaken and I could see him reaching for a bottle the minute he was alone in his own quarters.

I nodded indifferently enough, but inwardly I braced myself. On this morning, her purpose in wanting to see me would not be good. I walked alongside Aruba to the entrance of the pavilion tent, where two of her officers —colonels—now stood with machine rifles, doing sentry duty. He stopped at the tent flap.

"Go in," he said, "she's waiting for you."

I went in alone. Paula was alone also, wearing a filmy yellow dressing gown as if she had just risen from bed; but her face was hard and weary with the look that comes from being up and tensely awake for hours.

"Marc," she said, and her voice was pure industrial diamond in tone, "there's a paper over there on the desk. Sign it."

"Sign. . . ?" I went across to the desk and looked down. It was a neatly typed letter, several pages long, beneath the letterhead she had given me as one of her staff.

"Just sign it," she said.

"Not until I read it," I answered.

Our eyes clashed. Then she shrugged and turned away; but I could almost see the note her memory made of this, my balking at her command. It would be recalled when the hour was right.

"Of course," she said.

I bent my head to the letter again and read. It was like being unexpectedly hit in the stomach. Or, more accurately, it was like a sickening collision in the dark, running full tilt into a concrete wall you had known was there all the time, but whose existence you had put out of mind —an impact so unexpected and brutal it left you nauseated; because suddenly I understood Paula, saw her complete and naked in the glaring, fluorescent light of what she was planning to set me up for.

I read that I had been shocked by the irresponsible behavior of some of her soldiers in taking over the enemy area. But, over and above my shock, I had been aghast to see the criminal murder of certain innocent individuals among the defenders; artisans and mechanics, as well as other trained personnel, who had only been in the enemy camp under duress. The slaughter of these innocents was not only a heinous crime against them as individuals, but amounted to treason against the Empire, since the Empress was now deprived of the willing services of these people and many of her subjects would suffer because of that lack. Consequently, I called upon her formally to take action against the criminals responsible and see that they were brought to justice, since I, with the skills that had allowed me to halt the ravages of the time storm, could see more deeply and clearly than anyone into the terrible cost we must all bear because of the deaths of these innocents.

Suddenly, reading this, the pattern I had been building on Paula was complete. I saw the hell she had in mind not only for the soldiers responsible for delaying her here over the coming winter, but for anyone who had been around to witness this happening to her; and that told me more about her than she might have betrayed to me in two more years of my observing her.

I signed.

"I'm proud to do this," I said, taking the letter over to her. "It doesn't say anything I didn't feel myself. No wonder you're the Empress, Paula. You can even read minds."

She smiled and took the letter. I was by no means forgiven for wanting to read before signing, but for the present small moment, the smile was genuine. I would never have risked flattering her so grossly before I had stepped through the flap of this tent; but now I knew when and where she was vulnerable.

"Dear Marc," she said. "You understand."

She looked at me; and I understood, all right. Ironically, suddenly the moment I had patiently waited for, in which I could gain control over her by securing her physically, was with me. In this devastated moment she was available, if I had still wanted her. But the fact was, after reading that letter, I now would not have touched her with a shark-stick.

"More than ever before," I said. "Do you want me to let other people know I've written you this letter?"

She hesitated, but it was only the habit of caution operating in her. Again, if she had been herself, I myself would have hesitated to show her such rapid agreement. But she was not herself. That was the crucial truth that had broken out into the open, with the completing of her pattern in my mind just now. She had a flaw I had never really appreciated until now, a deep flaw that would cost her the rulership of the world that had seemed so possible up until now. Already, she was adapting to my own hint that I was eager to accept the authorship of the letter she held. Already she was beginning to make herself believe the attractive idea that I had indeed written it on my own initiative.

"If I just drop the letter with you and go out to spread the word, I know your officers'll be eager to back me up. I know they will," I said. "Then we can arrest the guilty ones and bring them to justice before they have time to fill the minds of their fellow soldiers with lies."

"Yes." She laid the letter softly down on the end-table

beside her. "Of course. You've got my permission to tell what you've written me. Justice should be speedy."

"I'll go right now, then," I said. "Wait a second, though. Maybe if you give me a written order to do what's necessary, I can make sure none of them escape. Or, for that matter, with that kind of authority I could do anything necessary in connection with the matter. . . ."

She smiled dazzlingly, seeing me setting the noose of responsibility for this so firmly around my own neck.

"Of course," she said.

She crossed the desk, wrote on the top sheet of an order pad sandwich, tore off the top sheet and pushed the carbon copy to the back of the desk.

"There you are."

"Thank you." I took it without looking at it and moved toward the door. "Probably I shouldn't waste time. . . ."

"No. No, you shouldn't. I have to rest now; but—see me after lunch, Marc. Dear Marc. . . . What would I do without you?"

"Come on, now. You're the Empress. You can do anything."

She smiled dazzlingly.

I went out. Aruba was gone, as I had expected him to be; and I went directly back to my own tent. Doc was off the couch and on his feet the second the tent flap fell behind me.

"We're leaving for home right away," I said. "I'll explain as we go. You armed?"

"My rifle's with the jeep," he said. He patted his shirt at belt level before and behind. "Belly gun and knife."

"Right. I want your help in bringing some blood-soaked criminals to justice," I said. "The Empress has given me special authority to corral the soldiers who committed atrocities on certain innocent people among the civilian population opposing us until tonight."

His eyebrows went up ironically. I reached into my shirt pocket where I had put the order after folding it up, still without having read it. I unfolded it and read it now, then passed it to him.

" 'Marc Despard has asked for authority from me, and I have given it to him, to do whatever is required . . .' " he nodded slowly. "All riiight!"

I took the order back from him and replaced it in my pocket.

"The first thing I want to do is check those future-built aircraft we captured," I said, "to make sure none of those responsible for the atrocities are planning on using them for escaping. They may even have explosives to destroy the aircraft they can't use. You're an expert on explosives. What kind do you think they might be able to get hold of for something like that?"

He grinned and patted himself at belt level again.

"Primer cord," he said. "It wouldn't take much to do a lot of damage—particularly if they know what they're doing."

"That's what we'll search the area for, then. Come along."

We headed out the door. The Old Man came with us.

"Want me to put him back inside?" Doc asked, as we stopped just beyond the tent.

"Why, no," I said. "Seeing him with us, they won't think I'm doing anything important. It'll serve to allay suspicions—Major!"

I called out to a short, swarthy block of an officer in his mid-twenties who was passing by. The fact that he was on his feet at all this morning meant that he had not been deeply involved in the celebrations of the night before. He came closer and I recognized him. There were only so many majors in Paula's army, in any case.

"Major Debrow? Sorry to interrupt whatever you're doing; but I've got a special job and I'm going to have to ask you to help. Take a look at this."

I passed him Paula's authorization.

"You see," I said, while he read it, "we want to move before these criminals take off on us—don't we, Major?"

His face did not agree. Someone who was unprejudiced might have found a trace of loathing in it for me, a civilian who called combat-battered soldiers "criminals."

"Yes, Mr. Despard."

"Good. I knew I could count on you, Major. We've got an idea that some of them might be trying to get away in some of the valuable future aircraft these people had. We're going to go and check. I want you to come along with us."

"Those planes are locked up, as well as being under

guard," Debrow said. "Nobody could get away with one of them."

"Let's make sure."

We walked toward that part of the former airport where the post-twentieth-century planes were kept. It was not a short distance, but eventually we clambered over a low barrier of sandbags and found ourselves not more than forty feet from the entrance to a separate hangar, around which perhaps a dozen apparently sober and competent male soldiers stood guard.

"Go get their officer and bring him here, quietly, so we can explain things, will you, Major?"

"Just what is it you want?" Debrow asked. "What do you want him to do?"

"I want to check the men on guard and have a look inside," I said. "And I want the officer with us when we do that."

Debrow went forward to the two soldiers on guard at the hangar door and was challenged. As he answered, I turned to Doc and saw him looking at me questioningly.

"I want you and me to take off from here in one of those planes inside," I said in a low voice. "I don't want the other planes left behind to be workable; and I want the soldiers on guard here out of action. I'll try to arrange it to give you a chance at them, one at a time."

"Just the two of us to leave. Not the major?"

"Not the major."

Doc nodded. Debrow came back, led us forward to the hangar doors and in through a small personnel door set in one of them. Inside was the large, dim, echoing interior of the hangar with small, pearly glowings in the gloom that were the future aircraft. To our right was a glassed-in office brightly lit with self-powered battle fluorescents, standing in for the built-in fluorescent lights in the ceiling, now dark for lack of power from the community's central supply.

Inside at a desk was a single thin, young officer with first lieutenant's silver bars on the straps of his uniform leather jacket. He got to his feet as we came in.

"Major?" he said.

"Lieutenant," said Debrow. "This is Marc Despard."

"I know Mr. Despard," said the lieutenant.

"And his . . ." Debrow glanced at Doc and the Old

Man, "servants. Mr. Despard has some special authority from the Empress for you to see."

I passed Paula's authorization to the lieutenant. The light blond eyebrows jumped several times while he was reading it, although the rest of his narrow face remained calm.

"Yes sir," he said passing the letter back to me. "What is it you want, Mr. Despard?"

"First," I said, "I want to check the future aircraft, without making a fuss about it. Just you, the Major and I, and Doc here."

I nodded at Doc.

"Doc," I said, "has had some experience in handling sabotage. If we find one or more of the aircraft has been booby-trapped, he may be of help to us in disarming it. This Experimental with us is called the Old Man. His sense of smell, particularly, is much more acute than ours, and he works well with Doc on jobs like this. Now, how many of the future planes are there?"

"Nine," said the lieutenant.

"Does anyone here know how to fly them?"

"Nobody's tried so far," said the lieutenant. "I believe the plan is to talk first to these people who had them."

"It seems to me I heard they weren't hard to operate," I said. "The criminals we're looking for may have heard that, too. These planes would buy them anything they wanted, anywhere in the rest of the world, if they could successfully steal them from the Empress."

I saw both officers looking at me oddly and wondered if I'd been laying on my image of self-importance too thickly.

"All right," I said. "Let's go then. Major, Lieutenant, we'll take three planes apiece. We won't take the Experimental on this first search. I'll keep Doc and the Experimental with me until they're needed. Do you have flashlights?"

"You mean hand torches?" said the lieutenant. "Yes, sir." He went to a locker across the office and came back with flashlights for Debrow and myself. Leaving the Old Man in the office, we went out into the hangar proper and split up.

I took the three planes closest to me, forcing the two officers to take the ones further over. In the illumination of the flashlight, the first aircraft I came to seemed to glow with an inner gleam of its own. It was made of some milky, semi-translucent plastic and looked light enough to float up in the air if it was breathed on too heavily. But in spite of appearances, it was solid and firm when I pulled open the door in its curving side and stepped in. Within, possibly because of the almost egg-shaped hull, there was more room than I would have guessed. I went forward to the control panel.

It was a simple-looking affair, a single small television-like screen inset in the panel and a five-key keyboard just below it. I pushed down one of the keys at random and the lights went on; not only on the panel but all over within the aircraft.

"Ready," said a voice.

I grinned. There had been no pattern at all to what I was looking at; and now, suddenly, there was very nearly a complete one.

"How do I take off?" I asked.

"You may pilot yourself, or instruct a takeoff and flight."

"Thanks. Go back to sleep." I punched the same key again and the lights went out. Experimentally, in the glow of the flashlight, I punched another of the keys.

"Ready," said a voice, as the lights went on once more.

"Go back to sleep."

So, that was it. The secret to flying these things. It was that there was no secret at all. I punched off again, the lights went out and I beckoned Doc to follow me. Together, we left the plane.

"All right," I whispered to him, "get busy taking out those other planes. I'll take my time with the two I've still got to look at. Meet you at the last one, the third one up straight ahead near the back of the hangar. I'll go as slow as I can, but don't let those two officers see you."

"They won't," said Doc and he evaporated in the gloom.

I took the Old Man and went on to the next plane and let myself in, then sat down before the control panel and turned it on. I had quite a little conversation with the computer, or whatever it was, on this second aircraft; and by the time I had finished asking questions, I had as good a general knowledge of this kind of craft as if I had kept one around for some years. They were ridiculously, child-level foolproof, and operable.

After I had wasted as many minutes as I thought I reasonably could, I went on to the third craft, poked about inside for a while, and then stepped out again. Neither Doc nor the other two men were in sight. I stepped around to the far side of the plane to wait; and a finger tapped me on the shoulder.

I whirled, stepping back instinctively as I did so, and found Doc grinning at me.

"All set," he said.

"Good. Come on then."

We walked toward the next plane over and found the lieutenant there, conscientiously examining the craft's undercarriage with his flashlight.

"Did you find anything, Lieutenant?"

He got to his feet.

"No sir. You, sir?"

"No luck for me, either. Maybe Major Debrow's found something. Shall we go see?"

We all moved over and found Debrow inside his last aircraft. After a moment he came out.

"Nothing," he said.

"I'm greatly relieved," I said. "Now, if you don't mind, Lieutenant, I'd like to examine the men you've got on guard here?"

"But why, sir? We didn't find anything."

"For that very reason. We want to be sure. The Empress wants us to be sure. Doesn't she, Major?"

"Lieutenant," said Debrow with a tight throat.

"Yes, Major. Yes, Mr. Despard. If you'll come up to the office, I'll bring in the men on the doors first—"

"You'll bring them in one at a time, Lieutenant," I said. "Is there another door to this hangar besides those in the front?"

"There's a small service entrance in the back wall."

"Good." I turned to Doc. "After we examine each one, I'd like you to take him out the back way and back to his post. See he doesn't talk to any of the others, particularly not to any who haven't been examined yet. You go out with the lieutenant here, so you'll know where to bring them back to. Lieutenant?"

"Mr. Despard?"

"I imagine you'll be taking the place of each of your guards as you relieve them. If Doc should come for you without returning the man he last took—if he comes for you alone—it'll mean we've found one of them. I'd like you to come back with Doc as naturally as possible, so as not to alarm any of the others we may find."

The lieutenant opened his mouth, glanced at the Major and closed it again.

"Perhaps," said Debrow, "it might be better if the lieutenant simply stayed here, Mr. Despard. It's a little unusual, his filling in for one of the enlisted men on post; and—"

"If you don't mind, Major?" I said.

"No sir," said Debrow slowly. "I don't mind, sir."

"Then we'll do it this way, I think. Lieutenant, will you take Doc out so he can get the first guard?"

They went off. I turned to Debrow.

"Major, how well do you know the lieutenant?"

"I've known him for several years. More than three years, I'd say."

"But do you know him well?"

Debrow looked at me with sudden caution. After a second he answered, slowly.

"I couldn't say . . . well, Mr. Despard."

"Yes," I said.

I left it at that. After a few minutes of silence on both our parts, Doc came back with the first guard, a chunky lance corporal five and a half feet tall and looking about the age of the lieutenant.

"Your name?" I asked.

"Lance Corporal Charles Onash, sir. Third Platoon, Fourth Company, Blue Regiment."

"Have you ever ridden a motorcycle, Corporal Onash?"

"No sir."

"Good. You can go. Take him back, Doc."

The next man had never ridden a motorcycle either. No more had the three after that. The fifth man we questioned had. I had to reach for some other mysterious question.

"Ever fly a sailplane, Private Mahn?"

"As a matter of fact, yes, sir."

"How about drive a hydroplane?"

"Yes sir."

Debrow shifted uneasily in the seat he had taken behind one of the desks. I was beginning to feel a little trapped.

"How are you on reading Sanskrit?"

"Sir?"

"I said, can you read Sanskrit?"

"No sir."

"All right," I said, with inner relief, "take him back, Doc."

"Sir?" said Debrow, almost a little timidly, after Private Mahn had left. "I'm afraid I don't understand . . . ."

"You will, in due course."

He sat back without saying anything more. The seven more enlisted men on duty there came through and I managed to send them all back after getting each one to admit he didn't know how to do something or other.

"Mr. Despard," began Debrow, after the final one had left. "That's all the men on duty here. Does that mean—"

"It means this situation is a good deal more serious than I thought. Are you armed, Major?"

"No sir."

"That's unfortunate. Well, we'll have to do what we can. I'll stay here. Will you go quietly to the personnel door we came in by, and stand just inside it. Lock it if you can, and listen for any sounds you can hear on the other side. If anyone tries to force it open, let them; but stand back out of sight and when they're through, go for help."

"Yes sir. But for Christ's sake, Mr. Despard, what's supposed to be going on here?"

"I can't tell you quite yet. I've my duty to Paula—to the Empress—to think of," I said. "Get going now. I'm going to step off into the shadows just outside this office and be ready to warn you if anyone who shouldn't comes from the other end of the building."

He went. I took the Old Man by the hand and followed the Major out, moving off to where the shadows hid us from him, but where we would be in line to intercept Doc, coming back from returning the last soldier to his post. From where we were, I could see the thin line of daylight showing around the personnel door, blocked out now and then by an uneasily shifting body standing just this side of it. Eventually, this occultation ceased, and a second or two later, Doc emerged alone from the dimness in front of us.

"All set," he said under his breath.

"All taken care of?" I asked.

He nodded.

"The lieutenant?"

"I saved him until next to last."

"All right. The Major's over by the personnel door."

"Was. I've taken care of him, too. He was the last of them."

I wanted to ask how many of them were dead, but the words stuck in my throat. It was a lifesaver to have a young timberwolf like Doc for a friend, but it was a little illogical to demand he be wolf and harmless at the same time.

"How about the aircraft?" I asked.

"The first one you looked at, I didn't touch," Doc answered. "The rest are set to blow any time you want."

"All right. I've got to see if we can get the hangar doors open easily. Otherwise, you may have to blow a hole in them—"

"No sweat there either. They're supposed to be electrically operated, but there's a chain block-and-tackle type dingus to use if the power's off. Can you fly that thing, Marc?"

"I can fly it. Or rather, I can tell it to fly itself and it will."

"Just checking," he said; and I could barely see his grin in the gloom.

"I don't blame you. I would too," I told him. I was very tired, suddenly. "Why don't you rig the other planes to destruct as soon as we're safely out of here, and I'll move the one we're taking up to this side of the doors? Then you open the door, hop in, and we'll move."

"Right."

He moved off. I turned on my flashlight and led the Old Man toward the aircraft Doc had specified as untouched. We climbed in, shut the door, and I depressed one of the keys.

"Ready."

"Move up slowly on the ground to the inside of the doors to this building. Or—to put it another way—move slowly forward along the ground and I'll tell you which way to turn and when to stop."

The craft stirred and seemed to slide rather than roll forward.

"Left," I told it. "Left maybe ten degrees. Now maybe five degrees more. All right, straight ahead . . . stop!"

We halted just inside the hangar doors. I opened the door of the craft and waited. In a moment, there was a faint, rattling sound to be heard through the opening; and the big doors slid apart to either side of the opening they guarded, and bright sunlight blinded us.

"That's good enough!" I called softly into the brilliance after a moment. But the doors had already stopped parting with just enough room for us to go through. I heard a faint thud and Doc was in the cabin, shutting the aircraft door behind him.

"All set," he said.

"Go!" I told the craft. "Straight ahead, out on the ground through this opening, take off and climb to three thousand meters. Head west."

It slid forward through the doors into the full sunlight. Without any run, it leaped suddenly skyward. There was a sound like a paper bag popping below and behind us. I glanced back and down to see smoke coming from the open doorway of the hangar building, dwindling rapidly to toy size below us. A second later, we were up where the roads looked like thick pencil lines and the landscape was starting to move backwards beneath us toward the sun half way up in the clear sky.

"That takes care of everything, I guess," Doc said. He came forward and pushed the Old Man off the seat next to mine—a move the Old Man took without complaint. It was surprising what the Old Man would take from Doc, nowadays. Almost as much as Sunday used to take from Ellen. Doc seated himself where the Old Man had been.

"Need any help flying, or anything like that?" he asked.

I shook my head.

"Then I'll get some sleep," he said, imperturbably. "This gadget's better than a locked door. No one's going to break in and surprise you in the middle of the air."

He curled up in the seat, closed his eyes, and dropped off.

I was not so lucky.

29

The aircraft out of the future did not seem to need any serious attention. I asked it for a map of the country, and it was displayed on the screen in front of me. On the map, I picked out the general area of our community, asked to have it enlarged for me, and so continued zeroing in and enlarging until I could identify our destination to the craft. Once this was done, I simply told it to take us there and land by the summer palace—which I described—and my duties were done. I would have liked, then, to curl up and sleep like Doc; but I could not. I could not even imitate the Old Man, who was half-dozing, opening his eyes every so often to blink at me, as if to make sure I was still there.

Instead, I just sat, watching the empty, clean sky and the slowly moving landscape far below. There was no sound of passage inside the plane and I felt like a fly trapped under an overturned water glass.

As long as we had been working to escape, my mind had been clear and sharp and purposeful. But now, the effect of the body adrenalin began to die out in me, leaving me feeling empty, dull, and ugly. The thought of the soldiers on guard who had undoubtedly died so the three of us could go free came back to my mind whether I wanted to think of them or not. God knows I had never wanted to be the cause of anyone's death, particularly now, since I had found that at least part of myself could blend with the rest of the universe. It was, in fact, that specific, blendable part of myself that I now felt I had betrayed, misused like a fine-edged tool put to some wrong purpose.

But what else could Doc and I and the Old Man have done, I kept asking myself? We had to escape, and the only route open to us lay over the dead or incapacitated bodies of at least some of Paula's warriors.

Did it? a jeering little voice in the back of my mind nagged at me.

All right, I told myself, what other way was there?

You tell me. You're the man who can see patterns.

I couldn't see one here that didn't involve violence.

Then you're not much good, are you?

Leave me alone, I told it. Get out of my head.

How can I leave you alone? I'm you. You're stuck with me.

There's a way out, I thought. And I became very cold when I thought it.

You haven't got the guts. And even if you did, what about Ellen and Marie and all the rest you'd be leaving for Paula to take her revenge on? You want their deaths on your conscience, too?

Paula—I forced myself to think of Paula instead. But that brought no relief either. Her image summoned up another sort of sick feeling inside me. Because I had been attracted to her. I actually had. The fact that she had challenged me with her unavailability had been a cloak for the fact that I wanted her anyway, had wanted her, in fact, from the moment I had first seen her getting out of her helicopter looking like a page out of a fashion magazine in a world now vanished forever. Having her would have been almost like getting that world back again.

Of course, I had known she had dressed like that deliberately, that the whole matter of her entrance on the scene had been cool-headedly calculated to produce the effect on all of us that it had. But knowing this didn't alter the emotional leap I had felt. Seeing her like that, I had been lifted out of the raw and dusty reality of my present into a gilded dream of a memory. I had suddenly been reminded of the tawdriness of the little world I was about to defend with my life. I had felt suddenly embarrassed by the workaday plainness of the two women who shared my life with me, and my handful of loyal friends. They were like coarse brown bread compared to angel food cake. They were like flat homebrew beer compared to champagne.

I had been attracted to Paula all right—from that moment. I could have convinced myself I was in love with her, given time. Given enough time, time enough to hang myself with, I could even have gradually forgotten my duty to go back and finish what I had begun with the time storm. Maybe, I thought now, there had been the thought of not returning in the back of my mind all along. So that when I raged at the possibility of Paula not being able to get her army—and me—across to Europe this fall, I was really raging against the delay of the excuse that being on the other side of the Atlantic would have given me, the excuse to put off escaping from Paula if and when word came that Porniarsk had succeeded in accomplishing the very large task I had set him to do.

Yes, it had all been there, hidden inside me, the impulse to throw away the golden light I had found for the gaining of an enameled tin ring. How purely tin, I had finally discovered when I had seen her in her tent that dawn, and she had directed me to sign the letter she had written for me.

At that moment, the last piece of her personal pattern had clicked into place for me; and I was forced to see her as she innately was. I had thought that there must be at least a touch of something Napoleonic under the display brightness that was her surface. After all, she conquered the larger part of the North American continent. She had a government, a standing army, and more accumulated resources than any other half-dozen communities in the world combined. Above and beyond this, she had an Alexandrian dream of conquering the whole world. There must, I thought, be something there that was unique and powerful.

But there was not. When I had stepped into her tent that morning, when I saw her appearance and the letter she had for me to sign, her pattern had been completed for me; and I realized that what I was looking at was an individual who momentarily, at least, had gone irrational under the pressures of defeat and disappointment. With the evidence of that irrationality, everything about her had fallen into place. She was neither Napoleonic nor Alexandrian. She was a borderline psychotic who had fallen into a chain of circumstances which allowed her to ride forward triumphantly on the crest of a mounting wave—as long as everything went her way. While luck was with her, she appeared to be inspired by genius. But when things went wrong, she had no plan.

Literally.

Those who were on her side were people. Those who were not were rag dolls to be thrown at the wall or have the sawdust ripped out of them if she was in a temper. She could wade in blood up to her elbows and it would not matter; because, of course, it was not real blood. It could not be real blood, because it belonged to those who were against her. That was the psychotic side of her; that was what had hit me like a swinging barn door in the face when I had stepped into her tent.

All the communities who had given in to her on her way here were composed of real people, of course. But Capitol had chosen to refuse her. Therefore, its population were not real people and she told her soldiers to kill them. But some of her soldiers had not distinguished between those she wanted killed and those she did not, and so obviously those soldiers were not real people either. Therefore, she would have Marc Despard find them and kill them. But Marc Despard would know that the idea to kill had come from her in the first place, which might make him think wrong things about her—things no real person would think. Therefore, it should be arranged so that it looked as if the soldiers' punishment were Marc's own idea, and then later she would use some new soldiers to kill him for doing such a thing. Then everyone would be happy again; because there would be nobody left but people who agreed with her. Real people.

Of course, this pattern explained why she had never let me or anyone else get close to her. Experience would have taught her that anyone she let get too close to her might end up disagreeing with her about something or other. I had thought I was beyond the point where any other single human being could scare the hell out of me; but she had done that, this morning in the tent. It had been like finding myself locked in a cage with a wounded tiger.

So it was someone like Paula that I had been willing to trade the universe for—the universe and everything else I thought I loved. I was sick: sick at heart and sick at mind. And to cure a bad situation I had now gone out and caused bloody deeds to be done myself. I who had seen the golden light had done my own wading in blood. I had sent Doc to kill. . . .

The pain of it was more than I could stand. I groped desperately for the unity—the golden light—and could not find it. I scrabbled and clutched for self-justification and found nothing. Nothing, but the wrong-end-to excuse of saving the lives of the few people that meant something to me. I had killed that they should not be killed. *"Nature, red in tooth and claw. . . ."* wrote Tennyson. The books I had drowned in during earlier weeks danced in my head; but there was no comfort in them. The only small, slim reason I could find for my living was to defend what I loved. At least, if there was no justification in doing that, there was no agony. Perhaps I could be simply pagan, and simply simple.

> *And how can man die better*
> *Than facing fearful odds,*
> *For the ashes of his fathers,*
> *And the temples of his gods?*

I had no ashes of my fathers, no temples and no gods. I was not Horatius, the ancient Roman of whom Macaulay had rhymed in these lines from his *Lays of Ancient Rome.* I only had my little tribe of one-time strangers to guard against all things human, temporal and infinite; and I wanted some comfort, some prayer to cling to. Like an overboard passenger hanging on to a life preserver, I clung now to Macaulay's four lines and the idea of a finish in battle, to end all, to wash all out; and I went whirling down into darkness, into dreams and final forgetfulness . . . .

I woke suddenly, it seemed a long time later, staring up into two close, concerned faces. One was the smooth face of Doc and the other the hairy face of the Old Man.

"Marc!" said Doc. "Are you all right? Were you dreaming?"

"Why? What?" My tongue was thick and dry. "What is it?"

"Your eyes were closed and you kept saying, *'I can't do it—I can't do it—'* and we couldn't wake you up," Doc said.

The Old Man nuzzled my face in relief. I got a noseful of his hair and realized he badly needed a bath. That brought me back to normality faster than anything else.

"Where are we?" I said, sitting up.

"I think we're almost home," said Doc. "You take a look. You know how this plane works. I don't."

I turned to the control panel and depressed one of the keys.

"Where are we?" I asked. "Show me with a mark on a map."

Obediently, the screen gave me the image of the last enlargement of the map I had asked it for earlier. A tiny image of the aircraft appeared on this and I peered at it for a second or two before I could see that it was actually in motion across the map lines.

"Looks like we're not more than a few minutes out," I said, "depending on how fast we're travelling."

I looked out and down. We still seemed to be at the same altitude; and, surprisingly, the sun seemed no higher above the horizon behind us than it had been when we took off. That would seem to indicate that we had been matching the earth's rotational speed—which was a good rate of travel, to be sure.

"I've told it to go in and land by the summer palace," I told Doc. I turned back to the control panel and spoke to it. "Land slowly. I don't want any of our own people shooting at us. And I don't want to scare anybody."

The craft took me literally. It came in over the summer palace at exactly three thousand meters of altitude and then descended vertically, and slowly. We took about twenty minutes to actually touch ground in the landing area, and by the time we did, most of the population of the community was on hand, standing off about fifty feet from our touchdown spot, with the community leaders in the front rank.

I opened the door of the future plane and stepped down to the earth—and they all just stared at me, as if I were a man from Mars. Then Doc and the Old Man came scrambling out behind me; and everyone poured in on us with a rush. I was surrounded, picked up and carried, literally, almost all the way to the summer palace entrance before I could make them put me down on my feet.

When I finally did get a semblance of quiet, I climbed up in one of the jeeps parked there, stood on the back seat and told them, as briefly as I could, that I had escaped from Paula, that she would be after me eventually, but should not be showing up for some weeks at least, and I would have more details for them tomorrow. But right now, I had to sort myself out and talk things over with the other leaders.

They were a little disappointed not to hear the whole story at once; but they dispersed to their various activities eventually, after I had promised a community-wide celebration for that evening. Finally, I got to go inside the palace with Ellen, Marie, Bill and the rest.

Over food in the same dining room in which I had told them I was going with Paula, I broke the news to them, bluntly.

"She's not completely sane," I said. "I don't mean she's out of her head all the time; she'd be less dangerous if she was. I mean that when it comes to certain things she'll do exactly what she wants, regardless of the consequences. Because when she gets to that point, nothing matters except doing what she wants. That's why I left; because sooner or later, she would want something and find me in the way; and that would be the end of me."

I told them about the letter she had me sign.

"The point was to hit back at the soldiers who had killed the experts," I said, "and to saddle me with the blame for doing it. Sooner or later, she would have used that blame to get rid of me. That's why I had to get out of there without wasting time. Because it could have been sooner. It could have been the minute the men she wanted executed were executed."

"But what'll she do now?" Marie asked.

"She'll send a force to bring me back," I said. "But maybe not right away, because she's understrength now. That's one reason leaving her now was good timing. Here, I can work with Porniarsk and maybe we can find a way to make the move forward before her people can show up here. I've been working on pattern recognition. I'm stronger in that area than I was. It's a fighting chance, anyway."

I looked over at Porniarsk, who had not been outside with the others when we landed, but who had come into the dining room since we had been sitting there.

"I should have sent word to you sooner," he said. "The fact is, I ran into this sticking point over a month ago, but I thought that it was something I could get through. Now, I don't know. Maybe the two of us can get through it."

"I'll come to the lab with you as soon as we're finished here," I said, between bites of the home-cured ham I was digging into. "But in any case—"

I looked back at the rest of them.

"In any case, everyone in the community who won't be needed for the monad gestalt, when and if we're ready to use it, better start making preparations to scatter, now. If Paula can't get me back, she'll raise bloody hell—and I mean bloody hell literally—with anyone connected to me she can get her hands on. Bill, Marie—"

They both looked at me, from farther on down the table.

"You'd better start making plans as to how supplies are to be portioned out, and where to, and how people are to take off. Also, Doc—"

"Yo."

"We're going to need a fast, a really fast warning system to give us as much notice as possible when we learn Paula or some of her people are headed this way. Maybe you can figure out something using that aircraft we came in."

"I think so, Marc." He looked at Ellen. "Right, Ellen?"

Ellen nodded.

"All right." I finished the ham and pushed my plate back. "Anyone have any suggestions or comments, before I head out to the lab with Porniarsk?"

"You need some sleep," said Marie. "You look dead. So does Doc."

I looked at her. The words were Marie-type words, but there was a difference about her which found an echo in the way she said them. However, I had no time to investigate such things now.

"I slept on the flight coming in," I said. "Doc probably could use some sleep."

"I slept last night," said Doc.

"Whatever," I said, getting to my feet. "Anyway, I'll catch up on my sleep later. Porniarsk? Ready to go?"

"Yes," he said. We went out of the dining room together, leaving the others behind us.

"It's an unusual situation," said Porniarsk, once we got to the tank in the lab. "It's the kind of stoppage as if the extrapolative element of this device—what you've been calling the computer—had encountered a logical contradiction, so that further extrapolations from this point would result in increasing error. But attempts on my part to find out what such a contradiction might be have produced no results."

"Let me look at where it stopped," I said.

He activated the tank. Once more I stared into the blue-grayness, with the little firefly points of light flickering through the space of it. For a moment, a small crawling fear woke inside me, a fear that in my step aside with Paula I had lost whatever had given me the ability to see patterns in the tank before. But then, slowly, the little points of light began to relate and group themselves into associations.

The pattern took shape. It was a strange and unfamiliar pattern, which was to be expected. But when I tried to go one step further and change my perception from that of small lights in a tank to the actual universe envisioned, as I had done once before, I could not do it. The small crawling fear came back, stronger.

"I can see what you've got there," I said to Porniarsk, finally. "But I can't seem to make it mean anything to me. I don't know what's wrong."

"You may just be tired," said Porniarsk. "Or perhaps you've been away from the device long enough to feel unfamiliar with it."

"Maybe."

I gave up and withdrew my attention from the pattern in the tank. Suddenly, I was dead tired. Tired right down to the marrow of my bones.

"You're right about one thing," I told Porniarsk. "I need sleep. I'll go lie down."

I went back to my own room, part of the suite I shared with Marie and Ellen. But neither of them were there now. It was only early afternoon, and they, with the rest of the community, would be hard at work. I felt a child's loneliness for someone to sit with me while I fell asleep; but I pushed the emotion away from me. I undressed, lay down on the bed, pulled a blanket over me and stared at the white ceiling, lightly shadowed now and then by the clouds outside reflecting from the window.

I was still dead tired; but I began to wonder if I would sleep. I lay there.

I woke to someone shaking me. For a second, I thought I was back on the future plane again and being woken by Doc and the Old Man. Then I saw it was dark outside the window and dark in the room, and the shape bending over me was female.

"Marc—" It was Ellen's voice. "I hate to wake you, but the whole community's waiting for you. If you can just come out and show yourself for a little while, you can come back after that and sleep as long as you want."

"Sure," I said. "All right."

I levered my wooden body up to a sitting position on the edge of the bed and she began to massage my neck, standing in front of me and reaching around behind my head. I leaned my forehead gratefully against the human softness of her belly, feeling myself come alive again to the warm pressure of her fingers kneading the stiff cords and muscles running up from my shoulders into the area behind my ears. She felt and smelled delightful; and I wanted to stay there for the rest of my life, getting my neck rubbed.

But she stopped after a while.

"You're awake now," she said. "Get dressed."

She was right. I was awake; and there was nothing to do but get dressed. I was standing on one leg, putting on my pants, when it came to me suddenly that what I had felt was second cousin to what makes dogs and other animals enjoy being petted and stroked by humans. Not the physical sensation alone, but the implications of affection and concern. For a second, I could almost feel what an animal might feel in such case—and there, for a second, the universe-identity almost was with me again. But the second passed, and it was gone.

I finished dressing. Ellen had already gone ahead. I followed down the corridors, out through the door, and stepped into the warm, early evening dark of outside. A barbecue pit had been dug in the landing area, and I could smell roasting meat. There were several other large fires, throwing sparks high in the air so that they seemed to mingle with the stars overhead; and the open space around them was filled with moving silhouettes and the hubbub of voices. For some reason, it reminded me of a small town in Mexico I had happened to go through once on vacation on an evening of a fiesta. I could not remember the name of the saint who was the cause of the fiesta; but it had been night, and fireworks were exploding high in the air over the town, their sparks raining down into the dark streets. Lights and voices had been all over the place, with people coming and going in the narrow streets, so that it all had a sort of incredible richness to it. I had wondered then where that feeling of richness came from; but of course now I knew where. Unconsciously, I had been reading the patterns of the fiesta around me the way those who lived in the area read them. I was picking the rich feeling up from them; and now I was doing the same thing, picking up the magic and warmth of the moment from the rest of the community, gathered here to celebrate the fact that Doc and I, and even the Old Man, were back safe.

I went forward into the crowd, and was recognized. The faces and bodies swirled around me, drink was shoved into my hand. I was mobbed and hustled and questioned and patted on the back and kissed until my head started to spin. Between that spinning and the fatigue I had, measured by the little sleep I had just had, I was not to remember most of the events of that evening. It was merely one long happy blur that ended when I finally groped my way back into my dark room and fell on my bed again, some hours later.

Ellen was there and I hung on to her.

"Where's Marie?" I asked after a while.

"She's still outside," Ellen said. "Sleep, now."

I slept.

I did not come to until late the next day. But in spite of that long, exhausted slumber, it was three days before I was really back in proper body and mind again. The night of the celebration with the crowd had healed me somewhat, in a way I could not quite pin down, but I felt more whole and healthy generally. I went back to Porniarsk's lab on the third day and tried the pattern of the tank again.

The first time I tried it, I was no more successful than I had been the first day I had come home. Still, my failure did not leave me with the sensation of being so helpless as before, and after a rest I tried again. This time I was also unsuccessful, but I got the impression I had come closer to actually envisioning the universe; and so I continued, trying and trying again, feeling that I got a little closer with each try—and a couple of weeks later I broke through.

Whatever barrier I had been pushing against went down all at once. Without warning, I was suddenly in the uni-

verse of galaxies and stars—and what I saw leaped at me
so hard that I was jarred out of it, back into the conscious reality of the lab and myself standing there, staring
into the tank.

"Why, hell!" I said. "It's wrong!"

"Wrong?" Porniarsk said. "In what way?"

I turned to the avatar.

"I don't know," I said. "I mean, I do know; but it
doesn't matter! Don't you see? Your device here shut
itself down because it began to turn up inconsistencies
within the patterns it was evolving from the patterns it
had evolved previously. Logically, there couldn't be any
inconsistencies, but there are!"

"I don't understand," said Porniarsk.

"Don't you? Look," I said, "this tank has been extending previous patterns that were correct and getting one
that is incorrect."

"Then you're saying the device has broken down? I
don't see how it could," said Porniarsk.

"No. It hasn't broken down—that's the point. *It's* not
wrong! What's wrong is reality. One of the factors the
device takes into account is the human—pardon me, I
mean the intelligent life—factor; and that factor logically
evolved is creating inconsistencies with the purely physical
evolution of the other factors considered. Don't you see
what that means?"

"I do not," said Porniarsk.

"It means somewhere up there in the future—at the
time we're looking at right now—intelligent life is doing
something about the time storm. Doing something at least
effective enough to produce inconsistencies with what
would have happened if the storm had just been allowed
to run its course. We've found them, Porniarsk! We've
found a time when they're able to do something about the
time storm!"

The avatar stood perfectly still, looking at me. He was
so motionless and his silence went on so long that I began
to entertain the outrageous thought that he had not heard
me.

"I see," he said, speaking just as I opened my mouth to
repeat to him what I had just said. "Then our search is
over."

"That's right. All we have to do now is figure out how

the monad needs to shift the immediate small factors so that at least this lab can move forward to that time."

"Is it possible?"

I had never actually stopped to doubt that it was possible; and his question took half the joy out of me at one blow.

"Of course it is," I said. "It has to be. We're away down at the end of the chain of storm changes. The forces dealing with this area have to be relatively light . . . ."

I ran down.

"We'll have to check and see, of course," I said, "Maybe we'd better do that first before I tell everyone what we've found and start getting their hopes up."

We were still checking several days later when Doc came into the lab one morning.

"I've just made a swing east in the plane," he said. He had become used to the craft now and he flew daily patrols. "There's a force of about a hundred and fifty of Paula's soldiers, about half on foot and half on horseback, about a hundred and twenty miles east of here. No motorized transport or anything more than carry weapons. They aren't wearing her uniforms, but they can't be any other troops. No one else on this continent can put together that many people and get them to move in formation like that."

"How did they get so close?" Porniarsk asked.

"They must have started out individually or in small groups," Doc said. "That's the only way I can think of. Then they rendezvoused someplace last night, so that this was the first day they've been all together. I'd have spotted them from the air otherwise. At the rate they're marching, they'll be here in less than a week."

I looked at Porniarsk.

"That ends the checking," I said. "All we can do now is go, and hope we make it."

30

There was something wrong in the atmosphere around the summer palace. I could feel it, but I could not take the time to pin it down. I set the rest of the community to packing up, ready to get out, and with Porniarsk, got down to the choosing of an optimum target nanosecond on the day before the soldiers were due to arrive. We wanted a time when the pattern of storm forces concerned with our small area would be as close as possible to the conformation I was going to try to force them into with the monad. My original idea had been to deal with as small an area as possible—probably only the lab itself and everything inside it. But as the situation developed, it turned out that the difference between restructuring the forces dealing with just the lab and those dealing with an area including the summer palace, mountain section and enough of the plain to contain the town and a couple of square miles outside it, was essentially no difference at all, in terms of the size of the forces to be dealt with.

This put a new complexion on things. It was the first good news I could remember finding in a long time. Now I could take along everybody, if they wanted to go. I was tied to the work in the lab, but I sent Doc out to tell the rest of the community that as things had turned out, they didn't need to run and hide from the soldiers unless they wanted to. Those who wanted to come along with the monad and myself into the future could simply stick around.

Having sent the word out I got back to work. Matters, for once, seemed to be all going in the right direction. The more I pinned down the force-changes to be made, the more possible they looked. Even setting aside the fact that I was much more pattern-experienced and more developed and mature than I had been when I had balanced the forces in the immediate area of the planet, what I now looked at was a much simpler job.

This, in spite of the fact that we would be moving an unguessable distance of time into the future. There was no way to measure how far, but thousands of years anyway in terms of the old temporal yardsticks we had used before the time storm. The reason for this was that, even taking in the area including the town, I was dealing with a very small patch of space compared to that which enclosed the immediate neighborhood of the Earth. What it amounted to was that I would be making a much larger temporal change—but in a very, very much tinier area than I had the time before. It was as if I multiplied by a factor of a few thousand, but then divided the result by millions.

So, matters in the lab progressed well; but nothing goes with complete smoothness. It was a good thing that Porniarsk and I were, if anything, ahead of our schedule for charting all the parameters of the shift as I had laid it out; because I found myself called away from the lab to deal with the human side of the move.

Without realizing it, I had hit everyone in the community harder than I had planned when I had sent out word with Doc that those who wanted to come with me could do so. Living with the time storm as I had been all this time, I had forgotten that only those who had been with me at the time of the balancing of forces originally would have any idea of what to expect from involving themselves in what I planned to do. Nor did they look on going far into the future as calmly as I did.

Accordingly, they were seething with questions that needed some kind of answers if they were to come up with their individual decisions. I found I had to call a meeting of the community as a whole to explain matters and answer those questions. We were too many to crowd into even the largest quonset hut, so the meeting was held outside on the landing area, with a public address system rigged by Bill for the occasion, with extra microphones on long cords, so that everybody could hear the questions as well as the answers.

I began by explaining the mechanism of the time storm as well as I understood it, and how this mechanism had affected us here on Earth. Porniarsk stood beside me in the jeep I was using for a speaker's platform, ready to answer questions himself; but no one asked him any. I think they were still a little wary of Porniarsk, whom few besides those in the summer palace had, in fact, ever seen.

When I finished that part of my explanation, I called for questions, but there were none. So I went on to explain how I believed that up ahead in the future, people—not merely human people, but 'people' in the larger sense, including intelligent, civilized life like that represented by Porniarsk's race—would finally come to grips with the time storm and find some way of stopping it. Finally, I repeated what I was sure they must know already, that I thought I had located such a time and I planned to go there. Those who wanted to go with me, could.

Once more I asked for questions. This time I got them —three hours or more of them, mostly unanswerable, by me or anyone else there at least.

Basically, they were unanswerable because what they all wanted most to know was what it would be like for them up there in the future. This was, naturally, something about which I had no more idea than they had themselves. It began to sink in on me as I stood there doing my best to answer them, what an unimaginable gulf exists between those who are obsessed by a goal and those who simply want to live as best they can. In a manner of speaking, I wanted only to arrive in Samarkand, and anything short of the moment when I got there was unimportant. The others were concerned with the possibility of tigers and robbers on the way, the availability of wells along the route, the quarters they would occupy once they arrived and the marketplace where they would eventually vend their wares.

I could not help them. Without realizing it, I had discounted myself completely from the price I was willing to pay to get what I wanted. They had not. They could not think like me; and—God help me—I could no longer think like them.

But I did what I could. I gave them words, explanations, until my throat was hoarse, and they went away discussing what I had said, sure that I had told them something of importance, but finding themselves still unsatisfied, and unreassured.

Porniarsk and I went back to the lab. With or without the extra people, I had to close with the storm forces when the proper moment came; and the moment was marching inexorably toward us.

We finished going over all possibilities by mid-afternoon of the day before the soldiers were due in. Doc had been checking the progress of our invaders from the air, at heights of ten to fifteen thousand feet. Whether they noticed him—the milky-colored aircraft was all but invisible to the ground at that altitude—or not, they continued to come on steadily, neither slowing nor increasing their first observed rate of travel. If they had been the total force that Paula could bring against us, it would have been a temptation to go out and meet them. A night raid or two on their camp, led by some of our people who had picked up special skills from Doc, plus a few good daytime ambushes, could have cut their strength to a point where we would have been able to defend against them quite handily. But Paula could keep after us forever, and there was no use wasting lives.

I had been worrying about what to do with the experimentals, now that some of us were moving forward in time and the rest taking to the hills. Paula was just the sort of person to kill them all on sight when she found out I had escaped, if they were left behind and undefended.

That problem, however, I found no longer existed. Apparently, when the Old Man had taken his interest in me, the rest of the village had started to disintegrate socially. Except for a few of the others who had formed alliances with some of the human families and were either going forward with these families or taking to the hills with them, the rest had long since wandered away from the village on their own and disappeared. It was a sad sort of diaspora to think about, because there was nothing away from here for them but the lives of solitary, intelligent animals; but there was nothing I, or any of our people, could do about it now. It could be, I told myself, that there was a consciousness in them that their race, as a race, had no future—just as it had had no past beyond a test tube. But that thought did not make me feel any better.

In any case, I had no time to think about experimentals now. This afternoon was the afternoon that had been picked for saying goodbyes. I made myself available out in the landing area; and they came up by individuals and families and groups to say farewell, not only to me, but to the rest of us who were going. I was surprised, and even a little secretly unhappy, to see the number who had decided to take their chances running from Paula the rest of their lives, in preference to following me forward. But, it was their decision; and better they make it now while they had the chance than regret that they had not made it, later.

Dinner time was to be the end of the farewells. We broke off finally and went inside. I had wanted to hold a meeting of the people who would be with me in the monad before we settled down to eat; but when we all gathered in the dining room there were some extra faces. One of these was merely Wendy, who had never shown any interest in being part of the time storm work, but who was welcome to the monad if she wanted to join. Also, there were her gangling young boyfriend, who was not welcome under any circumstances, and Abe Budner, our big, slow-moving Director of Food Services and former chef, whom I liked personally, but whom I had never thought of as being monad material.

"Abe," I said, as I sat down at the table, "no offense, but we're just about to start a business meeting. You and—"

"Marc," said Marie.

My mind suddenly became alert. By which I mean that it came out of the whole problem of the move into time and back to the everyday present of the dining room and the people now in it. I woke to the fact that Marie, Wendy, the boyfriend and Abe were all in hiking gear, rough clothes and heavy boots. I also became aware that there was a silence in the room, a tense silence on the part of everybody else that said that all of them there had known for some time about what I was just now recognizing.

I looked at Marie.

"You're not going?" I said.

"That's right, Marc," she said. Now that I really examined her for the first time in a very long, long period, I was a little shocked at what I saw. Her face was tired, and definitely now showed the signs of middle-age, the crow's-feet at the corners of the eyes, the sagging of the chin line. I had never really looked at her in all these months. I had never thought to look.

"Get out of here, the rest of you," I said, hoarsely. I did not specify who the rest were, but they all left the room except the four who were dressed to travel, and Ellen.

"Wendy and Walter don't want to go into the future, Marc," Marie said. "And I've decided to go along with them and Abe."

"Marie . . ." I said. The words would not come. Patterns flashed and clicked through my mind; and I saw what I did not want to see. If Marie stayed here, Paula would find her sooner or later; and Paula would remember that Marie had been one of my two wives. It was inevitable—no, it was not inevitable. Did I think I was a deity to deal in inevitability? But it was so overwhelmingly probable that the chances it might not happen were too insignificant to consider.

"Marie," I said. "Don't you understand? Unless you go with me, you'll land right in Paula's hands. Believe me, I know. You will."

"Even if I do," she said.

"Look . . ." I made an effort to get the emotion out of my voice and talk reasonably. "There's no point in throwing yourself away just because Wendy wants to stay. I know, she's young, and—"

"You don't understand," Marie said. "I don't want to go with you. I *want* to stay here myself."

Understanding suddenly struck me like a numbing blow. I had not fooled anyone, it seemed, except myself. I realized now that she and Ellen had known all along how I had reacted to Paula, and what at least part of my reason was for going off with her.

"Listen to me," I said. "About Paula and me—"

"Marc," Marie said. "You're going to have to understand. It's me who doesn't want to go into the future. It's me. I can't take this moving any more. I'm sick of it. I want to settle in one place and stay."

"With Paula hunting you down?" I couldn't believe what I heard.

"That doesn't matter. I'll be here, in this world, not in some other. Not starting all over again. I can't keep starting over and over again, Marc. You can. All right, you go ahead. But I want a little ordinary life for as long as I can have it, here, before the end comes."

I shook my head. It was all crazy. Vaguely, I became aware that even the ones who had stayed behind before had gone—Wendy and the boyfriend and Abe. All except

Ellen, and she was standing far back now in a corner of the room, almost lost in shadow. Marie came around the table to me.

"You never did understand me, Marc, did you?" she said. "You didn't understand me from the first; and you didn't love me."

"Maybe not at first," I said; and my voice had gone hoarse again. It was part of the general craziness that I should be standing here now telling her this while the other woman I loved stood back listening. "It's different now."

"Not different enough," she said. "Not to the point where you'd move one inch out of your way for me. Or anyone."

"That's not true."

"Then prove it. Stay here yourself. Don't go forward."

"Marie! For Christ's sake, talk sense!"

"I am talking sense. But you can't even hear me." She stopped and said nothing for a moment; then, surprisingly, she reached up and stroked my cheek with her fingers, very gently. "It's all right, Marc. You don't have to hear. You can't change for me, I know that. But there's a point beyond which I can't change for you. Nobody can make all the changes you'd like them to make, don't you know that?"

"I just want you to live," I said. "I don't want Paula to get you."

"I know, dear," she said. "But it won't work. I've got to stay; and even if you wanted to stay too, you couldn't protect me."

"Don't be so damn sure about that!" I said; and for an insane, small second, hope of straightening this out after all flickered alive in me. "If I decided to take Paula and all her army apart, it might take some time; but—"

"You'd be throwing yourself away on something other than what you're built to do," she said. "If things went that way, I'd have held you prisoner here, instead of you taking me prisoner into the future."

I didn't know what to tell her.

"Marc," she said, raising her face to me. "Say goodby to me."

The ghost of some giant hand took me by the neck and bent my head down to hers. I kissed her and her lips felt dry and strange, as if I had never known them before.

She hugged me, and I hung on to her in return until she used strength to break herself loose.

"There," she said, stepping back a pace, "it'll be all right. A big part of it is you just can't bear to lose anything, Marc. But it'll be all right in the long run. Goodby now; and be careful."

She went out. I watched the doorway through which she had gone, and when I looked around not even Ellen was in the room. I went out into the shadows of the evening and walked by myself for a long while.

When I came back inside, it was nearly ten o'clock and there were a great many things to be done. I called together the monad, which now consisted of the Old Man, Ellen, Bill and myself. Doc had volunteered to join us; and with Marie missing, I now more than wanted him, I needed him there. I went over the patterns with them, as best I could describe them. Not so much because the patterns would mean anything particular to them; but the more their minds could identify with mine once we were in action together, the stronger we would be as a unit, and the more certain I could be of doing what I had set out to do.

Most of the people in the community who were leaving had already gone by midnight, when the meeting broke up. I sent Doc out to check that everyone was clear of the area who did not want to be transported forward with the rest of us. It was one of those coffee nights, when everything is due to happen with the next day's sunrise, and the nerves feel stretched to the point where they sing like guitar strings at a touch. A warm weather front had moved in early in the evening, and the dark outside was still and hot. Only a faint rumble of thunder sounded from below the horizon, from time to time; and the lights among the buildings down below were fewer even than they might be at this hour on an icy winter night, so that already the community looked like a ghost town.

Doc came back.

"Everyone gone but the Mojowskis," he said, "and they were just leaving as I came up. Be clear of the area in another twenty minutes."

"Fine," I said. "Go on into the lab. Porniarsk's getting everybody into helmets and set to go. Tell them I'll be along in twenty minutes."

He went. I took one more turn around outside. The night air was so dark and still it could almost be felt by the fingers; and the mutter of distant thunder seemed to sound halfway around the horizon of the plain below. I had a vision of Paula's soldiers night-marching through the gloom to take us by surprise. But even if they had started to move the moment the sun was down, they could not get here in time. No one was moving in the streets of the town below. Those going with us would be in their homes, waiting.

I went into the summer palace and took a final tour of the building. The rooms seemed oddly empty, as if they had been abandoned for years. I stepped into the court-yard where Sunday lay for a moment, but without turning on the lights. As I stood there, a cicada shrilled suddenly in the darkness at my feet and began to sing.

I went back inside, with the song of the cicada still trilling in my head. It stayed with me as I went down the halls and into the brightly lit lab. Everybody was in place, with helmets already on. Only Porniarsk stood by the directing console, which he had moved out into the center of the room by the tank. I went to the tank myself, to make one last check of the patterns, for we had it set on the pattern of our moment of destination. There was no change in what I saw there.

I seated myself and took a helmet. As I lowered it over my head, the cicada sound was still ringing in my ears, so that it was like being trapped under there with it. I felt my strength flow together with the strength of the others in the monad and the memory of the cicada sound was lost in the silent song of blended identities as I opened myself to the time storm forces in balance around us.

They were there. They had been there all this time, waiting, quivering in balance like a tangle of arrested lightnings. I read that pattern at a glance this time and laid the far future pattern that I wanted like a template upon them. There was matching and overlap and disagreement between the two patterns. I reached out with the strength of the monad, pushed, and the two slid together. It was suddenly done, and over. There had been nothing to it.

I took off my helmet and looked around. The others were taking off their helmets also and, under the fluorescent lights, their faces looked pale and wondering, like the faces of children.

"We're there?" said Ellen. "But where are we?"

"I don't know," I said.

Then I noticed that around the corners of the drawn shades of the windows, the gleam of full daylight was showing.

31

We put up the shades; and the sunlight, which looked no different than any sunlight we had ever known, poured in. But outside the windows, all we could see was the same inner courtyard that held Sunday. Overhead, it was a half-cloudy day with thick white cloud masses and clear blue alternating.

We went down the corridors and out into the parking area. Below us, the empty village of the experimentals and the town were unchanged; but beyond a short distance of plain that surrounded these, high grasses now began. The stalks looked to be six feet tall at least and stretched to the horizon like an endless field of oversized wheat. The road was gone. What now was on the other side of the mountain behind us, we could not, of course, see.

Down in the town, there was still no one stirring. This was not surprising, since many of them might not yet have realized that the move had been made. There had been no sound, no feeling of physical movement when it had happened. It was difficult even for me to realize that this was the far future I had talked about.

"Shall I go tell them, below?" Doc asked.

"Go ahead," I said.

He hopped into one of the jeeps and drove off. I stood where I was with Ellen beside me, and the others, including Porniarsk, not far off. A moment later, we could see Doc's jeep emerge beyond the trees and drive in among the buildings of the town, stopping here and there while he jumped out and went inside.

Each time he came out again, he was followed by people from inside a building. Soon the streets were swarming, and the figures below were starting to stream back up the slope toward us. Half an hour later, there was an impromptu celebration underway on the landing area.

It struck me, caught up in it as I was, that I had had more shocks, and more large gatherings recently than in any time since before the time storm. Nonetheless, this last one—this arrival party, as it was named almost immediately—vibrated with something neither the welcome home blast, nor the information session had possessed. There was a relaxed feeling of peace about this occasion that I had not noticed before. It was a warm, almost a cozy, feeling. Moving about among my fellow time travellers, picking up patterns, I finally zeroed in on the reason for it. There was something held in common by all the people now around me that I had not thought to look for in them, before we made the move.

In a sense, those who had come with us were the adventurers among our community, the true pioneers. Those particular words all rang a little off-note, applied to the situation we were in. But what I mean is that, to an individual, those who had come forward with me were men, women, and even children who did not want to be any further back down the line of history than they had to be. In all of them, there was an urge to be at the very front of the wave, up where the race as a whole was breaking new ground.

Realizing this, something new and unsuspected in me warmed to them. It was a corner of myself that I had not even realized existed before. It was, in fact, the part of me that felt just the way they did. Even if I had known before we started that what we would all find up here would be the hour of Armageddon and the final end for our kind, I at least would have wanted to go anyway, to be part of even that, while it lasted, in preference to living out my life in any previous time, no matter how comfortable.

Now, here I was with perhaps a hundred and eighty people who felt the same way I did. Under the most unlikely set of conditions that could be imagined, I had unconsciously put together my own special tribe. I was so elated with this discovery that I had to talk about it with someone. Ellen was busy helping organize the food and drink aspect of the gathering, so I went looking for Bill.

I found him also busy. He had set up a table with some sheets of paper and was asking everybody to sign up

so that we could have a complete and correct list of who
had actually come through with us, since there were people at the last moment who had changed their minds either
for or against the move. The sign-up table, however, was
essentially self-operating, now that word of it was being
passed through the crowd, and I managed to pull him
aside.

We walked off a little way from the rest, and I told
him my discovery about the pioneer element in those who
had come and my pleasure in it.

"I can't get over striking gold like that," I said. "Stop
and think how small the whole North American population was after we got the mistwalls halted. And out of that
small population we've gathered nearly two hundred people who really belong up here, thousands of years ahead
in time."

"That's true, of course," he said.

His handsome, small face had been tanned by several
years of outdoor weather, and the same amount of
time seemed to have thickened and matured even the
bones of it, so that he now looked more competent and
mature. I realized that it was with him as it had been
with Marie. Just as I had not really looked at her for a
long time, so I had not really looked at him either; and he
had been changing under my nose.

". . . it shouldn't be such a surprise, though," he was
going on to say, even as I was noting the changes in him.
"Stop to think that the ones who gathered around us in
the first place were survivor types. You had to be a
survivor type to stay alive while the mistwalls were moving. Even if you were one of the few who were lucky
enough to stay put and have no mistwalls come near you,
contact with the survivor types around you afterwards
either made you like them in a hurry, or buried you."

"My point, though," I checked and glanced around to
make sure that none of the others were close enough to
overhear me discussing them in this clinical fashion, "my
point is that these people are a lot more than simple survivors."

"Right," said Bill, his brown face serious. "Look what
happened, though. After the time storm, our group began
to attract a particular type of people—those who had
heard of us and thought they'd like to be associated with
us. The ones we attracted were the ones who saw the

same sort of things in us they saw in themselves. So they came—but they didn't all stay. Those who didn't fit went off again. The community was a sort of automatic self-filter for a common type. Then, when it came down to a question of who wanted to make the jump forward in time or not, that decision shook out the last of the chaff."

I winced inside; though I was careful to make sure no sign of it showed on my face. He had labelled Marie with a tag I neither agreed with, nor would have wanted to hear applied to her even if I had agreed with it. At the same time, I had to admit he had laid out a good argument. I said as much.

"Time will tell, of course," he answered. "I'll say one thing, though." He turned and met my eyes directly with his. "I've never felt happier in my life than when I realized that it was a settled thing, an unchangeable thing, that I was coming forward like this."

"Well," I said, a little lamely. "I'm glad."

"I think even if Bettijean hadn't wanted to come along, I still wouldn't have hesitated."

I opened my mouth to ask who Bettijean was, and then closed it again. One more thing had evidently been going on under my nose without my noticing. I would ask Ellen later.

"I'd better get back to the others," I said.

After the celebration had begun to settle down a bit, I got up on my customary jeep-rostrum to tell them what we would be doing in the next few days. I said that we would start setting up the community again, here. Meanwhile, Doc would be flying surveys to locate other human settlements in this future world. He would, in fact, fly a spiral course out of this area; and the navigating equipment of the plane could be used to map the ground he covered, in the sense that it would store up information about it, which could later be recalled on the view screen of the control panel.

"How soon do you think we'll find other people?" some male voice I did not recognize, somewhere toward the back of the crowd, asked.

"I can't make any guesses," I said. "Actually, if I was betting, I'd bet they'd find us first."

There was a silence; and I suddenly realized they were waiting for me to expand on that.

"This is the future," I said. "Porniarsk and I found

evidence that up here they may be doing something about
the time storm. If that's the case, they have to be pretty
competent technologically. I'm assuming that sooner or
later, and probably sooner, the fact that we're here will
register on whatever sort of sensing equipment they've got.
For one thing, if they're aware of the time storm, they're
going to know that a chunk of their real estate suddenly
got exchanged by the time storm forces for a chunk
from the past."

There were a lot more questions after that, some serious, some not so, covering everything from what future
humans would look like to whether we should post guards—
against animals, if not humans—until we learned that this
was unnecessary. I turned that suggestion over to Doc,
who thought it was a good idea. The session ended with
Bill climbing into the jeep and making himself somewhat
unpopular by saying that he wanted to start tomorrow
morning getting a complete inventory of everything we
had left after those leaving had taken what they wanted;
and he wanted everybody to cooperate by listing their
own possessions.

I broke away from the gathering before it finally ended
and got together with Porniarsk in the lab. The view we
had in the tank was essentially the same as the one that
had been in it before our move. The difference was
that now it was real rather than extrapolated; and there
were minor corrections in its display because of that.

"Try it now," I said to Porniarsk. "See if we can extrapolate forward from here, now that it's the present."

He worked with the equipment for perhaps twenty
minutes.

"No," he said. "It's still hesitating over inconsistencies."

"Then we've landed in the right place—or time, I
mean," I said. "To tell the truth, I've been a little worried.
Between you and me, I half-expected the people from
this time to be waiting for us when we appeared."

"You were assuming that our activity of time forces
would at once attract their attention? I would have
thought so, too."

"And that they'd have means of getting here the
moment they saw it," I said. "If they don't, how can they
be advanced enough to do anything about the time storm
generally?"

"I don't know," said Porniarsk. "But I think there are

too many unknowns here for either of us to speculate."

"I hope you're right."

"About that, I believe I am. Beyond that, it's anyone's guess."

"All right," I said. "But if no one shows up within twenty-four hours, I'm going to begin to worry."

No one did show up in the next forty-eight hours. Nor within the forty-eight hours after that, nor in the week that followed. Meanwhile, Doc was coming back from his daily mapping flights and reporting no sign of other human existance. No habitations, no movement. We were evidently at the far eastern end of a mid-continental area of plains uniformly covered by the tall grass, like central North America in the time of the buffalo; though there were none of the bison breed to be seen now.

However, both the grasslands and the hardwood forest that began about sixty miles west of where our chunk of territory had landed, were aswarm with other game. Deer, elk, wolf, bear, moose . . . and the whole category of familiar smaller wildlife. The hardwood forest gave evidence of stretching to the east coast and had been in existence long enough to kill off most of the undergrowth beneath it, so that it had a tidily unreal look about it, like a movie set for a Robin Hood epic. Doc had landed in an open section of it and reported great-trunked oaks and elms with level, mossy ground beneath them, so that there was a cathedral look to the sunlight streaming down between the lofty limbs overhead.

I kept to myself my concern over the fact we were not being approached by the other intelligences of this future time. Our community was digging in, literally. Just as we had arrived here in daylight when we had left our former time period at night, so we had also arrived here in the spring; although it had been fall where we had left. A fair amount of planted crops had been lost behind us; and even without Bill's urging, a number of our people were eager to get seeds in the ground in this place. There would be no stores of pre-time storm goods to plunder for additional food and supplies in the time where we were now.

So the first week became the second, and the second the third, with no sign of other intelligent life to be found on the continent around us and no futuristic visitors. Gradually we began to adjust to the fact that we might, indeed, be completely alone on this planet of the future; and the life of our own community began to take up most of our attention.

It was a strenuous time. In addition to coping with the fact that here we would have to supply our own necessities, there was evidence that the climate in this future time and area would have colder winters than we had endured, back where we had been. Possibly, much colder winters. There was a good deal of work to be done to insulate buildings and expand the capacity of their heating units, whether fireplaces or stoves.

With the move, we had lost the small river from which we had powered our electric generator. Bill had said he could get some windmill structures built in a few weeks to give us at least intermittent current; but this depended on having the hands available to do the work. More immediate was the need for firewood. Right now the only wood available was on our section of a mountain that had come forward in time with us. One hard winter would deforest this completely. It was almost an imperative that we arrange somehow to bring fuel from the forested area sixty miles to our east, or move the community to it; and we had too big a stake in fixed property here to make that move in one short summer.

The result was that everybody worked time and overtime, including me. In a way, this was something I was grateful for; because it kept my mind off the fact that no one had contacted us. Doc had by now flown as far as the east coast and for some hundreds of miles north of what had once been the Canadian border. He had seen absolutely no sign of civilization. Everywhere, there was only wilderness visible from the muskeg conifer forest of the north, though the now-distorted pattern of the Great Lakes, down to the flat country north of the former Mexican border. A cold worry had begun to nibble at me that possibly Earth at this time was completely uninhabited and forgotten; and if that was so, how in my lifetime was I ever to contact time storm fighters who were light-years—possibly hundreds to millions of light-years—away?

So I was grateful for the hard work, in one way. In another way, it kept me from coming to grips with a second worry, one that was like acid eating away deep within me. With Marie's leaving, something in her had come out into the open that I had never suspected she felt. Now, I was aware of it in Ellen as well. Ellen was still there during the days; she was there beside me at night; but I could sense now that not all of her was there. Some part of her was being withheld from me. There was a wall between us, as there had been between Marie and myself, although I had never realized it.

I wanted to talk to her about it; but there was no time. In the morning we only had time to rise, dress, eat, and run. During the day there was no rest, no pause in which to talk. At night, there was only time for another meal, and sleep would threaten to claim us before we had finished refueling the weary, empty engines of our bodies. We fell into bed, opened our eyes—it seemed—a moment later; and another day's cycle was already rushing us inexorably onward.

But there had to be a break sometime. It came at the end of the fifth week, when the first of Bill's windmills began to power the generator, and a trickle of electricity came to make our lighting fixtures glow faintly against the ceilings and walls behind them. It was as good an excuse as any to give people a breather, and I declared a night and a day off.

For all the wonders of artificial light refound, there was little celebrating that first evening. All that most of us wanted to do was to sleep; and sleep we did, until late the next day. Then, in the noon sunlight, we gradually came out of our sleeping quarters to sit or move around slowly in the sun, either doing nothing at all, or turning our attention at last to something that had long gone neglected, that we now had time to check, clean, mend, or build.

It was the second of these activities that concerned me. When I woke, Ellen was already up and out of the summer palace. I got up, drank a couple of cups of black coffee and went looking for her.

I found her hanging out a wash on the upsloping hillside that lay on the opposite side of the summer palace from that which held the landing area. Coming around the corner and seeing her from a distance, I woke to the fact that she had necessarily taken over all of Marie's household obligations in addition to her own. I had been so used to having both of them around and being selfishly immersed in my own problems, that it had never occurred to me that Ellen would not be doing double duty in addition to her outside work with the rest of the community.

Nor had it ever occurred to me to help either her or Marie before. I came around a corner of the building and saw her from a little distance. I stopped, and for a moment I simply watched her, for she had not yet seen me. Then I went forward, picked up a pair of my own jeans from the basket and joined her in hanging up the rest of the wet stuff.

We worked side by side in silence.

"Look," I said, when we were done. "Why don't you sit down for a moment? I'll take the basket in, bring out a card table and some chairs and fix us a lunch. You just sit still. How about it?"

She looked at me. I had never been able to read the deep thoughts behind her face, and I could not now. But I noticed again, as I had come to notice since Marie had left, how Ellen had also changed with the years in between. She was still young—what had I figured out once, that she could not be any older than Doc and was perhaps even younger? But there was nothing of a girl left about her now; not even the ghost, it seemed, of she whom I had picked up in the panel truck long since. The Ellen I looked at now was a mature woman and another person entirely.

"All right," she said.

She sat down on the grass of the hillside, took off the scarf she had tied around her head and shook her hair out. She was wearing some old, autumn-brown slacks and a dark green shirt, open at the throat. Her neck rose in one straight column from the spread collar of the shirt, and under her dark hair, now loose about her head and shoulders, her eyes were blue-green and brilliant.

I took the basket and went into the house. I rummaged around the kitchen, trying to remember what she had shown a liking for, in the way of food. I had become a halfway decent cook in my years alone in the north woods before the time storm hit; but there was not much available here in the way of foodstuffs. We were all living off stored goods until fall, when the crops of our recent planting would hopefully be in.

I finally found a small canned ham, and with this, some canned new potatoes, and three of the highly valuable eggs from our community's small flock of chickens, managed to make a sort of ham and potato salad, mois-

tened with a spur-of-the-moment, homemade mayonnaise
I whipped up from the yolk of one of the eggs and the corn
oil we had in fair quantity. I also hunted around the palace
and found a bottle of Liebfraumilch that was not overage. There was no way to cool it, lacking electricity for
our refrigerator; but salad and wine, once I had the card
table and chairs set up outside with a tablecloth of sorts
on it, looked reasonably festive.

"That's good," said Ellen, about the salad, as we ate;
and I warmed clear through.

"Glad to hear you say so," I told her. "Do you realize I
really don't know that much about what you like to eat?"

"I like everything," she said.

"That's good. Because it'll be a long time before we
have anything like what we were used to before," I said;
and I went on about what we could expect in the way of
diet that winter, even if the crops went well.

I was talking around and about, trying to get her to
give me some sort of conversational lead from which I
could get onto the topic I wanted to bring up. She said
nothing, however, to help. Nonetheless, with the relaxa-
tion of the food and wine in me, I finally began to drift
on the tide of my own words into the area I wanted.

"There's two chances that might help protect Marie and
the others," I said. "One's that when Paula's soldiers
arrived and found the country changed where we'd been,
they figured I'd magicked everybody safely forever beyond
their reach, and Paula bought that idea when they told
her—"

"Do you really think she would?"

I hesitated.

"No," I said. "If she was completely normal, mentally,
I'd think she might. But part of her mind is never going to
rest, where I'm concerned; and sooner or later, word is
going to reach her of people who've met and recognized
some of our people who stayed behind. Then her hunt'll
be on again. All we can really hope for is a delay."

"What's the other chance?"

"That's the long one. If I ever do get into contact with
the time storm fighters here and get to work with them,
maybe I can learn some way to go back and make Marie
and the rest permanently safe from Paula—maybe by
shifting Paula herself to a different time."

Ellen said nothing. There was a little silence between us; and a fly that had discovered the empty wine bottle circled it, drowning.

"God help her!" I said; and the words broke out of me, all of a sudden. "God help them all!"

"It was her decision," said Ellen.

"I know," I said. "But I—"

I looked at her.

"How much did Paula have to do with her going?" I asked.

"Not much," said Ellen.

"You both knew how I reacted to—to Paula. Believe me, I didn't even know it myself. I didn't even realize it until after I caught on to what she actually was, head-wise, and then I knew I had to get out of there."

"Paula wasn't that important to Marie."

"You say that? If it hadn't been for Paula and how I felt about her, we'd still have Marie and Wendy with us."

"I don't think so," Ellen said.

"How can you say you don't think so? Marie never talked about leaving before."

"Not to you. She did to me, lots of times."

I stared at Ellen.

"She did? Why?"

"She told you why, when she left. Marc," Ellen said, "you don't listen. That's one of the reasons she went."

"Of course I listen!"

She said nothing.

"Ellen, I loved Marie!" I said. "Why wouldn't I listen to someone I loved? I loved Marie—and I love you!"

"No." Ellen got up from the table, picked up the empty plates and silver and started in toward the house. "You don't, Marc. You don't love anyone."

"Will you come back here!" I shouted after her. She stopped and turned. "For once will you come back and say more than three words in a row? For Christ's sake, come and sit down and talk to me! There's something here, in the air between us. I can feel it. I bump into it every time I turn around. And you're telling me that there was something like that between Marie and me and I didn't know about it. Come back and tell me what it was. Come back and *talk* to me, damn it!"

She stood facing me, holding the dishes.

"It wouldn't do any good."

"Why not?"

She did not answer.

"Do you love me?" I said.

"Of course. So did Marie."

"She loved me and she wanted to leave me? I didn't love her and I want to keep her? What kind of sense does that make? If you loved me the way you say you do, you'd explain it to me, so I could do something about it, about me, or whatever was necessary."

"No," she said. "You've got things the wrong way around. I love you without your doing anything."

"All right, then!"

"But you're asking me to change. Talk doesn't come easily to me. You know that. If I have to talk before you can love me, then you don't love me. You wanted Marie to change, too, but she couldn't. I can, but I won't. It's up to you, Marc, not me."

I stared at her; but before I could say anything more, a stranger walked around the corner of the summer palace and came up to us. He was a startling figure, a good four inches taller than I was, completely bald, and wearing only a sort of kilt of white cloth around his waist. Even his feet were bare. His features looked something like those of an eskimo's but his skin was brown-dark, and the muscles stood out like cords under the skin. He looked as if he had spent his lifetime exercising, not with barbells, but on the parallel rings and other gymnastic equipment. He came up to me.

"Marc Despard?" he said. He had no accent that I could put my finger on, but the timbre of his voice was somehow different from that of any other human voice I'd heard. "My name's Obsidian. Sorry we took so long to come forward and meet you, but we had to study you for a while, first."

32

He was offering his hand in ordinary fashion. I took it and shook it automatically. I had been expecting him, or at least someone like him; but the delay had been long enough, and he had appeared so suddenly that he had managed to knock me off balance with his appearance, in spite of all my expectations. I found myself going through the social routine.

". . . my wife, Ellen."

"Ellen," and he shook hands with Ellen, "my name's Obsidian."

He had a round, friendly face, a little flat-looking and mongoloid; and this, with the hairless skull, gave him something of a tough look.

"Hello," said Ellen. "Where did you come from?"

"We're perhaps two hundred miles from you."

"Just a couple of hundred miles away?" I echoed.

"We had to keep you from finding us while we were studying you," he answered. "You have to understand that we had to gather a lot of data on you in order to work out your language and customs. And, of course, we wanted to collect data toward understanding the accident that brought you here."

"Accident?" I said. "We came here deliberately."

He stared at me for a long second.

"You did?"

"That's right," I said. "I'd probably better take you down to see the lab and Porniarsk. Sorry, maybe I'm getting the cart before the horse. But after expecting you every day from the moment we landed here, and not having you show up until now—"

"Expecting me when you arrived?" Obsidian said.

We seemed to be talking at cross purposes.

"That's right," I said. "We came here because I wanted to contact you people who were doing something about the time storm—"

"Just a moment," he said. "Excuse me."

He disappeared.

He did not come back in a moment, either. He did not come back the rest of that day, nor the day after. It was nearly a week later that I stepped outside from the door of the summer palace that opened onto the parking area, and found him standing there, bright with the morning sun on his bare shoulders. Ellen stepped out just behind me.

"Excuse me for not getting back before this," he said. "But possibly I got off on the wrong foot when I first visited you. I've talked the matter over with a number of others, and we've decided that our data was much more insufficient than we thought. Would you be willing to sit down with me and tell me the whole story of how you came to be here, so that we can have that information to work with?"

"I'll be glad to," I said, turning back toward the door. "Do you want to step inside?"

"No. If you don't mind, no," he said. "Later on, I'd like very much to have the chance to look inside your summer palace, but not just yet. Can we talk out here?"

"Certainly."

"Good." He dropped into a sitting position, cross-legged on the grass.

"If you don't mind, I'll use a chair," I said.

"I don't mind," he said. "I'm very interested. Is it actually comfortable for you, sitting on that piece of furniture?"

"It's more comfortable than sitting the way you are," I said. "I can sit like that, but not for any length of time."

"I see."

I went inside and came out with chairs for myself and Ellen. We sat down.

"The chair was more a product of western culture in my time, though," I said. "In the east, even then, people would be perfectly comfortable sitting the way you sit."

"Thanks," he said. "That's the sort of data we appreciate."

"All right," I went on. "Where do you want me to start?"

"Any and all information you can give us will help," he said.

"Suppose I start with the time storm then," I said. "We're together on that, aren't we? You know what I mean when I talk about the time storm?"

"Oh yes," Obsidian said. "We're aware of the time storm."

"Well, we weren't," I said, "until it hit us without warning one day. I was up in a northern, wild area of a state called Minnesota in the north central part of this continent . . . ."

I picked up my own history from the moment when I had thought I was having a second heart attack and proceeded to tell it. I had thought it was something I could cover in an hour or so; but I had badly underestimated what there was to tell, and I had come nowhere near beginning to estimate how many things Obsidian would need explained. We began with the matter of my heart attack, which took some thirty minutes or so of explanation by itself, and went on from there, frequently dropping into what must have sounded like a vaudeville act built around the idea of two blind men meeting in the middle of the Sahara desert at midnight.

"But there's no evidence of any damage to your heart, now."

"There isn't?"

"You mean you don't know there isn't?"

. . . And so on, far into the night. After a little while, Ellen sensibly got up and left us to bring Porniarsk out to join us, and to call Doc to let the rest of the community know what was going on. Within a few hours Obsidian and I had a quiet, attentive audience seated in a semi-circle around us and consisting of everyone able to get from the town up to the landing area.

The talk went on for four days. Obsidian had clearly come with the intention of getting information, but giving little or none himself; but it proved impossible for us to communicate unless he explained something of his own time and civilization. He and I had nothing in common but the language his people had deduced from the first weeks of recording and then taught him to speak accentlessly, and by the end of the first hour, we were both realizing how inadequate this was by itself.

The words alone meant little without their connotative referents, and his connotative referents and mine were separated by thousands, possibly hundreds of thousands, of years. It was a curious sensation to hear a sentence made up of nothing but the old, familiar sounds and, at the same time, realize that I had not the slightest idea of what Obsidian meant as he uttered them. Luckily he was an intelligent person; and above and beyond this, he had a sense of humor. Otherwise the talks would have broken down out of sheer exasperation on the parts of each of us.

But he was bright enough and sensible enough to adapt, in spite of the consensus he had been sent out with, that he should listen but not talk. By the end of the third day, he was telling us as much about his people as we were telling him about us, and from that point on, the information exhange began to work, to a point, at least.

By this time we were once more talking privately; but with a tape recorder powered by a stepped-down automobile battery that had been charged by Bill's windmill generator. The tapes were duplicated and made available to the rest of the community. To hit the high points of the information they gathered, Obsidian and his associates here on Earth numbered under a thousand individuals belonging to a race of latter-day humans that were primarily scattered, very thinly indeed, across the habitable worlds of this galaxy.

These humans did not think of themselves, however, so much as members of a race, but as members of a larger community, including representatives of some millions of other civilized races with whom they intermixed. Individuals of these other races were also thinly spread across the same habitable worlds; and some of them, as well as some of the humans, were to be found as well in other galaxies or elsewhere in the universe—although when this happened it was because of special circumstances Obsidian had not yet explained.

The reason for all these individuals being scattered so widely was apparently that (a) the time storm had cut populations on inhabited worlds to the point where there were several habitable worlds for each individual of intelligence; and (b) apparently there were means of travelling not merely faster than light, but many times faster than light, so that even visiting other galaxies was not impossible. Obsidian shied away from my questions when I tried to find out more about this means of travel.

Evidently faster-than-light did not describe it directly in his terms; and he was clearly unsure of his ability to explain it to me at our present level of communication.

We had encountered a number of such points of noncommunication. The main problem was the complete dissimilarity of our referents, so that often we found ourselves talking at cross purposes. Some cultural differences only emerged more or less by accident. For example, it turned out that Obsidian was not his name—not at least in the way we think of "names." In the way we used that word he had no specific name. This was because he had a certain unique identity, structure, or value—there was no way to express it properly in *our* terms—which was recognized as *him* by his fellow humans and other race individuals who had met him and experienced this unique identity of his.

For reference purposes, in the case of those who had never met him, he was referred to by a code word or symbol that essentially told where he had been born and what he had been doing since. But this was never used except for that sort of reference. For ordinary communicative purposes he had a number of—nicknames is not the right word for them, but it is the closest I can come—depending on how the individual referring to him associated him. The most common of these nicknames, the one he favored himself, and the one generally in use here among his fellows on Earth, was a name that compared him to the mineral we call "obsidian" and since it had been established, during the month or so they had been recording our speech, that we would recognize that word, he had identified himself with it when he first met Ellen and me.

It was not just an arbitrary difference from us, this matter of names, it seemed. It was something much more important than that. The whole name business had to do with the different way he and his community of humans and nonhumans thought and worked; and until I could understand why they did their naming that way, a vital chunk of their culture would remain a mystery to me. Accordingly, I struggled to understand and to make him explain himself so that I could understand.

The name business had something to do with identity in that word's most basic sense, which was tied to occupation among them much more than it would be with us, which was, in turn, tied to a different sort of balance between individual and group responsibilities—which was all somehow connected with the fact that they had not approached us the moment we had appeared here, but had hid and studied us instead.

It had not been because they were in any way afraid of us. Fear seemed to have a more academic quality to Obsidian than it did to me. They had been obligated to be able to communicate with us before they could appear. Consequently, they had stayed out of sight of Doc in the plane—which was apparently not as hard as it might seem, since they used structures much less than we did. In fact, our buildings were almost a little forbidding to Obsidian, which was why he had refused my invitation to come inside the summer palace. Apparently, he was about as attracted to the interior of the summer palace as I might have been to the idea of a neighborly crawl through the tunnels and dens of a human-sized mole. Obsidian's people built observatories and such, but these were generally constructed without walls or roof.

Apparently they did not need as much protection from the weather as we needed. When I asked about this, Obsidian demonstrated how he could envelop himself in a sort of cushion of invisible warmth, apparently just by wanting to do it—although he insisted that the heat was generated by mechanical, not mental, means. But beyond this, it was obvious to me early in our discussions that he had a far greater tolerance for temperature extremes and the discomfort of his physical surroundings than I did. In spite of the chilliness of the spring mornings or the heat of the afternoon, he showed the same indifference to the temperature and wore the same kilt, no more, no less. It was not until the third day that I discovered he was only wearing that out of courtesy to us, it having been established by them that we had some kind of clothing taboos.

It was about the third day, also, that a great many other things began to make sense. Surprisingly, my ability to communicate improved much more swiftly than did his; so much so, in fact, that he commented on it with unconcealed awe. The awe was almost more unsettling to me than the other mysteries about him. It gave me an uneasy feeling, mentally, to think that these people of the far future might not be so superior to us after all; that they might, in fact, be inferior in some ways. Obsidian and I worried over the communication discrepancy together and finally concluded that, paradoxically, Obsidian was in a sense being inhibited by the fine command of the spoken language he had exhibited the first time he appeared.

It emerged that his group was not used to translating concepts. Sounds and symbols, yes. These varied from race to race among them in infinite variety. But, just as they could agree on the unique identity of any single individual, they were apparently able to agree on the perfect value of any concept, so that translation, in that sense, was never necessary. When we first appeared, they had set up recording devices to pick up every sound made in our community and channeled these into a computer-like device which had sorted them out and deduced the rules and vocabulary of our language, with the observed or implied denotative values of each sound. With this done, they had pumped the information into the head of Obsidian and set him to talk to us, confident that he could now communicate.

Only, he had run into trouble. The sounds he used turned out to have had meanings over and above what the language computer had deduced. In short, Obsidian and his fellows were in the uncomfortable position of people who have grown up with a single set of concepts, thinking there was no other, and who had then run into an entirely different set—ours. They were like the person who grows to adulthood before he discovers that there are other languages than the one he knows, and then has to struggle emotionally with the concept that anybody else can prefer some outlandish sound to what he knows in his heart of hearts is the only "real" sound for a thought or thing.

Because of this, his plans had gone awry. It had been planned that he would drop in on us, pump us dry of all other relevant data on us, feed that also into the computer, and come up with patterns of us in all departments, from which it could be figured how to adjust us to the culture of their time, if this was possible. Instead, here he was floundering at absorbing my patterns while I was picking up his, hand over fist.

Well, not exactly hand over fist. His patterns, unlike ours, were all logical and logically interrelated, which gave me a great advantage. But there were also abilities

and concepts in his area that he took for granted and I
could not get him to talk about because I had no way of
describing what I was after.

It was not until the fourth day that I finally achieved a
breakthrough in that respect; and it happened for a
strange reason. That mind of mine, which could never
leave a problem alone but must keep worrying at it and
chewing it over until either mind or problem cracked
wide open, had been at work on the two enigmatic con-
versations I had had with Marie, just before she left, and
Ellen, the day that Obsidian had appeared.

I still could make no sense of what they said. For all
my efforts to understand, my comprehension slid off the
memories of their words to me as if both had been encased in glass. At the same time I had a reason to keep
working at them, now. There was something in me which
I evidently could not see, as I could not see my own eye-
balls, except in a mirror, or the back of my head. There
must be something in me, I thought, like a dark area, a
shadow cast by the sensing mechanism itself, that was
keeping me from the closeness I wanted to have with
other people—and of all people, Ellen. I had been trying
all sorts of approaches to the problem, trying to find some
way of sneaking up on the unseeable, so to speak; and it
occurred to me suddenly as I was talking to Obsidian that
there might be a similarity between this problem and my
problem of communication with him.

I had tried evoking the golden light as a means of reaching an understanding of Ellen. But I had found that when I
tried to reach for the feeling of unity with all things for
that reason, it was as it had been in the plane after leaving
Paula's camp—I could not evoke the state of unity. It
came to me now that it would do no harm to try for it
once more in the case of Obsidian and his people, where
the emotional roots concerned did not go so deeply into
the dark of my own soul.

So I tried. It helped that I had grown to like Obsidian
in the last few intense days of talking. I thought I could
almost grasp what he described as that unique identity
element by which all other beings of his time recognized
him. So I picked a moment when he was trying to explain
to me what among them took the place of family structure, as we in our community knew it. I watched him
as he talked, seated cross-legged on the ground. His face

was animated and his hands wove patterns in the air. He had the attribute of seeming to be alive with energy even while he was obviously without tension and relaxed. It was an ability I had seen before in casual encounters with professional athletes in top condition.

I was hardly listening to what he said. That is, my mind was making automatic note of it, but I was comfortably aware of the fact that the tape recorder was catching his words and I would be able to review them again this evening in the quiet of the summer palace library. Most of my attention was concentrated on him as a complete entity; a sound-making, limb-moving individual extending energy to me in the form of sound and gesture. I squinted, mentally, to focus in on him in this sense; and when I had him in focus, slid on top of his image before me the emotional/intellectual gestalt that was my friend Obsidian, as I knew him.

The two melted together; and as they did I was able for the first time to take a step back from him and the present moment. I kept my point of view at that distance and slowly let the rest of the day soak into me.

We sat just outside the summer palace and I had my back to it; so that I looked past Obsidian, across the open stretch of the landing area and out over the descending slope of the trees to the town below and the tall grass marching in all directions to the horizon. It was, for once, a perfectly clear day; there was not a cloud in sight. But a small, cool wind was wandering back and forth across the mountainside where we sat.

I saw the treetops moving to it and felt the intermittent light touch of it on my face and hands, cancelling out now and again the warmth of the steady afternoon sunlight. It was too early for insects; but down on the wooded slope below me, a cloud of specks that were small birds burst up unexpectedly as I watched, to swarm dark against the far bright sky for a moment like a cloud of gnats, and then settled back down out of sight into the dark mass of the leaves below them again.

High up, another single speck swam against the cloudless sky. A hawk? My vision went out to the horizon and beyond. Slowly, I became conscious of a rhythm that was the beating of my own heart and at the same time the breathing of the world. Once again, the golden light began to grow around me and, once more, I felt myself touching all things in the earth, sky, and water, from pole to pole. I was touching all things, and I reached out to touch Obsidian.

I looked at him without moving my eyes and saw him in full dimension for the first time. For he was a part of the universe, as all these other things were a part of it; and that was what was at the core of his community's difference from ours. They were aware of the universe of which they were a part, while we thought of ourselves as disparate and isolated from it. That was why Obsidian's identity was unchangeable and instantly recognized by his fellows. It was because the dimensions of that identity were measured by the universe surrounding him, in which he was embedded, and of which he was a working part. All at once the gestalt formed, and I understood without words, without symbols, the different, fixed place he and all other thinking minds of his period had in this, their own time and place.

I had produced the golden light again and it had helped me find what I had been seeking. I sat, just feeling it for a moment—then let it go. The light faded, I came back into my ordinary body and smiled at Obsidian.

But he did not smile back. He had stopped talking, and he was staring at me with a startled expression.

"Obsidian—" I began, about to tell him what I now understood.

He vanished.

33

Once again, he did not come back for a while. He was missing all the rest of that day and through the next two days. Under the conditions applying up until five minutes before he left, I would have worried that I had somehow damaged the relationship building between the two of us, and between our people and his interstellar community. Following the moment of light and my sudden access to understanding, I was sure this was not the case; and I tried to reassure the other members of our group who were inclined to worry about his nonappearance.

"It's not explainable in our words," I told Ellen, Bill, Doc, Porniarsk and about five others of the community who had been emerging as leaders during the past few weeks. We were all sitting around the fireplace in the library on the second evening, with the windows open to the courtyard and the night sky outside. "But I'm sure I didn't step on his toes in any way. I can't tell you how I know it, but I know it."

"Why did he take off, then?" Bill asked. "Can't you give us some idea, Marc?"

"He recognized what I was doing—this universe association trick I've told you about. I've explained that the best I can, and I won't try to explain it any more now. You'll have to learn how to do it yourselves if you really want to understand."

"You'd better start giving us lessons, then," said Doc. They all laughed.

"I will," I said. "Seriously, I will. When we've got the time."

"Go on, Marc," said Bill. "Finish what you were saying. He knew what you were doing . . . and that's what disturbed him?"

"Not exactly disturbed, I'd say," I told them. "He was just surprised. He's gone back to check with his friends. The way they are—the way I now *know* they are—that sort of checking's a responsibility on his part.

"So that's why you're sure he'll be back?" Bill asked.

"Isn't that what I've been saying?"

"Porniarsk," said Bill, turning to him, "can't you help explain any of this? You're from a more advanced race than we are."

"By comparison with Obsidian and his associates," said Porniarsk, "I'm essentially of the same primitiveness as the rest of you. Also, you'll remember, I'm only an avatar. I've no creativity, and no imagination beyond what I acquired when I was produced in the image of Porniarsk. I'm not equipped to speculate or interpret."

"Well," said Bill. "Anyway, we've all got plenty of work to do while we're waiting for him to come back. Marc, you'll speak to him as soon as you can, about whether we can count on them for supplies or assistance in case we need it?"

"Yes," I said. "I can talk to him about that as soon as he comes back. I was afraid earlier that I couldn't explain what we wanted without muddying up the idea we intend to be independent here. We still do want to be independent and self-supporting, don't we?"

I looked around the room. I did not really need the murmurs of agreement from all of them. I only wanted to remind them we were all together on that one point.

"If it's only a station they've got here," said Leland Maur, a thin, black man in his mid-twenties who was an architect and our construction and mechanical engineering expert, "my feeling's that this world is ours by right of settlement anyway. Not theirs. We don't want to start off owing any piece of it to someone else."

That comment ended the business of the evening. We sat back to drink coffee and compare notes on how things were going with our individual work projects to get ready for winter; and after about an hour of this, most of us were ready to fold for the night.

The next day, Obsidian had still not come back. That morning happened to be the half-day a week we had begun to take off as a rest period, following the good effect of our one day holiday after the first windmill generator had been put into operation. We had found that there was a limit to the efficiency involved in working seven days a week. After several weeks of unbroken work, we ended up going through the motions of our labors, but getting less done in total than if we had taken a break and started in fresh again. Accordingly, that morning I could stay home with a clear conscience, instead of lending my strength to one of the work jobs down in the town. Ellen was also home and busy doing something with her clothes in one part of the summer palace. I took advantage of the chance to dig once more into the books I had been neglecting lately. But they did not seem to hold my attention, after all. The urge had been growing in me to try for the golden light state again and, once more, to try to reach toward Ellen as I had reached toward Obsidian.

I was encouraged in this by my success with Obsidian, and also by the fact I began to believe I was at last zeroing in on my inner search. The outer search had always been the time storm; but the inner search, I now began to suspect, went back to my relationship with Swannee—and my mother.

I put the book I was holding aside and looked out into the courtyard feeling once more for a unity with the universe. It did not come easily this time. It was almost as if it knew why I wanted it and was reluctant to help me in that direction. But slowly, as the minutes went by, first the room and then the courtyard and the sky I looked out on took on greater values of reality, as if I was seeing them with a dimension added, a greater depth, a *beyondness*, in addition to the ordinary height, depth and width of normal vision. My body slowed its breathing and its heartbeat and began to blend with the movements of the planet.

The light changed, the gold moved in, and once more, I had it.

I held where I was for some little time—perhaps as much as ten or twenty minutes, although in that state of concentration time seemed almost suspended—to make sure that my hold on the state I had evoked was firm. Then I reached out to feel Ellen, elsewhere in the palace.

My touch went out like a wave spreading up on a sloping beach. I reached her, felt her there, lightly, and started to enfold her—and something far out in myself jerked back, so that the wave of my feeling was sucked away again, abruptly and my touch against her was lost. All at once, the golden light was gone and the unity was destroyed. I was alone and isolated, in my armchair in the room, looking out through the glass window panes at a world I could no longer feel.

I sat there, dulled and numbed by my failure. But after a few moments, a miracle happened; because the door opened, Ellen walked in, bent over the chair and kissed me. Then, without a word, she turned and went back toward the door.

"Why?" I managed to croak as she opened it.

She looked back and smiled.

"I just felt like it," she said.

She went out, closing the door behind her; and I sat there with my heart rising like a rocket. Because now I knew. I had not succeeded in fully touching her; but I knew that I was going in the right direction now; because she had felt me trying. If I lived, I would reach her eventually.

Our half-day holiday ended with noon. I put on work clothes and left the summer palace to go down and help the people who were insulating and expanding our largest quonset, so that it could become a combination dining hall, hospital, and living quarters for those of us who might turn out to be too young, too old, or too feeble to live out the winter cold in the other, flimsier, buildings of the town. I had just shut the door of the summer palace behind me when Obsidian appeared in front of me.

"Can we talk?" he said.

"Of course," I said. He came first before any rough carpentry of which I was capable.

"We've come to an important decision, my colleagues and I," he said. "You remember I told you our original plan was to gather enough information on you so that we'd know how to educate you into adjustment with civilization? At least, educate you enough so that you could stay with us, here?"

"I remember," I said.

"I'm afraid I didn't tell you everything," he said. "There was an alternative I didn't mention. If it turned out you people couldn't be adjusted to a civilized pattern, we were intending to send you back to your own time, the time you left to come here."

"No, you didn't tell me that," I said. "But you didn't have to. We primitives can think of those sort of alternatives without being prompted, you know."

"Yes. Well," Obsidian looked uncomfortable, "as it happens, you've turned out to be in some ways more than we guessed; in fact, more than we bargained for. In particular, you're different, yourself, from anything we imagined. So, now we've come up with a third alternative. But for this we're going to need your agreement."

"Oh?" I said. He did not answer immediately, so I prompted him. "Agreement to what?"

"To an alternative that ties in to this desire of yours to get into the work of controlling what you call the time storm. Logically, it's unthinkable to expect someone from as far back in the past as you are to be capable of learning to do a kind of work that's done only by unusual, highly qualified individuals in our time. But because of certain anomalies about you, we'd like to test your aptitude for such work."

"Fine," I said. And for the second time that day my heart went up like a rocket.

"You understand," Obsidian said, "this testing in no way changes the fact that by no stretch of the imagination could we expect you to actually be able to work in the temporal area. It's simply a means of supplying us with data by which we can decide best what to do with all your group, here."

"All right," I said.

"Are you sure you understand? Our interest in whether you have any ability for temporal work is only academic."

"I hear you," I said. But my heart was still high inside me. Explain it any way he might, Obsidian could not hide from me the fact that, in offering me such tests, they were letting me come one step closer to the goal I had been working toward.

"Well, then," said Obsidian, "even if you're willing, there's a further question. Ordinarily, there'd be no need for you to leave your area, here. But in this particular case some special conditions are involved; so that to be tested you have to be willing to go some distance across the galaxy. Now, if you want time to consider this—"

"Thanks. It's not necessary. I'll be happy to go wherever being tested requires."

He gazed across the jeep at me for a full second.

"Are you sure you understand?"

"I think so," I said. "You want to know if I'm willing to be tested for abilities in time storm fighting. I am. You also want to know if I'm agreeable to going a large chunk of light-years to wherever I have to go to be tested. I am."

"You understand this means travel between the stars, through space?"

"Well, I'd gathered that," I said. But he did not echo my grin.

"I'm a little surprised," he said. "I understood from what you told me that you'd never been off this one world in your life."

"That's right."

"But you're willing to go, without thinking it over? Without talking it over with the rest of your people?"

"I'll check with them, of course," I said. "But they've been getting along without my immediate help while I've been talking to you. They ought to be able to get along without me for a bit longer. How long would I be gone?"

"In terms of time here, not more than a couple of your weeks. Probably considerably less. It may be a single simple test will give us an answer, once you've reached your destination. It's possible we might have to test further, but probably not more than a day or two."

"I see," I said. "The more ability I show, the more you'll go on testing?"

"Essentially. But Marc," said Obsidian, "if you've got hopes of our tests finding you to have very great ability in that area, I wish you'd temper those hopes. Believe me——"

"I believe," I said. "I'm also willing to go. We're agreed?"

"Yes," he said, slowly.

"Good. The thing you have to understand about me, friend Obsidian," I said, "is that I'll do whatever I decide is best. I'm not going to leave the other people here in a bind because I didn't bother to check. I'll check first. But I said I want to go, and I'm going."

"Forgive me," he said.

"There's nothing to forgive," I said. "It's just that this isn't a matter of group discussion. This is me, saying what I choose to do."

"All right," I said. "But it's not quite what I'm used to. You understand that? We have——"

"I know," I said. "You people've got a pattern of responsibility. So've I. And I won't violate my pattern any more than you'd violate yours. But I tell you, Obsidian, I want to go where your people will test me. The fact it's across space doesn't matter; because I'd go cross-universe as quickly as I'd go around this jeep to get that done."

I had gotten a little warm on the subject; and I was braced to have him react with equal emotion. Instead he only looked at me, a long, questioning look. Then he nodded.

"This means more to you than we'd thought," he said.

I stared back at him. Something other than the golden light was moving me now; a surge of feeling that was more like a tide, a running tide carrying me irresistibly forward.

"You don't understand me at all," I said, "do you?"

"No." He shook his head.

"All right," I told him. "See if it has meaning for you this way. I don't know who my remote ancestors were; but what moves me as far as the time storm goes, must go as far back as they do. There's something in me that's certain about one thing; that anything can kill me, but until I'm killed I'm what lives. And as long as I live, I'll fight. Come and get me out to face my special enemy, whoever that is; and while I can still move, I'll stay after it. When I'm finally done for, I'll still be happy; because I wasn't deprived of my chance to do something. All I want is that chance—nothing else matters; and here you come asking me if the fact I have to cross some space to be tested might make me decide against going!"

I had really moved off the high end of the emotional scale this time, but I saw now that at last I had gotten through to him. I do not think even then that he understood what I was talking about, but he had registered the charge of the emotion that had ridden on top of my words.

"How much time do you need before you'll be ready to go?" he said.

"Two—three hours, say."

"Good. One more thing. We'd like, since we're moving you this distance, to take advantage of the opportunity to do some testing of the avatar, as well. Do you think he'd be willing to come? He's had experience in cross-space travel, I understand."

"He has," I said. "I'll ask him. I think he'll want to come."

"Then I'll be back in three of your hours."

He vanished.

I turned back into the summer palace and went to find Porniarsk. It had not occurred to me until now to wonder what had been occupying him since we had arrived at our destination here in the future; and it struck me suddenly, now, that he had been busy in the lab all that time. But at what, I wondered? When I arrived, I found him working with the vision tank; and I asked him that question.

"I've been doing some charting," he said, waving a stubby tentacle at the tank. "I thought perhaps if I could establish specifically what the inconsistencies were that we noted, I might be able to evolve a picture of what's happening with the time storm at this future moment."

"What did you find out?"

"I discovered that, except for certain areas where the force lines of the storm still seem to be breeding, the universe in general has been brought pretty much into the same sort of temporary, dynamic balance that we achieved around this planet back in our earlier time."

"What about the breeding areas?" I asked.

"That's interesting. Very interesting," he said. "The force lines seem to be both breeding and healing—both increasing and decreasing in these areas. By the way, the areas I'm talking about are all out in the midsections of the galaxies. There's none of them down in the very center of a galaxy—in what might be called the dead core area."

"Dead core?"

"I thought you knew?" he glanced at me. "The center of most galaxies, like this one, is an area of very old stars, immersed in a dust cloud."

"Where's the closest activity to this solar system?"

"The blue-white supergiant star," said Porniarsk, "that you call Rigel seems to be one of the near loci. But the main activity close to us is centered on the star you call S Doradus in the lesser Magellanic Cloud, outside this galaxy, about a hundred and forty thousand light-years from us here."

"S Doradus is a big, hot star, too, isn't it?" I said.

"Like Rigel, one of the brightest."

"Sounds like a large, bright star is necessary. Can you tell why?"

"No," said Porniarsk. "All I know is that the lines of time storm activity in the area in question seem to center on S Doradus. And, then, there's the matter that S Doradus has stopped radiating."

"Stopped what?"

"It's no longer radiating. It's gone dark," Porniarsk said. "I mean by that, that if you were in the immediate neighborhood of that star, it would no longer appear to be radiating. From our distance here, of course, it still seems to be shining; since we're getting light that left it thousands of years ago."

My head began to spin. The distances, the star sizes, and the rest of the information involved was on such a scale that my imagination struggled to get a grip on it.

"I've got a message for you," I said, to shift the topic of conversation.

I told him about Obsidian taking me to be tested, and his question as to whether Porniarsk would be willing to go also.

"Of course," said Porniarsk. "I'd be very interested to see how they do such testing."

34

Three hours turned out to be less time than I thought in which to get hold of Ellen and the other leaders, explain what Porniarsk and I were going to be doing, and pack a suitcase. When Obsidian reappeared outside the summer palace at the landing area, he found about forty people —all who could possibly get up there to see Porniarsk and myself off. But it was not at the others he stared, or even at Porniarsk and I, but at the suitcase at my feet.

"Can I ask . . ." he began.

"My bag," I said. I guessed what was puzzling him. "Personal necessaries. Remember, I wear clothes, shave every morning, and things like that."

"Oh," he said. I had discovered by the end of our first day of acquaintance that the humans of his time had no body hair to speak of. "Of course."

Following this conversation, there was a great deal of kissing and handshaking all around. In fact, our community nowadays was more like one large family than anything else. I almost spoiled the occasion by laughing out loud at the spectacle of Porniarsk solemnly promising people that he would be careful and take good care of himself. It was rather like a battleship assuring everyone that it would keep a wary eye out for sharks and take care not to get bitten.

But even the saying of goodbys had to run down finally.

"We're all set," I told Obsidian.

"All right," he said. "Then, if you'll just stand close to me, here."

Porniarsk and I moved in until we were almost nose to nose with him, leaving a ring of unoccupied ground about ten feet wide around us. All at once, we were standing elsewhere, in a little open space between the trunks of massive elms spaced about thirty feet apart. We stood on something that looked like a linoleum rug, but felt underfoot like deep carpeting, a solid dark green in color. About us were some walls at odd angles, several large puff-type cushions ranging up to a size that would have made a comfortable queen-sized bed, and several of what looked like control panels on stands apparently connected to nothing.

I looked around.

"This is your living area and working quarters?" I asked Obsidian.

"Yes," he said. "I think you'll find it comfortable for the three of us. I can arrange the walls so that you can have separate rooms for privacy, if you like."

"Don't bother," I said. "I assume we won't be here long in any case, will we?"

"About the equivalent of five days of local time."

"Five days?" I said. "I thought we'd be leaving for wherever it is in a matter of hours, if not minutes?"

"Oh, we've already left," he said. He waved his hand and something like a picture window appeared between us and the trees to our left. The view in the picture window, however, was a view of black space, bright pinprick stars as thick as pebbles on a beach, and a blue and white earth-globe nearly filling the lower right-hand corner of the view.

I stared at the earth-globe and confirmed my first impression that it was visibly shrinking in size as I watched.

"I thought you said this was your working and living area?"

"It is."

"It's a spaceship, too?"

Obsidian waved a hand.

"I suppose you could call it that," he said. "Actually, it's more accurate to say it's simply living quarters. The process of travelling between the stars isn't much more cumbersome if we bring it along, however; and it's a lot more comfortable if we do so."

I turned about in a circle, on my heel.

"The trees and all," I said. "That's just an illusion?"

"Out here, yes," Obsidian said. "Back when we first arrived, of course, you were looking at the actual surrounding forest."

"When did we take off?"

"As soon as we arrived. But to call it a takeoff—"

"I know," I said, "—doesn't exactly describe what happened. Never mind. I'm not really interested in the mechanics of it, right now. All right then, if we really are going to be here for five days, I believe I'd appreciate a room of my own, after all; and I'd imagine Porniarsk would too."

"It makes no difference to me," said Porniarsk. "But I am interested in the mechanics of your space flight. Can I examine those control panels?"

"By all means," said Obsidian. "If you like, I'll explain them to you. They're for work back on the planet we just left, actually. Our trip will be handled automatically."

"I'm interested in all things," said Porniarsk. "This is the effective result of being the avatar of an individual, Porniarsk, who has always been interested in all things—"

He checked himself.

"—I should probably say, was interested in all things."

"Do you miss him?" Obsidian asked. "This individual of whom you were an avatar?"

"Yes," said Porniarsk, "in a sense I do. It's a little like realizing that part of myself is gone, or that I had a twin I now know I'll never see again."

The tone of his voice was perfectly calm and ordinary; but suddenly I found myself looking at him closely. I had never stopped to think of Porniarsk as having emotions, or stopped to consider what he might have lost in a personal sense by going forward in time with us.

"I should have asked you if you wanted to come with us," I said.

"If you had, I'd have answered yes," said Porniarsk. "The process of discovery and learning is what I was constructed for."

"Yes," I said.

I was suddenly very tired, with an almost stupefying feeling of fatigue. Part of it, undoubtedly, was the work schedule we had been keeping in the community these last few weeks. But the greater part was something more psychological and psychic than physical. In spite of Obsidian's insistence that the testing I was about to take was that and no more, I was at last certain that I had reached the last arena, the moment of final confrontation.

I was like someone who had trained physically for

months and years for one battle. I felt loose, light and
ready, but drained and empty inside, hollow of all but the
inevitability of the conflict toward which I was now marching inexorably. Not even enthusiasm was left—only a
massive and silent acceptance of what would be.

"I think," I said to Obsidian, "I'd like that private
room now, if you don't mind. I think I'd like to get some
sleep."

"To be sure," he said.

Suddenly, the white walls were around me. I had not
moved, but now I was enclosed, alone with the picture window, or screen, showing the innumerable stars and the
shrinking Earth. I turned to the largest of the cushions
and fell on it. For a second the lighting was still daylight
strong, but just before I closed my eyes, it dimmed to
nonexistence; and the space in which I now rested was
lit only by the star-glow from the window.

I slept.

When I woke, the stars in the picture window were
different. Not merely a little different; they bore no relationship to anything I had ever seen in the skies of Earth.
Puzzled, I lay there looking at them while gradually I came
to full alertness; and either automatically, or in response
to some way of sensing my urge for better visibility, the
lighting in the room slowly increased, back to the level of
sunlight. I got up, explored, and found a doorway that let
me into a bathroom, which was too good a replica of
what I was familiar with to be anything but a construct
created expressly for me by Obsidian.

Still, I was grateful for the fact that it looked so familiar. Part of my waking up had always been a morning
routine involving a sharp razor blade, soap and a good
deal of hot water. This out of the way, I left my private
quarters and found Obsidian sleeping quietly on one of the
larger cushions of the main area, Porniarsk busy doing
incomprehensible things with one of the control consoles.

"Good morning, Marc," be said, turning to look at me
as I came up.

"Morning, if that's what it is—" I lowered my voice,
glancing at Obsidian. "Sorry, I forgot about him sleeping
there."

"I don't think you need worry," said Porniarsk at ordinary conversational volume. "I don't believe he hears any

noise he doesn't want to hear until he wakes at the time he wants to wake."

I looked at Obsidian curiously.

"Good trick," I said. "What's the breakfast situation?"

"There's food of various kinds in a room there," said Porniarsk, pointing a tentacle at a doorway in one of the walls that had been there when we arrived.

I went to look and found he was right. It was a pleasant, small room, apparently surrounded completely by the illusion of the forest in forenoon sunlight. There were chairs, my style, and a table, my style; and a piece of furniture that looked like a heavy, old fashioned wooden wardrobe.

When I opened the door of this last piece of furniture, however, I found it filled with shelves full of all kinds of fresh earthly fruits and vegetables. There were fruit juices in transparent vessels, milk, and a pitcher of black liquid that turned out to be hot coffee; although what was keeping its temperature up was a mystery. There were no meat or eggs; and although I looked around carefully, I could not find a stove or any means of cooking any of the other foodstuffs. Well, at least the coffee was hot. I found a small empty vessel to pour it into and settled down to eat.

It was an interesting meal. There were no shocks, but some surprises. For one thing, the already-sliced loaf of bread I discovered turned out to be hot. Not toasted. Hot, like the coffee. The glass of what I had assumed was orange juice turned out to be slightly fizzy, as if it had been carbonated. There was no sugar and the honey tasted as if it had been spiked with vodka.

I finished up and went back into the other room. Obsidian was still asleep and Porniarsk was still at work.

"Have you eaten?" I asked Porniarsk. I knew he did eat; although Porniarsk and nutrition were something of a puzzle; because apparently he could go for weeks at a time without food. He had told me once that his bodily fueling system was almost as much a mystery to him as it was to the rest of us; since that was an area of information in which Porniarsk, the original Porniarsk, had no interest whatsoever. Apparently our Porniarsk, at least, had some way of getting a great deal more energy out of the sustenance he took in than we humans did. I had played with the picture of a small stainless steel fission engine under the thick armor plating of his body—although he had assured us he was pure animal protein in all respects.

"No," he said now. "There's no need. I'm greatly interested in this equipment."

"It looks like we built up quite a velocity while I was asleep," I said. "Where are we now?"

"That's the fascination of this," he said, nodding heavily at the control console. "Apparently, as Obsidian said, our trip's completely under automatic control. But this console, since he showed me how to operate it, has been furnishing me with information on our movements as we make them. Right now we're something like three million years in the past, and consequently, far displaced from your solar system—"

"Displaced?" I said. But even as I said it, even as he began to explain, my mind was jumping ahead to that explanation.

"Why, yes. Obsidian and his community," said Porniarsk, "have evidently done a superb job of, first, balancing the large areas of time forces; and second, an equally excellent job of charting specific force lines in between the balanced areas. In fact, I'm inclined to think that the process of balancing was designed to leave just the network of working force lines that remain. The result has been that, although they can't actually cross space at more than light speeds, by using the force lines they can jump distances equivalent to some hundreds or even thousands of light years, and arrive at their destination in a matter of hours, or even days. Watch the present stellar arrangement."

He touched the console in front of him with a tentacle tip. Another picture window appeared, showing the starscape beyond. My memory for patterns now was too good to be deceived. This was a different view again of the galaxy than the one I had seen in the other room on waking up.

"We should be coming up on another transfer, momentarily . . . " said Porniarsk. "There!"

The starview abruptly changed, without jar, without sound, and so instantaneously that I did not even have the sensation of having blinked at the scene.

"We've gone down the ladder in time in order to make large shifts through space," said Porniarsk. "In the smaller node of forces on Earth, the time jumps were also much smaller and the physical displacement was minor. Here, of course, when we take a large step forward or backward in time, the surrounding stars and other solid bodies move around us. What's that phrase I once learned from Marie about Mahomet not being able to go to the mountain, therefore, the mountain must come to him? Obsidian's people have learned to use the time storm to bring their mountains to them, instead of themselves making the journey to the mountains—"

He glanced at me. Porniarsk could not be said to have the most readable facial and body expressions in the universe; but I knew that hang of his tentacles well enough by now to tell when he was being apologetic.

"—I mean, of course," he said, "to refer to the stars and other solid bodies of the universe as 'mountains.' "

"I'd guessed you did," I said.

"I'm afraid I'm sometimes a little pedantic," he said. "So was Porniarsk himself, of course. It's a failing that often goes with an enquiring mind."

"Don't let it bother you where I'm concerned," I said. "One of my worst habits is telling other people what the situation is, at great length."

"That's true, of course," he answered, with gentle unconcern for my feelings. "Nonetheless, two wrongs do not—I believe our host is waking up."

He had creaked his head to one side as he spoke, to gaze at Obsidian, who now opened his eyes and sat up cross-legged on his cushion, all in one motion, apparently fully alert in the flicker of an eyelash.

"Are you rested, Marc?" he asked. "I finally had to take a nap, myself. Apparently Porniarsk needs very little sleep."

"Damn little," I said.

"We'll have a little more than four days more before we reach our destination," said Obsidian. "I'm looking forward to doing a lot more talking with you, Marc. I gather you've already come to a better understanding of the present time."

"I think so," I said. "Tell me if I'm wrong, but as I see it, all the intelligent races in the galaxy have joined together to fight for survival. Animate organisms against the inanimate forces that otherwise might kill you all off."

"That's a lot of it," Obsidian said. "We're concerned with survival first, because if life doesn't survive, everything else becomes academic. So the first job is to control the environment, right enough. But beyond survival, we're primarily interested in growth, in where life goes from here."

"All right. But—" I checked myself. "Wait a minute. I ought to give you a chance to get all the way awake before I tie you up in a discussion like this."

"But I am awake," said Obsidian, frowning a little.

"Oh. All right," I said, "in that case, suppose you start filling me in on the history of everything. How did this brotherhood of civilized entities start? What got it going?"

"As a matter of fact," he answered, "what began the getting together of races that later became the present civilized community was what you call—excuse me, I'll just use your word for it from now on—the time storm, itself. This was paradoxical; because it was the time storm that threatened the survival of all life, and here it made real civilization possible. . . ."

With that, he was underway with a flood of information almost before I had time to find myself a seat on a nearby cushion. In the next four days, while his house, so to speak, flitted through space from time force line to time force line, and Porniarsk watched that process fascinatedly with the control console, Obsidian drew me a picture of some forty-odd thousand years of known history—on the time scale of our galaxy—and an unknown amount of time before that in which life was nearly destroyed by the time storm, but in which the foundation of a universal community was discovered and erected.

"The process was instinctive enough," he said. "We tried to adapt to an environment that included the time storm, and, in the process, learned to manipulate that environment, including the time storm, as far as we could. Right now the time storm makes possible a number of things we couldn't have unless it existed. At the same time, by existing, it continues to threaten to kill us. So, we're doing our best to control it. Note, we no longer want to wipe it out; we want to keep it, but under our domination."

"Like taming a tiger," I said, "to be a watchdog."

He frowned for a second. Then his face cleared.

"Oh," he said. "I see what you mean. Yes. We want to tame and use it."

"So do I," I said.

He looked unhappy.

"I was hoping," he said, "that you'd be beginning to appreciate the difference between someone of your time and people of the present. We'll be arriving shortly, in a matter of hours in fact; and I thought that, maybe, with the chance we've had to talk on the way here, you'd be seeing the vast gulf between what you know and are, and what anyone from the present would have to know and be."

"It's not that vast," I said. "Now, wait a minute—"

He had opened his mouth, ready to speak again. When I held up my hand, he closed it again—but not with a particularly comfortable look on his face.

"All right, look," I said. "You've evolved a whole science. But anyone born into this time of yours can learn it in that person's lifetime, isn't that so?"

"Oh, of course," Obsidian said. "I didn't mean to sound as if the hard knowledge itself was something more than you could learn. In fact we've got techniques and equipment which could teach you what you'd need to know in a matter of days. But the point's that the knowledge by itself wouldn't be any use to you; because to use it requires the sort of understanding of the time storm that only growing up and being educated in the present can give you."

"What you're saying," I told him, "is that aside from the intellectual knowledge that's necessary, I'd need the kind of understanding that comes from knowing a culture and a philosophy. And the cultural part is simply the same philosophy expressed on a nonsymbolic level. So, what it boils down to is understanding your basic philosophy; and you've just finished telling me that that's been shaped by contact over generations with the time storm. All right, I've had contact with the time storm. I've had some contact with you. And I tell you that your culture and your philosophy isn't that much different from what I've already understood myself where the time storm forces are concerned."

He shook his head.

"Marc," he said, "you're aiming right at a disappointment."

"We'll see," I answered.

"Yes." He sighed. "I'm very much afraid we will."

Just as there had been no sensation of taking off when we had left Earth, so there was no sensation of landing when we got to our destination. Simply, without warning, Obsidian broke off something he was saying about the real elements of art existing fully in the concept of the piece of artwork alone—a point with which I was disagreeing, because I could not conceive of art apart from its execution. What if the statue of Rodin's Thinker could be translated into a string of symbolic marks? Would the intellectual appreciation of those marks begin to approach the pleasure of actually seeing, let alone feeling, the original statue with whatever microscopic incidentals of execution had resulted from the cuttings of the sculptors' tools and the textural characteristics of the original material? The idea was absurd—and it was not the only absurd idea that I had hear from Obsidian, for all his personal likeableness and intelligence, during the last five days.

At any rate, he broke off speaking suddenly and got to his feet in one limber movement from the cushion on which he had been seated cross-legged.

"We're here," he said.

I looked over at the picture window and still saw only a starscape in the picture window. Just one more, if once again different, starscape—with only a single unusual element about it, which was a large, dark area just to the right and below the center of it. Porniarsk was also watching the window from his post near one of the control consoles, and he saw the direction of my attention.

He trundled across the room and tapped with a tentacle at the screen surface over the dark area.

"S Doradus," he said.

Obsidian turned his head a little sharply to look at the avatar.

"Aren't we down on some planetary surface?" I asked Obsidian.

"Oh yes," he said. The starscape winked out, to be replaced with a picture of a steep hillside littered with huge boulders. The sky was a dark blue overhead and what looked like beehives, colored a violent green and up to twenty or thirty feet in height, were growing amongst the rocks. "The scene you were just looking at is of space seen from the vantage point of this landing spot. Haven't I mentioned that we nowadays have a tendency to surround ourselves with the type of scene that suits us at the moment, no matter where we are in a real sense?"

"You like the Earth forest scene yourself, then, Obsidian?"

"Not primarily," he answered me, "but I supposed you did."

"Thanks," I said. I felt gratitude and a touch of humbleness. "I appreciate it."

"Not at all. May I introduce—" he turned abruptly to face the several individuals who were now joining us from somewhere outside the illusion of the Earth forest.

There were only four of them; although my first impression when I saw them entering was that there were more. None of them wore anything resembling clothes or ornaments. In the lead was what I took to be a completely ordinary, male human, until I saw there was a sort of bony ridge, or crest, about three inches deep at the nape of his neck, running from his spine at midback up to the back of his head and blending into his skull there. He was somewhat taller than Obsidian. Next was a motley-colored individual with patches of skin almost as light as my own intermixed with other patches of rust-red and milk chocolate darkness. This one was less obviously humanoid, but seemed plainly female, and of about Obsidian's size. The third was something like a squid-crab hybrid, with the squid growing out of the back shell of the crab—and he, or she—or for that matter, it—entered the room floating on a sort of three-foot high pedestal. I would have guessed this third individual's weight at about a hundred pounds or so, Earthside.

The fourth was a jet-black, pipestem-limbed humanoid about three feet tall, with a sour face and no more hair than Obsidian. I was secretly relieved to find that everybody with a generally human shape, nowadays, was not someone I had to get a stiff neck looking up to. As they all came into the room, its area expanded imperceptibly until we stood in the middle of a space perhaps thirty by forty feet. The illusion of Earth forest now only occupied a portion of the perimeter about us. In the remaining space were four other scenes, ranging from a sort of swamp to a maroon-sand desertscape with tall, whitish buttes sticking up dramatically out of the level plain below.

I was so interested in watching all this that I almost missed the fact that Obsidian was trying to introduce me.

"Sunrise—" this was the individual with the neck crest. "Dragger—" (the particolored female); "one of the Children of Life—" (the squid-crab) and "Angel—" (the sour-faced, little black individual).

"It's a remarkable thing to be able to meet you," I told them. "I'd like you to know I appreciate the chance."

"Compliments are unnecessary," said Dragger, in a somewhat rusty voice. "I suppose we can call you Marc without offending you?"

"Certainly," I said. "You speak my language very well."

"It wouldn't have been practical to have you learn ours," Dragger said. She seemed to be the speaker for the group. "If you don't mind, we'll get on with the test. Would you give your attention to that panel just behind you?"

I turned. The panel she was pointing at was about three feet high by five feet long, sitting on top of a boxlike piece of equipment that had appeared with their entrance. As I looked, an elliptical pool of blackness seemed to flood out and cover the corner areas of the slab. I stepped close to it and found myself looking into, rather than at, the darkness, as if it had depth and I was looking down into a three-dimensional space.

As I focused in, deeper into the darkness, I saw that it was alive with shifting, moving fans of lights, something like the aurora borealis with its successions of milky colors spreading out over the northern sky at night. These lights I watched now moved much faster than the northern lights I was used to, and their pattern was much more complex. But, otherwise, they were remarkably similar.

They were similar to something else, too. I stared at them, unable to quite zero in on what they reminded me of. Then it burst on me.

"Of course!" I said, turning to Dragger and the others. "Those are time storm force line patterns, extremely slowed, but still force line patterns in action."

The four of them looked at me. Then Dragger turned to Obsidian.

"Thank you, Obsidian," she said. She looked back at me. "Thank you, Marc."

She turned around and began to lead the rest out.

I stared after her, and at the rest of them.

"Wait a second!" I said.

"Marc," said Obsidian behind me. "Marc, I said you might be working yourself up for a disappointment—"

"Disappointment!" I said. "The hell with that! I said they're force line patterns, and they are. Come on back here—Dragger, the rest of you. You can't just walk out. You owe me an explanation, if I want one. I've picked up enough about your time to know that!"

They slowed and stopped. For a moment they stood in a group, and I had the strong impression that a discussion was going on, although I could not hear a word or see a lip movement. Then they turned back into the room, Dragger still leading, and came to face me again.

"There is no explanation to give," Dragger said. "We wished to test you for a sensitivity we feel is necessary, if you and your group are to be allowed to stay in the present. Unfortunately, you don't seem to show that sensitivity."

"And how do you figure that?" I said. "You showed me a pattern of time storm forces in action, I told you what they were—where's the indication of a lack of sensitivity on my part?"

"Marc," said Dragger, "I'm sorry to say that what you looked at was not what you said it was."

"Not a pattern of force lines from the time storm?"

"No. I'm sorry." Once more she turned to go and the others shifted with her.

"Damn it, come back here!"

"Marc—" It was Porniarsk, now, trying to interpose.

"Porniarsk, stay out of this! You too, Obsidian! Dragger, you others, turn around. Come back! I don't know what the idea is, your trying to lie to me like this. But it's not working. You think I don't know time storm forces when I see them? Obsidian's been told what I've done and been through with Porniarsk here. You must know what I told him—or didn't you do your homework? If you do know what I told him, you know you can't get away with showing me a pattern of the storm lines and claiming it's something else."

The four stood facing each other in silence. After a second, Obsidian took three quick steps across the floor and joined them. They stood motionless and voiceless, facing each other for a long minute. Then they all turned to face me.

"Marc," said Obsidian, "I assure you, that was not a representation of lines of force from what you call the time storm. It was a projected pattern of conceptual rhythms common to all minds in our present-day culture. If you had shown a capability for responding to those rhythms, the pattern would have evoked some common images in your mind—water, gas, star, space . . . and so on. Apparently, it didn't; so we have to conclude that you don't have the capability to respond in modern terms. That's all. You don't gain anything by this insisting that you were looking at a representation of temporal force lines."

"I *see!*" I said.

Because suddenly I did. And suddenly I was so sure I was right that I went ahead without even bothering to check the words out in my head before I said them.

"In fact," I said, "I see a lot of things. One of them is that I understand you better than you understand me— and I'm going to prove that right now. You see, I know you can't sluff me off and send me back with that answer, if I say the proper words. Your responsibility reflex won't let you; and I'm going to say the proper words now. The words are—you and these people here, and everyone else you know, have one galloping cultural blindness. You're dead blind in an area where I'm not; and I can see it where you can't, because I'm standing outside your culture and looking in at it. Your whole set of rules is based on the fact that you can't deny me a hearing on that point. Now that it's been raised, you have to settle conclusively whether I'm right about what I'm saying, or wrong. If I'm wrong, then you can get rid of me. But if I'm right, then you, all of you, are going to have to learn different—from me. Am I right?"

I stopped speaking and waited. They merely stood there.

"Well?" I said. "Am I right, or aren't I? Am I entitled to a hearing or not?"

They looked at each other and stood for a moment longer. Then they all turned back to me.

"Marc," said Obsidian, "we'll have to consult about

this. In theory at least, you're right. You'll get your hearing. But now we have to talk the whole matter over, and that's going to take a little time. Meanwhile, because of the importance of your challenge to us, it seems you're going to have to learn our way of communicating after all."

35

It developed that the reason they had not tried to teach me, and Porniarsk for that matter, how to communicate in their way was because of an assumption on their part that, conceptually, we were not up to such education. But since I had now told them that I believed the shoe was on the other foot, and that I knew things of which they couldn't conceive, their original reason for not teaching me had become indefensible. In short, whether I could actually handle their language effectively, or not, I had to be given a chance to explain myself in it, so that the accusation couldn't arise that I had failed to make my point because I had not been given the chance to state it in fully understandable terms.

That much established, the actual process of learning turned out to be easy. As Obsidian had said, they had devices and techniques for teaching. Within twenty-four hours, Porniarsk and I could handle all four modes of their communication. These were sound; signal (limb-waving, etc.); attitudinal (which was really another form of signal, since it meant communicating with physical attitudes —body language); and modification-of-surroundings, which essentially meant communicating by playing games with the surrounding scenery, whether illusory or real.

These four modes actually duplicated each other. That is, they had each been single, exclusive methods of communication originally, and had been combined as amplifying redundancies. Actually, I would be able to make my argument completely in the verbal mode. But if I should be questioned on a particular verbal statement, I could now nail down what I meant by repeating what I had said in one or more of the other modes. In theory, any statement made in as few as two modes established its message beyond any possibility of ambiguity.

So, I was ready for argument in twenty-four hours. The debate was not called to order, however, for the equivalent of three more Earth days. I was not too unhappy about that because it gave me time to do some thinking. Under pressure, I had jumped to a conclusion, there in that moment when Dragger and the others had turned to walk out; and that jump had been genuine inspiration. But now I needed to build that inspiration up into a solid, cohesive argument.

When the meeting was finally called to order once more, the number of the universal community's members present had grown from five individuals to thirty-two. The space that arranged itself around us, consequently, was large and had sloping sides around the flat central area; so the spectators looked down on Dragger and me as if they were a crowd in a small arena or a lecture hall.

Dragger began by replaying what had happened on our first meeting. It was a little strange to stand there and see myself, in apparently solid replica, demanding that the five come back and listen to me. When this reached an end with Obsidian's last words to me, the illusory figures of our former selves winked out and Dragger turned to me.

"You're going to point out a cultural blindness to us, Marc," she said. "Go ahead."

"All right," I said. "As briefly as possible, then—the first evidence I noticed of a cultural blindness was during the first few days that Obsidian and I talked. We found out then that he had trouble understanding what I meant, in spite of the fact that he'd been trained by your equipment. On the other hand, I was understanding him fairly well, in spite of the fact that he was trying to gather information on my culture, rather than teaching me about yours. You might want to check your records on that, sometime, to see what I mean."

"We can show it," put in Dragger.

The illusory figures appeared again. This time, they were Obsidian and myself talking, back outside the summer palace. This was a bit of assistance I had not figured on. I stood there, as my image pointed out to Obsidian that he was like someone who had grown up thinking everyone spoke only one language and was having difficulty entertaining the idea that there might be other words possible for a familiar object.

The second set of figures disappeared.

"This started me thinking," I went on. "From the beginning, in your contact with us, you've assumed the only possible solution to my group existing in the same time with you people would be for us to adopt everything that was part of your culture and discard anything of ours that didn't fit. As with the language situation, your thought seemed to be that there was one, and only one, *right* way of doing things."

I stopped and looked at Dragger, giving her a chance to argue this point. But she said nothing and seemed to be merely waiting. I went on.

"As far as I can gather," I said, "you wouldn't have had any intention of testing me for present-day abilities, even to this small extent you tried here a few days ago, except that Obsidian had turned up a couple of anomalies in the characters of me and my people that—because it's a cultural imperative on you to base your conclusions on certainties—made it necessary to check. The first anomaly was that I said we have moved ourselves to your present time deliberately, using the time storm forces to do so."

I stopped again and looked at Dragger.

"Would you like to replay that particular conversation?" said Dragger. "Very well."

The figures of myself, Ellen, and Obsidian appeared before us.

"*. . . And, of course, we wanted to collect data toward understanding the accident that brought you here,*" Obsidian was saying.

"*Accident? We came here deliberately.*"

"*You did?*"

"*That's right,*" I answered. "*I'd probably better take you down to see the lab and Porniarsk. Sorry, maybe I'm getting the cart before the horse. But after expecting you every day from the moment we landed here, and not having you show up until now—*"

"*Expecting me when you arrived?*"

"*That's right. We came here because I wanted to contact you people who were doing something about the time storm—*"

"Just a moment. Forgive me," said the figure of Obsidian; and he disappeared.

The figures of Ellen and me also winked out of existence.

"That bit of conversation," I went on to Dragger and the rest of the audience, "shook Obsidian up, because here I was talking about deliberately making use of time storm forces back in a time long before anyone was supposed to be able to make use of them. The second anomaly, and the one that made it imperative that you test me, was the fact that Obsidian caught me making what I call a universal-identification—I note, by the way, that this is one area of my vocabulary in your languages that you haven't filled in for me. You have to have a term for it yourselves—"

"We have," said Dragger. "You just used it. We term it 'universal-identification.' "

"Sorry," I said. "My apologies. So you didn't deliberately leave that part of my vocabulary out, then. At any rate, the point is, once more Obsidian had discovered that I could do something that I shouldn't be able to do, being from as far back in prehistory as I was. But, making use of time storm forces to move in time or space, and the concept of the individual being able to share the identity of the universe or vice versa, are things you've believed belong to your time, not mine."

"So far," said Dragger, as I paused to look at her, "I hear nothing to disagree with. You must have more to say than this, though, I assume?"

"I have," I said. "Let's call me fish and you mammal, in the sense that I'm, in effect, your prehistoric ancestor. When you found I could breathe air the same way you did and had legs rather than fins, you had to classify me and those with me as something more than fish. So you thought you'd check me out to find if I was mammalian. But your first check turned up the fact that I'm an egg-laying creature. Since mammals, in your experience, don't lay eggs, you assumed I must be a fish, after all. It didn't occur to you that I might be something like a platypus."

I had used the human word for "platypus"; because there was no alternative in their four communication modes. It was true their spoken language gave me the building blocks to construct an equivalent word; but from their point of view, that equivalent would have been a nonsense noise. Dragger and the rest stared at me in silence.

"Platypus," I said. "An animal from my planet. A *monotreme*—" Now there was a word that was translatable into some sense in their language. Dragger spoke up.

"Just a minute, Marc," she said.

There was a delay while the audience got a thorough briefing on the fauna of Earth in general, and that of Australia in particular.

"It's understood, then?" I said, when this was over. "The platypus lays eggs, but nonetheless it's a hair-wearing, lactating mammal."

"Primitive mammal," said Dragger.

"Don't strain my analogy," I said. "The point is, there was a possibility of my people and me belonging in a category which your culture had made you blind to."

"That's an assumption," said Dragger.

"No," I said. "It's not. It'd be an assumption only if I was wrong about what you showed me having anything to do with the movement of time storm forces. Now, you were right in saying there was no connection between what you showed me and the storm. But in the overall sense, I was the one who was right, and you were wrong. Because the connection *is* there; and you're so culturally blind to it that I'm willing to bet that, even in these last three days, none of you have checked out the possibility that that connection might actually be there."

There was a second—only a second—of silence.

"You're correct. There hasn't been any check made of a possible connection," said Dragger. "On the other hand, we've nothing but your guess that the connection exists."

"I told you the last time I saw you," I said, "it's no guess. I'm neither fish nor fowl. I'm a monotreme. I've learned to use the time storm and to make a personal identification with the universe entirely without and apart from the history, culture, and techniques that you people have developed. I can read the time storm by reading patterns of movement. All movement falls into patterns."

I looked around the room at the spectators.

"You're probably not aware of it," I said, "but the ways

you've grouped and sorted yourselves around me, here, show certain patterns; and from those patterns, with what I now know about your culture and language, I can see a habit of social sorting by individual specialties or abilities.

"If I didn't have that cultural information, I'd still be seeing these patterns, I just wouldn't know what they implied. In the case of your groupings here, I now do know; and in the case of the time storm forces also, I do know."

"This is assertion only, Marc," said Dragger.

"No. It's a case of my being on the outside of your culture, so I'm able to see clearly something you're refusing to see. You people have struggled with the time storm for hundreds of generations. That struggle literally created your community the way it is now and dominated every element of it. It's quite true the panel you showed me was supposed to be showing patterns of conceptual rhythms common to your time and culture; and that I didn't recognize them as such because my own conceptual rhythms aren't like that."

I looked around at them.

"Marc," said Dragger, "have we waited these several days and gathered together here only to hear you admit that we were right to begin with?"

"No!" I said. "Because you're wrong. What I saw, and recognized, *were* time storm force patterns. You, all of you, couldn't realize that because you don't recognize how much the time storm's become a part of you over this long struggle—part of your body, mind, and culture. Your conceptual rhythms *are* time storm rhythms. You don't see that because they're so much a part of you; you take them for granted. I can see it, because I'm standing outside your culture, looking at you. I'm the most valuable mind you've got in this present time of yours; and you'd better appreciate that fact!"

I was almost shouting at them now. This was a strong statement in their terms; but I needed to wake them up, to make them *hear*.

"Don't take my word for it!" I said. "Check those conceptual rhythms on your instrument against the patterns of the time storm forces and pick up the identity between them for yourselves!"

I stopped talking. In my own past time, a moment of

this would have provoked a buzz of unbelief from the spectators, or outcries against my idea or myself—anything but the way these individuals reacted, which was in a thoughtful silence. There was no visible evidence that I had attacked the very base of the culture they had always taken for granted.

But I knew what was happening in their minds. I knew, because I now knew more than a little about how they thought and about their obligation to consider any possibility for truth which that same culture put upon them. I knew they had been jarred, and jarred badly, by what I had just told them. But my knowledge of that was about all the emotional satisfaction I was likely to get from the situation. As far as appearances went, they showed no more reaction than they might have if I had told them that I planned on not shaving when I got up tomorrow.

The meeting was breaking up. Some of the figures in the stands were simply disappearing, some were walking off through visible doorways, some were simply melting into the illusions of surrounding scenery. I found myself alone with Porniarsk, Obsidian, and Dragger.

"We'll check, of course," said Dragger to me. "Tell me, Marc, what is it exactly you want?"

"I want to fight the time storm. Myself. Personally."

"I have to say I can't see how that can be anything but a complete impossibility," she said. "On the other hand, there are always new things to be learned."

36

"They're a great people, Marc," said Porniarsk, once we were alone again in the ordinary configuration of Obsidian's quarters—which Obsidian had, by now, largely given over to our own private use. "You shouldn't forget that."

"You think they are?" I said.

I heard him as if from a middle distance. I was once more as I had been when we had just left Earth on the way here in Obsidian's quarters; like someone who had trained years for a single conflict. I was light and empty inside, remote and passionless, hollow of everything but the thought of the battle that would come, which nothing could avert or delay.

"Yes," he said, "they've survived the time storm. They've learned to live with it, even to use it for their own benefit, and they've made a community of innumerable races, a community that's a single, working unit. Those are great achievements. They deserve some honor."

"Let other people honor them, then," I said. It was still as if I was talking to him from some distance off. "I've got nothing left except for what I've still got waiting for me."

"Yes," he said. He sounded oddly sad. "Your foe. But these people aren't your foe, Marc. Not even the time storm's your foe."

"You're wrong there," I told him.

"No." He shook his ponderous head.

I laughed.

"Marc," he said, "listen to me. I'm alive, and that alone surprises me. I'd expected I'd stop living, once I was taken from the time in which Porniarsk existed. But it seems, to my own deep interest, that in some way I've got an in-

381

dependent life now, a life of my own. But even if this is true, it's a single life only. I was constructed, not engendered. I can't have progeny. My life's only this small moment in which I live it; and I'm concerned with what and whom I share that moment. In this case, it's you, Ellen, Bill, Doc, and the rest."

"Yes," I said. At another time, what he had said might have moved me deeply. But at the moment, I was too remote, too concentrated. I heard and understood what he told me; but his words were like a listing of academic facts, off somewhere on the horizon of my existence, shrunken by their distance from what obsessed me utterly.

"Because of this," he said, "I'm concerned with what you're planning to do. I'm afraid for you, Marc. I want to save what I've got no other words to call but your soul. If that's to be saved, sooner or later, you'll have to reconcile yourself with things as they are. And unless you do it in time, you'll lose your battle. You'll die."

"No," I said. The need for sleep was deep in me and I only wanted to end the talking. "I won't lose. I can't afford to. Now I've got to get some rest. I'll talk to you after I wake up, Porniarsk."

But when I finally woke up, Dragger was standing over the cushion on which I lay.

"Marc," she said, "your training as a temporal engineer is going to begin at once; and if you can absorb that, you'll be taken out to where the line of battle runs with the time storm forces."

I was suddenly fully awake and on my feet. She was going on, still talking. Porniarsk was also to be given the training. This was a bonus, because, in no way, had I dared to hope I could win for him also what I had wanted for myself. But now he, too, would have the chance. There was a comfort for me in the sight of his ugly, heavy bulldog shape. He was like a talisman from home, a good omen.

Obsidian took us far across space again. For the first time we came to another vehicle. It was like a raft the size of a football field, with some sort of invisible, impalpable shield, like a dome, over it to keep in an atmosphere that would preserve workable temperatures and pressures for the massive engineering equipment it carride. Barring the star scene that arched over us in every direction, it was like nothing so much as being in the engine room of an incredibly monstrous battleship.

All the way out to this star raft in Obsidian's quarters, and for nearly two weeks of Earth time after we got there, Porniarsk and I were force-fed with information from the teaching machines Obsidian had talked about. It was an unnerving process. We were like blank cassette tapes in a high speed duplicator. There was no physical sensation of being packed with instruction; and in fact, the information itself did not become usable until later, when contact with some of the actual engineering work going on aboard the raft tapped it, the way a keg of wine might be tapped. But at the same time, there was a psychic consciousness of mental lumber being added to our mental warehouses that was curiously exhausting in its own way. The sensation it produced was something like that which can come from weeks of overwork and nervous strain, to the point where the mind seems almost physically numb.

How Porniarsk reacted to it was something I had no way of knowing, because we were kept separated. Emotionally isolated by my own purpose, I was generally indifferent to what was being done to me, physically or mentally; and when, in due time, the process of information-feeding ended, I fell into a deep sleep that must have lasted well beyond the six hours of my normal slumber period. When I woke, suddenly, all the knowledge that had been pumped into me exploded from the passive state into the active.

I had opened my eyes in the same unstressed state of thoughtlessness that normally follows a return from the mists of sleep. I was at peace, unthinking—and then, suddenly the reality of the universe erupted all about me. I was all at once bodiless, blind, and lost, falling through infinity, lifetimes removed from any anchor point of sanity or security.

I tumbled; aware—too much aware—of all things. Panic built in me like a deep-sea pressure against the steel bulkhead of my reason, threatening to burst through and destroy me. There was too much, all at once, crowding my consciousness. Suddenly I had too much understanding, too much awareness . . .

I felt the pressure of it starting to crack me apart; and

then, abruptly, my long-held purpose came to my rescue. Suddenly I was mobilized and fighting back, controlling the overwhelming knowledge. I had not come this far in time and space and learning to disintegrate now in an emotional spasm. The universe was no bigger than my own mind. I had discovered that for myself, before this. I had touched the universe, not once, but several times previously. It was no great frightening and unknowable entity. It was part of me, as I was part of it. A thing did not frighten itself. An arm did not panic at discovering it was attached to a body.

I surged back. I matched pressure for pressure. I held.

But my mind was still far removed from my body, back on the raft. It felt as if, at the same time, I was floating motionless, and flying at great speed through infinity. My vantage point was somewhere between the island universes, out in intergalactic space. In a sense, it was as if I stood on the peak of a high mountain, from which I could see the misty limits of all time and space. Almost, it seemed, I could see to the end of the universe; and for the first time, the total action of the time storm activity became a single pattern in my mind.

"So, Marc," said a voice—or a thought. It was both and neither, here where there were no bodies and no near stars—"you survived."

It was Dragger speaking. I looked for her, instinctively, and did not see her. But I knew she was there.

"Yes," I said. I was about to tell her that I had never intended anything else, but a deeper honesty moved me at the last second. "I had to."

"Evidently. Do you understand the temporal engineering process, now?"

"I think so," I said; and as I said it, the knowledge that had been pumped into me began to blend with what I was now experiencing, and the whole effort they were making unrolled into order and relationship, like a blueprint in my mind.

"This isn't the way I imagined it," I said. "You're actually trying to stop the time storm, by physical efforts, to reverse its physical effect on the universe."

"In a sense."

"In a sense? All right, say in a sense. But it's still physical reversal. To put it crudely, in the sort of terms you're most familiar with, the normal decay of entropy began to stop and reverse itself when the universe stopped expanding. Then, when the farther stars and the outer galaxies started falling back here and there, they set up areas where entropy was increasing rather than decaying. Isn't that right, Dragger? So it had to be these stresses, these conflicts between the two states of entropy in specific areas, that spawned the nova implosions and triggered the time faults, so that on one side of a sharp line, time was moving one way, and on the other, a different way. So that's what made the time storm! But I assumed you'd be attacking the storm directly to cure it."

"We're after the root cause."

"Are you, Dragger? But this way—this is using sheer muscle to mend things."

"Do you know of a better way?"

"But—using energy to reverse the falling back of these physical bodies, to force them to move apart again? There ought to be some way that wouldn't require tapping another universe. Isn't that what you're doing—and tapping a tachyon universe at that? You're working with forces that can tear this universe apart."

"I asked you," repeated Dragger, "do you know a better way?"

"No," I said. "But I've got to see this for myself. I can't believe you can control something that powerful."

"Look, then," said Dragger. "S Doradus is only a thought away from us here."

It was true. Merely by thinking of it, we were there, with no time spent in the movement. Bodiless, with Dragger bodiless beside me, I hung in space and looked at the great spherical darkness that was the massive engine enclosing the young blue-white giant star called S Doradus. It was an engine that trapped all the radiation from that vast sun, to use it as a focus point, a lens in the fabric of our universe, through which then flowed the necessary jet of energy from the tachyon universe that was being tapped for power—to push not only stars, but galaxies around.

A coldness took my mind. Through that lens, we were touching another place where every physical law, and time itself, was reversed from ours. As long as the lens aperture was controlled, as long as it remained small and unvarying, the reaction between the two universes was under command. But if the lens should tear and open further, under the forces it channelled, the energy flow could flash to proportions too great to be constrained. The fabric between the universes would break wide open; it would be mutual annihilation of both—annihilation in no-time.

"You see now," said Dragger, "why we didn't think it was possible for you to do this work. In fact, if you hadn't been able to make the conceptual jump that set you free to survey the situation, like this, there'd have been no point in even considering it."

"Made the jump? Just a minute," I said. "This isn't something I've done all on my own. I must be getting some technological assistance to let my point of view go wheeling through infinite distances, like this."

"Of course you are," said Dragger. "But the only person who could make it possible for your mind to endure such assistance was you, yourself. You're strong enough to endure the sense of dislocation involved. We didn't think you were. I didn't think you were. I was wrong."

"I've got work I want to do," I said. "That helps."

"A great deal, evidently. At any rate, Marc, you're one of a select group now. Less than a millionth of one percent of all our people have the talent to do this work and endure the conditions under which it's done. Are you surprised we doubted that you could? An individual has to be born with the talent to be a temporal engineer. Evidently, you *were* born with it—millenia before there was such work."

"I didn't know about this," I said. "That's true enough. But there were other things that called for the same kind of abilities."

I was thinking of the stock market, of that part of me which could never rest until it had tracked down what it searched for; also, of that other part of me that had immediately recognized, in the time storm, an opponent waiting for me. . . .

My mind boggled suddenly and strangely, and shied away from finishing that particular thought. Puzzled, I would have come back to it; but Dragger was talking to me again.

"Are you listening to me, Marc?"

"I'm listening," I said. I returned my full attention to

the moment, and our conversation, with an effort. "Something bothers me, though. If it's pure technology at work, why is it talent's needed at all? Why is it only a few can do this? There must be more than a few who can endure the conditions, as you say."

"There are," she answered. "And that's why you've got one more strength you have to demonstrate. We need people with a special talent because when we move stars, and more than stars, we make gross changes in the time storm forces. We don't have any technological device quick enough to safely measure and assess the effect of those changes on the stresses by which we control the flow of energy from the tachyon universe. If the pressure against which we're exerting our energy flow changes suddenly, the flow can increase, the lens may dilate, and you must have guessed what can happen then, before any adjustment can be made."

"You mean the lens tearing open," I said.

"That's right. Only minds able to read the pattern of the time storm forces, directly, can see danger coming fast enough to correct for it. We who are temporal engineers have to direct our stream of extra-universal energy and, at the same time, make sure that it doesn't get out of our control."

She stopped speaking. Eyeless, I hung in space, watching the great darkness that was the engine, the dyson sphere enclosing S Doradus. My imagination pictured the unbelievable holocaust within that shell of collapsed matter and the Klein bottle forces, that made the core of a star millions of times the mass of our sun into a tiny rent in the fabric of a universe. I had thought I was equal to any dimensions that might exist in the battle I wanted to join; but the dimensions here were beyond imagination. I was less than a speck of dust to that stellar nucleus; and in turn, it was infinitesimal, to the point of nonexistence, compared to the two great opposed masses of energy between which it formed a bridge and a connection.

And I was going to share in the control of that bridge?

My courage stumbled. There was a limit, even to imagination; and here that limit was exceeded. I felt my view of the space around me growing obscured and tenuous. I was aware of Dragger, watching, judging me; and with remembrance of her presence, my guts came back to me.

If she could stay and work here, so could I. There was nothing any life born in this universe could do, that I could not at least attempt.

The view of the space before me, and the mighty engine in it, firmed. It grew clear and sharp once more.

"You're still with us?" asked Dragger.

"Yes," I said.

"Then there's only one more step to take," she said. "We'll test you on the line. If you don't succeed there, no one can help you. There'll be no way out."

"I'm ready."

We went forward, toward the dyson sphere. Bodiless, we passed, like thought through its material shell, through the Klein bottle forces, down into the sea of radiation beyond any description that was the enclosed star. We approached the core that was the lens. Here, ordinary vision was not possible. But with the help of the information that had been pumped into me, the lens area rendered itself to my mental perception as an elliptical opening, dark purple against a wall of searing blue-white light. The energy stuff of the other universe pouring through that opening, was invisible, but sensible. It rendered itself as a force of such speed and pressure that it would have felt solid to the touch, if touch had existed in that place and it had been safe to use it upon that inflow.

Dragger led me almost to the lip of the lens.

"Do you feel anything?" she asked.

"Yes," I said.

There was an odd counter force at work here. In spite of the tremendous outflow, I felt something like an undertow, as well, sucking us toward the lens. From where I felt it, it was nothing I could not resist; but I did not want to get closer.

"The downdraft," said Dragger—the word she used in her communication form was not a precise or scientific term, but a casual one, almost a nickname for what I felt, "does it bother you?"

"Yes," I said; for the touch of its pull toward the open lens filled me with uneasiness. "I don't know why."

"It bothers us all," she said, "and none of us is sure why. It's no problem here, but out at operations point it becomes something you'll need to watch out for. Now, meet the others working in this area."

She spoke in turn to at least a couple of dozen other identities. My stored information recognized the symbols that were their personal identification as they answered her and spoke to me. Our conversation seemed to be mind to mind, here in the heart of the star. But actually, as I knew, we were talking together through the purely technological communications center of the space raft where my body and Porniarsk's were. Most of those I spoke to had been at my full-dress argument session, previously. I was a little surprised to realize how many, there, had been temporal engineers; although, now that I thought of it, it was only logical that most of them should have been, since they would be the ones most concerned with me.

"Marc is going on line with us, out at operations point," Dragger said. "If he works out, there, we've got another operator. Marc, are you ready to go?"

"Yes," I said.

We withdrew from the lens, from the star and the engine. I had expected that I, at least, would be returning to my body on the raft, from which I would then go by ordinary, physical means to the operations point. But our identities instead started moving out along the energy projection from the engine, through interstellar space from the lesser Magellanic Cloud, where S Doradus was, toward our own galaxy.

"Your bodies will be sent back," she said.

"Bodies?"

I woke to the fact that the identity of Porniarsk had just joined us.

"Porniarsk!" I said. "You're going on the line, too?"

"Only as an observer, I'm afraid," he answered. "As I think I've said to you in the past, I lack creativity. And a certain amount of creativity is required for direct work in temporal engineering. But in all other respects, I'm qualified; and our instructors thought you, at least, might find me useful to have with you."

"Dragger?" I said.

"Yes?"

"Thank you."

"The decision wasn't mine," she answered. "But I think it's a good one. In spite of the fact you've passed all tests, Marc, you're still very much an unknown quantity to us. Aside from whatever advantage it'll be to you to have your friend with you, it'll make the rest of us feel more secure to know that there's an observer ready to tell us what happens if you do have trouble."

"Enlightened selfishness," I said.

"Of course."

The trip we were now taking was a curious one. My newly educated memory told me it would have been thoroughly possible to make an immediate jump over the hundred and forty thousand light-years of distance from the neighborhood of S Doradus to our own galaxy. But Dragger evidently had a reason for taking me over the distance slowly, following the route of the energy being sent from the engine to the retreating matter of our galaxy; and now I began to understand what that reason was.

The energy from the tachyon universe was not projected in the form it was received, like a light beam aimed over a hundred and forty thousand light-years of distance. Instead, it was converted to a time force line, itself —an extension across space of form without mass, which would not be converted back into energy until it touched the solid material at its destination; and even then, it would be absorbed, rather than felt, as an outside force, by that material.

The form in which it was extended, however, was designed to increase in cross section until it was as wide as the galaxy to which it was being sent. Crudely, then, the energy flow could be represented as a funnel shape, with the small end at the lens of S Doradus and the width of the funnel increasing over the light-years of intergalactic distance between lens and galaxy, until the large end could contain our whole galaxy, including its spiral arms.

We were following, then, alongside this expanding funnel; and as we travelled, I became acutely conscious of its steady growth, and of a corresponding increase in the uneasiness I had felt about the downdraft. And this was ridiculous; because here, with the energy converted into a massless form, there was no downdraft to be felt. Dragger's reason for moving Porniarsk and me this slowly along the route of the projected energy was becoming apparent.

I set my teeth against the reaction. It did not let itself be beaten down easily, because there was something very old about it; as if I had suddenly come face to face with a dire wolf out of prehistory, lurking among the shadows of some well-groomed, civilized park, at sunset. But it was only one more enemy to conquer; and gradually, as I faced it, it ceased to gain against me and then finally retreated. It was all but gone when Dragger spoke.

"How do you feel, Porniarsk?"

"I'm filled with wonder," said Porniarsk.

"Outside of that, nothing?"

"Nothing," he answered.

"And you, Marc?"

"Something," I said. "But I think I've got it licked."

She did not say any more until we came, at last, to the edges of our own galaxy and moved in among its stars, ourselves now within the mouth of the funnel.

"When possible," she said, "we give the individual engineer a sector of work that includes their own home world. Your sector, Marc and Porniarsk, will include the world from which Obsidian brought you to us. Just now, there's no work going on in it. For the moment, no changes in the temporal forces are appearing here, although the earlier forces aren't balanced fully except in the local area of your world where you balanced them yourself, we understand, back before we have records of the storm. But there are going to be forces building up farther in toward the galaxy's center in about nine months of your local time. You'll have that many months to study your sector. Your bodies are being returned there and you'll be able to spend some time in them. Obsidian's returning them and bringing in the equipment you'll need individually to work in this sector."

We were in sight of Sol, now; and to my eyes, the star scene had a familiar look that moved me more deeply than I would have expected it could.

"I was told of one more test to be passed back here," said Porniarsk.

"There's one," said Dragger, "but not for you—for Marc. Marc, in the final essential, the only way we'll ever know whether you can work with the time storm is to see you work with it. Only, if it turns out you can't, it'll almost certainly destroy you. That's why this is the last test; because it's the one that can't be taken under other than full risk conditions."

"Fencing with naked weapons," I said.

I had not meant to say it out loud, for one reason because I did not think Dragger would know what I was talking about; but she surprised me.

"Exactly," she said. "And now, I'll get back to my own work. Marc, Porniarsk, watch out for the downdraft, now that you're sensitized to it. It seems diffuse and weak out here; but don't forget it's always with you, whether you're in space like this, or down on a planet surface. Like any subtle pressure, it can either wear you down slowly, or build up to the point where it can break you."

"How soon will Obsidian return, so we can have our bodies back?" Porniarsk asked.

"Soon. No more than a matter of hours now. Perhaps, in terms of your local time, half a day."

"Good," said Porniarsk. "We'll see you again."

"Yes," she said. "Before the next buildup of forces that affects this sector."

"Goodby, Dragger," I said. "Thanks."

"There's no reason for thanks. Goodby, Marc. Goodby, Porniarsk."

"Goodby, Dragger," Porniarsk said.

She was suddenly gone. As we had been talking, we had drawn on into the Solar System, until we now hung invisibly above the Earth at low orbit height of less than two hundred miles above its surface.

"I'd like to go down, even without our bodies and make sure everything's been going well," said Porniarsk.

"Yes," I said; then checked myself. "—No."

"No?"

"Something's sticking in my mind," I said. "I don't like it. Dragger was talking about this sector being affected by a buildup of time forces farther in toward the center of the galaxy, in about nine months."

"If you'll consult the same information I had impressed on me," said Porniarsk, mildly, "you'll see that the area of space she was talking about is quite large. It'd be reasonable to assume that the chance of our own solar system being strongly affected by that buildup should be rather small—"

"I don't like it, though," I said. "I've got a feeling. . . ."

I stopped.

"Yes?" said Porniarsk.

"Just a feeling. Just a sort of uneasy hunch," I said. "That's why I didn't say anything about it to Dragger—

it's too wispy an idea. But I think I'd like to take a look at the forces of that full area from close up, out here, before I go down to Earth. You go ahead. It won't take me much longer to do that than the few hours we have to kill, anyway, before Obsidian gets here with our carcasses; and nobody's going to realize we're around until then. You go ahead. I'll be along."

"If that's what you want," said Porniarsk. "You don't need me with you?"

"No reason for you to come at all," I said. "Go ahead down. Check up on things. You can check up for both of us."

"Well, then. If that's what you want," said Porniask.

I had no way of telling that he had gone; but in my case, I did not wait to make sure he was. Even while I had been talking to him, the uneasy finger of concern scratching at my mind had increased its pressure. I turned away from the Earth and the solar system, to look south, east, west, and north about the galactic plane at the time storm forces in action there.

37

It was not just the forces themselves I wanted to study. It was true that they would have progressed considerably since I had last viewed them in the tank of Porniarsk's lab; but that tank had still given me patterns from which I could mentally extrapolate to the present with a fair certainty of getting the present picture of matters, in general. But what concerned me was how those patterns would look in the light of my new knowledge; not only of the engine around S Doradus and the lens there, but of the downdraft as well. The downdraft worried me—if only for the fact that it had had the capacity to disturb me, gut-wise as well as mentally, when I had encountered it.

The situation I found in the area when I examined it was one in which the sectors were established within force lines that had been stabilized by the universal community, so that they might be used by members of that community in physical travel amongst stars. I was now able to trace with no difficulty the first twenty-nine force line time shifts Obsidian's quarters had used in carrying us to the testing by Dragger and the others. I could have continued to trace them all the way to our destination; but right now, I was concerned only with the situation in the area to which Dragger had assigned me.

Between the force lines, stability did not exist—except in our own area around Earth where we had produced it ourselves. Struck by a sudden curiosity, I checked the Earth's balance of forces with what I now knew about the time storm and satisfied myself that the present balance was not my doing. My original balance had evidently lasted far longer than I had expected—in fact, for several hundred years. But since that time, it had been periodi-

cally renewed by an outside agency. I was puzzled for a
second that Porniarsk had not picked up this evidence of
outside time storm control earlier than the present period.
Then I remembered that the search had been made by
the computer mind of the tank; and undoubtedly Porniarsk, like myself, had never bothered to instruct it to
consider a continuing state of inaction, in what was already a nonstorm area, as an anomaly.

Within the fixed boundary lines of the stabilized force
lines set up to be used for cross-space transportation, the
time storm had gone on in its normal pattern of developing and spreading temporal disintegration, until
about three thousand years ago, when there began to be
evidence of periodic checking of areas threatening to set
off large-scale disturbances throughout the general, gal-
axy-wide pattern. This checking had apparently been so
minor as to be essentially unnoticeable, until the cumula-
tive effect of a number of such incidents began to show
evidence of anomaly on the large, general scale; and the
tank picked them up.

I studied the stabilized force lines; and I studied the
earlier, smaller evidence of disturbance checking. What
was gnawing at me, I finally decided, was the fact that
corrections which were too small to be important, taken
singly, could pile up to have a much more serious cumu-
lative effect on the stress situation of the galactic area as
a whole.

Moreover, this could kick back against the flow
through the lens and cause exactly the sort of tearing and
enlargement that was the everpresent danger there.

It was all very iffy. It was a chain reaction of possibilities, only—but I did not like the look of it. I swung
back and forth mentally over the force line stress pattern
in my sectors, trying to make it all add up in some other
way than it had just done; but I kept getting the same
answer.

What I was hunting for were those elements of patterns that would point me toward the evolution of one
particular pattern, less than a year from the present
moment. It was difficult and frustrating because, so far, I
had no idea what kind of ultimate pattern it was I was
after. All I had to go on was a subconscious reaction to
something I did not like; as when someone who spends

his life in the open, in the woods or on the sea, will step out of doors on a morning, sniff the air, feel the wind, look at the sky and say—"I don't like the looks of the weather." The day might even be bright, sunny and warm, with no obvious hint of change about it; and still, some deep-brain sensor, conditioned by an experience consciously forgotten, sends up an alarm signal.

I thought of calling Dragger and immediately saw the pitfall on that path. Dragger had warned me that the only way, in the end, to prove I could work with the time storm was for me to work with it. My starting at shadows, if indeed that was what I was doing now and there was nothing really for me to worry about, might strike her as just the sort of sign she had been talking about, that I could not deal with the storm.

She might even be right in thinking that. She had given me no reason to think there was any dangerous situation building up here; in fact, she had deliberately reassured me this was not the case.

Maybe, I thought, the best thing for me was to put it out of my mind and follow Porniarsk back down to Earth's surface. I had been paying little attention to time, but now I realized that at least as many hours had gone by as Dragger had said it would take before Obsidian was due back on Earth with Porniarsk's body and mine. I should go to his station now, pick up my body and go back to my own clan.

I turned and went. Mentally, it was only a single stride to Obsidian's quarters, in the forest east of our community. Obsidian himself was not there when I arrived, nor was the body of Porniarsk, which meant that the avatar must already be back home. But my own body was waiting for me; and I sat up in it on the edge of the cushion on which it had been lying, feeling the strangeness of experiencing the weight and mass of it under the pull of gravity once more.

As I sat up, the illumination of the room increased around me, responding to my increased heart beat, temperature, and half a dozen other signals picked up by its technology from my now activated body. I stood up and moved to one of the two consoles that still stood in roughly the same places they had stood on our voyage out.

I knew how to use these now. I touched the keys of one of them and stepped from the room in Obsidian's quarters to the spot on the landing area, outside the door of the summer palace, where Obsidian had always appeared.

The darkness about me when I arrived came as a small shock. Waking in the room at Obsidian's, I had not realized I might have come home during the hours when that face of my planet was away from our sun. For a second after appearing there, I felt oddly as if I had not come home in the body, after all, but as if I was still only a point of view, hovering there, as I had hovered in space a few moments past, overlooking the whole galaxy and all the stars that were now shining down upon me.

The drawn shades on the windows of the summer palace were warm with light. Everyone there would be celebrating Porniarsk's return and expecting me at any moment. I turned and looked away, down the slope to the town below; and under the bright new moon of midsummer, I saw the buildings down there had their windows also warmly lit against the night. I had been intending to turn to the door immediately, and go on into the palace; but now I found myself caught where I was.

The small, cool wind of the after sunset hours wrapped itself around me. I could hear it moving also in the distance, whistling faintly amongst the trees on the slope below. No night bird called; and the chill and the silence held me apart from the light and the talk that would be indoors. Out of the avalanche of printed words I had read during my mad period crept something more for me to remember. Not a quote this time, but a story—the French-Canadian legend of La Chasse Galerie. It was a myth about the spirits of the old voyagers who had died away from home, out on the fur trade routes, coming back in a large ghost canoe on New Year's Eve for a brief visit with their living families and the women they had loved.

Standing alone in the darkness, strangely held from going inside, I felt myself like one of those returned ghosts. Inside the lighted windows there were the living; but no matter how much I might want to join them, it would be no use. Like the ghosts of the voyagers, I was no longer one of them, within. I had become something else, part of another sort of place and time. It seemed to me suddenly that the small cold breeze I felt and heard no longer wrapped around me, but blew straight through my bones, as it did through the tree limbs below me; and

I thought that all my life I had been outside, looking at lighted windows, thinking how good it would be to be inside.

Once, I might have made it to there. God knows I had tried, with my mother, with Swannee . . . but now it was too late; and that was no one's fault. It was not even my fault, in a sense. Because at each fork in the road along the way, I had made the best choice I knew to make; and all those choices had led me here. If here was outside forever, still, getting here had led me to many good things, beginning with Ellen and the crazy cat and continuing to this same moment, which was also, in its own way, good. For if I was lonely out here in the dark, looking at the lighted shades of the windows and knowing I could not be behind them, I was less lonely knowing who and what were there, and that their lives, which were part of me now, could be warm and bright.

Thinking this, I felt some of the warmth come out and enter me, after all. I remembered that I had discovered before this, that there was no real separateness. I was all things and all things were me . . . and, with that bit of remembering, I began to move again into touch with the universe. I flowed out to be part of the breeze around me, the ground under me and the trees beyond me, part of all the houses below with their lights and separate lives. I felt the summer palace behind me and reached into it to touch everyone there. There was no light, but the gold came into everything again. I saw them all behind the walls at my back, the eternally sleeping Sunday, Doc, Bill, Porniarsk and Ellen. I saw Ellen and I touched her; and she was the key to all the rest between the walls of infinity and all infinities beyond those walls. I had a larger picture of this universe and all others now. I went out and out. . . .

"Marc!"

I turned to vanish, to step back into Obsidian's quarters; and even as I turned, I knew it was already too late. I came all the way around to face the summer palace and saw, darker shadow within shadow, Ellen there.

"Ellen," I said, "how did you know I was here?"

She came toward me.

"I know where you are," she said, stopping in front of me. I could barely make out her face. "I always know where you are. Porniarsk was back, and when you didn't come in, you had to be here."

"Go back inside," I said. My voice was a little hoarse. "Go back in. I'll be along in a moment."

"No you won't," she said. "You were going to leave and not come in."

I said nothing.

"Why, Marc?"

Still, I could not answer. Because suddenly, I knew why. What had been niggling at me all the time I had been studying the force lines now suddenly rearranged itself from a possibility to a certainty, from a suspicion to a knowledge, as the absolute vision of my unity with the universes took hold.

I had been turning away because I knew I would not be coming back.

"Why?"

I realized, then, that she was not asking me why I had been leaving. She already knew it was because I would not be back. She was asking me why I would go to something from which I would never return.

"I have to," I said.

She put her arms around me. She was very strong, but we both knew she could not hold me there. The whole damn universe was pulling me in the other direction. There always was Doc for her, I thought bleakly, looking down at her. I had seen the way he felt about her. But I was wiser now than I had been; and I knew better than to mention that to her now.

"I do love you, Ellen," I said.

"I know you do," she said, still holding me. "I know you do. And you don't have to go."

"I do," I said. "It's the time storm."

"Let somebody else do it."

"There isn't anyone else."

"That's because you've made it so there isn't."

"Ellen, listen." I felt terribly helpless. "The whole universe is going to blow wide open unless I do something."

"When?"

"When?" I echoed.

"I said, when? Ten years from now? Ten months? Two weeks? Two days? If it's two days, take the two days—the first two, real days of your life—stay here and let it blow."

"I can't do that."

"Can't?" she said. She let go and stepped back from me. "No, that's right. You can't."

"Ellen . . ." I said. I stepped toward her; but she moved back again, out of reach.

"No," she said. "You go now. It's all right."

"It isn't all right," I said.

"It's all right," she repeated. "You go."

I stood there for a second more. But there was no way I could reach her, and I had no more words to say that would do any good. She already knew I yearned to stay. She knew I wouldn't. What was there to tell her beyond that?

I went. It was like tearing myself down the middle and leaving the larger half behind.

I stepped back into Obsidian's quarters and turned to the console to put in a call to Dragger. There was a little delay, and then Dragger's voice spoke to me out of the air of the softly lit room, with its cushions and its nighttime trees all around.

"Forgive me, but I'm working now and can't be disturbed. Leave word if you want me to call you back."

It was a canned message.

"This is Marc," I said. "Call me as soon as you get this message. It's critical."

I sat down on the cushion I had gotten up from earlier and sent my mind back out among the stars.

The forces of the time storm were still out there, waiting for me. Now that I came back to them with the additional insight of my momentary contact with the universe, outside the summer palace, what I had only suspected before showed as not only certain but unavoidably obvious. But whether I could convince Dragger and the other engineers of its obviousness was by no means certain. My conviction rested on my own way of interpreting the forces, which was different from theirs.

The time storm was too much in their blood and bones for them to hate it and love it the way that I did. For I did, I realized now, both hate and love it. I hated it for what it had done, for the millions of lives it had swept out of existence. Or perhaps they were all still in existence somewhere else—locked up in little dead end universes—my wife; Swannee; and all those Ellen had known; Marie's husband; Samuelson's family; and the countless others erased by moving mistwalls, not only on Earth but all through the universe. But I loved it, even as I hated it, for being my opponent, for giving me an enemy to grow strong in fighting.

So it was because of both the love and hate that I could see where it was trending now; and it was because they saw it only as a technological problem that I feared the temporal engineers like Dragger would not. I traced the lines of my suspicion again now, through the network of forces, out beyond my sector, out beyond the galaxy and the influence of the one lens I had seen, until I had checked it out against the storm across all the viewable universe. What I feared was there, all right. I could trace the paths of my suspicions, I could see the connections to my own satisfaction, but I could not turn up any solid evidence to present to the engineers.

I was still searching for something to prove what I believed when Dragger called me back.

"Marc?" her voice sounded in my mind. "You had something critical to talk to me about?"

"The time storm's going to get out of hand," I said. "It's going to get out of hand right here in our own galaxy, and possibly in a number of others throughout the universe, at the same time. The pattern's already evolving out of the patterns of the last thousand years. You've already got evidence of it. You told me there'd be increased activity here in nine months or so, my local time. That isn't just going to be increased activity. It's going to be activity that's quadrupled, sextupled, a hundred or a thousand times increased, all at once."

"What makes you say so, Marc?"

"The character of the patterns I see evolving."

There was a little silence.

"Marc, can you describe what you mean by 'character'?"

"The color, the feel, the implications of the patterns in the way they form and change."

There was another silence.

"None of these words you mention have any precise meaning for me, Marc," she said. "Can you describe what you're talking about in hard concepts? Failing that, can you give me the concepts you're talking about in more than one mode?"

"No," I said, "because these verbal symbols of your language only approximate my personal meanings. I'm translating verbal symbols from my own language. Symbols that have special value derived out of my experience, my experience with all sorts of things outside your experience, my experience with buying and selling shares of stock in a market, with painting pictures in varied colors, with understanding what is written and carved in the name of art, with thousands of things that move intelligent and nonintelligent life, and make it the way it is."

"I think I understand," Dragger said. "But to convince me you're right about this coming emergency you're talking about, you'll need to give me evidence in terms and symbols I can value and weigh exactly as you do. The only symbols like that are in my language, which you now also know."

"I can't explain things your language hasn't any symbols for."

"Then you're saying that you can't convince me of what you guess is going to happen."

"Not guess. *Know*."

"If you know, show me how you know."

There was an emptiness of desperation in me. I had known it would be like this, but I had hoped anyway. Somehow, I had hoped, the gap would be bridged between our two minds.

"Dragger, don't you remember how I explained to you how I'd learned about the time storm by a different route than the rest of you? That route gave me a view of it you others don't have; and that view gives me insights, knowledge, you don't have. Don't you remember how I convinced you I had a right to be tested? And didn't I pass those tests?"

"But have you actually passed the last part of that test, now?" Dragger said. "Or are you finding some incapability in yourself in actual practice, an incapability which you hide from yourself by imagining there's an emergency condition building, that none of the rest of us can see and you can't substantiate?"

"Dragger," I said. "I *know* this is going to happen!"

"I believe you think you know. I don't yet believe you're correct."

"Will you check?"

"Of course. But if I understand you, my checking isn't likely to turn up any evidence that agrees with you."

"Check anyway."

"I've said I will. Call me again if you find something more to prove what you say."

"I will."

She said no more. She had gone then. I said no more, either, merely hung there, a point of nothingness in open space. The conclusion was the conclusion I'd feared. I was alone, as I had always been, as I still must be.

Dragger would check, but find nothing to convince her I was right. It was up to me either to find something she could understand, or stop the time storm myself.

It was the latter that I'd come to, eventually—I might as well face that now. It had been inevitable from the first, that the time storm and I should come to grips at last, alone, like this. I had come this far forward in time to find the tools to fight it and the allies to help me. I had not found the allies after all; but I had found some tools. Thanks to Dragger and the others, I knew that the storm could be affected by massive use of energy. Thanks to myself, I now knew that all things, all life, all time, were part of a piece; and if I could just reach out in the right way, I could become part of that piece and understand any other part as if it was part of me.

The thought was calming. Now that there was no hope of outside help, the solitary and abandoned feeling began losing its edge in me. It was ironic that I had come this far forward to find help who could handle a time storm I believed was too big for me to handle alone, only to discover that, while the help was here, it would not aid me. But now the irony no longer mattered. All that did was that I was back at ground zero, alone; and there was no need to waste any more effort on false hopes.

If anything was to be done, I would have to do it, by myself; and if nothing could be done, nothing could be done.

I felt more at peace than I could have dreamed I would, at this point. The unity with the universe came on me without my reaching for it, and I hung bodilessly in the midst of the galaxy that had produced my race and myself, sensing and touching all things in it. I had thought of failure as inconceivable. Nothing was inconceivable. Ellen had said to let the universe blow and take what time remained for myself, even if it was only a couple of days. It would be more than a couple of days, of course. It would be months, at least; and each day of that could be a lifetime if I lived it touching everything around me.

Ellen had been right in her own way, and I should have told her so. I thought of going back now and saying it—and then I realized that she was reaching for me.

"Ellen?" I said; as I might have spoken to Dragger.

No words came back. She could not speak to me in symbols, because she did not have access to the technological equipment of the engineers. But across the touch between us, I could feel her thought, even though it was not in words.

I shouldn't have let you go like that, she was telling me.

"It's all right," I told her. "I'll come back."

No, she told me, *you mustn't come back. Not as long as you still think you can do something and want to do it. I want you to do what you want to do. I just didn't want to cut you off; I didn't want to be separated from you.*

"You don't have to be," I said. "You never have to be separated from anything as long as you can really hold it in your mind. I didn't know that before; but I know it now."

A sudden discovery moved in me.

"Ellen," I said, "where are all the short words, and the short speeches? You're thinking just the way everybody talks."

It just always came out the other way, she answered. *But I talked to you like this, in my head, from the very beginning, from the first day you picked me up.*

"I should have known," I said. "Anyway, I know now. Ellen, I'm coming home."

No, she told me. *You mustn't unless you're sure you don't want to stay at all. Are you sure?*

We no longer talked in a place where there were any rooms to hide what I did not want her to know.

"No," I said. "You're right. There may not be anything at all I can do, but I want to try. I've got to try."

Then try, she said. *It's whatever you want, because I'm with you now. Aren't I with you?*

"Oh, you are," I said. And I reached, forgetting how I was bodiless, to hold her.

With that she came to me, like a wraith but real, across the light-years of space from our little planet, to where I now floated. And with her came another wraith, a bounding, furry shape that bounced against me and sandpapered my face and hands with its rough tongue and crowded between our legs as we clung together.

"Sunday!" I said.

Of course, Ellen told me, *he was always there if only you'd reached for him.*

With them both there, with the three of us—we three ghosts—together once more, my heart broke apart with happiness and out of the broken pieces rose a strength that spread and towered in me like a genie let loose from a bottle when the Solomon's seal is snapped. There was no universe or combination of universes that I was not now ready to attack, to save what I now held; and I reached to the ends of all time and all spaces. So—at last—by the one route I had never dreamed existed, understanding dawned to me.

"I should have realized it," I said to Ellen. "It's one and the same thing, the time storm and what's always been inside me, what's always been inside all of us."

38

"What's been inside you?" Ellen echoed. She was still not speaking to me by the physical route Dragger had used; but what she said was now so clear to me that my mind supplied her voice as if both it and my ears were physically present.

"The storm," I said, "the struggle. The fight to understand, and be understood by everyone else in the face of the equally strong need to be yourself and yourself only, that unique and completely free identity that never was before this moment in time and will never be again, once you're gone. 'I've got to do that, say that' the identity says, 'otherwise I can't grow, I can't make.' 'No, you can't do that,' say the other identities outside your skull, all also struggling to grow and be free. 'If you do that, I won't understand why. I'll take it as a threat. I'll isolate you; or I'll fight you.' So, before each action, along the road to each goal, there are all the interior battles to find a way of compromising what you want, and need to do, with what others will accept your doing. The storm within. Everyone has it; and the time storm without is its analogy."

"I don't see that," said Ellen. "Why?"

"Because both storms are the result of conflict between two things that ought to be working together. Like a couple of millstones, badly adjusted, chewing each other up, throwing off stone chips and sparks instead of joining to mill the grain between them."

"But even so," said Ellen, "why's that important, here and now, and with you, particularly?"

"Because I never knew how to quit, to give up," I said. "When I ran into the inner storm I couldn't stop trying to

406

conquer it; but because it was inside me, because it was subconscious, instead of conscious, I couldn't get at it. So I made everything else a surrogate for it—the stock market, the business, my heart attack . . . and at last, the time storm."

"Even so, what good could it do to fight other things?"

"It could teach me how to fight. It could help me discover and forge weapons to fight my inner storm with. And it did! By God, it did! I've found the answer to the inner storm."

"Not fighting," said Ellen, very positively.

"All right. That—yes. But there's more to it than just not fighting. The full answer's in the unity of everything. Reaching out and becoming part of everyone and everything else. It was you and Sunday who first broke me in to being a part of someone else without struggle. You were both completely dependent on me, so it never occurred to me that I had to adjust myself to suit you."

"There was something besides that," said Ellen. "We cared for you."

"I know," I said. "I know. I took that for granted too. I'm sorry, I didn't know any better than to take it for granted, then. I didn't begin to know any better until Sunday was gone and I suddenly found the big hole in myself where he'd been. I didn't realize then why it hit me as hard as it did; but actually, something of myself had just become suddenly dead. If Sunday hadn't been killed, just then—"

I broke off, looking instinctively for her face before I remembered she was not there in the body to be seen.

"Would you have gone off with Tek, then, if Sunday hadn't been killed?"

"I don't know," she said. "If I had, though, I think I'd have come back. I never loved Tek. But I couldn't make you hear me or see me."

"I remember—" the wraith of Sunday jumped up to hug my bodiless spirit with nonexistent forepaws and tried to lick my face that was not there. "It's all right, Sunday. Down, cat! I'm not feeling bad now; I was just remembering something. . . ."

"But the time storm's still there. You mean you can give up on it, now?" Ellen asked.

"I think I could—now."

"But you don't really want to."

"No," I said. "The truth is, no. If I give up, nothing'll be done; and that means the end, for all of us."

"You're sure it does?"

"Yes. There's been a situation building up for a few thousand years now, ever since the temporal engineers started working with the storm. They've been trying to cure an imbalance between energies in this universe by importing more energy from another universe, to shore up the weaker of the two energies here. It's worked for a while, but it's also been creating the potential of a bigger imbalance if the scale should suddenly tip the other way, and the weak side become the strong one, with all that extra, imported energy added to its natural advantage. And I think it's about to tip—in this universe at least—in about nine months."

"The engineers don't know this?" Ellen asked. "You're sure about that?"

"They know it, but they don't realize how great the reaction can be."

"In any case, what can you do by yourself?"

"I don't know. I need to think. Quiet, cat. Leave me alone for a few minutes."

Sunday stilled. His ghost body lay down with crossed paws, on nothingness, and resigned itself to patience. I still held my vision of unity with the universe, that had come on me after I had finally faced the fact that there was no hope from Dragger or her colleagues. I had found what I had stumbled toward and struggled for all this time; and now I wanted to live, as even more I wanted Ellen, Sunday, and my universe with everyone in it to live. It went against reason that I could have come this long journey through life and time without picking up the skill and knowledge to do something about the situation. Somewhere, there had to be a chance; and if there was a chance, my blessing/curse of being unable to turn away from an unsolved problem should keep my mind hunting until I found it.

"If I'm right about the parallel. . . ." I began at last, slowly.

"What parallel?" said Ellen.

"The parallel about the time storm being an analogy of the inner storm. If I'm right about that, and I had to get outside myself to find the key to my inner storm, then. . . ."

Ellen said nothing.

"Then," I went on, after a moment, "the answer to the time storm has to be outside too. Outside the universe— outside *this* universe. If I go outside this universe, I ought to be able to see it."

"But how can you do that?" asked Ellen.

I did not say anything.

"There's no way you can do that, is there?"

"Yes," I said, slowly, "there is. There's the lens."

"What lens?"

I told her.

"Marc!" said Ellen. "Are you crazy?"

"It's the only way to get outside."

"But it's the center of a star—and worse than that. You'd be burned up before you got into the lens."

"I'm not material at the moment, remember. It's my mind only that'd be going."

"But even if you could go through this lens without being destroyed, there's the problem of getting back. How could you do that?"

"I don't know."

"Why don't you check the idea out, first, with the temporal engineers?"

"They might want to stop me; and maybe they could," I said. "They can't help me, Ellen. The time storm's too much inside all of them, just like my inner storm was too much inside me. I'm the only one who can do anything; and the only thing I can think of to do is go through the lens."

She said nothing for a moment. The wraith of Sunday lay waiting, trusting, leaving it all up to me.

"If you don't, we all die?"

"I believe so."

She sighed.

"Then you do have to go. There actually is no choice," she said. "All right. I'm going along."

"I don't think you can," I said. "Where are you? Back down in the summer palace asleep?"

"I'm in my own bedroom at the summer palace," said Ellen, "lying on the bed. But I don't think I'm asleep."

"You're there, though. I'm here. Tell me, can you feel the downdraft?"

"The what?"

I explained what it was. She was quiet for a little while after I finished. Finally, she spoke.

"No," she said.

"I thought so," I said. "I'm probably reaching down to you, as much as you're reaching up to me. You see, I really am out here—in a sense. I'm an energy pattern projected by the engineering devices of the temporal engineers. I can go from place to place at faster than light speeds only because I can turn off my projection in one spot and turn it on at another."

"If you're a pattern of energy, then the energy coming through the lens *can* destroy you! Or at least, change you. Energy *is* material."

"Maybe. I've got to try it, anyway."

"There has to be some way I can go with you!"

"I don't think so; and that's good. Because then I couldn't stop you from coming; and there's no sense in both of us . . . going."

"Let's try and find a way. Wait a bit. You said we had nine months."

"Nine months before the axe falls; but it may be already too late to stop its swing. I can't wait. I've got to go, now."

"Wait just a little bit. Come back home for a couple of days, or even one, so we can talk it over first."

"If I did that, I might not go after all. Particularly not now, with the two of you around. Ellen, I've got to go. I've got to go now!"

We flowed together, we ghosts. She held me. Sunday held me. I held them.

"All right, go then," she said at last. "Go now."

"Goodby," I said. "I love you. I love you both. I'll be back."

"You'll be back," said Ellen.

I pulled away from them and shut them out of my mind. I was alone among the stars; and, by reaching out for it, I could feel the funnel of energy and also the downdraft— weak, as Dragger had said, way out here, but unceasing, relentless.

I let the pull of the downdraft fill my mind. I let myself go with it. At first there was nothing; it was like floating on a lake. Then I noticed a slight movement, a drifting, and I became aware of the fact that I was dropping down below the galactic plane. I revolved and saw the direction of my movement, toward the Lesser Magellanic Cloud and a darkness there enclosing a young, blue-white giant star, a darkness I was still too far off to distinguish.

I let myself drift. . . .

The plane of the galaxy receded above me. I was in intergalactic space. There was nothing to measure the speed of my movement now, but I sensed that it was increasing. I was falling faster and faster, down the funnel of extra-universal energy, reaching from the lens at S Doradus to our galaxy.

I fell a hundred and forty thousand light-years; and time became completely arbitrary. It may have been minutes, and it may have been months, that I fell with steadily increasing velocity until I must have been travelling faster than any pulsar measured in my early, original time. I think it was probably minutes rather than months, or at least hours rather than months, because I could feel that my acceleration was not merely steady, but steadily increasing all that time. I had no ordinary way to measure this—I only knew it, with some measuring back part of my mind.

It became plain to me, finally, that I would not see the lens before passing through it. By the time I would be close enough to make out the dark circle of the engine among the lights of the lesser Magellanic Cloud, I would be only a fractionless fraction of a second from entering the tachyonic universe, too small a moment of time for perception. I relaxed, letting myself go. . . .

And it happened.

There was a shock that felt as if the subatomic particles of the energy pattern that was my identity were being torn apart and spread through endless spaces. Following that, incomprehensibility.

I was afloat in darkness, streaked by lines of light that shot past me on every side almost too fast to see. Other than these, there was nothing. But the darkness had a value and the lights had a value—even if I could not read them. Feeling stricken and dismembered, I floated helplessly, watching the shooting lights.

I had no power of movement. I had no voice. I could find no means by which I might measure the time, the space, or anything else about me. If I had indeed come into the tachyon universe, I had arrived completely helpless to learn what I needed to know, and helpless to take the knowledge back with me. Look about as best I might, I could see nothing left to me but to give up; and the only reason I did not do so immediately was because I was not sure if I was even able to do that.

I floated; and gradually, like a shocked heart starting to beat again, my ancient weird woke again in me. I could not give up, because even here, I was still lacking the reverse gear I had been born without. Alive, dead, or in living pieces less than electron size, I was still committed to chewing at any cage that held me until I could gnaw a way out.

But what way was there? Where do you begin when there is no starting point on which to stand? A journey of a thousand miles may begin with a single step; but where to begin—if you are not standing still, but skating across eternity in total darkness, with meteor-like lights flashing all around you? I hunted through myself for something to hang to, and found nothing. Then Ellen came to my rescue.

"Remember?" she said. "When you first found me, I was lost like that; and I found a way back."

She was not speaking out loud to me. She was not even talking in my mind, as she had as I hung in space, normal space, just before I had come here. It was the Ellen which had become a part of me, speaking to me out of a corner of myself, as Sunday had come bounding back from death to hug me with nonexistent paws, out of a corner of myself where he had been all this time, without my realizing.

"If I did it, you can do it," Ellen-that-was-me said. "Do it the way I did it before. Take what there is, and build from there."

She was right, of course; and I drew strength from her. If she had been able to do it once, she was able to do it again. Therefore, I could do it, as long as she was part of me. I drew certainty from her and looked about once more at what I had.

I had the darkness and the lights. The lights were totally incomprehensible; but with Ellen's certainty that I could build with them, I started to watch them. They were too momentary to form patterns . . . or were they?

I floated, watching; and the watching became a studying.

All that underwent change fell into patterns of altera-

tion, eventually. It was a long time resolving to my understanding, but finally, I began to see the elements of
patterns in the streaking lights. They were not entirely
random after all.

If they had patterns, they were part of a larger identity
in which such patterns could be held, a larger identity
which was the universe of their context—whether that
universe was as small as an atom of an atom, or larger
than all other universes put together. If this was so, then
there was a relationship between the universe that held
them and the patterns that it held.

What I had learned in my own universe could be the
key here, also. Incomprehensible as this place was, the
unity of every part of it with the whole, the identity of
every part of it with the whole, might be certain here, as
it had been where I came from. If this was so, I had to be
a part of this universe and it had to be a part of me, simply because I was now in it. Therefore, its patterns had to
be part of me also, as understandable as my own physical
speech in action when I was back in my old body, because
a part of the whole cannot be either strange or alien to
the whole, as I had found.

"Now you see," said Ellen-that-was-me. "And, since
you see, all you have to do now is reach out and touch."

She was right again. There was no cardinal here,
perched on a bird feeder; and the golden light was lost and
left behind in another infinity. But she was still right; there
was nothing to stop me from reaching out and trying to
touch, to connect with, that of which I was now a part.

I reached. I felt outwards for my identity with this
place surrounding me, just as I had felt in my home universe. Identity was slow coming; but in the end, it turned
out to be only one step more than I had needed to make
in reaching out for identity with Obsidian and his peers.

I touched something. It was something, or some things,
with an ability to respond. After that, it was only a matter of mastering the necessary patterns to communicate
with them; and in this they met me halfway. Apparently—
I say apparently, because the situation does not translate
into words easily if at all—the distinction between living
matter and nonliving matter was not the sharp division
existing in our own universe. Instead, the important division was between those, or that, which had finite lifetimes and those who, or that which, did not; and the

lights I had been watching were each a single lifetime, lighting up from the apparently brief moment of its birth until the moment of extinguishment at its death.

But what seemed so brief was not necessarily so. Looked at from another viewpoint, what seemed to me a momentary lifetime could have existed the equivalent of billions of years in our universe. Also, to live here was to communicate; so that, in the end, I myself lived to communicate and communicated by living. It was a long moment for me, because I had a large job in making them understand what I wanted them to know about us and our situation.

But the time came when I got through; and after that, no more time was needed. I was left, with my mission accomplished, but myself isolated.

The only way I had of telling that I had gotten the message to them was by the change I could observe in their patterns. For, of course, there was no way they could speak directly to me any more than I had been able to speak to them. Actually, the most I had been able to do had been to signal crudely in their direction; like someone on a hilltop waving flags to people in a valley far below, to direct their attention to a distant danger. It was not just the mechanism of communication that was lacking between them and me—it was the fact that not merely our thinking processes, but our very existences, were too different.

So, there I was successful, but stranded. I had no conception of what might now be left to me; for I had no conception of what I might be, here, in this different universe. It was possible that, here, I had an incredibly long life before me; a slow, almost imperceptible decay into extinction like that of some radioactive element with a half-life measured in millions of years. It might be that I was only seconds from extinction, but that the vastly different perception of time would make this into a practical eternity. It might be that I was truly immortal here and would exist forever, observing and apart from a universe filled with a life for which "alien" was an insignificant, inadequate word, but unable to end.

Curiously, none of these prospects bothered me. I had done what I had set out to do and, in the larger measure, I was content. The only sadness left in me was because I could not tell my own people that the message had been carried, the battle won. Battles, I ought to say; because in coming here, in managing to get my message through to the life of this place, I had finally got outside myself, finally seen myself in full reflection, and come to the inner understanding I had been trying to find all along.

My hunt had been nothing more than the human search for love. Only I had been afraid of finding it even while I was pursuing it. So I had made sure to create masks for all those I encountered, so that if I became attached to any of them, my attachment would be to the mask and not to the real being behind it. That way, if the person betrayed me, it did not matter, because I had never really known them anyway. There was no way the living person behind the mask could sink emotional hooks into my soul because it was to the mask I had committed myself. In retrospect, I had put a mask on my mother and sister. I had put masks on Swannee and Marie and Paula. Those whom I feared I might love I gave unlovable masks. Only to those I was sure were unable to love me did I give masks that I could love.

It was a fail-safe system. It was only when I forgot to use it that I got tripped up. The crazy cat and the idiot girl—who would have suspected in the beginning that either of them would be able to reach through and tear me up inside? True, I had wakened to the danger in the girl and tried to put a mask on her, but by that time, it was too late. Meanwhile, the crazy cat had already got to me. When he was killed, for the first time in years, I hurt; and, hurting, I came back to life, whether I wanted to or not.

Now I was grateful for that return to life, because what I had been doing was wrong. It was against instinct and could only have led me nowhere finally, but to a dessicated hell of sheer loneliness that was at the opposite end of the spectrum from the contented isolation in which I now hung. This way I was alive. The other way, I would have been dead. The golden light had been first to give me the answer; but then, I had still struggled against it.

39

I was in my own bedroom of the summer palace. For a moment, the terrible thought came that the whole thing had only been some sort of dream. But then, I knew better.

I looked around and saw Ellen, standing beside my bed with Porniarsk and Dragger.

"Hello," I said to Ellen, and my own physical voice echoed strangely in my ears. "I'm back."

"Yes," she answered.

It was the sort of answer I would have expected from her. I lay there, savoring the familiar goodness of it, feeling warm and comfortable, while the three of them stood watching me with a careful concern, as if I were some sort of carefully brooded egg which was about to hatch and which might produce something strange. I thought over half a dozen things to say; decided against all of them and simply held out my arms to Ellen, who came and hugged me.

"How did I get back here?" I asked, finally, when she let me go. Outside of feeling as weak as dishwater, I seemed to be fine.

"We brought your body here right away," said Dragger, speaking twentieth-century English now, as well as Obsidian ever had. "Just as soon as we caught you. We were barely in time to keep your identity from going through the lens."

I stared at her.

"No, you weren't," I said.

At that, Dragger looked embarrassed, like someone caught in a lie, which surprised me. I would not have thought it possible for her to show that particular reaction; and I would not have expected myself to be able to interpret it, if she had. But there was no doubt about what I was seeing now.

"At any rate," she said, almost defensively, "we trapped your mental energy pattern in time to keep it from going through. Something else *could* have gone through, that was a part of you, though what it would be, there's no way of telling."

"His soul," said Porniarsk, firmly and clearly.

"Call it that, for the moment, then," said Dragger. "At any rate, it's been some eight of the local days here, since then."

"Eight days? Is that all?"

"That's plenty," said Ellen.

"It felt like. . . ." I began, and ran out of words.

"Temporal differences," said Dragger, more briskly, "or possibly differences in temporal perception? It'll take a great deal of study."

"But you did it, Marc," said Ellen. "Whoever they are in the other universe, they've been sending messages in through the lens. The engineers here understand now. They're cutting off the inflow of differential energy and doing something with the downdraft instead. It's going to work out. It's all going to work out."

"You were right in the first place, Marc," said Dragger. "We were too much a part of the time storm ourselves to realize the forces that were building up."

"It's interesting," put in Porniarsk. "When you get down to it, there's nothing in such great supply that it's inexhaustible, no container so large it can't be filled."

"And that's true for a universe as well as boxes, bags, oceans, and galaxies," said Ellen.

"I should say, however," Porniarsk corrected himself, "it may be that the human spirit is inexhaustible. Time and work will tell."

"You were right, as I said, Marc," Dragger repeated. She was apparently determined to make her apology, or say her piece, whichever it was. "We were too close to the problem to see it properly. Are you interested in the details?"

"You could say that," I answered. I pulled the pillow up behind me and propped myself up against it. I got it crooked, but Ellen straightened it out.

"Essentially," Dragger said, "you were right in assuming that it was a mistake to import energy into this universe

from another one—Ellen told us what you told her, before
you tried to go through the lens."

"The energy already stored in the increase of entropy
by matter falling back in toward itself," I said, "can be
tapped to push it out again, instead of using the energy
flow from the other universe."

"They told you about it over there, then?" Dragger
asked.

"They didn't tell me," I said. "When you've seen both
universes it becomes obvious. Theirs is the opposite of
ours. There, something travelling at the speed of light is
standing still. When you started tapping the differential in
energy between their universe and ours, you triggered off
the equivalent of an entropic decrease in their universe,
where normality was a continually increasing entropy and
a collapsing universe."

"Ah," said Dragger, "that explains it."

"Explains why you've got to work with them to pump
back the energy you've taken from them?" I said.

"No," said Dragger, "we're already doing that, of
course. It becomes possible if we use the downdraft to
trigger the release of energy stored on this side, as you
said. No, I'm talking about a message we got from them,
thanking us for solving their problem."

"Oh," I said.

"Apparently," said Dragger, "they don't realize that
you weren't deliberately sent to them as our representa-
tive, and that your concern was to solve the problem here,
rather than altruistically offering to aid them with their
problem."

"I see," I said.

"All this is rather embarrassing to us," said Dragger.
"There's little we can do to set the record straight with
them—at least until communications between the two universes become more sophisticated and we understand
their conceptual processes better. In time, no doubt, we
can make it clear to them they owe us no gratitude. But
that still leaves us overwhelmingly obligated to you."

"I don't know what you can do about that," I said. "I
was interested in saving this universe for myself and those
I now know I care for. Wait—"

"Yes?" Dragger said.

"There's one thing," I said. "One of the things that
Porniarsk and I hoped for from the beginning was that

you could do something for a leopard who used to be a
friend of mine. He was killed, and Porniarsk put him in a
state of timelessness, hoping that, up here in our future,
you people would know how to reverse time for him back
before the moment he was hurt and killed. If you could
do that for me—"

"Oh, yes," said Dragger. "Ellen and Porniarsk both
told me about this; and we've looked at the body of the
creature. I'm afraid there's absolutely nothing we can do
with that."

"I see," I said.

"Life isn't something that can be created simply by an
alteration of the temporal matrix, forward or back. You
have to have noticed," said Dragger, "that when you
passed through a time line—a mistwall, as you called it in
the past—and through time lines in travelling with Obsidian to your testing, that your movement in external time
did not change your apparent age or state of health—"

"All right," I said. "Yes, I understand. All right. Let it
go then."

"But what I was going to say," went on Dragger, "is
that life is apparently a concept; and, given the concept,
the rest isn't difficult. As you discovered yourself at the
time you had your conversation with Ellen, in space, before you went to pass through the lens—"

"Oh, for God's sake!" said Ellen, exasperatedly.

She went to the door of the bedroom, opened it, and
put her head out into the corridor.

"Doc!" she called.

"—you were able to summon up a complete conceptual gestalt of your leopard, probably largely thanks to
your developed ability to recognize and think in patterns.
We've theorized that what you did was to put together in
your mind a critical number of behavior patterns of the
leopard and this triggered off a creative whole. Now, given
this, of course, it's simple for us—"

"I should have thought of it myself, of course," said
Porniarsk. "I'm ashamed that I didn't."

"—to build a duplicate of the physical body to which
that conceptual gestalt belonged. As Porniarsk says, this
much was possible even in his culture, back in that early
time. So, we took the completed pattern from your unconscious several days ago—"

Doc appeared in the open doorway. A black, furry

thunderbolt shot past him, flew through the air and landed on top of me, stropping my face with a file-rough tongue. The bed collapsed.

"Oof!" I said.

I had intended to say, "Will you get the hell off me, you crazy cat?" but I didn't have the wind. He had knocked it all out of me. It didn't matter.

ABOUT THE AUTHOR

Born in Edmonton, Alberta, Canada in 1923, GORDON R. DICKSON moved permanently to the United States in 1937. After attending graduate school in the Midwest, Mr. Dickson became a full-time writer, and at this point, has over a hundred and fifty short stories, thirty-three novels, including four novels in collaboration, six collections of short stories, and the editing of several anthologies to his credit. His major work is the Childe Cycle, a cycle of twelve novels, three of which are historical, three contemporary and six set in the future. Writing began on the Cycle in 1956. Four of the future novels—*Dorsai!, Necromancer, Soldier, Ask Not,* and *Tactics of Mistake* are already published, with writing presently underway on the last two of the future, and the first of the historical novels. All twelve books, when completed, will connect to form a single "novel of thematic argument," a literary form conceived by this author. President of Science Fiction Writers of America for two consecutive terms from 1969-1971, and recipient of the World Science Fiction Award ("Hugo Award"), the Science Fiction Writers of America Nebula Award, the E. E. Smith Memorial Award for Imaginative Fiction and the August Derleth Award of the British Fantasy Society, Mr. Dickson is one of the most esteemed members of the science fiction community.

RAY BRADBURY

America's most daring explorer of the imagination

☐	11932	S IS FOR SPACE	$1.
☐	10750	SOMETHING WICKED THIS WAY COMES	$1.
☐	11997	THE HALLOWEEN TREE	$1
☐	11957	THE ILLUSTRATED MAN	$1
☐	11930	DANDELION WINE	$1
☐	11931	R IS FOR ROCKET	$1
☐	10249	TIMELESS STORIES FOR TODAY AND TOMORROW	$1
☐	11942	I SING THE BODY ELECTRIC	$1
☐	2834	MACHINERIES OF JOY	$1
☐	11582	THE WONDERFUL ICE CREAM SUIT & OTHER PLAYS	$1
☐	11945	THE MARTIAN CHRONICLES	$1
☐	2247	GOLDEN APPLES OF THE SUN	$1
☐	10882	LONG AFTER MIDNIGHT	$1
☐	10390	A MEDICINE FOR MELANCHOLY	$

Buy them at your local bookstore or use this handy coupon for orde

Bantam Books, Inc., Dept. RBS, 414 East Golf Road, Des Plaines, Ill. 6001

Please send me the books I have checked above. I am enclosing $_____
(please add 75¢ to cover postage and handling). Send check or money orde
—no cash or C.O.D.'s please

Mr/Mrs/Miss _____

Address _____

City _____ State/Zip _____

RBS—10/78

Please allow four weeks for delivery. This offer expires 4/79.

OUT OF THIS WORLD!

That's the only way to describe Bantam's great series of science fiction classics. These space-age thrillers are filled with terror, fancy and adventure and written by America's most renowned writers of science fiction. Welcome to outer space and have a good trip!

11392	STAR TREK: THE NEW VOYAGES 2 by Culbreath & Marshak	$1.95
11945	THE MARTIAN CHRONICLES by Ray Bradbury	$1.95
02719	STAR TREK: THE NEW VOYAGES by Culbreath & Marshak	$1.75
11502	ALAS, BABYLON by Pat Frank	$1.95
12180	A CANTICLE FOR LEIBOWITZ by Walter Miller, Jr.	$1.95
12673	HELLSTROM'S HIVE by Frank Herbert	$1.95
12454	DEMON SEED by Dean R. Koontz	$1.95
12044	DRAGONSONG by Anne McCaffrey	$1.95
11599	THE FARTHEST SHORE by Ursula LeGuin	$1.95
11600	THE TOMBS OF ATUAN by Ursula LeGuin	$1.95
11609	A WIZARD OF EARTHSEA by Ursula LeGuin	$1.95
12005	20,000 LEAGUES UNDER THE SEA by Jules Verne	$1.50
11417	STAR TREK XI by James Blish	$1.50
12655	FANTASTIC VOYAGE by Isaac Asimov	$1.95
02517	LOGAN'S RUN by Nolan & Johnson	$1.75

Buy them at your local bookstore or use this handy coupon for ordering:

Bantam Books, Inc., Dept. SF, 414 East Golf Road, Des Plaines, Ill. 60016

Please send me the books I have checked above. I am enclosing $_____
(please add 75¢ to cover postage and handling). Send check or money order
—no cash or C.O.D.'s please.

Mr/Mrs/Miss_____

Address_____

City_____State/Zip_____

SF—11/78

Please allow four weeks for delivery. This offer expires 5/79.

Bantam Book Catalog

Here's your up-to-the-minute listing of ov
1,400 titles by your favorite authors.

This illustrated, large format catalog gives
description of each title. For your convenienc
it is divided into categories in fiction and no
fiction—gothics, science fiction, westerns, my
teries, cookbooks, mysticism and occult, biogr
phies, history, family living, health, psycholog
art.

So don't delay—take advantage of this spec
opportunity to increase your reading pleasu

Just send us your name and address and 5
(to help defray postage and handling costs).

BANTAM BOOKS, INC.
Dept. FC, 414 East Golf Road, Des Plaines, Ill. 60016

Mr./Mrs./Miss_____
(please print)

Address_____

City_____State_____Zip_____

Do you know someone who enjoys books? Just give us their names
and addresses and we'll send them a catalog too!

_____

Mr./Mrs./Miss_____

Address_____

City_____State_____Zip_____

_____

Mr./Mrs./Miss_____

Address_____

City_____State_____Zip_____

FC—9/78